This book is for you if...

This book is for you if you are a reader who loves to explore alternative ways of thinking and complex psychological thrillers.

It is for you if you want or need to understand what is it like to live with:

- Asperger's Syndrome; Autism; Attention Deficit Hyperactivity Disorder; Obsessive Compulsive Disorder;

- Suicidal tendencies;

- Panic or anxiety attacks;

- Thinking differently to other people;

- Deep communication challenges;

- No understanding of the consequences of your actions;

- A serious lack of confidence;

- Daily lifestyle challenges;

- Inherent sensory issues; and

- Amplified or multiple sensory awareness and emotions.

It is the story of a man who was groomed by a paedophile in his adolescence but who fought to survive his ordeal, without once emulating his evil mentor. The story expresses the fact that children and adults who are most likely to succumb to being victims are: those who think differently; are diagnosed on the Autism Spectrum; have the condition Alexithymia; or are yet to be diagnosed. It reveals the details of this adult's ordeal, the life-changing burden it created and the methods he sought to overcome the many lifestyle challenges and issues he experienced.

This story will give hope to people with similar conditions or people who have been labelled with unnecessary and unwanted labels. Anyone who has faced any form of abuse will be able to learn what those life skills are to help themselves or other people overcome their life challenges. This book may help parents to learn modern tactics to ensure their children's safety; know the signs to look for; and what to do about it.

The author believes his book will prove beneficial by not only helping the lives of other people with similar life challenges but also by informing acquaintances, employers and friends about their condition. He hopes that parents, teachers, psychologists, the medical profession, police force, social services department staff and supportive institutions - who help people with emotional disorders and mental conditions - will be able to tap into the new *Aspie and Me* web platform which accompanies the book - to help people develop life skills they might otherwise not be aware of. Here, the author shows that having a relationship with an Aspie can be beyond your wildest dreams.

Things you can do at **www.AspieandMe.com**:

- You can interact with the *Aspie and Me* story

- Read hundreds of comments that analyse incidents and situations

- Look at alternative strategies

- Learn modern tactics to ensure your children's safety

- Know the signs to look for and what to do about it.

The author also encourages readers to take a look at his earlier website **www.lifewithoutlabels.co.uk**, which takes readers on a surreal journey into the heart of the creative mind. If you are reading this book as a neuro-typical (non-autistic), you may begin to resonate with some of the issues the story raises and perhaps think that you are not so neuro-typical after all?

The author's underlying message in this story is that society should no longer tolerate any form of abuse - be it within families or from employers or any other organisations - as more people make public their stories.

All characters in this book are fictitious.

What other people are saying…

"I first met Laurence Mitchell some years ago at a business networking event. This was his first experience of this kind of gathering. The moment came when Laurence was expected, like all of us present, to stand up and tell the assembly something of himself and his work. He was completely unable to get a word out. It was as if he had been struck dumb. As a voice coach, I immediately recognised the symptoms of a chronic stammer. After the meeting ended, I assured him that his communication problem could probably be considerably improved, if not completely cured.

Laurence worked with me over a long period, arriving at a point where, on many occasions, he was able to control his stammer. However, he was, and still is, convinced that he has within him some kind of demon who gains control of him if he indulges in a diet of high sugar content, one of his prime addictions. There is no doubt that he is on the Asperger's Syndrome spectrum and exhibits many of the known traits of this. As an experienced video producer and on-screen presenter, I was able to help Laurence to appear in a series of videos over a period, in which he could showcase his extraordinary knowledge of antiques and in particular Meissen Porcelain. In this subject, Laurence is a world authority.

Laurence also received considerable help and support from my wife, Catherine Palmer, a relationship coach and practitioner of The Radiance Technique (TRT), which is the authentic Reiki. Through learning this hands-on self-help process, Laurence was able to achieve a more balanced outlook when he was in a particularly serious addictive state.

Although Laurence is now much abler to communicate with others since I first met him, he tends to be constantly focused on himself and his own personal thoughts and feelings. This is something that makes genuine relationships a great challenge for him. Since Catherine and I moved away from Britain almost three years ago, our communication with Laurence has been very sporadic and we have been unable to meet with him on any of our rare visits to the UK. I therefore do not consider myself in a position to give any kind of judgement about his current state. All I am certain of is that enabling him to handle his acute stammer and feel able to expose himself to a wide public in his videos has greatly helped his complex and sometimes tortured life."

Valentine Palmer, international voice and presentation executive coach, Academy of Communication, RADA, London

"There are two main themes in what Laurence has mentioned. The first one concerns the power of music, generally positive but sometimes (as with earworms) negative. The second theme is the difficulty people with autism may have with understanding emotions.

Ten or fifteen years ago, a number of psychologists were busy claiming that people with autism would have musical deficits; in one well-known formula, that they would be unable to 'get' music. They justified this claim on the basis of a theory that music making originated as a kind of social glue: one might summarise this as 'the society that plays together, stays together' hypothesis. On this basis, their reasoning - in a very simplified form - was as follows: 'Aspies have no social skills, music is a social phenomenon, therefore Aspies won't have the skills to understand music.'

The problem with this logic was that it assumed that because people with autism were not good at social relations (and this was admittedly part of the definition of autism), they therefore had no wish to have social relations. It also assumed that music, having originated in social activity, could only act within a social context. Both of these assumptions turned out to be wrong.

Ten years ago, I began my research in psychology by investigating the 'Aspies don't get music' claim. Up to that point, some experimental work had been done with autistic children and music, but nobody had sat down with autistic adults and asked them what music meant to them. When I did this, I soon found that far from being unable to get or appreciate music, music was often most important in their lives. For many of them, it was a vital support to their well-being. In effect, they had devised their own programmes of music therapy. This is shown by some of the comments they made to me.

Laurence's other theme is difficulty with understanding emotions, both one's own, and other people's. This often goes hand in hand with a difficulty in regulating one's emotions.

The fundamental cause for this, I believe, lies in the common factor, that of difficulty in labelling one's internal mood states. This is not a mental illness, but psychologists describe it as a 'trait': that is, a characteristic of individuals, which tends to be fairly constant through life. People who seem to experience emotional arousal, but have difficulties recognising the nature of the arousal, have what is called 'type II alexithymia', alexithymia being a word of Greek origin (it was coined by Peter Sifneos, a Greek-American).

Alexithymia simply means 'being without words for emotions'. Language is so important to humans that without the ability to label our emotions, our social interactions as well as our happiness can be severely compromised. I found a high level of alexithymia in my participants.

By the way, I doubt whether earworms are linked to alexithymia. They seem to be too common in the general population for that. Nor do I think earworms are specific to people with OCD, for the same reason.

One other point Laurence made was that people with autism are often seen only as having deficits, and no account is taken of the positive contributions that they can, and wish to, make to the world. I quite agree with this comment. Some people have argued that a degree of autism is an asset in enabling a person to break away from commonly held views and to think in a new and original way. It has even been claimed that Isaac Newton and Albert Einstein were autistic, and that this was a necessary part of their ability to develop their revolutionary ideas.

I do not know whether this view is true or not. It may be a little extreme. But what I am sure of is that people with autism can make a real contribution in the workplace, provided their employer understands that certain allowances may need to be made for them. Firms are obliged to make such allowances for an employee who cannot climb stairs, but it sometimes seems to be beyond them to do so for a person who needs - for example - to work in quiet surroundings without distraction. Forty years ago, people in wheelchairs were unable to get work. Let us hope it does not take as long before things change for people with autism."

Dr Rory Allen, Department of Psychology, Goldsmiths University of London

"What I admire and cherish most about Laurence Mitchell is his passion for life, learning, people, nature, growth - and living life to the full. He is a passionate spirit who, like many, has a remarkable life story - and so I'm so thrilled that he is sharing some of that life learning through this book.

I first met Laurence many years ago long before I knew anything much about autism and Asperger's. We had a conversation and I knew from the start the secret was to engage with Laurence as the wonderful spirit soul that he his rather than any of the labels - honouring the person I was speaking to and learning directly through them. We had many rich conversations on the mind, spirit, thoughts and inner peace.

Over the years since, he has dedicated much of his time and energy to understand the worlds of those touched by Asperger's and to being in a space where he can help people to live rich, full lives by embracing life. It has become much of his life's work.

Laurence has seen the seasons of life but he is mindful that, as I would put it, 'the sun is shining whether you see it or not'. Enjoy the rich journey through the seasons that this book shares and enjoy the warmth and light it offers."

Rasheed Ogunlaru, Coach, Speaker and Author
Soul Trader - Putting the Heart Back into Your Business

"I have known Laurence for about ten years now, initially through business networking and more recently as a client of mine. He has always come across as an intelligent, thoughtful, professional man. He has survived numerous enormous challenges, which he has sought to overcome or at least manage to the best of his ability. He is able to articulate well about his autism and is keen to work on himself in any way he can, be it on his mind or his body. He has struggled with his sexuality all his adult life, ever since a bad experience as a teenager, and has fought and overcome predatory inclinations. He's had low self-worth and we have worked a lot in this area. He has shown tremendous willpower and determination to do what is right for him, including recently going virtually sugar-free. I am so proud of Laurence for completing this book and hope it will inspire others with autism to realise that help can be sought to either overcome, or at least manage their challenges, enabling them to reach their potential too.

Go gently, Laurence."

Diana Powley SQHP/MPNLP, Dune Hypnotherapy

About the Author

Laurence Mitchell has had a lifelong challenge with behavioural traits that prevented him from fulfilling his goals. At the age of forty-nine, he was diagnosed with Asperger's Syndrome and ADHD.

If his diagnosis was not bad enough, his wife took her own life in 2004, leaving Laurence to look after his three children. Social services deemed his condition too dangerous to be fit enough for the role of a responsible parent and considerations were taken to put his fourteen-year-old daughter into care. His two other children were old enough to look after themselves.

At a point of despair, desperate to be recognised as a responsible parent over the next couple of years, Laurence was supported by the advice of a specialist Asperger's support school to learn how to live with the condition and to get on with his life.

During this period, he began to take an interest in personal communication. In 2006, he was introduced to a life coach who showed him a unique way to live a life free from the labels that had so long trapped him. He decided to devote his spare time between his antiques business in researching as much as he could about the communication challenges people suffer on the autism spectrum. He went on to launch, in 2008, an autism resource, www.lifewithoutlabels.co.uk, as well as speak at major professional autism conferences internationally.

However, Laurence was holding onto a dark secret, which he was scared to reveal for fear of being thrown into jail.

Simultaneously, with increasing press coverage about Aspies being deemed 'dangerous people' and the victimisation of Gary McKinnon, in 2015 Laurence struck up the courage to report to the police a historical incident where he had been victim to paedophiles since the sixties.

But he had an unanswered question: why him? It was only later, during subsequent investigations, he discovered a condition present in not just people with autism but neuro-typicals too, Alexithymia. Could it be a simple cue, a facial expression, that attracts paedophiles to their victims and, being autistic, the sensation is amplified or exaggerated, making them more of a target?

In part, *Aspie and Me* is Laurence's story based on real life events. His passion is to tell other people that they are not alone. It is time for them to bear their souls and he will do his best to offer his guidance and emotional support.

Contribution from the author's mother

My memories of Laurence as a baby and toddler was of a very happy little boy, busy, inventive, with intense concentration on whatever he was doing. It was when he went to nursery at the age of three that his carer drew my attention to his difficulties, especially his inability to mix with the other children. There were signs of other problems, and he eventually attended weekly child psychiatry sessions that resulted in a diagnosis of insecurity and lack of confidence. This continued until he was nine years old when they could not help him any further. Autism was not heard of in those days.

Considering all his difficulties during the years, I am amazed and full of admiration at his perseverance and dedication on his long and arduous journey to the completion of this book.

Acknowledgements

My special thanks to my mother for her phenomenal patience. She was aware of the immense challenges that writing *Aspie and Me* imposed on my life, yet throughout she has been a pillar of emotional strength and support.

During the 1960s and 1970s, life in the antiques trade was like living in a jigsaw puzzle of communication and character peculiarities that traders ignored because simply getting along with buying and selling antiques was the nature of the beast during a period where money grew on trees. There are portions of this story that could not have been completed had it not been for my many business colleagues, including the Camden Passage Mob, many who are now my good friends.

Special thanks to Linda Wheatley and her daughter Sarah, and Ivan Macquisten, past editor of the *Antiques Trade Gazette*.

Special thanks to Richard Mills, Research Director, and Deepa Korea, former Chief Executive Director, of Research Autism, for inviting me to speak at their conferences.

Also, Carol Povey, Director of the Centre for Autism at the National Autistic Society, and Geoff Nargis Soppet of The Autism Show.

Special thanks to Jeffrey Salmon and Stephen Osborne.

I thank Wendy Yorke, my literary editor and book coach, for her attention to detail, her professionalism and her patience in working with me on what was a very complex manuscript, www.wendyyorke.com

Chris Day, my publisher, www.filamentpublishing.com; Durwin Banks, the British linseed farmer www.thelinseedfarm.co.uk; and Colin Sugden and Bivek of Artistic www.artistic-uk.org.

Also, I thank Allen Landau, Craig and Cindy Emmerson, Herb Jeffries, Gerry High and Denise Diamond.

Finally, in memory of Rhys Morgan, a very talented mind who passed away far too young.

The challenges of living with
Asperger's Syndrome

ASPIE and ME

A psychological thriller based
on true life experiences

LAURENCE MITCHELL

Published by Filament Publishing Ltd
16 Croydon Road, Beddington, Croydon,
Surrey, CR0 4PA, United Kingdom.
+44(0)20 8688 2598
www.filamentpublishing.com

ISBN 978-1-912256-27-3

Printed by IngramSpark

CONTENTS LIST

PART FOUR: CONSOLIDATION - TRAVEL AND SEX ADDICT   **215**

PART FIVE: FINALE - SCHADENFREUDES AND MURDER   **281**

Foreword

I've known Laurence for some thirty-eight years through my involvement in the art world. We were always very friendly but only on rare occasions did we mix socially. He was always awkward but never once did I nor indeed anybody else in my circle think that the awkwardness was anything other than eccentric behaviour. It has to be said that the vast majority of art world participants could easily be described as eccentric so it was never anything that majorly stood out other than oddness.

Perhaps one thing that in retrospect, and in the light of the relatively recent Asperger's diagnosis, did stand out was his immense knowledge of his chosen genre and how he communicated with relative ease with important collectors who, like us, would have been totally unaware of his condition.

When you read any of Laurence's emails, you'd believe that they had been written not by an Oxbridge scholar but by the Professor of English himself, such is his use of syntax and command of words. Believe me, there have been many times that I convinced myself that I was not reading Laurence's own words and that he had received help such is the dichotomy of his written work when compared to speaking to him 'face to face'. This I find one of the most interesting facts I have learnt about Asperger's through my long friendship with Laurence.

What has not surprised me is the immense effort that Laurence has put in to learning about every aspect of autism not only for his own deeper understanding, but also to ensure that a wider audience can gain information thorough his knowledge and acceptability from other people. I pride myself on a relatively good sense of humour but it took Laurence's diagnosis to fully explain to me why he did not find my topical jokes as funny as others seemed to find them. It seemingly came across as rude but with my greater understanding of Asperger's, I now realise that it's par for the course.

As bad as I am at not phoning people as regularly as I ought to see how they are keeping, Laurence has always made that extra effort to continually stay in touch over nearly four decades, and thank goodness he has because life would be a far duller affair for my family without him.

Jeff Salmon, British businessman, art and antique dealer

Author's Note

My story has been by no means an easy write. Originally eighteen hundred pages repeated several times, as though every page had been placed through a scanner without my knowledge, perhaps an amazing Aspie acumen.

However, there are other people in my life I had to think about in fictionalising my story. My children, in particular, and their emotional safety.

My reporting to the police took immense courage not knowing what to expect, and it may appear to the reader that Aspie is addicted to sex. Like many addictions, unless treated it can be pervasive and damaging. The emphasis about writing about the sexual innuendos is intended to illustrate how damaging sexual and other types of related abuse are to people who think differently and whose senses are amplified because their sensory system is wired differently in their brain. Where I have written about the main character's sexual experiences, driven by his need for 'love searching', the key message is focused on understanding the diversity of anxieties and meltdowns that occur, and how the Aspie in me manifested them.

Furthermore, imagine as a fifty-five-year-old adult being confronted by the impossible; a real live T-Rex and being able to feel its breath. Try to appreciate the intense fear of no escape and the real feel of finality from immediate consumption by its cavernous jaws. Take this example of extreme amplification of the senses into everyday life; as a child watching an embarrassing television scene, then imagining being a part of that scene. I would run out of the room until my anxiety died down. It was probably very evident to bullies of all sorts, mental and physical, that I was a vulnerable target. I experienced mental turmoil long before any physical pain.

Laurence Mitchell, October 2017

Terminology

Ambisinistrous; clumsy with both hands, probably caused poor motor skills.

The Aspie Continuum; a surreal world behind Aspie's wall, where he always feels safe.

Bar Mitzvah; the coming of age when a Jewish boy is officially recognised as being an adult.

The Bishops Avenue; London's billionaire road.

Eidetic memory; the ability to recollect an image so vividly it appears to be real.

Groomed; made an emotional connection with a child.

Katana; traditional Japanese sword used by the Samurai.

Monteith; a large bowl with a scalloped rim, where six or eight wine glasses may be suspended by the foot.

Nabeshima; highest quality Japanese porcelain originating in the seventeenth century.

Neuro-diversity; those people on the spectrum who think differently to the average person.

Neuro-typical; non-autistic people.

Salieda Kakiemon; credited for discovering amongst the easiest production of porcelain making in Japan, during the early seventeenth century.

Schadenfreude; a person who relishes another person's misfortunes.

Seppuku; Japanese ritual suicide by disembowelment.

Shul; a synonym for synagogue or temple. Shul means school in Yiddish. In America, a temple is the same as a synagogue.

Yakuza; members of Japan's murky criminal underworld.

PART ONE:

THE BEGINNING - TRIGGERS AND PAEDOPHILES

Prologue: Aspie, Hartley and Rea

Aspie first came in contact with Rea after reading an advert he saw in the personals column of his local paper. The advert read *Personal Services, Tantric Massage.* He was curious as to what tantric meant?

In particular, Aspie only had eyes for anything in a skirt that had the biggest pair of jugs, preferably on a shapely body. His ideal massage was one that ended with some kind of sexual innuendo given by the big-bosomed masseuses he desired. Yet, his sole reason for visiting such women was misguidedly seeking them for only one reason; abundant love and attention as other people sought a dating agency. He hoped for an engagement ring to put on their finger.

Since being a child, Aspie felt he lacked one principle function that all humans sought to survive, and that was love, and he travelled to the end of the world to find it if necessary. Lying on a massage table gave him his satisfaction and thinking time to escape his overwhelming presence.

Yet, it was ridiculous to think he crammed in a massage for every day of the week because at last he had found someone who listened to his most intimate sordid and perverse fantasies. Someone who assured him that whatever was discussed remained within her four walls, and this meant soon he would find a way to coerce her into becoming his wife.

H. Rea, it's troublesome to me that I appeared to go through the same routine. I came to you, I got naked, I lay on your massage table, then I became aware I'd entered the battle zone. Was it going to be me who came out the victor, or was it Aspie contriving to manipulate me into his world rife with unending sexual innuendos?

Let's try to do something different tonight. How about we celebrate with some jazz and fine food in Highgate Woods? Although I must warn you that Aspie is not going to like it one little bit.

A. Are you fucking out of your mind, mad, stupid, got a screw loose, or something else? You are going to get us locked up for a very long time. You can't tell the world about your relationship with me?

H. What you mean to say is our secret. You're not talking about me, you are talking about you. Use the singular when you have something to share with me.

A. Fuck off, you demented pervert!

H. Most certainly, I am not a pervert now, shut up otherwise you will ruin our story.

R. I don't understand - is it normal for you to talk to yourself while you are with company?

H. If I do, I am not aware of it or perhaps I am, but afraid to admit it.

R. This, whoever you say, sounds quite a nasty and selfish person?

H. I know, it's not something I expect you to relate to now but perhaps, later on, you will understand that there is Aspie and there is me. Now let me begin towards the end of my story where upon I reflect what I believed were going to become the last moments of Aspie's life, only it gets worse.

R. Surely there can't be anything worse than death?

H. Wait and learn.

Chapter 1: Death Wish

H. The suicide gene wasn't an Aspie concoction. If he could have had his way, he would have ensured he had the 'action-everything' gene, that's how his mind worked. I, on the other hand, regularly suffered unending dangerously intrusive panic attacks where I was confronted with a real live monster from Loch Ness. The only way I can describe them is akin to sleep paralysis; you wake up inside a dream while you are asleep. Instead, you are experiencing your most horrific nightmare. You are aware only of a complete emptiness. What was once brain matter has ceased to exist, entirely void of all thought.

I wondered if it was drummed up by some innate jealousy, like a magician conjures a trick, the slight of hand but with him it's slight of mind. It happened for the first time thirty years ago in Tokyo from a concoction of alcohol and drugs with Aspie watching to see if I could survive jumping from a second floor balcony. The alternative was remaining in my nightmare wondering whether I had arrived at Hell's doorstep. To enable you to relate to my experience, I want you to imagine you are the last living creature on earth, just you and nothing else. The last of every other species of life are gone, the oceans now bare rock. You are completely alone and you have to ask yourself the question; 'Is there any point in living?'

I believe there is no ideal solution to my question, yet Aspie's need insisted that he found one. He was a survivor, so he believed. His plan was to beat death at its own game. He got as close to his own suicide as he could because his plan didn't work out to his advantage and there was only one last thing left to do; commit the perfect murder.

He believed he could succeed because he had no relationship with his conscience. This scenario took place during a period where my life lay in tatters, although I had a pretty good life before this. I wanted peace of mind and to ensure Aspie was out of my head for good.

R. I don't really know what to say other than I disagree; there is always the will to find an alternative even if you are, as you say, in a state of mind that Aspie has his hand so far up your arse, he is controlling your lips.

H. My story is only just beginning and assuming you have more of an understanding of Aspie's personality, it's purely a guessing game how his next innuendo is going to materialise or manifest. Seriously though, as preposterous as I might sound, I didn't have an inkling that the next two events I would be facing were going to be the nightmare of nightmares. Almost as though if you could take every detrimental incident and event that had occurred during my entire life, these two are the culmination of the whole.

Aspie vindicated; he had no choice, totally my doing, driven to necessity. I, on the other hand, believed he had gone past that point of no return brought on by terminal exhaustion, the ultimate anxiety where all forms of reasoning are thrown out of the window. Whether I liked it or not, now a delirious and delusional shell of a madman to which I was about to face the truth, my life was about to be exterminated because he saw himself as his very own Schadenfreude.

It reminds me of a Jason Statham movie, wearing an immovable wristband that is a bomb. Aspie saw himself as a death warrant, whose own hate is worn around his neck and can only lead him in a direction he knows I never want to go in; to darkness and desolation. But it is too late for him since he has become a slave to his hatred that can only lead to another distraction and, somehow, do I have the unearthly resolve to break free?

R. You've obviously achieved that because you are here to tell your tale?

H. Yes, however if this is what you call a close call, I hope there is never going to be a next time.

A. That, my friend, is something you will never know.

R. How does Aspie almost cause your undoing?

H. Attempted suicide followed by murder.

R. Wow, I imagine that does beat the lot.

H. Yes, and it began from something so trivial. Reminds me of one of those James Bond films, where James is being invited to play a game by his captor in which either one of their lives might be terminated. The two of them are sitting at opposite ends of a table with their hands on a machine that delivers electric shocks. As the game increases, so does the prize, but the downside is the strength of electric shocks.

The beginning of the day wasn't anything out of the ordinary, although it was going to be a long day and a lot of travelling on trains. Aspie insisted I find the cheapest ticket available for purchasing our return ticket to Birmingham to view an auction that was being held two days later. After the viewing, we cycled back to the train station before setting off for the stop at every station so Aspie could make a nuisance of himself. He had to jump on and off at every platform as though he had something to prove on our return home!

But as you have learnt, Aspie rarely does things to the norm more so; another ruse. It hadn't been my intent, you can call it what you want, but you need to remember when I am Aspie, he makes the decisions. He doesn't distinguish between doing this or robbing a bank because consequences aren't something he thinks about. Those are left to me. The game planned for that afternoon was primed for beating the Revenue Inspectors at their own game. From his perspective, it was another fare avoidance technique arriving home without paying the correct fare. My original plan was to board and purchase the ticket but Aspie intervened and concocted what he thought was a bright idea. At night the chances of the station being manned was very remote.

R. That to me is blatant fare dodging. What you are about to tell me is you were travelling from Birmingham without a ticket?

H. The intent to dodge the fare had until then gone like a tee. Aspie had me purchase a single ticket. Pulling away from the station, I decided I needed the loo. I never expected to see the Ticket Inspector, far more lenient than the Revenue Officer, otherwise I would have been issued with an on-the-spot fine.

In my mind, I have returned to the Eastern Coast of America where I often travelled on Amtrak, and heard the words, 'Any more tickets please?'

I asked the Inspector whether we had gone past our station and said that I had a bad tummy, hence my dashing to the loo. It reminded me of flying on the typical cheap ticket we purchased while cavorting around the US, this time flying from LA to New York. I required the perfect excuse to visit the antique shops in downtown Chicago. When our plane touched down in Chicago, we were allowed to de-plane but not to leave the terminal. I waited until our plane left the gate until Aspie had me rush up clutching my stomach with the excuse, 'I'm so sorry - had diarrhoea', making sure the airline staff could see a rather unsightly brown smudge on my left leg. It wasn't the first time he came up with that ruse and it was unlikely to be the last.

So, now our next stop was in the heart of the countryside where we were told to cross to the opposite platform and take the next train back. Little did I know that my desire to live an illustrious life could have just as easily terminated a few miles away. Aspie was unprepared to buy another ticket, given his plan had failed, and this left us with only one choice to cycle home. By now, it was pitch black, but that was okay because Aspie decided we use the cycle path. As for trying to reverse Aspie's madness, it became completely fruitless. He decided we can use the reflection of the lights from the nearby estuary. It was as though the Devil had taken over from God and decided I was going to teach those sneering bastards a lesson they would never forget.

My angst with Aspie was how he appeared to have a thirst of provoking tenuously dangerous situations that appeared to follow us every day. I wished they came with a second chance so that I could land on Go - as if I was playing the game Monopoly - but I rarely did.

I had this fold-up bike that travelled with us wherever we went. We had been downtown that afternoon and were taking a shortcut, cycling back to our hotel through a rather deserted industrial area close to Miami Airport. Because of the unfamiliarity to the area, Aspie drummed up thoughts of being chased by a pack of wild dogs, and of course this became a reality and we find ourselves cycling for dear life while growling dogs are hard on our trail. But then they are no longer dogs but instead T-Rex, the most terrifying of my childhood fears, while the threat to us was very real.

R. That must have been scary nevertheless. I can't believe the Hartley I know allowed this to happen. Surely you have the sense to be aware that in pitch black you are taking on a suicidal risk?

H. The truth in my mind was blighted by Aspie. I was void of all conscious thought. A dilemma with a no-win situation. We were in the heart of the country on unlit roads and the last thing I needed was any of his unhelpful witticisms. But as luck would have it, he couldn't understand why I was making so much fuss.

A. Wasn't it exciting?

R. Seems to me with the two of you, that's like the pot calling the kettle black.

H. Anyway, Aspie didn't think about the occasional dog walker or pedestrians, and I can't remember how many we had cycled into while being shouted at - 'Fucking lunatic!' - let alone the occasional honking from cars as they drove past the madman. Then, without warning, our worst nightmare happened.

R. Did a car hit you?

H. No, I saw a flashing blue light. The last thing I needed to see, but I knew it meant trouble. 'What absurdly dangerous stunt do you think you are doing cycling without any cycling lights, dangerous enough along this path, the estuary's water is very cold at this time of the year, and I doubt your bike will easily float?' shouted the police officer. 'You should be thankful we've finally caught up with you. Thought you could get away with this regular jaunt of yours? How many calls we've had from drivers who had to get out of your way, let alone the mayhem you caused. At least the locals will be grateful we have at last caught the village idiot; such a shame stocks were done away with but perhaps a night in the cell will make you think twice. At the very least you might wake up in the morning!'

'Yes, Officer, you are right,' Aspie interrupted, insisting there was a reason for his lunacy; he had hijacked my mind. Can you imagine, I had no choice in the decision, knowing jolly well the sheer stupidity of us cycling at night in pitch black without lights didn't fall within Aspie's protocols, rather a necessity to pull off dangerous stunts. I am grateful I am able to stop him from what he wanted to say; always with him there was an ulterior motive. Anyway, here I was contemplating the night in a cell!

R. I would have called that a saving grace, the reason you are here to tell your tale, better than taking your bike for a one-way swim in the estuary?

H. Wishful thinking would be a fine thing but very far from the truth. We were about to be arrested.

R. My sentiments, your life saved!

H. Instead Aspie was excited at the prospect of a night in a cell. I didn't realise but there were going to be many an opportunity for him to keep that promise. While I was told my predicament was my own doing, or Aspie's way, suicide. That night I did wonder whether we would make it out alive. Would make interesting reading in the papers and whether the policeman would still have his job!

R. I bet that was a pleasant walk?

H. Except I was treading Aspie's territory knowing he had no interest in listening to advice, be it the policeman's or anyone thinking about the scary creatures of the night reappearing, lunacy an understatement particularly as we still had a couple of miles of road cycling. Do you think he really cared about the copper's advice? Aspie didn't do walking bikes. He didn't care about running into people, let alone cars for that matter. It wouldn't have surprised me if the police got another call about Aspie's belligerent attitude and we weren't picked up and arrested on the spot. Fortunately, luck was on our side when we eventually saw the lights of our home.

Yet, the irony of all that had occurred was because of Aspie's concocted idea that behaving like any normal citizen purchasing the correct fare was beyond his way of thinking. Any chance I had of a good night's sleep that night was thrown out of the window as he planned his revenge and at this point I had to realise I was residing with a deranged psychopath.

R. Then I do have something to worry about. Aspie is liable to do away with me and carry on with life as though nothing happened.

H. I would hope not, I would have thought I have the impetus to ensure that could never happen.

R. Guarantee?

H. Even that.

R. That's a relief, I do prefer feeling alive. Anyway, from what I understand, we have now reached the last chapter in your story?

H. That would be correct if I didn't have to tell you the whole story as I cast you back to the day before the worst moment of my entire life.

Chapter 2: Florida

H. In the Northern Hemisphere, the beginning of May marks the
rites of spring. I thought the day marked a rather auspicious
occasion since we were visiting the Cummer Museum in
Jacksonville. This was a remarkable achievement since I was
doing something I had long wanted to do. When you have an
Aspie sharing your life, trouble follows you everywhere and
rarely does any day go the way you expect it to. Distractions are
a part of the culinary requisites of the daily routine of the beast.
Therefore time management let alone keeping a diary doesn't exist
in his world. At last, I had found an opportune moment to get my
own way and not dwell on the fifteen years it had taken me.

Floridians, as they are known, are blessed to live in their sub-
tropical paradise. The day we chose to make the drive was
typical for the time of year. Any thunderstorm spent rarely
anything more than a fleeting visit.

The night before, Aspie made certain a Corvette Convertible
rented via the concierge desk downstairs in the lobby was
waiting to whisk us away. While I am not going to digress and
tell you what happened two nights before, because that will
ruin my story, what I can say is we were staying where we were
because she had failed to open her legs and he needed to do
something to burn away his disappointment.

Aspie had the knack of finding us opulent places to stay at
bargain prices and spending the night at The Biltmore in Coral
Gables was little short of that. The resort was known for its

rich and famous past residents, as well as the notorious and decadent. Within a short while of arriving into the cavernous reception area and being completely mesmerised by the hand-painted frescoes on the barrel-vaulted ceilings, I was catapulted into a world beyond. I opened my eyes to find I am mingling with President Franklin and the Duke and Duchess of Windsor, while tragedy almost stabbed me in the back as I bumped into Al Capone and I wondered if I'd wake up in the morning.

For a fleeting moment, I dived head first into Aspie's world and the reason that compelled us to stay here. The following morning, I awake having rested the night away on the lushest of pillows wishing if I could have my way, I would dive back into my dreamlike world and be swallowed up by another innuendo. However, I'm not to be beaten by exhaustion as I forced my feet onto deep woollen pile and, moments later in the shower, I felt rescued by the strongest jets of water pounding me from every angle wide awake. Moments later, any jet lag remaining became as recumbent as the past, hardly noticeable.

Aspie reminded me of my call of duty. For the next hour, I swam repetitively the entire circumference of the 600,000 gallon, 22,000 square-foot pool; the largest in the United States. Only then was I able to dip into our prize. Breakfast on tap; simulating a dog's inability to masticate Aspie's performance was seeing how many silver dollar pancakes oozing with freshly poured, real, organic maple syrup he can swallow whole. Only after he'd savoured a taste of everything else on the buffet table did he decide his gullet was full.

I began feeling more relaxed, when some thirty minutes later, at precisely 8:13 in the morning, we were heading eastwards along the 836. Our drive should have been like the clear blue sky, without interruptions. However, ten minutes past the toll booths, what I should have pre-empted was that this was to be the first of the day's many distractions, as I was hit by a barrage of inappropriate thoughts from Aspie and we missed our turn-off.

Early on in my life, I learnt that to do whatever I intend achieving requires giving up a piece of me to Aspie, giving in to his whims and rarely driving a direct route. We should have turned northwards along the I-95 and connected to the Turnpike at Sawgrass to save a good three hours. Instead, it didn't surprise me that we were heading eastward along MacArthur's Boulevard in the direction of South Beach so Aspie could say a wow to the large cruise liners that berth there. Whenever Aspie is in control, failure didn't exist because a backup plan was permanently on tap. Without warning, our car grinds to a halt in front of Star Island and the vehicles behind begin honking. I should have realised Aspie was too absorbed looking at the homes of the super rich on the left side of the car. A fleeting reminder of the luxury life of cruising was also on the right-hand side; albeit we were forgetting about the other road users building up behind, who were fast getting irritated.

A few moments later, there was no point giving Aspie a dirty look as we pulled into the parking lot of the largest health food store on the corner of Michigan Avenue and Fifth Street. Long ago, I learnt to muster the resolve to allow him to wander around for a good hour musing himself in his daily madness, The Aspie Continuum. Otherwise, I had to succumb to the unnecessary tug of war of not deviating further from our day's journey by visiting every remaining health food store we discovered during past visits to compare values.

This action of his was more about reminiscing about another venture of ours that never took off the ground: importing health food into the UK. But I drew the line and marched out of there when I heard; 'What the fuck do you think you are looking at, you demented pervert?' as the Spanish woman at the till felt his deviant eyes undressing her cleavage.

Back into the Corvette, I knew another madness meant our detour would continue northward along Ocean Boulevard. Here, Aspie imagined a sign on our car advertised; *'Large breasted women wanted for virile Englishman in South Beach.'* Moments later, we were driving past the Hilton Fontainebleau, chatting with high-class hookers who I could ill afford, while he was thinking how he could whisk them away with his temptress thoughts. Another ten miles, we passed Bal Harbour Shopping

Mall, which was normally a must to visit. Only when the road dead-ended past Dania Beach Bouvelard opposite John U Lloyd Beach State Park did we have no choice but to make a u-turn, which reminded me of many others in the career of my life.

During the eighties, if antiques were your game, Dania was the place to be. Here, antiques of every description made their way from the doyen of the dying into the hands of the hundreds of antique dealers who sold along the couple of blocks south and north of Dania Boulevard. It's a mistake every dealer knows well. We bought a bargain once in a shop there but then were smitten to revisiting every time, in case other bargains showed up, which they rarely did.

By now we should have been fifty miles north. Just like the visit to the health food store earlier, another hour was wasted before we were continuing in the direction of our destination in Jacksonville.

You'd think, after all these years, I'd know Aspie's tricks, distractions and misdemeanours but not before too long I found I'm distracted once more. Sadly, a repetitive trait I have yet to change. Our next distraction was the perimeter of Fort Lauderdale Airport because we drive into the incorrect lane and notice people watching, after making a right-hand turn onto Las Olas Boulevard hoping some wench was going to jump into our car.

After another thirty minutes of stopping and starting at countless stoplights, we turned off the A1A on to Atlantic at Delray Beach, where we went through the same routine as in Dania and purchased a rare antique Meissen Vase at a bargain price.

My qualm with Aspie was his desperation to find what he doesn't have in his life and, for my peace of mind, I found myself drawn to knowing his ultimate goal of settling down won't be achieved until he has found his happiness. How many times must we venture into the territory of the super-rich wherever we go? Small memories of eating dinner set against the surf at a luxury resort and waking up to endure him taking me on another distracted journey, while he fantasised about living in one of the mansions belonging to Donald Trump; or driving down Worth Avenue, Palm Beach because it made him feel worth something.

Anyway, eventually we continued our laborious drive through Daytona Beach and, passing through Cape Canaveral, Aspie had to show how man he is. A reckless decision, cavorting with my life, for a quick dip in alligator-infested waters simply to feed his adrenalin and, of course, ignoring the warning: '*You are likely to be eaten alive if you swim here.*'

Eventually, I was able to come out of Aspie mode and drive the remaining one hundred and eighty-five miles of our journey from Miami to Jacksonville, along the Ronald Regan Turnpike before it continues as the I-95, with no further distractions.

A. Hang on a moment, do I exist? That you are able to get your way this time driving the most boring route because that fucked-up date of yours decides you are not for her a few hours after you had met the bitch. You're not going to pin that mistake on me. You drive the scenic route because otherwise you have to pay me some attention. Then you have the audacity to drive with the top down at ninety mph with the stereo blaring, which tells me I have no meaning in your life.

H. The irony is Aspie had me out here on false premise, a blind date. But she refused to open her legs and let him in and he blamed me. We'd just stepped off a ten-hour flight convinced that because her Go-Date profile read psychotherapist, she would be sympathetic to his needs. No difference to a lion tamer mauled by a lion because the lion doesn't know any better. Aspie cannot relate to a trait in him that she doesn't like so we were driving down to Islamorada, where we were supposed to be spending a sensual weekend together. Coincidentally, we run into some of her friends and had dinner together. During dessert, she breaks the bad news and she wants me to drive her home in my jet-lagged state. That night, I slept with fifteen cats. What a fucked-up psychotherapist!

Now, miles after we begun our journey, we are miraculously stepping through the entrance of the Cummer Museum in Jacksonville. The cultural tragedy in my tale is that so many fine collections in museums we never see because Aspie sends me somewhere to satisfy any one of his innuendos, knowing if killing was on the menu, he would be up for it.

A. I kind of like the idea of doing some killing.

R. Surely he must have some positive attributes? Are you trying to convince me there are two of you, one is good and the other evil?

H. Now you are beginning to get it. Even I can't comprehend the vile things Aspie gets me intertwined in. Try to imagine that during my life, I must have spent on therapy what other people earn in their lifetime.

R. That sounds a bit far-fetched. You couldn't have spent that much?

H. During my nightmare days, Aspie has therapy several times a week. Convinces me it is his necessity to keep alive. Saying he is pure evil, is being kind.

A. That's me. I love it. The best thing about me is being talked about.

H. Repetitively the same story, although different scenarios where Aspie controls every move.

A. If I dare be candid, manipulative; yes, controlling; no. I got so bored having to listen to your whingeing about being a victim of childhood sexual abuse. I think it bemused the psychiatrists, hasten to say even gave them some orgasmic satisfaction. I enjoyed it when the only answer they can deduce is that you live in a world rife with psychosexual fantasy. Shame you didn't see things my way? Given my circumstances, I decide I have no alternative but to become a killer, although not in my wildest dreams did I imagine I had the capacity.

H. There you have it, in a nutshell from the horse's mouth, so to speak. Assume I am of two personalities, you thought you heard Aspie interrupting. In the physical sense, it is only me.

R. Okay, I get it, if I notice a change in your tone or you are talking gibberish, you will let me know when you transmute from Dr. Jekyll into Mr Hyde?

H. I don't think you are getting it. A moment ago, Aspie mentioned he is a killer, forced to act because no one listens or comes to his rescue! I do appreciate your difficulty in acceptance of a story, which I write as unbiasedly as I can. You may not understand the context but I beg you to not ridicule or put Aspie down. Hopefully you will be able to grasp the gist of my story and when it appears I am talking to myself, understand that it is Aspie interrupting.

A. Hartley the pervert, Hartley's a fucking pervert!

R. Okay, you, or rather Aspie, have murdered someone, and that was an example of one of his outbursts you mentioned. Should I be scared that you will share your story then you will dispose of me?

A. Don't be so silly, Hartley wouldn't, although I might!

H. He does love his sick jokes! Anyway, I hope you have the time for lots of massages?

R. Hopefully. We can also learn why Aspie had so much influence on you?

H. In that case, all the more reason for Aspie to join in. My only concern is him having a loving relationship with the impossible, deplorable, disgusting and putting conjectures or fantasy to one side, then you will believe me when I say I am no storyteller!

R. Ah, Hartley, I know you well enough to know you are not that type of person. I want to reiterate earlier sentiments. I am not judgemental. You tell me your story, however you see fit, and let me be the judge of whether it makes sense or not. Remember, regardless of what you share, you can always count on me being your friend!

H. Okay then, if I jump from one scenario to another, which appears out of context, that is Aspie talking. Now, I feel the urgency to return to a part of life Aspie loved to bring up.

Chapter 3: The Trigger

H. I suppose had I been a normal kid, camping was something to look forward to. Except I had no knowledge then of Aspie. My mother had been informed that, after five years of therapy, I should have grown out of whatever I had gone through in my adolescent years. Yet, unbeknown to us all, he survived!

A. That's a nice thought, sarcastically speaking. Does this mean I'm preferred dead?

H. It was only a few weeks past my twelfth birthday and my mother did not know she was sending me into very unsafe territory. Aspie, still the child in me, preferred the security of her cuddles and he considered the camping holiday as his punishment.

During this period of my life, my mother was doing her best to ensure I had friends, without much success, other than children of close friends we often went on holiday with. I was being sent alone to the summer camp hoping I would find new friends. However, I returned home after the camp feeling like very damaged goods, having succumbed to the worst type of trauma any adolescent can be put through. So traumatising it had a profound affect on all my relationships and my marriage, as well as terrorising me every day until my last dying breath.

A. All I was doing was showing my contempt when I was yanked out of your father's Spitfire. Can you blame me for getting back into the boot and being yanked out again? You know how much I lusted the safety of your bedroom? Then the awful audacity of guzzling down a lunch of worms, when I was forced to eat with two hundred other children in the long white tent by the entrance to the camp.

H. That man looked so absurd, dressed in black shorts, striding backwards and forwards with a baton in one hand, as the commandant of the camp.

A. Absurd, but what he did with you pre-empted my lifestyle of deriving sordid pleasure from the experience he gave you. That the wrath of God descended on you when he stood on the table and announced; 'All you boys have been brought to me today so you can learn what being a man is all about. For a select seven, you will have me as your Scoutmaster. The rest of you will be under the watch of the other Scoutmasters during your stay at our campsite.'

It was ironic how Goliath's eyes seemed to zoom directly on you as he said, 'You see, this boy here is a wimp. If any of you want to be recognised as such, take a leaf out of his book. By the time I have finished with him, I can promise he will be every part all man.'

H. Already I was feeling humiliated, two hundred and more pairs of eyes gazing in my direction.

A. It was quite lovely that I endeared to you the ability to be hypersensitive. The way he grabbed hold of the tuft on your head and said to everyone, 'You see, this is something I won't tolerate. This means any crybaby I find will be expected to clean up the shit everyone else leaves behind. To enforce my message, this includes licking the shit off my arse if need be.'

H. Bad enough when his tongue licked the skin of my left cheek as if this was an omen to being a marked boy.

A. Perhaps for you, yes, but I had no idea how vile it was feeling his hot breath on your neck. I calmly savoured the sweat of his tongue thinking, Hartley my boy, you are going to die today. It was after he told everyone to go and erect their tents, unbeknown to you he had another erection in mind.

Goliath told you to close your eyes, count to one hundred and he would be waiting by his tent the other side of the wooded area. I knew you felt conspicuous and counting to one hundred quite unnerving, knowing his comforting words fuelled his deception. I found amusement when he had a completely different type of activity in mind. That memory is there to serve penance on you for the rest of your life and give me something else to savour. What you never expected in your wildest nightmares was seeing Goliath completely starkers spread-eagled waiting; with you totally unaware of what he had in store for you.

'Are you shocked by what you see, Hartley? Don't be shy, come down and sit with me; it won't bite. You think you are the first boy to go through this initiation process? All I am doing is initiating you into your manhood during puberty, whereas most boys have to wait well into their teens. You are here by request of your parents who can say to you when you arrive home, "How proud we are of you, Hartley." Come down and sit next to me, son, it won't bite you. Now, that's a good lad, wasn't difficult, was it?'

H. Sometimes, I wonder if Aspie even knows how to portray his own feelings or can comprehend how uncomfortable I felt, not that one utter of a word was able to be spoken from my lips, and worse was to come.

What happened next is what you might expect to hear if you were called to sit at court and listen to the prosecution who were there to see some fiend put away behind bars. You will hear words that horrify you, words that advocate a scene beyond belief, yet which were very real for me. Then the defence cut in with their own version of the story trying to make out that what occurred was no more than adolescent fantasy attempting to make an innocent man marked for life. The sad truth is I was humiliated by the most extreme vileness no one should be allowed to be a victim of. Sadly, I was that victim and I had to endure being told by him, 'Imagine if I have to tell all the other boys in the camp what a real wimp you are? What are they going to think?'

It was the afterwards when I told Aspie I couldn't live with the memory. I wanted to kill myself because I didn't want to be alive succumbing to reliving the horrendous torture. It reminded me of a cliché about God having to allow the worst atrocities to take place so he could understand man's pain. What about mine? The disgusting unthinkable thought that I had been raped. After it was over, he told me I must not mention a word to anyone and I had to report to him each and every night before I went to bed, when he would give me my punishment for allowing him to do what he had to do or the goblins would come and get me. It was annoying. I had to take the jibe from the other boys constantly jeering at me, 'Hartley can't sit properly. We wonder why,' becoming my recurring nightmare!

What was so sad was that instead of the epitome of my life and enjoying the fruits of adolescence, I instead had to endure Aspie finding my emotional pain so very entertaining.

A. I think you misunderstand me. It's my need to experience everything that life has to offer and, from my perspective, I assumed our experience was your initiation into adulthood. How could you have expected me to relate to you being violated? How many times do I have to repeat my inability to differentiating between right and wrong? After all, building a relationship of trust with my most trusted friend is what I'm about.

H. So finding me perched up a tree later wasn't a big deal? You remember when I was ten, I was lucky I didn't break my back when you had me climb that oak tree overlooking the cricket field because you wanted to get a better view of the match? I had no inkling I had to be on guard of your never-ending inquisitive mind being always forgetful about potential dangers. That's a great one, isn't it? Fun until the branch broke. Fun when I felt the searing pain as the branches giving away below left bloodstained scratches along my arms and legs. When I woke and wondered how I was going to walk my bike home because I hurt so badly all over? You humiliated me. I was mortified, like a wounded animal hiding for my life. You have no idea what you made me go through, or what he had done to me. I couldn't stop running into the darkness of the forest, running until exhaustion overtook me. I thought the darkness offered me safety, except this couldn't have been further from the truth! It was the most eerie rustling I was hearing. No idea your senses were far more sensitive than most boys of our age. It was as though I was picking up the vibrations of everything that was the terror of the night with some infested monster having me for dinner.

I was grateful when I reached the lower branches of the tree. I climbed until I could climb no further. I had never climbed a tree that high before. I was pleased when the noises I heard became muffled sounds rapidly disappearing. I had no idea until the following morning, when I heard a voice from below saying, 'What the hell are you doing up there? Do you know the worries you have caused?' Scoutmaster Jack said he had shouted out something to you and you got upset and before he could stop you, you ran into the forest. 'We shouted out your name, but you didn't answer and now you have caused so much unnecessary concern.'

They grounded me the following day and my punishment was cleaning the latrines.

Looking back on that summer holiday with the Forest Club, I wanted to curse my parents and have nothing to do with their friends who had suggested it.

Yet, I thought how ironic is it that the Forest Club was supposed to be the more socially adept version of the Scouts with less rules and regulations. I was told they were a community promoting equality and opportunity for children from the lesser walks of life. But instead it was run by paedophiles preying on naive kids, camouflaged in an organisation deemed to be safe. And I was unaware that what had occurred to me was only the main course, and dessert was going to be served during the following summer holiday.

I was barely thirteen years old when my becoming of man, the Jewish ritual, my bar mitzvah, was set to be the weekend after I returned from an exchange holiday to Denmark. My parents thought it was a good idea to teach me to become worldly by going to stay with my Danish penfriend who I had never met. Aspie must have been laughing his head off, as he watched me futilely trying to protest to my parents to get me home, during the only phone call I was allowed.

Initially, I was excited but it was the boredom of the Dutch and Danish countryside, devoid of any hilly scenery that Aspie became bored by, goading me into believing he had to think up some hiatus plans to make our stay more interesting. His sentiments were particularly portrayed when the ancient ugly duckling of my friend's mother threw open her front door to greet us with, 'Nice to meet you, but would you mind going out and buying a new face?'

After the exhausting coach ride, the old gizzard made the best suggestion that I get an early night and I was able to escape to my solitude. At breakfast, she gave me a thick slab of ham I couldn't eat, to which Aspie was so contemptuous, he threw the plate of food onto the floor. With the screaming of her illegible tongue bellowing, I ran out of the room screaming, 'Please, get me home!'

While each day brought a feeling I had been confined to solitary confinement. But what occurred during the second night, I had not the inkling would become akin to a penance for every day I lived. The following night, Aspie had me lie wide awake while his acute sense of hearing picked up the slightest creak of the floorboards. A hint of a whistle in the wind, a vibration of the glass in the window, and I begun to imagine my worst nightmare, a Pterodactyl working in cahoots with a T-Rex carrying me away until it was drop time into cavernous jaws ready for its dinner below. I screamed out aloud. The witch from downstairs ran into my bedroom sort of muttered in illegible English, 'What's wrong?' I saw by the expression on her face I had disturbed her relaxation. Anyway, she took me by her hand and led me into her living room and placed me on a sofa where she was sitting. It was then Aspie pursued his master plan.

A. Knowing the paedophile Scoutmaster had groomed me well, by telling me about things I could do, which other people deplore so much they run away in disgust, he told me it was quite natural for boys of my age to practice in readiness of reaching sexual maturity.

I knew how conspicuous Hartley felt sitting there on her sofa dressed in his brown-striped pyjamas knowing exactly his sentiments was for a fairy to whisk him home and open his eyes to the safety of being in his mother's arms. But I knew too he would never forgive me for what I was about to make him do.

H. I feel the urge to cut in here. What you are learning is that Aspie derives pleasure out of fucking up my life.

A. I agree on that one, mate! It was so enjoyable watching the contorted grimace on her ugly face. I felt she should have realised that watching television in a language you couldn't understand was no entertainment for you?

H. You had to take over with your menacing mind. Make me feel vulnerable and even more conspicuous as you drummed up your vile thoughts of what occurred the summer before. I wanted to run away from you. It was almost as though I was serving a penance staying with her. Yes, I do know you would have liked to have stood up and have me walk over to her and open my fly and thrust my penis into her face, but of course, you were a little subtler than that. You thought she wasn't going to notice your subtle taunting. Goading me until I finally snapped and I am unable to stop myself taking my hands and drawing my flies apart and pulling my penis out so it dangled there. It took her a while to notice, but then her abhorrent expression said the rest. She screamed blue murder and jumped up, pulled me by my left ear and dragged me back into my bedroom, cursing in her illegible language.

A. Remember my want to experience everything includes the paedophile grooming you to carry out his deed?

H. You do have a sick mind, don't you?

A. Honey, whether it is you or me. You see, you weren't doing what I had originally hoped you would do. My role in your life is to adhere to what you do best. You were coerced into doing something you didn't wish to be involved in. It was unfortunate for you, and my good luck. Thank your lucky stars she didn't call your parents to scream at them for allowing their perverted son to stay with her.

R. The tragedy of everything you are telling me is these very sick people cultivate vulnerable people because of their own sexual inadequacies. They were most probably sexually abused in their childhood in the first place. Then the indignity of believing they have every right to expect you to experience their own emotional torment.

H. Do you think I'm one of these vulnerable people?

R. Perhaps you are? From what I have gathered, easily influenced by the Scoutmaster to groom you. People like him should be locked up in solitary confinement for the remainder of their lives. They're mentally sick people, who all parents have to be very wary of. You, in your prime of your adolescence, had no knowledge of Aspie. Think about how terrified any one of your age would be devoid of any mental illness. How such deviant minds have only one sole purpose to get off on making you one of their converts.

H. I am pleased you have these sentiments because while I have three children, I have to live with punishing anxieties. Traumas I suffer on a daily basis and I believe my only solution is taking my life.

R. Don't you think that is a bit extreme?

H. For my children's sake, it is something I hope not to do. However, running away from my anxieties, I sometimes wonder if there can be an alternative.

It's not that I don't enjoy what Aspie has to offer me. You say he has been groomed; does this mean sexual perversion is something I have to accept will be a way of life for me? He would love us to fall in love with each other, have sex on a daily basis and live happily ever after. But I wonder how easily you can get used to his abnormalities?

No doubt you are already aware if you had small breasts, we wouldn't be having this conversation. But I wouldn't be lying on your massage table and, where sex was concerned, you would have to forget about foreplay since it would be a straight-in-and-out affair.

A. That's nice, you blind fucker. Shows how much you care about our relationship. I don't think you have any inkling of the emotional trauma I had to endure, particularly my inability to disassociate the entire sequence of discussion being forced down my throat. I am warned and brainwashed into believing that the female genitalia is God's heinous error when designing Eve. On one hand, wanting to give Adam a chunk of beauty, but on the other, a part of her anatomy to detest. So, where does that leave me, so young and innocent? Is it a crime that you could include my naivety into the transgression? Then having the audacity of him seeing me as his little bit of entertainment as he coerces me into believing sex is dirty, while female is genitalia the opposite of beauty.

Can you really believe I wanted to continually sexually expose myself to the world, yet that is what he had me do? Thank you. Blame me because I accepted the pervert's humour as being an unkind genuine truth. My fault, my inability to distinguish between fact and fiction, I rest my case!

H. I can only thank my lucky stars that I must have had an angel sitting on my shoulder looking after me. Groomed, yes; succumb to the pervert's hypnotic brainwashing, no, although at times, so dangerously close.

Chapter 4: Jacky

H. We are now moving the clock forward to the other poignant incident that rebirthed more of Aspie's torture. It was as though my wife Jacky's last supper with her mother was the ultimate endurance test for me. When a person's state of mind, their health, love, happiness, trust, value to their children, siblings, family, friends and other acquaintances are of little consequence and in a sense, a real macabre horror story; when a person decides they are beyond hope, that no one whatsoever is coming to their rescue and their desire, the final step they will ever make towards ultimate peace of mind for their physical self, is oblivion.

The culmination of this one act served me with a terminal prison sentence I should have never had to endure. Instead, I wanted to prove beyond reasonable doubt that the psychiatrist was proven guilty of misconduct. He was the one who had sectioned Jacky and then decided it served no purpose, instead believing that being looked after by her mother was the healthier option. It's common knowledge that antidepressant drugs can make you worse before they make you better. I spent six weeks discussing the matter with legal representation. I wanted some kind of retribution and to make him pay.

On the evening I am referring to, Jacky's mother made her the most loving of meals. She sat there looking so relaxed and pleased to be out of the hellhole, the mental hospital that had ensured her safety from herself, so I had been told. They watched television together and she bid her mother good night. The following morning, she was looking forward to the beautiful clear sky and the radiant waters of the Atlantic Ocean. It was the one thing her mother was always overjoyed about - she had taught Jacky as a child to become a strong swimmer. At the breakfast table, she looked a million dollars, dressed to impress as she ate the meal her mother had prepared for her.

A few moments later, they were sitting in her mother's car with her mother unaware of the hell that was about to descend. As Jacky put on her safety belt, the little demon sitting on her shoulder took over and Jacky said, 'Mother, please could you drop me at the beach? It's been such a long time since I have had a good swim.'

They were the last words her mother heard her daughter speak. Her determination and destination was a one-way swim to her eternity. She thought it would relieve the pain of living and hopefully, a bright new world lay in the waiting. A world where her soul could rest in peace and her spirit rekindled into a new life with unique adventures. It was when she didn't come back from her swim that her mother became alarmed and called the police. The coastguard later confirmed the worst.

By the time I reached the five-year milestone of marriage, I felt well endowed to be living the life of a family man irrespective of the trials and tribulations Aspie put me through. By now, Aspie had me well entrenched tiresomely commuting around the world searching for the most profitable antiques to secure a quality life for my family, while I supposedly always looked forward to arriving home and being in the company of my wife and children.

Sadly, Aspie had other plans for me that blinded me from understanding what commitment really means. My memory is of that night when I returned home, sensing a sign of sadness in Jacky's eyes. I tried to reassure her by saying how much I loved her, that we were a team and would be together to the day we die. Except Aspie prevented me from hearing the underlying tone, her repetitiveness of the same words often repeated: 'I am not so sure.'

I now fast forward to my erroneous dating escapades to Miami, amongst the many cities we regularly visited. Little did I know

Aspie had planned an adjunct of what was to follow, hopping from one blind date to another with a big chunk of water in between where I worked and lived. When he came across that advert in Go-Date, it spoke of a new life in a place where he felt most comfortable. The date he liked looked exactly like a woman who deserved to be his wife. In Aspie's eyes, there would be no courtship, she would know straight away they were going to be an item.

Except what happened was the opposite. Aspie almost pulled out his fingernails in frustration after repeating the same question. 'I don't get it. What have I done wrong? We have just met and you decide you don't like me without giving our relationship a chance.'

Being so quickly rebuked, I needed to seek some solace and I planned a drive up to the Cummer Museum in Jacksonville, knowing it wouldn't be long before I heard Aspie whingeing about feeling forgotten. Sadly, his boredom threshold was virtually non-existence even on days his ADHD rarely showed its face. With our visit to the museum behind us, the following day, mindful we needed to find a bargain at an antiques show, I felt a little warning sign that something terrible was about to happen.

We were in traffic at the time and the shunt forward was hardly noticeable, but the fact was the other driver shouldn't have been driving alone. Barely sixteen, just passed her driving test the day before. But for me, it broke a well-established record of twenty-five years of renting cars in America with no accident. After the little car fracas, Aspie and I found a motel for a good sleep before our three hundred mile drive to Miami airport the next day.

The unexpected phone call when it arrived threw me into an incomprehensible state of irrationality. Not even Aspie's impeccable and uncanny ability to assist me was helpful.

R. I cannot imagine in my wildest dreams how you must have been feeling, let alone how you coped?

H. Who could, yet somehow I knew I had to muster the strength to.

When my mobile rang, I was doing about forty mph and since I wasn't expecting any calls, it was a bit of a shocker hearing the words, 'Your wife has gone.' It was all my father said. In a fraction of a second, I felt more like a crumbled biscuit whose parts were now scattered onto the floor. It hadn't mattered that I had taken my hands off the steering wheel because my whole body had turned to jelly as I tried to recapitulate those four words.

When my car finally comes to a stop, it was lying at an acute angle somehow perfectly balanced over a deep ditch. I thought I hadn't blacked out, but before I could reverse and get back onto the road, a couple of drivers thought I'd a heart attack. 'Are you okay?' they said.

I couldn't answer. There was no strength left. The will to continue had all but left me. Worse were Aspie's sentiments trying to tell me that Jacky was 'a fucking stupid cow.' Because in my heart I knew she had done something I worried she would actually do.

'I've called for an ambulance,' I remembered one of these other drivers saying to me, and I must have mumbled.

'No, it's not necessary, I'm okay, just let me be. I've heard some rather bad news.'

'Sure?' They both asked to confirm I was all right.

I gestured, because I didn't have the strength to speak again.

A few moments later, both an ambulance and police car show up. My blood pressure was taken and I was given a thorough check to make sure I was fit to drive.

It was the emotional shock of what she had done that wiped out any strength I could muster. Just like you see on the TV, some nerve gas is dropped and everyone is instantly paralysed. It was the same for me, hearing words I had difficulty believing.

A. I knew I was right all along. Knowing her the way I did, it's all a test. She wants to see what she means to you. I know people like that. They coerce you to believe something terrible has happened to them and then you are left to patch up her broken pieces.

H. It's exactly what I would expect of Aspie; tough love, comes with the territory to make me even guiltier, as if I had neglected supporting her. Back on the road, I needed a chauffeur but the reality was, I was in a fucked-up state of mind.

'Go and have a strong black coffee,' the officer almost ordered compassionately.

I knew I was not in a fit and mentally stable way to drive to the airport, yet somehow I had to summon the emotional strength for the six-hour drive. During the five mile drive to the coffee bar, I couldn't stop crying. The tears were running down my cheeks and forming blotches of damp patches on my shirt and shorts. How was I supposed to make the drive that was demanded of me when my tears felt like the torrent of water that flows over Niagara Falls?

Whenever I approached any oncoming traffic, I somehow tried to cover my face, too embarrassed to let any stranger see how I was expressing my feelings. My erratic driving, moving from one lane to another, must have been obvious. I was the driver to be wary and stay well clear of. Before not too long, I saw in my rear-view mirror blue lights flashing.

'Son, what are we going to do with you? Perhaps you are too distraught to drive? I know I shouldn't be telling you to do this but a strong shot of whiskey may be the thing for you. I carry a small bottle in case of emergencies. But don't tell anyone I was the one who gave you a swig, and you have to promise me it be a small one?'

'Thank you, Officer, I feel so much better now. It has helped to perk me up, and I can tell you I'm now ready for my drive home.'

A. Knee him in the nuts, that you are not his son and order him to get the fuck out of your face.

H. You do say the right things at the right moments, don't you?

It is at tense times like this when I find it very disconcerting living with Aspie, not knowing how he will react to what is nothing more than normal concerned conversation. Then having to contend with the officer saying, 'I hope I didn't hear what I think I heard? Look, dead people don't talk, and although I know this is a sore point with you, I am sure your kids don't want a dead dad to contend with too.'

I didn't say anything, while Aspie murmured, 'Okay. I will do exactly as you asked of me before. You can even follow me if you want to and I am going to go directly to the coffee shop.'

'It's okay, son, I trust you,' the officer said as he was turning away. 'I can take it that I won't be meeting you in the morgue?'

H. 'No, sir, thank you, sir. That I can promise you, sir.'

I felt so isolated, miles from anywhere. Every alternative route went through my mind like finding a local airport to get me to my connecting transatlantic flight. The trouble was, even the closest airports of Orlando and Tampa were a good three-hour drive away.

I contemplated getting a connecting flight to New York. Whichever route I took, sod's law won. I wasn't getting home before tomorrow afternoon. It would be a sad, sleepless and empty journey home.

I thought it was best to make it safely to Miami and have as relaxed a day as was possible.

R. You made your flight?

H. Not exactly the way I had intended. You see, while this entire fracas was going on, Aspie decides I wasn't giving him enough attention. Irrespective of what Jacky had done, worried he was getting left out of the picture, he needed to act immediately. I sometimes joke that Aspie doesn't take any prisoners, just victims. Now bear in mind it is quite late in the day, and a few days before we arrived in Miami for a date Aspie fuck-ups.

A. That's kind of you. Blame me when anything doesn't work out for you.

H. Anyway, knowing Aspie always has a backup plan in place when things don't go well for him, normally a visit to the nearest massage parlour. On this occasion, he recalls Melons, another Internet profile he hoped I would have a relationship with. Her nickname fitted the bill of his ideal woman imagining the stimulus of gorging his head between her mammary glands. Anyway, three hours later, after we turn up at her place where she makes us welcome, she introduces us to her sister to whom Aspie believes a more enlightening relationship would be in the making, since she looks even more beautiful with the same curvaceous body. Thankfully we get offered a bed for the night, regrettably not hers while I had to get used to Aspie's jibe, hoping she would get the hint.

A. And why not, being in such a fragile state it should have been common decency for her to allow me to rest my head on her breasts. She had the biggest pair I had seen for a long time. Given your circumstances, she could have obliged!

H. Of the other things I forgot to mention is Aspie's annoying habit of interrupting with poppycock, just to be heard. I was feeling very fragile and the first thing I wanted to do was call home. Melons told me I can do so on condition when I return home, I send her some money to cover the costs of the calls.

R. Did you?

A. No way! Her email read only $25, so I decided what's the big deal? Actually Hartley deleted her contact details!

H. Something I feel I have to inform you about him. Our marriage began a catalyst of not learning about what he couldn't achieve. Simple thank you notes for all the gifts we received from invited guests took months to reply to. Meanwhile, I had to fend off annoying expressions by guests who decided I hadn't the courtesy to thank them for their generous wedding gifts. The truth be known, it was Aspie who found difficulty in putting a stamp on the envelope and the chore of sending the thank you note placed inside. Leave it to Jacky to do and it would never be done, amongst the first of Jacky's traits I learnt to get used to. It was my mistake of visualising the perfect marriage between Aspie and Jacky; one a misfit and both without organisational skills.

We left Melon's home feeling refreshed, and by the time Aspie had said his words at the Virgin counter, I think the agent in charge would have liked to stuff him in the baggage hold! True to the picture of what an Aspie is. He walked straight to the first class check-in, ignored two travellers standing in front of the counter, recognised a manager and came straight to the point. 'I just learnt my wife died; this means you're going to upgrade me?'

It was quite brash on Aspie's part. He believed in being confident in what you ask for and it worked this time. At the very least, I was grateful we were not sitting in cattle class that night.

R. I don't get it, what is the fuss of standing in a line. Everyone has to do it, so why not you'?

H. I will tell you why. A few years ago, I needed to get to a bank to draw out more cash than I could at any other cashpoint. We arrived in the branch and Aspie had me march up to the counter and demand the cash he required. Except we are met with our first problem; I didn't have any form of identity. 'You have no problem in what I ask, do you?' he demanded of the cashier. Had there not been a panel of glass between her face and his, I am certain their noses would have met. It was unsavoury enough, me listening to Aspie giving her some of his lip when she couldn't identify my bank details by my name alone.

All of a sudden, at the top of his voice - just to get the whole bank's attention - he shouted, 'No, you don't. You are not going to tell me that you are unable to find my personal information. Any idiot knows even an imbecile working here can find it. You're not going to tell me that your banking system is that fucked-up?'

'Please, sir, it is not necessary to use such language.' The cashier tried to implore.

'Don't tell me what I fucking can or cannot say,' Aspie added under his breath hoping she could not hear him, 'you fucking bitch.'

In front of Hartley was a very tearful cashier. Not in her wildest dreams did she ever imagine she would be confronted by verbal abuse, and she said to him, 'I am sorry, but you are going to have to excuse me for a moment.'

She added, 'I have never been spoken to in such a rude manner,' to her senior colleague, who tried to calm the situation with this belligerent customer. Aspie reiterated what he had told the younger of the two clerks, hoping the information he repeated to the more senior clerk would make it easier for her to find his personal details. But he was wrong.

'I am sorry, sir, but I have entered the information you gave to my colleague and there is no record of your account details. It would be better next time if you ensure you always bring your cheque or paying in book with you into the bank preventing this incident re-occurring.'

Aspie immediately went in for a frontal attack in his loudest raised voice.

'You do know what autism is, don't you?'

'I am sorry, I don't, sir,' was her reply.

That's a shame because it would have explained the breakdown in communication. By this time, we had our own audience; a dozen or so irate customers, some ready for a quarrel because of the rude man at the front of the queue. Aspie always had to have the last word, so he continued.

'It's a pity you are unable to find my personal details because now I will be forced to run through the freezing rain outside to my car to retrieve my cheque book because you pitifully refuse to be customer friendly. Therefore I can assume, can't I, that I can regain my position at the front of the line on my return?'

Suddenly, I felt an outstretched hand on my right shoulder.

'Look, mate, if you don't want my fucking fist through your teeth, just get the fuck out of my face.' The irate man said displaying an expression that he meant business.

'Jim, there's no point you getting so angry, can't you see we are dealing with a mental retard. It won't make a difference to him what you do or say!'

A. Fuck the lot of you!

H. I had to put up with Aspie a few moments later with his chequebook brushing his way through the crowd as though there was only him and no one else.

R. I imagine that couldn't have gone down well?

H. Too right! With him barging his way back to the front of the queue, with the audacity to add, 'You don't mind, do you!' I had long ago learnt never put it past him saying his worst, knowing embarrassment was part of his way of insisting every Tom, Dick and Harry were brought into the conversation.

A. It's something I will never understand. I've got every right to behave the way I do and also to say that Jacky was a stupid fucking cow! How the fuck do you think you were going to responsibly look after your children on your own? Wasn't I enough on your plate?

H. That's funny hearing that coming from you. I wish it could be that you are dead and gone, then at the very least I might have some normality in my life. No, don't say anything. I know you will say that is your sentiment too. But you know, because I do have you in my life, that it will be very challenging looking after four children.

R. It's odd how you have just referred to Aspie as one of your children?

H. What little I have told you about his interfering is just like dealing with a young child who doesn't know any better.

R. You must have been very pleased when the plane touched down in London. Bet you couldn't wait to see them.

H. I wish it were that simple. But for me, being the supporting father was entirely another matter.

R. Why?

H. Simply because my children didn't want to see me. They felt I had let them down. Remember I was away dating. From their perspective, I must have been seen as the bastard father who, if he had given their mother unconditional emotional support, would have been there for her on a daily basis and she might still be alive.

A few years later, when I was able to discuss with my boys their relationship with their mother, Tim admitted, that while I was travelling abroad, he became his mother's confidant. When he went off to university, Sam became his mother's crutch.

R. That's shameful. Surely a mother shouldn't share such intimate details about your private lives?

H. Tell me about it. In her state of mind, she needed to mentally unload; bearing in mind, as soon as Aspie brought home what she considered unwelcome presents, she had no choice.

R. You mean to tell me, Tim knew all about your various sexual liaisons?

H. There were no secrets barred. They always had a very good relationship. He could never do any wrong in her eyes, even though he made our lives hell throughout his adolescence.

R. Don't all our children do so as they are growing up?

H. If we lived on a council estate in a run-down part of town, I wouldn't have thought anything better of him. Jacky showered him with presents most kids of his genre don't get to have. I think part of the problem was Aspie getting the hump, when I couldn't relate to her emotional needs.

Their mother had taken her life and they were being deprived of the only parent they badly needed for support. There was nothing I could do to help them adjust to her unwelcome departure!

A. Poor fuckers. If they had an Aspie like me around, I would have ensured Jacky was reincarnated; that would have got them thinking.

H. A typical Aspie remark! Talk about the worst type of cruelty. I was deprived of my own children for the remainder of the day and for two nights. It was the look on their faces that told me what I didn't want to know. I knew they wanted what I couldn't give them. I felt useless; whatever I said couldn't have any meaning. Empty ashen faces all dressed in black. My poor mother-in-law could barely mutter, "My beautiful baby, gone."

A. Fucking bitch, the way she looked at you. Her stare freaked me out. I knew if the boot were on the other foot, she would have preferred you dead!

H. Exactly the sentiments I expect from your mouth. It is only natural she would have preferred her baby alive and I lying in that coffin.

Tragically, she had got her comeuppance, the peace of mind she had been waiting for so long. Yet, in front of me, laid out and dressed in the funeral parlour, she looked so eerily handsome, frozen in time. For what appeared to be eternity, but was likely to be no more than a passing moment, all I wanted to cherish were the mesmerising memories before I said my final goodbye. Even though Aspie vied her with his contemptuous eyes. As I stood there, I caressed her right cheek. It was so cold. I gave her a gentle kiss on her lips, hoping if there was a beyond, she would be aware I cared, before I said my final goodbyes. 'She's so beautiful,' is how I wanted to remember her as I took myself back in my head to the very first time I had set my eyes on her.

Chapter 5: That Most Beautiful Day

H. I was twenty-eight years old and a member of my local health club in Birmingham. I'd go there with Jamie, my training partner, who'd often comment why I had to strain lifting the heaviest weights. 'You know, lad, you are getting stronger and stronger.' I replied I was not a lad, I am Hartley, and he laughed. I didn't understand him but I accepted this was his way.

I told him when I was lifting the heaviest of weights, it got rid of my pent-up aggression and anxieties. Little did I know, this was Aspie stirring uncomfortable memories from my childhood. As weird as it sounds, I had to relentlessly check inside every drawer of every cupboard, wardrobe and under the bed, in case of a lurking monster; unaware while in Aspie nightmare mode, he was very much alive and kicking.

I began telling Jamie how lonely I felt and wanted to be like him with a wife and kids.

The next thing I was aware of was him calling his mates to come and join us and telling them they had to hear what I had said. 'Guys, you have got to listen to this. Hartley thinks we are the lucky ones because we are married!'

'Yeah, yeah, yeah!' they all shouted simultaneously.

'Why don't you tell Hartley the truth? Tell him he's the lucky one who can choose who he wants to lay, and if he really wants a piece of our advice, then he'd better wait another ten years before he gets himself hitched up like us.'

'You hear that, Hartley? They all think you are fucking crazy. Do you really want to emulate any of us? Here's the bottom line. You know how often I have told you how lucky you are being single? For one thing, we are a few years older than you and look at what happened to me? I wish I could have learnt a lesson and walked away from Joanne, but I didn't. I did the honourable thing and married her so she wouldn't have to raise Harry on her own. That was fourteen years ago and now we have three little Harrys. I'm only thirty-eight, and you know I can't always accompany you to the gym. It's even a luckier night when I get to go out for a drink on a Friday night with all the guys. Is this the fuck of a life you really want to become of you? Okay, if you do want to get married, do as the boys say, wait until you are forty. Then you can say you have really lived a life!'

In one way, I knew Jamie spoke sensible words but it was Aspie who was coercing me to believing finding a good woman, getting married, having some kids and becoming a family man was a well worth it headache.

It was while the two of us were walking out of the club through the reception area that I suddenly stopped abruptly. 'Look at the jugs on that bird sitting by the bar! Now she would make me a fine wife!' I said to him. We laughed as we walked out. Those were the days I drove a Ferrari, another of my mistakes.

R. A mistake, owning a Ferrari at twenty-eight? It seems to me you'd made it into the big time!

H. One of my life challenges having Aspie in my life was being coerced into believing the bigger or grander my possessions are, the more ideal our relationship could grow. Mind you, I did enjoy the moment I turned the key in the ignition and felt the roar of the 365 horsepower engine the car was famous for.

I remember saying to Jamie, 'You tell me a girl who is going to turn down a fine hunk of a man like me who boasted an everlasting sex drive, favourable bank balance, a luxury two-bed pad in Highgate, an antique Steinway concert grand piano in the living room and a view overlooking all of London to die for.'

'You are really crazy, aren't you, Hartley? Don't you ever stop trying to make us all jealous because you met a nymphomaniac in Israel? You can't stop boasting about what you got up to with her. Isn't that more of a reason not to want to settle down and carry on making fun of us?'

R. Nymphomaniac?

H. I will be talking about her a little later in my story. Anyway, as soon as I had dropped Jamie off, I couldn't get out of my mind the bit of crumpet sitting by the bar, hoping that the next time I went to the gym she would be still sitting there.

You have no idea that while I was living in the fast lane, travelling abroad as I did, I had so much competition with Aspie, knowing the last thing he needed in his life was getting less of my attention. While thinking sensual thoughts about the girl with the big tits, I had to contend with Aspie drumming up thoughts that my bedroom had been invaded by goblins. This meant I had to watch a horror film and then, with barely three hours sleep, I was grateful to hear the alarm go off at 4.00am for my early morning flight to New York.

R. I didn't know transatlantic flights left so early?

H. You don't know Aspie very well, yet. Once you have learnt my story, you will realise he was responsible for anything that normality isn't. The club opened at 5.30am and that is where we headed with the ridiculous assumption we were going to walk through the front doors and there she would be sitting. Then it would be a case of strolling across to her and saying, 'Hi there, my name is Aspie and I want to put my head between your enormous tits before I get on my flight to New York, so I know whether or not you are wife material!'

R. That's a great turn-off line. No doubt she wasn't there that early?

H. Sadly, no. That opportunity arose as soon as we returned from New York, and I decided to drop into the gym and saw her sitting at the far end of bar. I summoned up enough courage to walk across to where she was sitting but regrettably, it was Aspie who spoke first - on purpose whispering - and hoping she would find the tone of his voice amusing. But instead his words were in bad taste.

'Cat cut your tongue?'

She replied, 'Are you aware that you are known to have a very big mouth?'

'Who, me?' I answered, feeling rather shocked.

'Yes, you. I would much prefer you went to the men's changing room, find a mirror to talk to and you can spend all night gawking and staring into it at your heart's content!'

I remembered how I almost choked, gulping down my drink of cider as I said to her, 'Excuse me, who's woken up on the wrong side of the bed, eh?'

'I am sorry. It's been a bad week or two. I'm working freelance here as a beautician and the past couple of weeks, I've hardly made any clients. I know I shouldn't have barked at you like that, but there is one thing I have noticed. You do appear to stare a lot,' she said to me.

'Stare? You have got me on that one. Anyway, would you mind me staring at the most beautiful woman I have seen in the world?'

'Go away, you are trying to flatter me?' she answered.

'No, I am not. I always say what I mean and I wouldn't say you are the most beautiful girl in the world unless I meant it. If, as you say, I have been staring at you, then I have to say yes, I do admit to you that I have been staring. But only because of what I said a moment ago. I could have used the perfect excuse that I was jet-lagged because since the last time I saw you, I've been on a business trip to New York.'

'Wow! New York! I wish I'd been there with you,' she replied.

'Any chance of your phone number?' I asked.

'No, I don't think so. Look, I know we got off on the wrong foot, but you do appear to be a bit weird and I don't give out my phone number, especially to a bloke who hasn't even given me his name.'

'Oh, my name, why would you want to know that?'

This is where Aspie took control of our conversation.

'Are you joking me?' she replied.

'Why would I do that?'

Now try to relate to the many things Aspie doesn't do too well with. Whenever he believes someone is speaking out of place or untoward, he gets the hump. It is as though he believes he is getting rebuffed, so his way out of the situation is to walk out the front door of the club without saying another word.

Later, I got this story from Jacky, although at that time she didn't know my name. She had told her mother about her strange experience, meeting Aspie at the gym.

'Hi, Mum, the weirdest thing happened to me today. This strange bloke comes up to me and makes some stupid weak remarks, unaware he's staring at my tits, and then asks me for my phone number without telling me his name! I have got to admit, I had difficulty keeping a straight face. When I said to him, "Are you joking me?" and asked him for his name, instead of simply giving it to me, he walked out of the club. Mother, I have to say, this was one of the strangest experiences I have ever had with a man. You know I have been out with quite a few men in my time, but none of them that rude! Mind you, I had noticed him staring at me and, without a doubt, I fancied him, but I don't think after that experience I would ever want to entertain a date with him?'

'You know, darling, these men will do anything to get a date and you know this is a fabrication because their only real interest is to get you into bed, and then it will be all over. I suggest you leave it as one of life's experiences, and if you ever meet anyone like him again, just say, "I am sorry, you are not my type."'

H. I remember about a week later returning to the club and seeing her standing at the bar and asking if I could buy her a drink. She said to me, 'After the experience you gave me the other day, I don't think so.'

I had forgotten it was Aspie speaking, so I said, 'Excuse me?'

'You mean you don't even remember?' she replied.

'Nope!'

'Then there is no point in continuing with the conversation.'

'Why not?'

'You are beginning to bore me. Normally when two people meet, it's the norm to exchange names. This is the second time you have cornered me, been extremely rude, and last time when I asked you for your name, you turned round and walked out the door. I hate to say it, but you are the weirdest man I have ever met. Anyway, do you think you could tell me your name without getting upset?'

'That's no problem.'

'So?'

'I'm sorry, I don't understand what "so" means?'

'Look, this is getting absurd. I'm a woman and you are a man. Men are usually the first to introduce themselves! I have never met anyone like you before. Anyway, my name is Jacky, what is yours?'

'Oh, it's Hartley. Why didn't you ask me that before? Now can I have your telephone number?'

'Look, I don't want to appear offensive, but I hardly know you and strangers are not people I give my number to.'

'I don't really understand the remark you have just said. Why would I be offended? I decided to come up to you to say hello because every time I see you, you are sitting here by the bar. The other day I was with my mates and as I was leaving the club, I saw you sitting alone. So please tell me what's so wrong about wanting to chat to you?'

'You know this conversation is really going nowhere. I am sure you are a very nice guy, but at this time I am on my tea break and I came out here to the bar to have a quick puff and spend some time on my own. Once again, you have come along and ruined that chance. If you don't mind, since I have a client to see in a few moments, I would just like to be left alone so you are going to have to excuse me.'

Perhaps you are beginning to grasp that there is me and there is Aspie. We are two different personalities living under the same hat. Anyway, a little later on, once we got to know each other, Jacky told me about discussing her experience with Aspie with one of her clients. Once she had returned to the massage room, her client asked her why she was so disgruntled.

She said, 'Peter, you can't believe it, the other day I saw this guy staring at me.'

'What's wrong in that?' he replied.

'There's something more, but I just can't get a grasp what it is. He's got some strange mannerisms as well as being too persistent for my liking.'

'Jacky, have you ever thought he is just a shy and lonely guy, and perhaps he has difficulty in expressing his feelings? Maybe he believes he has found the woman of his dreams: you! I would, as I think any normal man would too. During the time I have got to know you, you tell me you are ready for a new relationship, and perhaps this guy is the one.'

'You know what, Peter, I think you have hit it on the nail and have exactly expressed my fears. I wouldn't mind so much if he was discreet, but he is full on in my face as though he doesn't seem to care. As much as I value your comments, I don't think there's a chance of that happening in a million years, thank God.'

I hope you are beginning to grasp a picture of Aspie. Sometimes I prefer thinking of him akin to Jekyll and Hyde; both friend and foe, depending on his mood.

Anyway, here I am back with Jamie and his mates feeling very disgruntled. They recognise my unrest because I am still acting out the Hyde effect, and with this in mind, all the more reason for them to continue goading me.

'Hi, Hartley, how's it going today. Shame you can't find the woman of your dreams, eh?'

I was grateful to Jamie who came to my rescue. 'Come on, lads. Don't be so heartless. You know Hartley is jealous of us having wives.'

The following day, exhausted from jet lag, I sleep for eighteen hours. Meanwhile, Jacky's perfectly voluptuous figure suited Aspie's needs and I knew she was the perfect woman I wanted for a wife. So, we both got what we wanted, or did we?

Chapter 6: A Sample of Aspie

H. During my next visit to the fitness club, things began to get off to a better start when Jacky walked over toward me. Because I had mentioned I was an antique dealer, she asked me if I knew anyone who could repair her earrings. I told her I could help on the condition she went out with me.

R. You said a moment ago, "or did we". Would you mind expanding on that?

H. Yes, it's a bit of a sore point. Physically, we were attracted to each other, but mentally and unknowingly, we were each other's nightmare. I never knew she suffered with depression, while Aspie's mannerisms lead her - later - to ask herself why the hell she had decided to become my life partner.

When I met Jacky, it was during a period when money grew on trees. Whenever Jacky visited my flat, she saw a wardrobe full of exclusive brands lying in a heap on the dressing table as though I didn't respect my possessions. The whole attire of the bedroom suggested wealth with an antique bedroom suite crafted in the finest Satinwood workmanship, silver-plated handles and the most luxurious super king-size bed. Meanwhile, the breathtaking views from my flat included seeing the whole of London down to the North Downs in Surrey.

If what Jacky saw was not enough to capture her imagination, then adjusting her eyesight to an antique Steinway grand piano sitting smack in the centre of the living room. She thought, if this was a place she could die, then Hartley had to be the right man to do it with. Little did she know this metaphorical thinking would have dire consequences later on in her life, let alone that her first baby would be conceived here too.

My naivety in realising how Aspie resided in my life was as volatile as relating his most fevered exhibitionisms, irrationalities and argumentative attitude, similar to an unexpected erupting volcano. An example was when Jacky agreed to live with me and Aspie demolished the kitchen units, explaining to her that our baby-to-be couldn't be looked after in a kitchen built of the most antiquated of units.

R. I imagine that went down well with her?

H. Exactly, but meanwhile OCD created wealth in our life. I had acquired a brilliant business acumen and the art of profiting from buying and selling antiques. Basically, to understand Aspie, I had to be aware he resented being at the bottom of the chain of command and the profit margins my customers put on top of the prices they paid me never failed to agitate him. My only saving grace was my unawareness to his unjustifiable antics. He had me spying on my neighbours, often having to listen to their repetitive jibes: 'Beware, Aspie is on the prowl, hide the invoice books!'

My angst with Aspie was his indiscreet manner and not caring about making it blatantly obvious he didn't care whether they discovered him rifling through their invoice books or not. Worse still was that customers who were gay didn't adhere well to his antics. You know similar temperaments to you women, who say something they consider inappropriate and irreparable damage will be done. My shop became the plague to them to be bypassed as all costs.

A. I always appreciate thanks being sent my way, although I disagree with Hartley intimating I didn't retain any learning capacity. Since I required him to initiate this in the first place, and if he didn't then I couldn't be expected to do so on my own account.

H. By now I only had around six years of experience as an antiques dealer, having left philately far behind. It's a sad fact because I believe I had a genuine talent and wished I could have retained knowledge of buying and selling stamps rather than just forgetting it. Sadly, Aspie never gave me that chance.

A. Bollocks, don't blame me for losing your ability to remaining a philatelist! You just presumed that you couldn't learn on my own accord, so there was no point in teaching me in the first place.

R. Is it true what Aspie has just said?

H. True, from the perspective of me losing interest, which disguised him taking on any of the blame. The most outrageous of all his jealousies was that no sooner had I made money out of my specialism than I was stopped dead in my tracks. I can't begin to tell you how many arenas of specialisms I moved in or out of on Aspie's account.

R. What do you believe pre-empted this getting you nowhere attitude of his?

H. In a nutshell, it got him my attention, as well as leading me astray to believing I was building a sustainable interest in virtually every possible profitable genre in world ceramics and oriental work of art. The irony of how I was learning about the antiques trade differed exponentially from those eight years I enjoyed as a young professional philatelist. It seemed my learning capabilities back then were far more enhanced than when I embraced the world of antiques. Converting from being a mere schoolboy collector to immersing myself in the world of philately appeared to be a doddle. I wonder if all Aspies are collectors of sorts? My reason for collecting began because I found the huge variety of colourful stamps very fascinating. The quirky idea of sticking the stamps onto mounts by licking the adhesive backs and mounting them onto pages that became stamp albums possibly assisted my motor skills.

However, the change in my luck happened when I met a teenage philately protégé. From the moment our eyes met, it was love at first sight. Zachary's success was due to being a second-generation philatelist; his father was in the trade too. I began working a Saturday job with Zachary and it wasn't long before I learnt from his experience and became successful in my own right.

While moving into the field of antiques dealing meant getting used to buying from every Tom, Dick and Harry, for me this was a daunting task because I didn't have a mentor like Zachary teaching me the ropes. Because we were selling to every Tom, Dick and Harry from overseas, the idea of travel became very addictive for Aspie; except unbeknown to me, he had an ulterior motive, which was looking for a bride masseuse to become the perfect wife for him.

Aspie is all about control as though I was entirely under his spell. You see, Aspie's attitude is akin to a double-edge sword. It required one hundred per cent of my attention. While I was making money he wasn't getting any attention from me and he could not emotionally cope with my difficulty in finding a girlfriend. Parting with my money got him what he wanted and why I sometimes considered him to be a controlling freak of nature.

Particularly, when Aspie realised I had left the world of philately to become an antiques dealer, it was as though it was one of my life's single biggest mistakes. From his perspective, he was breaking his own rules - learning from scratch - something he sadly resented.

While on paper I was bringing in the bucks, cash appeared to be free falling out of a hole in my pocket, which I wasn't aware of.

To Aspie, everything in my life appeared to be dominated by the same rule. The one he had taught himself when the nursery school teacher found him staring at the wall where he felt safe, exploring the infinity of the void that was his mind. Here he existed without interruption from anyone telling him otherwise. During my day-to-day business activities, on the other hand, he felt everyone was mocking him and somehow I had to put up with his rule presiding over my good business acumen. His infinite world equated being bigger to being more advantageous and smaller equating to the least, where value is concerned. It took me about ten gruelling years of emotional angst to get him to accept that small could be of greater benefit than big, because it fitted better into the collections of my customers.

Moving on a few years to another occasion, a few months after meeting Jacky, when big matters occurred. While I was not going to explain how Aspie developed his relationship with bigger being the better, all I can say is that big breasts was part of the reason, as well as having a correlating relationship with a big clock I was ordered by Aspie to hand deliver to one of my customers.

Whenever I do anything that Aspie believes he has not given me permission to do, he disappears into his world of infinite possibilities. As ironic and sad as it sounds, if Jacky had small breasts, we would not have been an item. The same criteria existed in everything we did together. When I was a philatelist, it was all about the highest catalogue value. As an antiques dealer, his criteria for the majority of our purchases was based on an object's size or profit, with the exception of rarities that often came in small packages, like cups and saucers, cream jugs or teapots etc. These were the only exceptions he accepted to his 'the larger, the better' ruling.

His ideals were based on our business exploits during the seventies and eighties when it was easy to identify with the huge worldwide demand for decorative objects of desire. Where bigger meant a higher price tag. So began an addictive search for the biggest of everything. I could, on any one buying trip abroad, buy as many as fifty items while Aspie curled each of his fingers and toes, working out how much we were going to make as though he was a computer capable of multiplying great numbers. This clear example of OCD I was unaware could be repeated repetitively while driving, on a plane, or while sleeping, or anywhere boredom took over, offering me little respite.

Another example occurred after I had meet Jacky, when I sold this large French tortoiseshell and brass inlaid bracket clock, almost as big as she was tall. The customer bought it on the condition of delivery door to door in Johannesburg. Bearing in mind I had to cover the cost of delivery, he had set me up with a dilemma and brought into the sale bad karma by saying I had to take Jacky with me, otherwise I would risk returning home to find her in another man's bed. Ultimately, this he would have preferred!

I always ensured we travelled in style, staying at the best accommodation I could afford. The Hilton was no exception. One day, we had just eaten a good breakfast and Jacky went to the bathroom. When she comes back, she asked me why my hands were behind my back. My answer was that I was getting down on my hands and knees and asking her to marry me, inserting around her finger a makeshift engagement ring. She hesitated for a moment and then, with an almost shock of disbelief, looked down into my eyes and actually said the words she had been waiting so say: 'I would love to.'

From Aspie's perspective, his instinct was to utilise the most despicable tactics because he didn't want anyone - regardless of their demeanour - to have a relationship with me. So, Jacky and I walked out of the hotel and suddenly it was as though some terrorist had pronounced his arrival, flung themselves with all force between an elderly couple who had been enjoying holding hands. For Aspie - living in his own world - the couple were invisible to him. The instant look of disapproval from Jacky demonstrated her discontent. 'I'm supposed to be marrying the rudest man I have ever met. I don't think so,' she said, while simultaneously chucking the makeshift engagement ring I had just given her on the ground.

A. From my perspective, I couldn't see why she was making so much fuss. I could see an elderly couple behind me but I had no idea I had actually brushed them aside. So what's the big deal? Women get upset by the most mundane of things.

R. You mean Aspie had no shame?

H. You know, at times I felt such utter despair because Aspie was so prevalent in my face. I contemplated a way out to be rid of him once and for all. It was sad because I was once the epitome of success, but he could wreak vengeance at any time since any form of kindness or sympathy was beyond his comprehension.

A. You expect me to show you some kindness. You don't have to share me with the rest of the world, you belligerent bastard.

H. Yes, there are days I felt contemptuous towards him when he breathed down my neck waiting for prime moments to show his indifferences. I just wish he could have been less confrontational and not taken every argument so seriously. My only recourse was to go along with his untoward ways; he won, whichever way I decide.

Sometimes I compared Aspie to a cantankerous viper. Once it sets its teeth into its victim, it never lets go; as though knowing survival is dependent on its first strike.

Thank God, by the following day, all had been forgotten because Jacky decided to put her indifference to Aspie's peculiarities to one side. After all, love is supposed to conquer all. Nevertheless we didn't have long to wait until the next episode, which occurred en route to Durban during a visit to a safari park.

It was like a story picked up by the media about tourists mauled by lions. I had forgotten to fill up with fuel and we were empty bang in the middle of the lion reserve. Fortunately, we weren't on the lion's menu that day because the park rangers were close to hand. So Aspie decided to find another way to put my life at risk and dive into the shark tank on the beach in Durban while Jacky went off to buy ice creams.

R. No paramedics to take you to a lunatic asylum. Sorry but it is hard to believe some of the far-fetched things you come out with. Did Aspie not realise you could have been eaten alive? Actually, I don't expect you to answer that question. Didn't Jacky think something was amiss? You must have been soaked to the skin?

H. Fortunately, we were next to showers. And there was something else Jacky had to get used to; an entire holiday without searching for a distraction, especially a profitable one, didn't exist in

Aspie's world. Fortunately, the following day we found an antiques shop and I bought this rare eighteenth century Chinese dish made for the Emperor Ching Lung that paid for our holiday several times over. At least the remaining ten days of our holiday was enjoyed in style and any more Aspie misdemeanours forgotten about.

I appeared to be in the epitome of my life - going from strength to strength - and with a wedding to look forward. However, reality was somewhat different. From day one of buying and selling my first stamp, I saw Aspie as a moneymaking machine. But inside my body, I was unable to understand the strange feelings and mannerisms. For all the positives going on in my life, there were many more negatives. Just as Aspie almost caused Jacky to disown me, he had a similar technique of losing me customers. Part of Aspie's character, his demure and decadence and communication challenges, that were invisible to me, meant anyone who didn't fit his norm saw his all too obtrusive label that read, *Gay people are not wanted here.*

R. Why?

H. He lived in a world where assurances and certainties drove him, and as successful as I was, I felt like damaged matter. I was financially getting richer but everything Aspie presented in my life gave me problems. Especially for those customers who were regulars at my competitor's shops and spent tens of thousands of pounds, but chose to veto my shop because of Aspie.

He did everything he could to find out as much as he could about them; pounding on their hotel rooms as though his intent was sharing their bed. I had to get used to the jibes behind my back. 'Such a shame Hartley's social manners are so unappealing. It's no wonder customers give him a miss when they deserve a little more privacy and peace of mind.'

R. I suppose you have heard this said to you before; business people have their private lives too. I wonder how they felt after Aspie invaded their privacy. Likewise in personal relationships, women love men who are independent and show a strength of character. It sounds like they saw this lacking in you.

H. Yes, thinking about it, our marriage reminded me of a constantly erupting volcano like Stromboli. There were the quiet times when our lives were always enthralling with happiness and then the explosions when Aspie erupted into play. When business was good, Aspie was less in my face, but when he saw the opportunity of missing out, he showed the side of him I preferred not to see.

Chapter 7: All About Aspie

R. Changing the subject, given that you compare Aspie giving you mayhem in your business activities and personal, what predisposed your marriage going wrong?

H. Hmmm, when Aspie was born. While this may make no sense to you, it's about Aspie's inability to be aware to other people's life challenges, just his own, with this culminating in sexual tensions between him and Jacky.

R. I don't think you mentioned anything to me about this part of your life before.

H. Okay, let's start from the beginning.

A. Hey, I think it's about time for me to butt in. You say your mother knew we were different to other children. Okay, what about me? How many babies grew into normal children when they were born six weeks premature, spent their first week of life in an incubator and are deprived of their mother's breasts for a further week? I reckon this absence of essential nutrients so early on stimulated my avid interest in mammary glands.

This rather spurious episode was followed by my having to accept normal would never exist in my life. I didn't have to wait for long because at eighteen months I became a guinea pig for medical science's latest Draconian approach for a cure for knobbly knees when leg irons were forcibly fitted to my legs. Not exactly the Christmas present I was expecting. Is it any wonder I developed a degree in cursing?

While the other children in my nursery class were defined as normal, I was only beginning to learn how not to wear nappies.

Then the audacity of learning I was not of Earth-born, an alien so to speak, I heard my mother being told. 'We can't really put pen to paper as we, that is I and my colleagues, think that Hartley believes he has found a novel approach to learning, counting the tiles on the floor and the wall and gesturing with his hands, as though he has literally gone off into some far away fantasy world. We have tried our best but every time we sit him back with the other children, it is as though an invisible thread pulls him back to where we found him, staring into some sort of void.'

What the teachers don't know was I saw the plethora of my class as being among the genre of fucked-up retards, not me. Have you got any inkling what it was like facing a string of child psychiatrists who informed my parents there was a place in the local zoo for me? That's what it felt like when I was placed on a pedestal and subjected to regular visits to establish what genre of the human species I might be. Guess what? Eventually my mother is told the exciting prognosis that I was experiencing growing pains that would dissipate during my adolescent years! However, the shrink, gesticulating with her hands crossed under the table, was holding a cross, praying. The real truth was that she and her colleagues were dumbfounded. They had turned to God for answers and prayed to the miracle maker, hoping he could come to my immediate rescue. All very well, but Hartley's parents were atheists.

How am I expected to respond to all this fucking great news? With open arms to the idea any normality lay in the lap of fucking God? That I was blessed to be a great catch for every Tom, Dick and Harry who wanted to impart heinous deeds in my direction? Worse, that I was programmed to believe normality didn't exist and I was a one of a kind in the Godforsaken universe? I rest my case!

R. It is a lot to swallow. All I can really say is, poor you!

A. Poor him? You should be saying poor me. If he could have got those sluts to swallow me more often, then I could have danced my way through life far happier than his life could ever be.

H. I don't think, looking back on those childhood years, I could have reiterated it in better detail than what Aspie has just said. I can imagine any autistic kid would be considered akin to being born an alien and would have looked to child psychiatrists for the answers that sadly were not forthcoming. On the plus side, they were scratching their heads because I could do amazing calculus in my head. Mind you, they wouldn't have been able to relate to what having an eidetic memory was back then.

I had to wait until Aspie was diagnosed as lacking in confidence and fraught with insecurity issues. The reality was learning to accept that, whether I liked it or not, I was in the early stages of embarking on a vocation of being a loner and accepting his growing pains were developed from his inaudible version of Tourette's Syndrome. When words like fuck or cunt sprung forth, these invariably occurred at funerals, weddings or in a multitude of public places where people or children were around. Although, fortunately not shouted out aloud, they reverberated inside my head continuously, while meanwhile Aspie was laughing his head off.

A. I don't think Hartley ever understood me. All I asked of him was to be in control of his actions! Mind you, I did enjoy it when you allowed me to go into action in your local fish and chip shop. That poor girl serving us didn't know where to put her face when I asked for three cunts and chips! Your mates couldn't contain their infectious hysterical laughter.

H. When I look back on my childhood, aged three, Aspie chose to go for a solo tour of Birmingham, crossed main roads as though I owned all the confidence in the world. When my mother and father caught up, I was found screaming my head off. How I broke my arm was put down to Aspie's earliest ability of self-injury. How they lost me was down to Aspie's connection with ADHD; now you see me, now you don't!

Meanwhile, Aspie was growing his attachment to peculiarities. For example, when I refused to use the johns at school. These were anxious times for my mother who had to share her time between breastfeeding my sister and the ordeal of having to knock on strangers' doors so I could use their loos. No doubt these people must have wondered why Aspie had to inspect their latrines. If they weren't up to his expectations, my mother had to knock on more doors until he found the one that was acceptably clean enough for him.

Yet, this was another Aspie quirk carried into my adulthood. During a family holiday in the Lake District when I was ten, while Mother entertained my sister at a local children's farm, Father decided to introduce me to adventure. That day we hiked to the summit of Skiddaw, the third highest peak in England. During our descent, I developed an awful tummy ache and was desperate for a clean loo to satisfy Aspie's needs. Any normal kid would have dropped his shorts and done the business. Instead Aspie felt aggrieved that the sheep were watching while I just had to wait, watching another anxiety attack in the making.

I have mentioned to you that Aspie had his talents. However, it was a shame I was unaware of the armada of angsts developing, especially when he was left alone with strangers. Being in a classroom of children and listening to a teacher, who to him spoke in an alien language, was part of the sensations that made him feel uneasy. Take my piano lessons for example, when learning to play, aged four, my early lessons were with a cousin and Aspie felt safe. However, the next teacher appeared more apt at teaching homosexuality and paedophilia from the many parts he groped while he sat next to Aspie on the piano stool. This caused Aspie more angst and developed a close proximity complex.

R. Are you certain your piano teacher was what you thought him to be, or is this made-up fantasy?

H. His intentions appeared not just to teach me to play the piano because when he stood immediately behind or beside me, I felt a pressure from some part of his body generally caressing me.

There are the memories too of the lodgers who regularly came into my bedroom. While I hoped nothing immoral occurred, I used to get my thighs squeezed, my face caressed and hands put on my backside.

When I later in my childhood met up with the Scoutmaster, I was already very frigid and an easy target.

R. No wonder your schedule for coming to see me sometimes seems years apart and at other times weekly or monthly. There's rarely a dull moment, although it would make a healthy change if you could talk about something more positive.

H. I think you know the answer to that question. I come to you with the intention of unloading unwanted thoughts. However, as soon as you get to work on my body, I become so relaxed and overwhelmed by a peace of mind. Whenever Aspie had to have his say, it felt like I was Jonah about to be swallowed by the whale.

During my puberty, our family doctor believed the only way forward was placing me in the leg irons I mentioned because my condition was being blamed on being born six weeks premature. X-rays confirmed a no-win situation. While some species have the ability of metamorphosis during their puberty, such as a tadpole being born a fish and later becoming a frog, evolution may be responsible for reshaping Aspie's brain, but my condition was defined as congenital malformation of the bones in my arms. Through puberty, the bones in my arms had developed abnormally. The physical pain was incomprehensible and the sole reason I missed out on so many days of sex education that was potentially responsible for my inability to recognise when Aspie befriended Schadenfreudes!

While my parent's atheist beliefs told me a story that God didn't have any role in the manufacture of Adam and Eve, they couldn't explain why Aspie was ambisinistrous.

But my parents went to Jim Ryan, a very accomplished complimentary practitioner, who during the next eighteen months, doused me in a combination of Naturopathic,

Osteopathic, Homeopathic and Acupuncture techniques pretty unknown in the West. He also put me on a vegan diet. The end result was that my symptoms were alleviated and I believed I would no longer grow into a gorilla.

R. Can you share more about your childhood?

H. Hmmm, sometimes questions asked of me, I have difficulty answering. As far as my mother was concerned, I was the perfect son, even though Aspie demonstrated all sorts of behaviours she didn't like seeing in me. My diet was a constant concern. She was constantly battling Aspie's preference for junk food versus healthy. He insisted on eating fish and chips from the chippy but not her home-cooked food. Aspie refused to eat anything that produced uncomfortable sensations, be it because of texture, taste, colour or smell. The slightest sign of gristle or blood caused Aspie to puke. Having to cook two different meals for me and my sister didn't help her situation. Aspie always wanted mealtimes to be completed quick so he could quibble off to find a quiet space and withdraw into his world. Only when my father's mother brought home her apple pie did Aspie bring more normality into my life. Meanwhile, the child psychiatrist told my mother, 'It is hoped Hartley will be rid of his symptoms while going through his adolescent years.' She knew she had been let down and psychologically there were symptoms beyond her understanding.

R. I asked you a question before which you appeared to avoid. Do you normally digress away from talking about your father?

H. We have a complicated relationship. Father was less tolerant than my mother and he was often exasperated by Aspie's behaviour. While my mother looked after us from my father's perspective, I must have been the most insincere child unaware of his business difficulties. When I look back, it is so sad. Jack, the husband of my mother's oldest friend, was my father's business partner, and together they owned a successful children's book publishing company. We spent many a weekend visiting their home and spending time with their three daughters of similar ages to me and my sisters. However, comparing how both our families lived, their lifestyle contained more luxury, with a nicer home and more thrifty with money, compared to my father who Aspie considered to be very frugal. What Aspie couldn't relate to was my parent's upbringing in a world where poverty was rife and their parents saving what little they had for a rainy day.

R. Yes, your father's sentiments are justifiable and obviously Jack was not getting what he wanted out of his marriage. It's the fall out from people that does the hurting most people find unreasonable, although affairs normally happen for a reason.

H. My mother's friend never recovered from the acute health deterioration trauma that preoccupied throughout her life. When I look at my mother, who gave up her life to look after Father during his twenty-five-year battle with multiple sclerosis (MS), I wonder whether the emotional losses she suffered from losing half her family during the Blitz built up her resilience.

R. How old were you at this time?

H. Bang in the middle of succumbing to becoming a victim of pure evil.

R. You are referring to being sexually molested?

H. Yes, becoming the pet of a man whose only interest was his sexually grooming his victims. Not something I'm proud of; the emotional damage way off the scale.

R. Grooming is strong language. How did your parents take to what happened?

A. I think I am more apt to identify with that than Hartley. How you went all coy when the paedophile told your father after he had come to collect you from the camp; how much you enjoyed your experience, leaving you feeling a real man. He was almost besotted as he was driving us home and you were on the back seat with your hands cupped over your ears. All Father was interested in was learning about what you liked the most? However, my aspirations about Hartley could have been different if he had the moral strength to report the beast.

H. I was a very sick boy, having to endure severe growing pains.
Some children's genes just give them abnormalities that are
nothing more than bad luck. It's something I never thought
about; perhaps the stress of what the paedophile did, wreaking
sexual havoc, set off the weird growing pains in my arms.
Therefore Mother's only interest was finding a short-term
solution to a serious impairment and 'reporting the beast' was
the last thing on my mind, even though very intrusive anxiety
attacks were very real. I can remember every evening when my
mother came into my bedroom to tuck me in. She was unaware
that Aspie was sending me on an endurance test. Reminding
me of T-Rex's running amok in my bedroom was his way of
wearing me out until exhaustion become sleep.

Add in the business of me missing out on sex education, my
chance of a platonic friendship was literally zilch, given my
relationship with self-esteem.

85

PART TWO:

DEVELOPMENT - YOUTH AND PHILATELY

Chapter 8: Becoming of Man

H. My father explained to me that bar mitzvah is called the becoming of man. When a boy becomes a recognised adult in the Jewish faith. He explained about the service; the expected studying for the ritual service; and the accompanying party and presents in recognition of my achievement. However, I was unaware that Aspie was even more jubilant than me.

A. I had every reason to be. It was another opportunity to create mischief. I couldn't afford you getting so immersed into studying; what about time for me? The plethora of presents had no meaning for me, but didn't we have so much fun when I fucked up your studying?

H. Yes, I felt so sorry for Mr Josephs. The moment he saw it was me, he knelt down and prayed to God.

A. My turn to speak. Wasn't I just besotted by Grandma Hetty's amazing chopped liver, kneidlach soup, apple pie, pickles and strudel? Best of all, she went along with playing hide and seek with the food she made, knowing if she didn't hide from me, there would be nothing for anyone else.

H. My grandmother was a wonderful friend to me. I remember the day she passed away, struck down by a stroke. I was so deeply sad.

On the other hand, Aspie couldn't relate to my mother's mother. He couldn't relate to her ill health or her immense emotional wounds, which time never healed; the distraught lives delivered by the hands of the Nazis when one of their bombs fell on her home during the Blitz. Gone were Judy, her husband, a son and his fiancée, and a sister. It was no wonder such emotional loss transmuted her emotional frailty into illness. Aspie despised her so much, he compared her to a cantankerous witch who was compelled to chase him around our garden on her broomstick, believing that when she caught him, the ugly gizzard would wave her wand and turn Aspie into an ugly toad. Now that's a thought - would have Aspie left me alone, if he had to live his life as a toad?

I was grateful when a park bench was erected to commemorate the neighbours who died along with my mother's family as a horrific reminder. Luckily for my mother, she like so many other children she were evacuated to Bedford, where coincidentally my father was also sent.

Meanwhile, at the time of my mother's loss, the Orthodox Jewish method of dealing with emotional grief was not to talk about it. Perhaps a good reason to believe God had forgotten about her and why she decided to join my father's faith in atheism.

Some years later, my parents and a cousin jointly authored a book about one great uncle's journey from the marshlands of Polish Russia to where he settled to live in New York. The story told how the majority of Jewish souls lived within absolute poverty and were treated by the authorities as vermin to be marred for all the atrocities that were carried out. While the majority of those Jews escaped, New York became their desired destination, but until they arrived they did not know where they would end up. While my great uncle found himself in New York, both my grandparents arrived in London, grateful that God had spared them from a fate worse than death. However, their lives were harsh and they were penniless, making ends meet via the generosity of the more comfortably off relatives; Orthodoxism became their saviour.

My father's parents survived the Blitz, with my grandfather finding trade as an accountant, which gave my grandma her freedom to spend her days making Jewish dishes.

Nevertheless, Aspie coerced me into becoming an oddball wandering round the world wondering if there was anyone else like him. In a strange and unrelated way, you could say it was how I ended up seeing you regularly, especially when you taught me all about tantric massage. I was naive until then; how could massage be so sensually stimulating?

R. I think you are misunderstanding my intentions. There is nothing morally wrong with tantric massage. I think Aspie concocted all sorts of ideas and compared me to whores who walked the streets, whereas I was a very experienced masseuse who offered a variety of massage techniques. It's just that with the sexual stimulus at the end, it helped pay the bills and, to be honest, in my opinion there was nothing morally wrong. I would add that it even helped men's relationships when sex got boring with their partners, as it did for you. Regrettably, having Aspie in your life meant all things became amplified and you didn't know how to handle his addictive sexual desires.

H. You see, Aspie, what you have turned me into?

A. This is something else. I don't like why you have to be so ungrateful. Many a man would love to have my sex drive; the fact that you might not be able to handle it is an entirely a different matter!

R. I asked you a little earlier about life at junior school?

H. The other paedophile, yes! He made sure Aspie believed he had it in for him. 'Jew boy' became my pet name. I remember how I found the hard wooden seats so uncomfortable. Aspie was accused of fidgeting and being a nuisance, as a distraction to the other pupils, and I was sent to the headmaster's study.

Try to understand; I felt like David encountering Goliath for the first time. Of course, no sling, which Aspie would have enjoyed! It was when he got up that Aspie found his 6'6" height intimidating and he thought he was about to be canned. It was my misfortune to say to the headmaster, 'You are not going to cane me, are you, sir?'

R. What did your headmaster say that was so demonstratively bad?

H. He told the entire school about the little boy who came to his study and asked if he was going to be caned, to which he replied, 'Not in my school.' I wouldn't have minded had he not been looking in my direction with his finger pointed and a couple of hundred pairs of eyes bearing down on me.

R. In my opinion, you felt punished for something Aspie had said and your headmaster had reiterated it to emphasise that his school condoned caning. That Aspie is unable to distinguish between fact and fiction became your punishment, knowing there was a likelihood of further bullying. No doubt not an easy situation to mentally assimilate being in your shoes?

A. That was fun for me, wasn't it?

R. I don't think teacher's back then had any inkling that they were delivering long-term emotional damage. In many ways, as adults we forget how it was for them when they were our age. They were brought up in the war years and therefore they experienced harsher attitudes where the iron rod was in force for any punishment. When the headmaster pushes your bottom, it was nothing more than demonstrating part of their authority and quite acceptable back then. Today, it would be considered sexual abuse.

No doubt making friends was the last thing on your mind?

H. I popped my mother that question and I saw tears in her response. It ingratiated me with a little more of my life story and the child psychiatrist she took me to - who was attempting to put together the composite parts of the jigsaw puzzle - that described the mental condition, that was Aspie. Back then, autism was virtually unknown, and no doubt I was a very introverted child who required as much emotional love as she could muster. The trouble was the final time I saw the psychiatrist, he said, 'Hopefully, whatever condition Hartley has, he will grow out of during his adolescent years, and Aspie will be gone.'

A. That's kind of nice hearing you want me gone.

R. What about having any friends?

H. Barely more than two, one of who was a neighbour's daughter who tried her utmost to befriend me. It was something about her eyes. Apparently we often bathed together and splashed around as though we were having fun, although she was a couple of years older. Perhaps what occurred back then might have procured the reason Aspie chose I lost my virginity to an older woman. However, our friendship was not to last since, after a couple of years, she moved away.

There was two friendships I remember; Frank, from the local housing estate, and Clive, whose parents ran a care home for the elderly, waiting for death's door to open. That was back in the days of Solihull High School, when venturing into the city centre reminded me how some cities were not dissimilar to Harlem in New York, but on a far smaller scale. Venture there if your desire was to become a disappearing species. Anyway, they thought Aspie would fit in well with the other one thousand and forty-nine pupils, another reason they thought it was the best choice of schools for me. I wish I could have been forewarned; it could be compared to the pogroms, except its local residents fought back rather in Jewish Poland, where fighting back was met by a fate worse than death because all Jews were considered no different from a lump of shit to be wiped from the sole of a passing soldier's shoe. My classmates from the likes of Jamaica targeted Aspie with their manipulative bullying.

However, at junior school my mother felt it was her duty to take me there and home again, but at Solihull Comprehensive it was too far away because of her employment responsibilities. In an ideal world, no sooner had I left my mother's arms than I yearned to be back in them again. In the time in-between, it was as though I was wearing sign that read: 'Conspicuous boy requires to be bullied every day because Aspie has a need to experience the mental pain and torment.'

R. That is a hard one to see given your height. I would have thought you could have easily stood on your own two feet. School couldn't just have been all bad?

H. I think it has more to do with handling too many negative memories than any other period of my life. Think about it; when we are at school, we are there to learn. We are not there because we want to be. For me, it was like I was on trial and my punishment was the severe mental bashing Aspie received daily.

A. You are a poor old fucker, aren't you? Do you expect me to have sympathy for your fragile personality? Your living in fear left me no choice but to be the very victim you wanted to be. Shame you couldn't have stood on your own two feet; shown who was boss rather than the wimp you disappointingly were!

H. I also wasn't able to relate to bullies coming from a background where their parents had a shoddy upbringing and were unable to offer their children stability. How many of these children would have experienced being the victims and the only way they knew how to fight back was with their fists, or worse, with knives.

Midas, a West Indian from such a family background, knew how to undress Aspie's mental defences, layer by layer. He turned me into feeling like I was a useless rag doll and to do as he pleased. Our unfortunate relationship began when he walked up to Aspie and said, 'You, Jew boy, and I are going to become the best of friends.' My first lesson was learning about the only profession Jews were allowed to be a hundred years ago, bankers. He decided to give Aspie an experience he'd remember by getting him to empty his pockets and deciding what I kept and what Aspie would lend him.

So, what do you think is worse, being beaten up or experiencing ongoing mental torture?

A. I'll tell you what I think; it was so beautiful back then. I relished experiencing the self-harm.

R. I think any type of bullying has no place in this world. Sadly, the foundation as to whether we become accustomed to being victims or being able to fend for ourselves has already been implanted in our genes. Although I hinted at your size, I hadn't considered the weaknesses of your mental durability, and in my opinion, out of the two, this is by far is the more malicious.

H. Among the most trying parts of my relationship with Aspie was his inability to think for himself. He needed me to come up with the answers before he asked the questions. Being bullied became par for the course, and whether I liked it or not, it perpetuated throughout my life. It began at school and perpetuated into my business years as well. Even after my diagnosis, no mental defence made me feel safe from Aspie's indeterminable ways.

R. How could you be expected to know? Any eleven-year-old kid is going to be rather mixed up. It was difficult enough to come to terms with strange and rebellious feelings emanating from the emotions of puberty during adolescence.

H. I know Aspie would say that his life was cut short to adulthood by the very traumatic and mentally damaging events that occurred. Religion played a part in teaching him that he had left his youth behind and was recognised as a fully-fledged adult.

R. Your bar mitzvah?

H. The bullying that occurred at school was a result of being recognised as a freak of nature, as though this was the age when Aspie was making ready to show to the world his true identity. As though safety was when he withdrew into his very own Tardis where he could simulate Dr Who.

A. That's a new one for me. I never considered my wall to be a Tardis, but then I always knew I was from a superior race.

R. You were discussing your congenital condition in your arms created havoc at school, but in what way?

H. Aspie fell into the category of referring to who he thought the majority of people on the planet were, while neuro-typical is a neologism for Aspies.

During puberty, the bones in my arms saw abnormal growth that caused terribly painful cramps mimicking paralysis. These continued relentlessly months at a time and, unluckily for me, although no doubt enjoyable for Aspie, I continually missed weeks of school, unaware Aspie extenuated all aspects of my symptoms, particularly an exaggerated pain threshold. It was inevitable that my education suffered and, most of all, I missed out on the vital sex education.

While Midas exacted his mental torturing, another boy called Pete, a rather stout 'Jack the Lad,' had already made his presence known to Aspie. He enjoyed tormenting him with his fists as though I was his plaything, waiting to see how long it took for my physical structure to crumble. I remember one day how the deranged boy took a hammer to my head in a metalwork class. Luckily for me, it must have hit a spot where my head had some resilience.

Often, I used to think the culmination of my experiences of Aspie's role in my life had gained credence to being labelled as the most mentally retarded giant on the planet who was looking forward to the day I would be mentioned in the *Guinness Book of Records*.

A. So much trivial fuss, I can never understand. I saw your bullying as a sign that this is the life you wanted. I would not have developed into the wimp had you been able to stand on your own two feet, just as at junior school. 'Take it on the chin,' as the headmaster said to you; because I could have turned out far more resilient to the bullying you experienced. I rest my case.

Chapter 9: Aspie Talk

R. You will have to excuse me but I still can't get my head round the idea that there is you and there is Aspie; even though he played an integral part of your story. It doesn't help that he made no distinction between your weaknesses or strengths. He simply adhered to whichever he felt more comfortable with. So, although it might appear that other people coerced you, I see Aspie's role as extenuating your circumstances. No doubt bullies recognised your weaknesses and engaged basic scaremongering tactics. Knowing what little I know about Asperger's Syndrome, I imagine they created a nervous atmosphere for you that affected the way you were able to grasp learning. If you don't mind, I prefer just addressing you. Although I believe I would be correct to assume he is the weaker-minded of your two characters?

H. I think your grasp sums up my general learning, irrespective of subject matter.

R. Something else I have been meaning to ask you. Why do you think of your father as not having your interests at heart?

H. You are going to have to give me some thinking time. It is as though we are born of two different breeds. Even though as a parent I am certain he showered me with as much love as he could, I have always wondered whether Aspie perpetuated bad memories he preferred to forget forever. Essentially, when Jacky took her life, it was as though she replaced what was best left forgotten; vying her in the same manner and refusing to acknowledge suicide was beyond her control.

Likewise, my father had a low tolerance to Aspie's behaviour, and this played on his mind, and he might not always have been able to show himself as the loving parent he wanted to be. It is possible his own health caused the development of untreatable stomach ulcers that would hamper his health throughout his life. As you are learning, my father was often exasperated by communication frustrations with Aspie that at inopportune times looked like we were about to annihilate each other.

But how Aspie might have aggrieved his tormentors because they saw in him his talent of fidgeting as attention seeking. Jack, the school's psychopath, prized himself in terrifying every victim within arm's length with his prize catch, sadly being Aspie. He was some mean machine. I only found out after he left school, he managed to knife one kid in the back and spend a number of years behind bars.

Needless to say, his bullying made me feel like being in captivity vying Aspie as competition and garnered my life with his unkind bullying conjuring up the likes of T-Rex manifesting and terrorising me throughout my life. In my opinion, Aspie in a macabre way hoped he had, among his capabilities, the ability to emulate Jack's ways.

R. You mentioned at the beginning of your story that you believe Aspie was capable of murder. Seems rather dubious?

H. I think those views emanated because Aspie got himself so traumatised. The capability of murder existed because of uncontrollable rash decisions and he was unable to grasp the consequences of his actions. Had he acted in this manner at school, the bullies would have left me alone. However, I was grateful to a gentle gorilla who, being twice the size of Jack, became my protector in disguise.

R. I think we as children have to quickly adapt to the bad apples at school; I am referring to the Peters and the Jacks. I am only reiterating what you said a little earlier. Aspie portrayed the weak character because it got him the attention he desired.

H. It was like a repeat performance of junior school; with a few friends wanting to have anything to do with a loner who attracted bullies, not exactly safe company to be seen with. Then they had the audacity of blaming me for everything that went wrong in our life.

I remember reiterating to my only friend Bob what occurred at my bar mitzvah with Aspie resenting learning Hebrew. Why couldn't he understand why he fussed about making an effort be rewarded with money and presents in exchange?

But, of course, Aspie decided to be coy, as though he hadn't heard what Bob said, which only infused Bob, as though he was being questioned by the Spanish Inquisition. But this lingo of Aspie's is typical of the way he behaved until Bob told him to fuck off and then my nightmare began; thinking I had lost a good friend.

Fortunately, on the whole we had a good relationship with more laughs than indifferences, although one incident almost ruined our friendship period. Since we both lived close by, we often met on the bus to school, although Bob's father took him by car whenever it rained. By chance one day, Bob said if it rained the following day, his father would be happy to take me too. When I told my mother, she told me the importance of making sure I turned up at Bob's home fifteen minutes early and thanking him for the lift.

Being unaware of Aspie's non-relationship with time management meant Aspie having to make a rash decision. There lay a rather busy dual carriageway directly in between our address and the safest crossing meant an extra half-mile on our journey so he decided on talking the shortest route. It was as though there was an erupting volcano between me and Bob because Aspie disregarded any safety and made a dash between passing vehicles.

Luckily for me, I turned up early. Unluckily for me, fate intercepts when we are dropped off at school and Aspie assumed because he heard Bob thank his dad, there is no need for him to do the same as well! My life became littered with many such incidents and I had to endure the nuances of the people Aspie upset.

The following day, I sense a complete coldness in Bob that I felt I did not deserve. Aspie is relentless to get an immediate explanation. I gave up counting how many times he repeated to Bob, 'Why are you giving me the cold shoulder?'

I was shocked by Bob's reply. 'You are a fucking shit and that's what my dad told me to tell you.' I was reduced to feeling the horrible sensation in the pit of my stomach as Aspie voraciously exaggerated the sensation, yet I had no idea what Aspie's mistake was. Then Aspie replied by asking Bob why his dad ordered him to say such unkind words to me because he barely knew him.

Bob said, 'It's your disgusting mannerisms. He tells me you have no shame and that it's only common decency to offer your thanks when taken to school.'

My angst with Aspie was that he was completely unaware that saying thank you was almost self-obligatory. So he tried to make amendment by saying to Bob, 'If your father is so mad over something so small, tell him I am sorry for not saying thank you, and in the future I will not forget to do so next time.'

But Bob replied, 'You don't get it, do you? There's not going to be a next time. The times for thanking him are now long gone. My father also said in giving you this punishment, he is hoping you will learn a lesson.'

Because Aspie didn't adhere well to his mistake, he refused to accept Bob's father's view and argued his point until Bob decided to end his friendship with me.

R. Now I can relate to Aspie's attention-seeking habits creating a wedge between you making long-term friends through his unacceptable behaviour.

H. You know, we as parents know so well how our kids make or lose friends from the most absurdest of reasons. Fortunately, at the beginning of my third year, I made friends with Henry, the new kid on the block, who temporarily replaced Bob.

Henry was two terms older and spoke in a lingo that Aspie compared to a foreign language, although it was English with an accent, but enough to make Aspie feel a little uncomfortable. Henry was also a good six inches shorter than Bob and nearly a foot shorter than me. No matter his lack in height appeared more assertive than Bob.

Anyway, Henry enjoyed his pranks and Aspie was the perfect candidate. These pranks were performed when I was old enough to learn to drive. Henry had already passed his driving test and coerced me to believing he could help me learn. But as he does, he slipped the gears without me being aware and my engine over-revs and he laughed his head off.

Although Aspie found Henry an oddball, when we were ready to enjoy the big wide world, I lost my relationship with Bob permanently.

Getting back to Aspie's confrontation with Bob, not once did his father offer to take me to school again. Although Bob and I were still friends of sorts, another Aspie incident reminds me how easy it was for him to coerce me into believing he had devised a novel way of offering us protection from the bullies. This time, it was a case of the headmaster reading out what was not going to be tolerated with severe punishments in the future. If we were hoping for a medal, Bob and I received the school's gold medal for turning up late for both morning and afternoon classes more than any other pupil in the past. Sadly, any thought that truancy was seen by the bullies as something to be proud of was short-lived. Instead, it just recapitulated Aspie's relationship with them.

R. So far, you have only really mentioned detrimental things that occurred at your school. While bullying must have made life very tough for you, and you have my sympathy, surely there had to be something you excelled at?

Chapter 10: Music Music

H. In a nutshell, music played a very benevolent role in my life. I could even say for certainty that without music, I would have joined Jacky on the other side. My father's mother, a retired piano teacher, obviously handed down in her genes a musical talent which enabled my father to form a jazz band and which Aspie could listen to forever. Although I passed grade eight piano at the Guildhall College of Music, learning to play jazz didn't do it for Aspie. Classical music did.

A. Now tell everyone how I fucked you up from advancing in music, even though in every way I emulated the character Dustin Hoffman plays in the move *Rain Man*, as well as my other talents, including having the best voice in the school choir.

H. That was something else, that made me stand out like a sore thumb in class because Aspie could calculate the size of the universe in my head, and our maths teacher and the rest of the class gawked at us in astonishment. But Aspie's ability to sing classic opera was way out in the universe as far as this ability was concerned.

R. Though you were handicapped by Aspie's frustrations, music still became one of your preferred subjects. How about a demonstration?

H. That's the worse thing you can ask me. Aspie suffered terrible stage fright. But yes, you are correct, Aspie was musically very gifted. While Aspie traumatised me with his inability to practice regularly the basics first, rather than taking on impossibly difficult pieces, he might have been able to focus on his singing capabilities as well. Aspie had an outstanding voice, so our choirmaster told us, and we were given leading roles in some of the smaller operatic productions. It was only after my voice broke that Aspie decided practising to the level required to become a professional was too hard. Instead he hijacked me with this crazed idea that I could pick up playing every instrument in the symphony orchestra. Our teacher Miss Charleston decided our aptitude was so good at the performances that passing A level music would be a doddle.

R. Hang on, a moment ago you told me you failed all your exams. What happened about O level music?

H. The teacher wrote a letter to my mother but she didn't explain I was a musical savant, and although I hadn't passed my exam, I was competent enough to take A level music.

From here on, Aspie displayed his remarkable ability. During that first term, we learnt off by heart every note of the first movement of Wagner's *The Mastersingers*.

A. So I do have positive acumens after all? I am pleased you recognised your appreciation in all aspects of my musical abilities.

H. And that remark was Aspie feeling the need to say his little bit.

R. You mean attention seeking, a rhetorical question?

H. Aspie and I didn't know a volcano in our midst was about to erupt, although he was unaware he'd set it off. The headmaster brought in a new school rule that adhered to the teachers too. 'No smoking would be tolerated on the school grounds'. Miss Charleston decided bollocks to his rule. It was to become our last spring term. I didn't know then what waking up on the wrong side of the bed meant. But Miss Charleston walked into the classroom with a fag drooping. She bent down and puffed into my face. As she got up to walk away, she grabbed hold of the tuft of my shirt and yanked me over her desk. 'You little fuckface, yid-nick, shit brat, you think you can ruin my life as a teacher? I had to listen to the headmaster tell me if I ever smoke in class again, I would be suspended.'

Anyway, it was about a month into the term when my mother told me the news. She said, 'Miss Charleston called today with some bad news. By being so late into the term, they accidentally had you on Cambridge curriculum and they now regret that it is too late to change to Oxford.'

I was no longer studying for A level, and my career in music had come to an abrupt halt.

When I look back at this time, I feel sad. Father's younger brother was hiding a dark secret, schizophrenia. I was unaware that music was his solace and masked his depression. A gifted man living in a world he felt wasn't for him, but he sadly planned an appointment with the Devil. Apparently he got himself into a one-way taxi and then jumped from a busy bridge onto the motorway below.

During my worst angst with my father, while Aspie had his amazing calculating talent with numbers, if anyone asked me to work it out on paper, I was left in a complete quandary. Father had it in for me because I wanted to focus Aspie's creative talents on the arts, whereas he insisted I study English grammar, French and maths. But, he refused to accept that what I wanted to learn, as well as not being able to come to terms with Aspie's inabilities. He thought they were excuses and during the next two terms, we hardly spoke a word to each other. Whenever he came into any room we sat in, his presence caused Aspie to run out and slam the door shut. Often I was forced to listen to father reiterate, 'No son of mine is going to learn art and music. Useless subjects, only useless people learn, and that is what you will become, useless.'

It had been a number of years since father had to rethink where his own business activities were going to take him and now he was heavily involved in developing business games. Another reason he forced me to study subjects he felt I would benefit from; even join him in what he was doing, but sadly Aspie thought word processing was a load of balderdash.

The remarkable thing about my father's business at that time was his business partner, Jack Ferguson, a man with a brilliant mind and recognised among the earliest genre of computer algorithm developers. Aspie got on really well with him; they both shared the oddball acumen together. I recall how Jack cared little for his personal appearance, unshaven, flies undone, shirt hanging out, overweight, chain smoker, splitting image of Aspie, who even today, unless I notice, is likely to do the same.

Examples of this peculiar aptitude of Aspie materialised when I was well into my career as an antiques dealer. One Friday morning, I turned up at Bermondsey Antiques Market at 5am. One of my mates came up and asked me why I couldn't afford a decent pair of shoes. I look down and discovered that one shoe was black, the other brown. Personally, I think it was about Aspie's attention seeking.

A. And why not? The way I saw our relationship developing was about only you. What about me? So I concocted things to show your mates I was daft. A simple way for me to derive satisfaction and the only way I finally got your attention.

H. I call it belligerent and selfish. On another occasion, I remember my wealthy great uncle inviting me to an upper-class networking event. He said words to me that I didn't understand at the time. 'Please be proper.' Only with hindsight was I to find out that Aspie intervened when we were introduced to the Chairman of Barclays Bank by asking him, in front of a number of colleagues, whether he was interested in investing in a project of his.

It is with much regret, that I was unable to recognise this unfortunate trait of his because I was guaranteed many repeat performances. Always, I learnt about it when it was too late. Among the challenging responses I had to succumb to getting myself used to was that when Aspie was in town, so to speak, I had to be on guard to mishaps that can occur completely out of the blue for no apparent reason.

This was very evident just after my wedding, when it was time to thank the guests for their most welcomed presents. It took six months to send these thank you notes out because of Aspie's attitude. You see, from his perspective, I was the breadwinner and therefore my role in our marriage was to oversee everything in that department, and sending thank you notes to the guests was Jacky's responsibility.

After a number of months of arguing who bore the responsibility, we decided she would post the thank you notes as long as Aspie stuck the postage stamps on them.

R. I can guess what occurred next. You didn't keep to your part of the bargain and she went ahead and posted the replies without postage.

H. It was Aspie's doing.

A. Damn right, had to make sure things got put into perspective, didn't appreciate being thought of as the dogsbody. Why should I take the blame just because Jacky decided to teach me an early lesson so she posted the notes as I had left them. Except sticking the stamps onto the envelopes was entirely a different matter. Mind you, I did enjoy the cursory looks I received from some of your colleagues.

H. My only recompense is another little story to share with you, Rea, about when I was delivering the clock I mentioned earlier.

When I met Jacky, she lived with a flatmate. While Jacky and I were enjoying the warmth of South Africa, Jacky's flatmate was almost dying of frostbite. Eventually my future mother-in-law went to the poor girl's rescue since every utility that was connected to their flat was cut off because of Jacky's failure to pay the bills. Little did I know of this inability of hers, which matched Aspie's lack of organisational skill.

R. They say that a mother-in-law is an invaluable commodity.

A. Isn't he lucky!

H. Anyway, getting back to my story.

So, here I am, halfway through the winter term of my fourth year, as I began to come to terms with the fact that anything that required complex thinking is beyond Aspie's coping mechanism.

It was like living several years of a tug of war event, trying to work out: who did the talking; who did the thinking; and who was doing the actioning. Then having to contend with neither of us making any real headway and constantly bickering with each other. It was quite maddening how much time I spent going over the same stuff, as though there was a reason for Aspie's madness.

Thinking about this, it is beginning to make more sense to me. You may recall the difficulties my mother had in my toilet training back in junior school. I have just realised it wasn't about the toilets. It was more because the toilets were the most likely room to be tiled. A tiled floor or wall became Aspie's imaginary skyscraper or spaceship and he got lost in counting all the rows of tiles. Whenever we travelled to New York, I never got away from Aspie stooping as we walked past skyscrapers and counting the windows and floors. Likewise, sitting down on the loo, he got absorbed in his imaginary world, imagining the tiles were great monoliths, and this helped strengthen his ability to demonstrate amazing calculation.

Chapter 11: Learning Issues

H. I am not trying to repeat myself, talking about the difficulties my father had in relating to my uncanny ability to calculate incalculable sums in my head instantaneously, yet be gormless at algebra. This was another part of the Aspie madness. Take geography. Aspie became stuck on any particular graphical page illustrating any type of building with brickwork, as though this temporarily gave him the opportunity of withdrawing into his world. The problems I encountered with English were due to the dyslexia I wasn't aware Aspie had, despite having to repetitively write lines after class.

However, in metalwork, Aspie showed a talent I could have done without because he enjoyed destructing anything I built. When it came to putting back together, his mind went blank. This left me to realise Aspie's talent fell within the constraints of art and music.

I remember how my art teacher looked at Aspie, while scratching his head wondering how on earth he was able to draw meticulously straight lines of the Eiffel Tower from memory and any other tower around the world in miniature to scale.

R. Yet, it seems that even though you remember Miss Charleston as being transient in cutting your musical career short, she couldn't prevent you from your musical accomplishments.

H. I was approached by members of my class who had formed a pop group and wanted a piano player to join them. Aspie immediately acted like a snail, by curling and withdrawing back into his shell, while making out that playing the piano wasn't something he excelled. He hated pop or rock music. Little did I know, this unsociable and selfish acumen of his was to become emotionally costly throughout my life.

A. Just doing my job. You see, something else you didn't seem to want to learn was that I tested you for a reason. It was the only way for me to learn. Don't teach me then I don't develop, right?

R. I think I'm slowly building up a picture of the difficulties you encountered at home and at school. It sounds like life wasn't at all easy for you: your growing pains through your adolescent years; and trying to develop a relationship with Aspie who was often more of a hindrance than anything else.

H. You can say that again. You can add to your list, his being responsible for an endless supply of abnormalities and innuendos that were beyond my scope of reasoning.

A. Mine too, mate!

H. Home life was quite a battle, and living in Aspie's shoes was very tenuous, to say the least. This dream caused Aspie a lifelong sentence of problems, because to him it was illogical that I was Jewish. This dream could also be disguised as the perpetrator of many of his anxiety attacks, even though they gave away the appearance of feeling emotionally warm and friendly.

Meanwhile, irrespective of Aspie's dislike towards my father, I was grateful to my father putting me through my bar mitzvah, although trying to understand God and respect my father's atheist views contradicted his beliefs. It gave me a lifelong dilemma; where does God sit in his relationship with the universe, religion or creation? Aspie extenuated this problem by giving me the most vivid of dreams, where I saw myself sleepwalking on a bed of hay to find Jesus bending over me saying, 'All will be well and you will always be safe.' To this very day, this dream remains as vivid as if it had occurred yesterday.

R. I believe there is a soul and a spirit attached to a higher consciousness. While we are in the present, we are in the material physical form of this consciousness. When we are ready to leave the world, the physical body dies, leaving our soul to interact with the spirit and live on in an eternal consciousness.

H. Reality was that my father was Jewish and enjoyed the fruits of tradition: the yearly gathering of the families for the traditional Seder nights, the first at his parents, and the second night at cousins of my mother's. It was sort of nice to believe that God actually existed, even only momentarily, in the form of Elijah, even though Aspie whispered into my ear to distract me, 'Did you see the rippling of the wine in the goblet?'

True to his colours, Aspie betrothed many issues in many walks of my life. He didn't adhere well to the idea that I could be Jewish and atheist. He also ensured that I suffered anxiety every Shabbat. Whereas non-Jews go to church on a Sunday to pay their respects and pray to the almighty, Jews go on a Friday night. Of course, I was the hypocrite, a bad Jew, not tolerated by the more Orthodox sect of the Jewish population.

During the couple of years preceding my bar mitzvah, my father forced me to be respectful towards the more holy holidays. This meant attending Shul on Rosh Hashanah, the Jewish New Year, and experiencing Yom Kippur, the day of atonement and fasting for the day. Aspie, of course, ensured I obeyed or I would feel the wrath of God! This was how I began my journey into the Jewish religion. Whenever I either walked or drove passed Jews on their way to Shul, I had to somehow make myself invisible, otherwise God would punish me.

I now digress a couple of decades forward, to two more examples since they fit here well. Often when I visited my Jewish accountant, in conversation, Aspie interrupted quite brashly with the words Jesus Christ; which caused me unending embarrassment. I began to sweat profusely and, with an anxiety attack in the making, be out of my accountant's office as quickly as possible, as though I was about to receive a disrespectful look from him.

Another pertinent incident occurred flying to New York on Yom Kippur after I got married, when God handed me my punishment. We were flying at forty thousand feet in the sky, and without warning our plane drops thousands of feet nose-diving towards the ground. Pandemonium erupts among our fellow passengers as oxygen masks fell from above and the contents of overhead compartments are strewn throughout the cabin. I decided I better start going to Shul on a Sabbath lest I wanted a repeat performance. For twenty-five years, I refused to fly on a religious holiday until I woke up one morning and wondered why all the other poor bastards on my flight had to suffer on my account.

Other memories during my teenage years were more spasmodic. One of my sisters regularly took her two boys on camping holidays. But with my experiences with the Scoutmaster, camping became no man's land for me, although this may have more of a relationship of finding a campsite with tiled walls than anything else.

A. Can you blame me from wanting the more luxury things in life? I certainly could have done with more Club Med holidays. Mind you, better than the year before, when we got a hiding for pinching a bag of sweets.

H. I was eleven at the time. Apart from vague memories of holidays in Brittany and Normandy, it was always the holiday to remember.

R. I am still having difficulty in understanding the context of your relationship with Aspie. For the most part, you are using 'we' then occasionally you use 'I' instead. Please explain why you appear to jump from one aspect of your story to another. If this is typical of him, I am not sure any normal person can have a straightforward relationship with him.

H. Actually, I have to admit it is a difficult one that boils down to a lack of confidence. Just as you are confused, I too have my dilemmas with him as well. It reminds me of another incident that occurred later in my adult life. I bought a Range Rover because I knew Aspie would enjoy its off-road capabilities. Often the playground at my children's school was used as a car park. It was exactly the same as when Aspie was behind the wheel of my Ferrari and decided to test the car's power on a wet road and hit a tree. After heavy rain, the car park became a deluge of mud, and since Range Rovers are advertised as a car that can go anywhere, Aspie decided to reverse the car into the middle of the mud and get stuck. All I wanted to do was shut my eyes tight and hope none of the neighbours were around as the AA pulled my car back onto the road.

R. I sympathise with you. However, I hope you don't mind when I comment on where Aspie fits in?

A. Well said!

H. When I was eleven, our holiday of a lifetime was the Club Med resort in Palinuro, Italy. My mother's brother's family travelled with us, and I was a lone boy with three girls. We went via Paris and on first sighting the Eiffel Tower, Aspie was amazed. I had no conception how Aspie gauged size, although I wondered when he sat in front of the walls that made him feel safe if it was the infiniteness of his imagination that he had a relationship with. When we stood under the iron monolith, Aspie was already racing towards the top in his mind, yet we were still standing firmly on the ground. Little did I know this was the premise of OCD and the need to explore everywhere simultaneously.

A. Yes, that was the one thing that I could have done with to bolster my self-esteem; be recognised for my accomplishments.

H. No sooner than my father walked us through the turnstiles at the entrance to the stairwell, Aspie was racing ahead. Father, on the other hand, was out of breath and hoping I was safe. My disappointment caught me unawares when I realised that to get to the top, we had to take to the lift. I knew this was the least desirable option for Aspie, who could easily have climbed the girders to get upstairs. If the Eiffel Tower experience hadn't been breathtaking enough for Aspie, we then caught a train to Naples, and exploring twenty carriages was even more exciting!

While at this early stage of my life I wasn't aware of the abundant conundrum Aspie attested me to, I learnt pretty fast if I was going to be one up in my relationship with him.

A. That's nice, I thought we were a team. Now I have to be aware you are ganging up on me.

H. No doubt that my father, in a gentle sort of way, wanted to throttle me. 'Can't you be still for a moment? Wait until we are settled before you go exploring. There's going to be plenty of time to see the scenery.'

I was grateful my designated seat was up against the window. No sooner had we sat down that Aspie had already delved into his world, his head pressed hard against the window, fascinated by the carriages of the train parked next to us, imagining them just as he did whenever he finds the time to delve into his world of tiles and the beyond.

By the time the train rolled out of the station, my cousins appeared quite content reading their various books or scribbling away in their picture books. Already though, I could feel Mr Ants in his Pants, while my father was wondering how to glue him to his seat. Anyway, there was another dogma in the making. Among the annoying habits I endured with Aspie was lack of confidence. Had I been able to overcome this, I might have been the youngest teenage millionaire.

A. There you are, doing it again, whining about my failures, whereas you should be blaming yourself. You mentioned control, but now it is you who are contradicting yourself. Why is it, I seem to have to reassure you, for me to be able to action any response I need you to initiate it in the first place? You don't have an answer for me, do you? Well, I will answer for you. Had you the courage to find a way to buy that first house you saw, then yes, our dreams would have come true with retirement at a vastly young age.

R. What is Aspie jabbering on about?

H. In his book of thinking, life is merely a numbers game. It was as though he had been born with an uncanny awareness of any value associated with money. During my teens, his eyes gawked whenever we drove along roads like The Bishops Avenue. Somehow, Aspie egged me on about Dr. Choy's home being an opportunity to make a huge profit fast. At that time, his home was on the market for £75,000, a mere snippet compared to today's market. It didn't help that we had friends in Avenue Road in St. John's Wood; one of the other well-known expensive streets in London. While my father might have had negative feelings about the wealthy, Aspie was counting numbers I was blind to.

However, these distractions of Aspie's were only to deliver even more mortal wounds: my ability to be able to use his kudos wisely. If I could have thought that my encounter with the paedophile early on in my life was to be a one-off, I was blindly mistaken. More mental torment lay ahead.

I often wondered whether my path in business somehow mirrored my father's inability to succeed in business. The subtle difference he didn't have an Aspie to wreck his ability and albeit circumstances instead chose the path of becoming a teacher in Business Management. Perhaps it is quite normal that people who are very talented hide the sin of depression. How easy it would have been for me to compare my wife, already in her childhood, the gift of dancing on TV, with my father's youngest brother, who was a brilliant pianist. How many celebrities we learn about, who battle depression, and the ones who lose their fight, who come with a very creative past.

Perhaps the lack of confidence I saw in Aspie invisibly followed me everywhere I went. You may recall me discussing some school friends hoping I might be their valued piano player for their pop group. I just fell to pieces and couldn't give them a performance that gave them confidence I was their man.

Chapter 12: An American Intervention

H. I am only too aware of having to repeat the following adage how the Americans would attempt to save my soul. I suffered in my life from the authoritarian ways of Grandfather, who my father got regularly put down by as well. My mother told us a story about after they were married, when he built a chest of drawers but my grandfather told him the wind would blow it apart so he proved to him that it will not by standing on the top. Of course, the inevitable occurred and my mother was crying her eyes out, upset by how intolerant my grandfather was.

My grandfather often walked in the rose garden in Regent's Park and found his solitude when he walked there. He sat down on a bench with his body bent, head bowed between his hands. Apparently, when he opened his eyes, he found a young man giving him a concerned look. 'Just musing about the past,' my grandfather said, when he noticed the young man with the New York accent was reading a book called *The British Prime Minister*. He was so impressed by his interest in British politics, they struck up a conversation. Within minutes of their meeting, two strangers, with fifty years apart in age, became the best of friends, and the next thing we know, Carl is sitting having dinner with us that evening. By the time dessert is put on the table, he is no longer going home at the weekend because now he was invited to extend his stay and live with us. Suddenly I have a new friend, who became a best friend because of his unorthodox American ways I found quite amusing.

Nevertheless, as much as he was a friend to me, Aspie had no qualms telling him that if he kept smoking in his company, he would alienate himself. You see, Aspie's contemptuous side wanted me for himself. He couldn't afford anyone becoming too friendly because he thrived on me giving him infinite affection. Aspie willingly hoped my new American friend was going to be gone soon and out of my life for good, and did his best to pave the way for that to occur.

A. Damn right. I didn't like Carl's abhorrent addiction to those cancer sticks; it kept reminding me of when your father took us to the coal mine in Ebbw Vale. He didn't expect me to complain about his chain smoking. It smothered my lungs.

H. I will talk later on about my stay in New York. Meanwhile, Carl had got himself a job working at Columbia in their London office and lodging with us. I was seventeen at the time, and barely a couple of months after I passed my driving test, my mother suggested I took Carl on a driving tour with some of the money I had made out of the stamps.

We made our drive during the Christmas holidays, and I convinced Carl that the climate in Wales was warmer than England so he managed to come without appropriate clothing. Aspie's turn for fun came when Carl decided to smoke and insisted keeping his window closed. But our real fun occurred the following evening after he had complained he had caught a cold. Aspie told him that the best remedy was gulping down a tablespoon of Tabasco sauce to warm his soul and rid him of his cold. You should have seen the grimace on his face. Funniest thing we had seen for years.

By the time another year had gone around, Carl had gone back home, although destined for a work placement in Phoenix, and that was why decided Phoenix was the city of my dreams.

Now I must wind the clock back two years. If I thought I was rid of the paedophile the forest folk introduced me to, I was in for a nasty surprise.

I was invited to the ninth World Youth Festival in Sofia, Bulgaria and our first stop was Budapest, where we were allowed to spend the day looking round the city before our onward travel. We were going by train to Sofia, where thousands of other youths from all corners of the world were to be involved in a variety of ceremonies and sports activities.

Where the festival was taking place, we had access to all the sports equipment that was on offer. There was a high diving board Aspie fell in love with, but when I was getting out of the pool, his hand reached down to pull me out. I saw his sneer but I couldn't get up and run away from the paedophile's clutches. Sadly, Aspie took it to heart and, without any warning, it was as though he had dived into the heart of the volcano. No sooner had my head entered its belly than the pain that was delivered made me feel like I was being instantly consumed by its stomach of lava. Apparently, when I came to, I was told I had been out cold for a couple of hours. The doctor who checked me over said, apart from a bruised rib or two, some bruising on my pelvis and a gash on my forehead, I was fine. Aspie insisted we visited a hospital to get me X-rayed. However, we were told it would be safer to wait until we got home.

What had actually occurred was that in my rush to get away from my oppressor, I had dived in to a lap pool immediately adjacent that was barely a metre deep. When we eventually returned home, about a week later, X-rays showed I had fractured my left wrist and pelvis.

However, life continued and at sixteen years old, I went off to New York, so excited about going to a city that had a skyscraper taller than the Eiffel Tower. It was funny; as a child, going to a country where they spoke unBritish English, Aspie and I couldn't relate to the odd stares we received when we asked where the nearest tube was or how fast the lifts were in the Empire State Building.

It was funny to hear Carl's dad say, 'Son, I do like your new friend Hartley, but getting used to his lingo is something else.'

It would seem that Aspie was getting well versed into training for the Aspie Olympics. I recall Carl's father telling me to stay away from the black ghettos in Jamaica, or risk returning home in a coffin. Just my bad luck and Aspie's good fortune, there was one a stone's throw away from where Carl lived.

Among the weaknesses of my relationship with Aspie was his need to experience everything the world had to offer. We were suddenly aware of a group of youths with sticks and knives, chasing us like all of hell was on their tail. Had I panicked, the outcome could have been somewhat different.

It was down on the island of Manhattan Aspie found a particular affinity. The layout of the city reminded him of the tiles on the wall of the loos he often sat in. To Aspie, each of New York blocks conformed throughout the city as though designed by Rain Man. Blocks that ran north to south conformed to an exact seventy-five yards. Comparing to London's irregular blocks, he wondered what madman had brought together that design.

The one-way traffic system was also more attractive than the streets of London. To any New Yorker, who might have been watching him pace each block, they might have wondered how long it would be before this mad Englishman met an untimely end. Basically my stomach churned since Aspie rarely looked to see in which direction the oncoming traffic was relative to us. It was as though he had a unique ability to spin his way along every window of every floor along every skyscraper block. When it came to crossing between blocks, his acute sense of spacial awareness came into play, regardless of drivers honking their horns as they screeched to a halt.

During the years we were commuting to New York regularly, I took it for granted that it was an Aspie thing, counting the windows on every skyscraper we walked past. When I wanted to drag him away from that feat, I had to offer him something else to be addictive about, such as how many subway stations we passed through before the end of the day.

The trouble with having Aspie in my life was that he took everything for granted. The following year, it was music to Aspie's ears when Carl invited me to spend the summer with him. His home was shaped like a flying saucer, ready to take off. An unbelievable circular monolith close to Camelback Mountain built on two floors, sixty feet in diameter, overlooking the entire metropolis. While staying there, I was surprised that the landlord, Greg, allowed Carl to drive his vintage Mercedes convertible, more so when I was trusted to take it out for a drive, except it was Aspie who sat in the driver's seat.

A. Yes, carry on the story. I just love what comes next, the look on his face and the denial in yours. I still thrive today on such sentiments.

R. You smashed up his car?

H. I didn't, but Aspie did have an incident in it.

A. Just like you to exaggerate the truth. I wasn't in the car, so how could I be responsible?

H. What Aspie has just said is one of his typical remarks, bending the truth. The fact was, I was speechless, embarrassed as to how Aspie was responsible for Greg's windscreen cracking and not realising it was his relationship with ADHD. Why Aspie is virtually able to walk across the busiest junction safely with his eyes closed, yet completely blind to his immediate surroundings? Where we parked was on a slight slope and it was inevitable that Aspie forgot to apply the handbrake correctly. I thought it was better to tell the truth than make up our contorted story that his car had rolled down the hill because a circus troupe had parked next to it and an elephant had swung its trunk against the windscreen, hence the damage!

This incident reminds me of another incident twenty years later, which was my fault for allowing Aspie to have an irresistible lust of gadgets. Joe's Electronics specialised in hi-tech auto gadgets. I had already spent a couple of grand on a top quality deck and tuner, and was shown an amazing remote control that would start any car automatically. Except Aspie had decided it would work on my car. One evening, we parked outside my parents' home and one of my uncles wanted to know why my car was facing the side of his bonnet with a dent in it and wondering what ghost could have started it!

R. It appears to me that Aspie was partial to concocting stories just to appease him on any given day. What you mean to say is this device should never have been purchased in the first place.

H. Sadly among Aspie's predicaments is his inability to recognise truth from fiction. He believed anything that was said to him. When we purchased the device, we were advised such a disaster might happen. But we never knew we were the guinea pig in the device's trial! Hence why at first I attempted to convince Greg that somehow on its own accord, his car had rolled down the hill and that was how the windscreen cracked.

R. And that was the end of that?

H. It was only the end of that when I coughed up for a new windscreen.

R. Of course, that was no problem for you being the rich kid you were.

H. Sentiments with hindsight, I wished I could have adorned. But there were hidden facets in our relationship that I have yet tried to explain. Aspie was so confident about his aspirations, he had no room for consequences. In business, this meant not getting outdone by our business mates was not going to be on the cards daily.

I have to understand they were a good half a generation older, already had beautiful homes and drove Rolls Royces. While I, the new kid on the block, and Aspie required to outdo them. He made me purchase a Ferrari. Exactly the type of the car waiting for an accident to happen, and we didn't have long to wait! Three days after its purchase, Aspie decided to see how the bodywork fared and wrapped it around a tree!

A. It is so easy to pin misfortunes onto me! If you are going to tell a story, please tell the whole story. It is the parts you leave out that I believe had real relevance. How often do I tell you I was unable to distinguish right from wrong, good from bad, or truth from fiction. Fundamentally, I looked to you to correct my errors before I learnt from my mistakes. My issue with you is whether that day will actually occur. If you insist on boasting about my mishaps, I will have no choice but to pass on the buck your way.

H. Already I have talked a good bit about my life story, including my unfortunate encounters with undesirables, too many to talk about. It was as though as soon as Aspie realised he was different from other boys of his age, he decided to display a label that read, *I'm over here. I'm who you have been looking for, and now you have found me.*

I have no real understanding or explanation as to why I was attracted to people I didn't want in my life, but little did I know I had little choice. Already there had been every type of bully, mental, physical and sexual abusers. Perhaps I had to accept that anyone who had an anxiety with society made a beeline in my direction and there was not a damn thing I could do about it. Furthermore, this was the antithesis of what was to come.

If Greg's car was the bread and my incident with it was the butter spread thinly, then there are plenty more incidents for me to tell you about, Rea.

The following summer, it was my luck that the night before my flight to LAX, my parents received a message from cousins that read, 'Something has cropped up. Can't pick you up from airport, suggest you find alternative accommodation.'

We had landed and were waiting for our luggage to arrive when Aspie noticed a cafe and decided to sample every sweet cake on offer. I can't blame him for his sweet tooth, since Grandma Hetty made delicious Jewish delicacies, and you know how the saying goes: 'Once bitten, forever smitten.' In a way, it was a misfortune she lived halfway between school and home. You can imagine how much Aspie scoffed. Actually, normally I arrived an hour before Grandpa had dinner. It wasn't as though I could turn up at any time, dare I interrupted her routine. Six o'clock on the dot, she went into the hallway and shouted out, 'Marv!' and momentarily he was sitting in his seat at the head of the morning room table. The dining room table was reserved for special occasions or when my uncle played the grand piano.

Basically, I had about half an hour to visit before Grandma prepared his dinner. I wished I could have adopted the rule one serving means only one serving, because Aspie invariably went searching for his second or third portions. I often imagined the way some of my desserts were drooling with maple syrup was in competition with calories Elvis Presley ate.

Anyway, after we had feasted, leaving me feeling as sick as a pig, this was when my troubles began unaware of the overdose of sugar, which was probably the responsible agent. I suddenly became aware of people staring at me, while Aspie was convinced they are staring at my label that read, *'I'm over here waiting for you.'*

It occurred a few weeks before, when unknowingly I was being groomed. Had it been a woman looking in my direction, I may have returned her stare. Except she was a man and one who Aspie found very attractive, and within passing a few stations, we become friends. What I didn't realise, my hard luck, was that to him, I was another piece of meat being prepared.

A. And my good fortune!

H. I had no idea that because Aspie had given off inappropriate facial responses, without warning I felt the hand of the pervert squeezing one of my thighs as though an inoffensive friendly gesture. Momentarily, I heard an American voice saying, 'Do you mind me tagging along? I am a stranger in your city and if you could show me around, I could get to know you better?'

Of course, I was naive about him, asking me lots of personal questions. He quickly found out I was visiting LA and he handed me a piece of paper with a number on it that read, 'Should you ever need a place to stay, you will always be welcome.' I wish someone had warned me that what it meant was that I would become a gay rent boy for the night I stayed there!

A. Can you blame me for wanting you to try out homosexuality? It might have found us a new, well-paid vocation. Perhaps bisexual would have been more exciting than just wanting sex with pussies. So, yes, I wanted to see your reaction when he placed his hand on your crutch. Just my luck, your mind was not set in that direction.

H. Sometimes I wish I could have ignored Aspie's lewd remarks. Anyway, feeling somewhat unbalanced, wondering where my first night in LA was going to be, I eventually succumb to knocking on Joshua's front door. Although I did think it was strange when I heard someone say, 'Our sweetie pie has arrived.'

It might have been enjoyable for Aspie, being fucked in every position in the Kama Sutra, but I had no intention of learning the rudiments of gay rent boys. When I eventually arrived at my mother's cousin's home, I told them about my unfortunate experience without discussing the rather embarrassing details. Instead, I told them about meeting this American guy on the London underground, who told me should I ever visit LA, I was welcome to stay with him and why I accepted his invitation, because I thought I had experience of America, having stayed with Carl the year before last and spending the summer with his family in New York. Only afterwards, I mentioned how one of them announced me as 'our sweetie pie' which was nothing more than Californian lingo.

'My dear Hartley, LA is a far cry from London. Here you can find every genre of the population and turning up at stranger's house is asking for trouble,' said my cousins.

They went on to say if I didn't want to compromise my safety, next time to stay at a motel. So you see, I was becoming a worldly traveller at seventeen. If I thought life experiences were going to bring me some solace, how wrong I could be? Did that answer my own question?

If I wanted to moan at Aspie, he ensured I got my comeuppance. What a fuck-up. By the beginning of the autumn term, while most of my fellow pupils of both sex had returned with no doubt amazing stories to share with their friends, I felt as flat as a squashed tomato, even brain dead.

Chapter 13: The Getting Nowhere Job

H. Now you know Aspie pretty much fucked up my education at school, pre-empting me to leaving at the end of the lower sixth spring term. What I wasn't looking forward to was spending my summer holidays visiting the local Job Centre. Given my lack of qualifications, the only jobs offered were working for the local council as an apprentice road sweeper, dustman or sweeping the floor of my local Tesco store. Aspie chose the latter, hoping he would never run into any of the neighbours.

Unbeknown to me, luck was on my side. The way everything was laid out along the aisles simulated Aspie's tiled wall thinking and he found himself back in his imaginary world, so from his perspective, he felt safe in his job. From the store manager's perspective, I appeared to be staring into oblivion! By the end of the first morning, I was called into his office and told to look for a new job.

I didn't think Aspie fared too well back at the Job Centre when asked what he wanted to do. His reply was, 'Anything that will make me a boss one day.' At my next job, I managed to fair better, that is sarcastically speaking. It took me all of three days to learn that Aspie could never work for anyone as a salesman, which we quickly found out at Whiteley Department Store's Menswear department.

A. It was just up my street. To me, it was no difference from stacking rows of different types of clothes, or comparing to rows of windows in skyscrapers. I loved counting them all.

H. After three days, the manager asked Aspie which planet he was born on. Not the sort of question you ask an Aspie because you are likely to get an out of worldly reply. Aspie's answer was, 'Earth, silly.' You can imagine how his very perplexed manager looked at me in such a way as though he had seen a ghost and said, 'Son, I don't think you are suited to this job.'

R. Now, I bet you are going to tell me that Aspie replied, 'I am not your son,' and from what I am learning about the way he responds, answers, or asks questions to questions, that should never be asked in the first place. Did he leave the manager even more bewildered?

H. You got it. Can you believe it was only mid-week and I was about to be offered my third job at a menswear shop around the corner in Westbourne Grove where I didn't fare any better?

A. But fun for me. I felt back at home into my world.

H. Yes, that's something else I had to get used to fast. Suddenly, it felt like I was in Hampton Court Maze. Rows and rows of tightly contained suits, jackets and trousers of different sizes, designs and colours meant ever more distraction. What to look at and where to look in such a confined space fuelled Aspie's mind. Just like at Whiteleys, I was supposed to learn the salesman's lingo, unaware it was not in Aspie's list of capabilities. The following morning, I was asked if I really wanted to become a salesman. That was the manager's first mistake. The next question the manager asked, he realised his mistake too late, not expecting the bellyful of Aspie's reply. The manager said, 'Look, son,' to which Aspie said, 'How can I be your son?' At this point, I could almost lip read the manager murmuring under his breath, about his luck to have been delivered a retard.

My manager wanted to be as helpful as he could and said to me, 'Look, it seems you have difficulties communicating with customers so I have tried to make it easier for you, by writing out what you need to say when any customer comes into my shop.' Written on the piece of paper were the following words; *Hello, sir. How can I help you, sir? What of my stock are you interested to see, sir? Let me see how I can help you, sir?*

That night, it was as though I was going back to school because I had been asked to reread what was written on the paper repetitively. Not in my wildest dreams did I think that working meant homework too.

The following morning, the first thing the manager said to me was, 'Got it?'

Again, it was Aspie who answered. 'What am I supposed to get, sir?'

Rather than bite my head off, I could sense the manager was trying to be as diplomatic as possible. 'Look, the reason I gave you the sheet of paper with words for you to read was so you know how to speak to a customer. For instance, whenever any customer comes into my shop, I always say, "How can I help you?" And I expect you to say exactly the words I do.'

By the end of the day, the manager must have felt very sad to have to say to me, 'I am so sorry, son, it does not appear you are cut out to work here.'

Where luck was on my side was that my boyhood interest in stamps saved my bacon. However, I didn't mention that I experienced one other job that pre-empted my journey into the world of philately, except Aspie's aspirations were about to show a serious flaw. He didn't do standing on the street with a placard round his neck advertising 'We sell stamps' to unwitting tourists who are in dire need of being conned.

A. Typical! There you go again, blaming me for your inadequacies. It was proof that once money is thrown in your face, you foolishly became part of that machine.

H. The truth is somewhat different. In a way, I had been led down a blind alley. I was told I could become a philatelist. What Aspie had ensured I didn't hear was that I was expected to do remedial work, be the tea boy and any other dirty work. My new assignment reminded Aspie of cleaning the latrines at the campsite and no Jewish scumbag deserved to being treated in this manner. Suddenly, my new employer was compared to the paedophile headmaster at my junior school or Irish Jimmy, the maths teacher, giving himself a hand job with my entire class jeering him on. It was a tug of war to prevent a repeat performance of exposing myself in Denmark. I heard the words, 'Get away from here, you fucking freak of nature.' Little did I know that by now Aspie had been holding onto his crutch as though he was holding onto his life! That it was protruding and there was a damp patch, which made me feel so awkward, while he was laughing his head off.

R. I think part of your problem was Aspie's coping mechanism with your past, be it the sexual deviants, predators or other unpleasant encounters. The culmination of emotional damage was too much for him to bear. Reality hit you just like the bullet that leaves the sniper's gun accurately hitting its mark. In this case, unequivocally it had become the culmination of your lifetime experiences. It is little wonder how terrified you were. Perhaps Aspie was Jekyll and Hyde. Let's change the subject and get onto something lighter. What about romance? I assume, like most other teenage boys, you had interest in girls.

H. I know it might sound strange to you, but Aspie didn't do girls. He couldn't afford me having any girlfriend because he believed he would be snuffed out of my life and not getting my attention. Things only began to get easier for me when I began my fifth year when most of the other pupils got rid of their adolescent nonsense. The boys thought of him as an anti-social freak of nature because he preferred girl's stuff like gymnastics or yoga, rather than football or rugby.

R. You still haven't answered my question. Are you telling me you had no girlfriends?

H. Aspie enjoyed girlish activities because he enjoyed gawking at their breasts.

A. You got me there on that one, and why not? I had hoped it would help you to understand at an early age that girls could only do you the best of good.

R. I think you felt safer with girls because we females are more easily able to be more responsive to people who are more sensitive about feelings and emotional issues. We would have sensed you had plenty of these and felt sorry for you.

H. Sorry for me? Whenever I think about it, Aspie would have loved any of the girls to have taken me by the hand and said, 'Let's go and have a fuck,' except the truth was I would have been scared out of my wits to have any relationship with sex involved.

R. I think sex for the first time for anyone is scary, and particularly with your vulnerabilities, even more so.

H. But for me, what the paedophile had brainwashed me into believing was that sex was dirty and the female genitalia was the work of the Devil himself. Even getting undressed in a male changing room in full sight of male genitalia, Aspie ensured I found it disturbing. During those earlier years of my childhood, there were few girls I was in contact with other than my cousins. Mind you, I often laugh about it now because when I was young, I shared a bath with both of them. Only at junior school was there one girl I played with but this was more so because she was a neighbour.

Nevertheless this attitude towards feeling comfortable chatting to girls made Aspie very uneasy. Shauna was a good example. I was fifteen at the time. We were sitting in the science lab and she was diagonally opposite me. I reached out to see if she would do the same and hold hands. I had no idea Aspie felt too embarrassed! Talk about falling in love at first sight with every Tom, Dick and Harry wearing a skirt. I didn't know why I had these feelings or how troublesome they would become throughout my life.

I didn't know Aspie had also betrothed me with eidetic memory. It was something about her eyes that I couldn't help myself stare into and be returned a stare I didn't know what to do with. Perhaps I should have known this was teenage love at first sight and we could have been an item.

A. Love at first sight, mate; fucking fool were my sentiments. It was as though all the years of telling you I could only learn through you had been flushed down the toilet. If only you could have had the courage to say hi, made that first move. So sad I had to contain myself to settling down to you constantly staring back at her; so frustrating!

H. Sadly, I have to agree with Aspie's sentiments.

R. We all have to move forward past our shyness.

H. Aspie's not most people. Relationships with girls couldn't work out for us! Even my first date was the ultimate sabotage!

Although my mother was very supportive knowing about Aspie, she introduced us to the Jewish Youth Voluntary Service, where boys and girls met in an informal atmosphere and participated in different social events and volunteering work. Our volunteering included visiting the homeless in the East End of London in the middle of the night, taking them food. In a strange way, Aspie felt he had an affinity with their neglect. Among my new group of friends were a number of attractive girls and the first one Aspie picked me to have an interest in was Shauna. Whilst the boys might have thoughts about getting into the girls' knickers, it was a sickening notion to Aspie, given the terms the paedophile had endeared him be groomed with.

It was my mother's Orthodox Jewish neighbour who arranged a blind date for me with another girl called Melanie, who was my age and from a reserved and orthodox family. Aspie asked my mother how he should kiss her good night. It was the ineffectual look that my mother saw in his response that told her the difficulty Aspie was going to have. The date turned out to be a real fuck-up.

R. I don't really understand. You went on a date and you were rebuffed; it happens all the time. Just something we all have to learn to grow up with.

H. I don't think you understand the seriousness of what occurred. What went wrong that night could even be said to be life-threatening.

R. Surely that's a bit overstating the facts? I would have thought you should have been able to gauge when the timing was right? Are you trying to say she rebuffed you and you tried to commit hari-kari?

H. Far worse than that. She must have thought I was a wimp when we didn't even get to snog in the back row of the cinema. You need to remember sharing my life with Aspie was living in a world where normality ceased to exist.

I mentioned a moment ago eidetic memory that on the ideal occasion can be very conducive, but on the other hand, he remembered everything. Imagine anywhere we travel, Aspie had mesmerised every landmark we past. Could be in the form of a bush or a tree, or the colour of the bricks on a particular building or as mundane as a lamppost, even a puddle as daft as it sounds. It was as though he had his very own inbuilt compass and therefore the chance of getting lost was very slim and we didn't require a map to get places.

R. Sounds more like you should be a billionaire by now.

H. Not so simple. Aspie's brain behaved like a supercomputer; the only difference was it didn't have fuses to blow and naturally the downside was the inability of coping with memory overload. Imagine remembering everything that ever happened to you from the moment you are born: good; bad; right; and wrong. His memory was indifferent too. How would you cope with all of these memories, simultaneously? Perhaps now you are getting my drift.

Both Aspie and I are naive when we have any understanding related to sexual emotion of being rebuffed. It reminded him of a shop sign he noticed that read 'Massage Parlour'.

A. I love it when I hear my name being mentioned. You said it yourself. You know why I fucked up your date. If you like another pièce de résistance, I had the time of my life that night.

H. It was Aspie's good luck and my bad fortune that I was making more money in a week buying and selling stamps than most boys of my age made in a few months, and that evening I had £50 in my pocket.

Anyway, we arrived and there is an open sign pinned to the front of the door, to the right, 'Please ring'. Aspie rung the bell and barely a few seconds later an attractive girl opened the door suspiciously and put her face between the door and the frame. 'Can I help you?'

'Your sign said massage and I would like a massage.'

The girl eyed me up and down. 'Are you sure you can afford a massage?' she continued.

Aspie asked her how much a massage cost. She replied ten quid, to which Aspie replied easily affordable. Opening the door further, I saw the girl appeared to be about ten years older than me. Being naive, I couldn't have understood her revealing dress showing her ample breasts, which were advertising her intention. She asked my name, to which Aspie replied as always, 'Why do you want to know that?'

Ignoring Aspie and attempting to appear polite, she made the mistake of saying, 'I'm Honey.'

Aspie replied, 'How come you are a jar of honey?'

R. I think I am getting a little of an idea of what life was like for you back then. Aspie took anything said to you literally.

H. He had no way of not knowing and there are still occasions he does this to me today.

R. Must make life trying for you at times.

H. That it does. Honey was among my favourite foods and it would have been quite normal for him to look at her and wonder why she had been given Honey as a name. She asked me how old I was and then led me into a small room about eight foot square with barely enough room for the massage couch and a small chair with standing room for me to get changed. The problem was, I didn't know what to do next.

She told me to get undressed and lie on my front and to cover myself with the towel that was hanging on the chair. Aspie asked her what clothes he should take off. She replied he could take off what he liked. I got worried when Aspie insisted I removed my underpants too. By the time Honey returned to the massage room, I was lying on my tummy worried that the small towel was barely covering my buttocks. She now returned with more buttons on her shirt undone, showing even more of her breasts than before.

As I felt a sexual arousal, Aspie reminded me of my first wet dream. These feelings were alien to me, since I couldn't understand why my penis was getting strangely harder or how I should explain my embarrassment to Honey. She began the massage by pouring oil down my back and legs, saying, 'That feels good, doesn't it?'

You have to remember, this was my very first sexual experience in front of a girl, having no idea her delicately light touch was deliberately bringing on an erection close to the point of an orgasm. Eventually, I said, 'Can't I lie on my front a little longer?' to hide my embarrassment.

She replied, 'If you don't turn over now, I won't have enough time to do your front.' While it was obvious to Honey what her intention was, I was quite naive to her asking her next question. 'Would you like relief?'

Aspie answered, 'For what reason?'

At this point, Honey left the room to tell her mates about the weird guy she was massaging who had no idea why she wanted to massage his penis. She returned, took my left hand and cups it over one of her breasts and asked me if I wanted to have my penis massaged. When I said, 'Okay,' I no idea it required an extra £5.

It was Aspie who replied, telling me that by making me cum, he would feel very happy. Much of my naivety about learning sex education at school was due to my congenital condition in my arms that meant I missed most of those lessons. I was unaware that masturbation was a healthy bi-product of the sexual intimacy between myself and the masseuse or that I was in a brothel.

This is why my visit to the massage parlour created an addiction for Aspie. He parted with a little bit of my money and he could get as much sexual satisfaction without getting involved with a girl. Worse, the paedophile had won his bet.

R. Not so happy an ending after all.

H. Aspie took everything I did by its face value. In a nutshell, he felt he had no choice but to follow my cue.

R. That's what I call tough love. You poor old thing!

H. What didn't help were certain incidents at the Jewish Youth Voluntary Service. Going round to different friend's homes and watching other boys making it with girls.

A. Was I'm supposed to know that Sharon was the prize. Worse was when I heard, 'Sorry, mate, it's the man who makes the first move that gets the prize; getting your dick into the slit between their legs!'

H. At this stage of my life, how could I possibly have known the complexities that Aspie would bring into my life? His total non-understanding of body language or of facial expression. It was at another gathering that Sharon offered me some sympathy when she asked me what was wrong, and I replied that I didn't like the jokes that were made and I had feelings for her but did not know how to express them. All I wished for was her cradling and stroking my head. I couldn't explain it but it made me feel safe. I did get the oddest looks though while Aspie was frequenting massage parlours; my request was having my head massaged.

As you will learn, this difficulty of talking to girls interfered with my working day. Aspie coerced me to believe paying a few quid for sexual massage beat attempting a relationship any day.

Yet, here's the weird thing about having these massages that really irritated me. It was like Aspie was imparting his very impulsive behaviour that evoked T-Rex and other types of intrusive thoughts terrorising me if I didn't comply.

Chapter 14: The Job That Worked

R. While not on purpose trying to change the subject, what was life like for you dealing in stamps?

A. You dumb fucker, you don't know what she is trying to do to you, diverting your attention? She is perverting you to tell the world our little secrets.

H. Sometimes I feel like I need to be saved from Aspie. Anyway, these were the fun days of my life, as well as giving me an introduction to the pitfalls and dangers of big business.

The first time I had a yearning for earning money, I was eleven, a Saturday job working for a friend of my father's, at his Dutch cigar import warehouse, where I was introduced at an early age to the aroma of cigars. I was paid ten shillings per hour. The following year, I had the nerve to ask for a raise and was surprised when my wage was doubled to £1 an hour. I had learnt the art that if you don't ask, you don't get.

How my stamp dealing caper began, was one day I happened to be wandering around St. Martins Lane and Strand Stamp and Coin Centre, which my father had introduced me to a couple of years before. I was sixteen and it was simply Aspie's obtrusive way of overlooking philatelists dealing with their customers, which gets us noticed by one of the dealers, and he asked me if I was interested in a Saturday job.

'Now, young man, I have been noticing you milling around my stand these past few weeks, and through the observations I have been making, it would seem you ask a lot of questions without buying anything. But that is okay, I have no qualms about that. Have you left school yet?'

I think he was taken aback by my ignoring his question and Aspie asking him how much he could sell me the Silver Wedding Pound for. It was a big stamp that Aspie assumed, with a high denomination, meant it was worth more.

I interrupted and said I really liked the colour of the King George V twopenny blue and asked how much it was.

'Son, this conversation is getting a little bit absurd. I am the one who is supposed to be asking the questions. Not wanting to appear to be rude, but are you a little deaf?'

A. I replied, 'Sorry, but if you were asking me a question, I can only concentrate on one thing at a time. Anyway, I like the colour of that twopenny blue.'

'Will someone help me string this guy up and hold his head in place so his eyes are focused on my attention?' the poor man said.

I replied, 'Got it, you mean me?'

'That's right, I mean you. Good, we are making a head start. Now, my name is Zachary and these are my stamps. Please can I have your name?'

I replied, 'Why didn't you ask that in the first place? My name is Hartley, what's yours?'

'Zachary.'

'I like the name Zachary.'

'Hallelujah, we are actually getting somewhere. praise be the Lord.'

'How much are the two stamps I asked the price of?'

'The Silver Wedding Pound will cost you £3 and the blue stamp, you don't want to know the price, is very expensive and it is not in the best of condition. It's £150.'

After about ten minutes, I asked Zachary if the price I had been given was the best price and if I could take it away, appreciate it and pay him in the morning if that was okay.

He replied, 'Young man, as a rule I don't normally allow customers to take stamps before they have paid for them. But you appear to be a genuine person and I am going to take the chance you are honest too. Yes, you can pay me tomorrow. But please make sure you come back with £3 in your pocket.'

H. I think I must have pleasantly surprised Zachary because Aspie was true to his word. The following morning, we were waiting for the centre to open and no sooner than he had opened up, we slapped the £3 into his hand. I told him I had sold the stamp to a neighbour for £3 and ten shillings, and asked him if he had more stamps to sell me. From that moment onwards, every weekend we became best buddies. During the week at school, I yearned for less of Aspie's interference; at the weekends, Zachary taught me the rudiments of becoming a professional philatelist. But, while Zachary and I got on well together, Zachary's baby face disturbed Aspie, as I mentioned earlier. Earlier on in our relationship, Zachary introduced me to his assistant, his father, who told me about Zachary's background. He had given his son the best education he could afford, sent him to Sussex's top public boys schools, and once he had completed his school exams, he decided to follow his father into philately.

Comparing father to son was like comparing chalk and cheese, leaving me hoping I'm not looking at Aspie in another fifty years with a big bulging beer belly. Rarely did a day arrive when Zachary's father turned up looking dishevelled with his shirt hanging out of his trousers, his collar button undone and his tie hanging down, as well as his flies open as though what remained hidden was getting ready for action. It was as though Zachary had a duty to take over his father's humorous role with his own antics. He worked hard during the day but acted the fool afterwards in the pub.

My future wasn't to be the boy who thought his voice was so outstanding he would one day be singing at Covent Garden

Opera House or unluckily sweeping the streets. Instead, a stone's throw away I was learning the trade of a philately at the St. Martin's Lane Stamp and Coin Centre. While I had failed miserably being employed, Aspie's acumen of making money as a philatelist was emerging. Zachary told me, 'You stick with me, lad, and 1 will show you how easy it is to make money.'

During the years I knew Zachary, I learnt the rudiments of becoming an entrepreneur, but I was blind to Aspie's talent of reversing any of my successes.

R. Although I never had a son of my own, I am only too aware that the hobby of stamp collecting is very much a boyish thing. Do you remember at what age your interest developed?

H. About twelve; it was a fascination with the different coloured pieces of paper that represented different countries. Perhaps because of geography, my other enjoyable subject, was the reason collecting stamps became an interest during my early teens. Also, the meticulous way I endeared much time sticking mounts on to stamps and pasting them to pages. Aspie saw insight into learning the art of buying and selling stamps because he was able to get bogged down and be completely absorbed and happy. I learnt from Zachary that the majority of albums full of hundreds or thousands of stamps had little value. It was best to distinguish between the rare and the common, as well as learning mounted stamps had less value than the unmounted.

As I began handling more quantities and improved my expertise, I began learning that condition played an important part and the sought after stamps could be worth far more than the catalogue value.

About a year after meeting Zachary, I began my first adventure in philately when he invited me to attend my first stamp auction accompanying him to the basement of the Strand Palace Hotel, where weekly auctions were held. He took us to our designated seat, as though it was a vantage point for viewing all the lots around the salesroom. By following his cue, it helped shape my level of confidence, although I had to contend with Aspie trying hard to sabotage my achievements, unaware of his ulterior motives.

R. Visiting massage parlours?

H. I wish it hadn't developed into a hobby Aspie craved, but that was how it panned out. Anyway, at the auction, Zachary bought his first lot for £240, several boxes full of albums and loose stamps and British postal history. I asked him, 'Would you do £60 profit?' He was delighted and said, 'That's my boy, absolutely! That is why we are here, to give each other a helping hand. You give me a profit on what I buy, and I give you a profit on what you buy.'

Fifteen minutes passed with Zachary and I continually looking at the contents of the box. Eventually, Zachary was the final owner at £1,840, and I taking home £800 in cash. Meanwhile, Zachary told me our private arrangement had to be kept secret between ourselves. Anyway, my meeting with Zachary proved far more fortuitous than I ever could have imagined. By the age of seventeen, I was also gaining my first business partner.

R. You have never mentioned anything before about a business partner?

H. It's complicated. You could almost say that Aspie had been my everything partner, business and personal built into one. But when I met Zachary, he shared the expenses of premises with a man called Matt, a numismatist who dealt with another dealer, Terence, who dealt in coins.

R. Who is Terence? It seems I need the senses of a hawk to keep a track on the different people in your life. You hadn't mentioned Matt or Terence before?

H. I suppose it's because I have few memories of Matt as I didn't develop an interest in numismatics. How my relationship with Terence began was because of his dealing in coins. What I wasn't to know was that two Aspies were about to encounter each other for the first time.

A. That was fun!

H. Another pertinent thing I don't think I've mentioned was that Aspies often talk their own language in tones that can make anyone listening quit trying because they speak in monosyllables with no variation in tone. I hope this makes sense to you?

Since the first time Terence and I met, and all of our subsequent meetings, it was as though he had just unlocked the door of his Tardis and was born into the world from a bygone era. Yet, between then, and the last time I saw him again about thirty years later, it was as though he was wearing the same clothes he got out of bed in when we first met. Terence was a couple of years older and employed by Inland Revenue. Dealing in coins was his hobby, and after I got to know him, he often told me that working for them would be a thing of the past, but that his work experience - buying and selling coins - would benefit his CV.

This is when Aspie took over our conversation.

A. How come the letters C and V can help you with your future?

No doubt a fly on the wall would have been surprised by Terence's reply: 'A CV is not ordinary letters, it is your Curriculum Vitae.'

'What is that? Sounds like a spaceship from another planet?' Aspie replied.

'Are you trying to be funny, my friend?' Terence said.

'I am not your friend. I have only just started talking to you,' Aspie continued

'Would you like to be my friend?

'I would like to be your friend.'

'Okay, you are my friend.'

H. Zachary suggested to Terence that it might be a good idea for us to exchange names otherwise our conversation wasn't going anywhere. The trouble was that Zachary hadn't realised, until it was too late, that neither of us could understand what was asked of us. It was as though Terence and I spoke in unison and we both asked Zachary where would our names go and how would we find them. Then to add chaos into our communication,

Terence added, 'Does exchanging names with my new friend mean he will have my name and I will have his?'

Poor bewildered Zachary said, 'I don't know what's wrong with you two but before I have a heart attack, and please don't ask me why I might have one, the purpose of exchanging names is that if you, Terence, tell your name to Hartley, he is going to know your name and vice versa.'

But Aspie jumped in before I could reply! 'How dare you! My name is not vice versa!'

Poor Zachary continued. 'Or course it isn't, Hartley. Hartley, say hello to Terence, and Terence, say hello to Hartley.'

It could have been like a choir because they both simultaneously repeated their names, and finally Terence knew my name was Hartley, and I knew his name was Terence.

Then he said to me, 'You know, mate, you do stamps and I do coins. I've noticed you milling around here for a while now. Would you be interested in sharing the cost of a table in one of my local markets on a Sunday morning in a place where collectors go to? It's called Collectors' Corner at the eastern end of East Street Market. You pay for half of my thirty shillings and this means it will cost you fifteen shillings. We open our table at 8am, can you do this?'

Of course, Aspie was thinking in a different direction and said so. 'Open a table. What do you mean "open"? Do you mean you open the table and we crawl inside?'

Poor Zachary was still trying to understand us. 'What is it with you two? Look, this opening a table is business talk. The two of you are going to share a table. You will have one half of the table and Terence will have the other half, and when you are ready for business, you will be opening the table, that's how it works.'

I then asked the logical question of what if it rained. Stamps don't do well in the rain. But Terence told me our table was under cover. The idea of setting up my new business in a market really appealed to me. Those Sunday mornings we visited were akin to the mysterious world Aspie so enjoyed, walking into a dimly lit cave, books and manuscripts adorned the shelves along the narrow corridors with even little room for pint-size me to walk. My memories are clouded now because property developers have changed parts of the area. I wish that signs could have been erected as evidence of a once thriving Jewish community in that neighbourhood.

At the time, Hannah, a distant cousin, was the first of my piano tutors when I was five. Long after she gave up tutoring, she turned to composing. Whenever we visited the little bookshop, my mother took me to see what bargains could be bought from Petticoat Lane around the corner. By the time I set up my own stall, I already had familiarity of market life, where bargains could be had on many of the stalls. However, it was only after a few weeks of walking from Elephant and Castle on the Northern Line and walking down the length of East Street Market, that I learnt how looks were deceiving.

While I can look back on those times, it was to be decades later until that I understood how most of the stallholders were from working-class backgrounds and had to work very hard to sustain their families. By the time Terence had introduced me to his family, what I became very aware of was that we were a very different story to the retail businesses along the High Street.

The first time he introduced me to his mother and his home overlooking a railway bridge in the heart of the slums behind the Walworth Road, it was a cultural shock for me. It made me feel how lucky I was and how tough his upbringing must have been. Wallpaper literally hung off the walls with much grey brick protruding. It was hard to believe that the councils allowed their tenants to live in such squalid conditions. His family's real sadness came about when an explosion ripped through their home one day from an unknown cause taking out whatever remained inside. He was playing with mates, his mother had gone to the market and his sister was left playing in the room she shared with him; and that was left smouldering when they returned. That was the worst part, seeing the smoke and the firemen nodding their heads, and then hearing the dreadful news they didn't want to hear. Her daughter, his little sister, had her life cut short.

His angst with society had more to do with being forced to live in such hellish conditions. He saw his secondary occupation as a means to escape and the fruits of working for society as a means for 'beating the system.'

We were living in an era where we could adapt the tricks of our trade and not be confronted by technology. The computer hadn't been invented and there were no mobile phones. One day in the future, he told me he would be in a better place financially than he was. It was while we were working together, sharing the stall, he told me that whatever spare income he had, he gave to his mother.

I remember our first Sunday morning together. The table cost was thirty shillings split between the two of us. On a bad day, my takings were £6, but on a good day they were £75, with a high percentage of profit. Soon I was building up customers and getting a taste of market life, while during the week I returned to St. Martin's Lane Stamp and Coin Centre north of Trafalgar Square to spend more time with Zachary.

While I enjoyed spending my rewarding days within Zachary's lifestyle, it was as though I was tied by an invisible thread to Terence. He kept an invisible watchful eye on me. It was as though he suspected he was missing out on some moneymaking action! Yet, within a couple of years, we went our own separate ways. Certainly every Sunday when we worked at our stall in Collectors' Corner, it must have been very strange to any fly on the wall spying on how we got on together. In a way, I can compare it to how ducks behave. You see them waddling around. Apparently, unbeknown to me, this was one of our own quirks. We waddled everywhere, and if by chance we wandered in to see Zachary and Matt, he said, 'The duck twins have arrived!'

Chapter 15: Fools and Their Consequences

H. I mention about the duck twins although Aspie resented the older duck's authoritarian ways based on that he was more experienced in the ways of the world. However, I looked to Zachary for my inspiration and mentoring, while Aspie saw Terence's mannerisms as inferior to his, and I had to contend with a little conflict between the two of us.

During those few years I hung out with Zachary, he groomed me in the world of philately and a sort of social life. We spent evenings fooling around playing harmless pranks that at best got the media's attention and at worst almost got us locked up. Zachary's favourite attention-seeking game was Dare. Each of us drew a straw and, depending on who chose the longest or shortest, we had to carry out a dare. Since Aspie couldn't relate to right or wrong, I had no idea we might get ourselves in some serious trouble. The dare for that evening was going into a local pub of our choosing and pretending to be a barman and serve drinks to customers. For my peers, their dare went perfectly well but when it was Aspie's turn, he was caught by the manager and we ran for our lives.

Fortunately Zachary had prepared a backup plan. Another of Zachary's wayward friends was Lord John. Looking as dishevelled as Zachary's father, he got between me and the manager, swaying with a bottle in one hand and a glass in the other with drink spilling everywhere, while Zachary bellowed for me to follow. Fortunately for us, the area between St. Martin's Lane and Covent Garden was strewn with alleyways for our escape!

Terence though did appear to have his unusual ways of doing things so he never joined in with our games. Anyway, I am digressing a little and you might find I occasionally bring your attention back to Aspie's unawareness of consequences.

R. Although I am sometimes at a loss to what you are trying to tell me, the picture I appear to be getting is Aspie's mannerisms made you stand out like a sore thumb. It seems Zachary and your peers had more observant skills, knew the risks and were more alert to what they could get away with. But for you, it appeared that when things didn't go your way, it was yours or Aspie's fault. I wonder whether you are the type of guy who had a relationship with bad luck? With the incident at the pub, given your relationship with Aspie getting shouted at, to you it must have felt like it was World War Three.

H. Just because we didn't get caught didn't mean we wouldn't try again at the same pub. And there was a next time, but at least we posted someone across the street to make sure we would have a clean escape should the occasion arise but fortunately for us, it didn't.

During those turbulent and crazy years, we all had so much fun. Lord John, for example, who said he was named this because he came from an aristocratic heritage. He said he was educated at Eton and he regularly showed up dressed for the occasion at Zachary's shop but then spent the entire day doing absolutely nothing.

His antics reminded me of a Christie's sale fifteen years ago, when Lord Bath of Longleat turned up wearing period clothes. Life for Lord Jim appeared to evolve around the shop. Any quiet day was rarely that. Had the *Guinness World Records* had a place for pranks, he sure knew how to win the title.

Needless to say, we set up a prank, which managed to get a blurb in the evening papers. Looking back to that day reminds me how we had chosen the hottest and sweatiest day of the year, a far cry from when we commuted to the US and enjoyed the cool air conditioning that didn't exist in London. Our prank had a purpose because where Zachary's shop was located was beneath offices and above we saw plenty of heads peering out of the windows hoping for a whiff of fresh air. That afternoon, we sat Lord John down with a cap on his lap in front of our shop and he began singing. For those who had the misfortune of no choice but to listen, a fine voice was something he was not talented with. Nevertheless a combination of good timing, bad singing and lousy playing was as irresistible on our part as was playing our April Fools in the middle of August. You couldn't begin to imagine the sight for sore eyes. Our bedraggled unshaven man wore a very torn suit which, on closer inspection, had dribble that could be seen forming blotches over his shirt, and he was sitting with a guitar, singing to his heart's content. It was fun for us to listen to shouts from up in the offices. 'Please get him to stop.' To any passer-by, it would have been a sight of disbelieve. We had already planted him with fivers and pound notes. Later that afternoon, he got a surprise visit from the local press, amazed how a busker who sang in bad taste accumulated so much money into his hat. In all, it counted up to around ninety quid.

The story he told people was that he didn't do this every day of the spring and summer months. He chose to sit in a very prominent place where he was likely to cause a nuisance. Knowing this, he got paid to shut up. Today had been an exception as, because of the warmth, more people seemed to be hanging around. He was asked how fivers got into his purse and he said they were from people who loved him.

Although that day was a first and last for Lord John, he acquired a small write-up in *The Evening Standard*. Thankfully, there was no way we could let the cat out of the bag. So we all went away with smiles on our faces, and the papers knew they had been had.

Talking about April Fools, it was fortunate for Zachary it only came around once a year. Seeing that Terence's full-time job was working for the Inland Revenue, during the next two years we played the ultimate April Fools on him. Although Zachary didn't have an Aspie in his life, he shared one trait; disorganisation that made our April Fools prank the more easier to play.

Early on the morning of the following April 1st, it was a Saturday. Terence managed to get hold of the Queen's stationery and put an official envelope through the letterbox of Zachary's shop. When Zachary opened the envelope, he read a letter duly signed by the Inspector of Taxes saying, 'I will be visiting you this morning at 11am to inspect your books.'

We knew what a horrible joke we had played on him, when a sign on his front door read 'Closed' and the remaining part of his morning was spent trying to put some order into his cramped office at the rear of the shop. At ten minutes to midday, we wandered in together and asked him how he got on with the tax inspector.

'How do you know?' he answered. A short look into our eyes told him what he didn't want to know. 'You bastards!' Then there was that short lapse of time when he didn't know whether to laugh or cry, and whether because of nerves or the need to give an appropriate answer, he said. 'I think you two did me a favour.' We all spent much time laughing together that afternoon.

You would think lightening doesn't strike twice in the same spot. But with Zachary anything was possible, so the following year it had to be our pièce de résistance. A similar envelope arrived in his letterbox, and typed on the front of the envelope were the words; 'To the Honourable Zachary Jackson. Your attendance at a Garden Party at Buckingham Palace is required at 11.30am this morning.'

During that past year, Zachary had taken an avid interest in politics and had told us one day his vision was to become the Liberal MP for Kemp Town. We knew the last thing he wanted was anything that could tarnish his political record. You might wonder how in between arriving at his shop at 9am and going to Buckingham Palace at 11.30am, he managed to secure an outfit? We were fortunate a hiring shop around the corner and this meant we could video his performance from a safe distance as he stepped out of a taxi wearing the full outfit.

We should have felt sorry for him, but were both in hysterics watching him show his invitation to one of the police officers outside Buckingham Palace who couldn't understand why someone in a morning suit with his top hat was convinced the Palace were holding a garden party that day.

That was when our Zachary played his part to the tee. He was always very good at seeing the funny side and we were amazed that we were able we take him for a ride once again.

In all, we split our life between London and Brighton until I was aged twenty-three. During this time, Zachary was doing his best to find some normality in his life, being that he had managed to get his girlfriend pregnant and he was focusing his attention on politics and running his business while being barely twenty-three. However, after fathering his child, it seemed that being a parent was not something he aspired in. For Zachary, it was time to move on. Since many of his clients were American, it was time to do battle there and he took up residence in Montana. I lost track of him until a certain incident, which took place on US soil and meant he had no choice but to return to his motherland.

About six years ago, while exhibiting at the Miami Beach Antiques Show, I learnt about consequences when catching up with Zachary. The man who knew how to beat consequences at his own game unfortunately got his comeuppance. Had I been as unlucky as him, I might have found myself being prosecuted, but his misdemeanour was plainly unfortunate. Whether it could have occurred in the UK, I am not so sure because we antique dealers had our morals but it was different in the US where Zachary was trading. Zachary and other philatelists were carrying out a knockout, unaware the FBI was watching.

One of the Americans was being investigated by the FBI for tax evasion during a divorce and made a deal to shop the ring. All in all, the FBI went back twenty-five years into the records of the members. Zachary, although he made his escape, was hoping for a Presidential Pardon because he couldn't return to US soil.

The story I was told by a new customer, who was also a member of that ring, was that one of the lucky dealers got suspended from dealing in philately for eighteen months and fined $150,000, while some of the major players were fined substantially more.

I know that Aspie was waiting to laugh in my face because of a story about me almost getting myself into a similar situation when I was eighteen years old. As you are aware, Aspie took everything he heard on its face value, rarely considering a project on its merits alone because he was unable to know how. This inability of his got me into serious trouble on many occasions. One incident stands out amongst the crowd when I almost was taken for the ride of my life.

The previous six months saw British stamps rise in an incredible bear market, the average British stamp rising a remarkable one thousand per cent within six month. This period added thousands to the value of my stock every week. I had an inkling stamps were rising too fast in value so when the crash came, I was fortunate to get out but not come out unscathed. Having watched what I hadn't sold go down in value by fifty per cent overnight, it cost me nearly £20,000.

Coincidentally, the Beltman Brothers were a Yorkshire based investment company offering investors thirty-two per cent per annum return on their investment in stamps. That was the upside to the scheme, working in their favour. The downside was investors couldn't cash in until after five years and they offered me a job for £300 a week plus commission.

While the economy was in boom years, their business flourished and their investment holding was worth more than forty million. A lot of money in those days! I came so close to saying yes to their offer, especially with Aspie continually taunting me, saying, 'Three hundred quid was a lot of money. You've got to be mad to turn that down, and at the least being a salaried man, you will be guaranteed a life of luxury.'

The incident reminded me of being caught off guard by the paedophile who helped me out of the pool in Bulgaria. Aspie panicked and I almost suffered my comeuppance. Now the boot was on the same foot and I had already had three bad experiences and didn't want a fourth. On this occasion, it was my good fortune that I said no to the offer although I could have picked up a very handsome commission. Nevertheless, when the economy swung into recession and too many concerned investors decided to cash in at the same time, they were unable to liquidate so much cash. No employee escaped unscathed, the police launched an investigation, and serious fraud was discovered. No doubt I would have been among those spending a couple of years behind bars, while the Beltman Brothers were sentenced to eight years.

R. Sounds like those days were something else, with you and Aspie not being aware of the consequences?

H. I think Aspie coerced me to believe I was invulnerable to any future loss, and while I was making lots of money, spending money on his needs was a small price to pay. It was inevitable I felt some of the pain from losing so much money; half of all my earnings went down the tube in three months. Furthermore, I tried to warn my customers that the inflationary bubble could burst at any time without warning. Needless to say, my customers were not as notably upset pursuing the idea; their investment was for the long term.

Meanwhile, all of this had gone to Aspie's head because, being relatively meaningless, convincing me that surviving such a drop of value I had to be recognised as one of London's new elite philatelists. Except this did not preclude him from having to build up a profile of integrity and trust. He naively thought that being a professional meant exactly that.

I spent in total eight years as a philatelist, during which time I thought I developed very good business skills buying from Tom and selling to Paul, Jim or Frank.

Chapter 16: Illicit Dealings and Bullies

H. I have already discussed illicit dealings to which Aspie
unwittingly had a relationship. What I haven't mentioned are
those people who instigated them in the first place. Fortunately
this time, we have luck on our side. Only the dealers dealing in
big numbers got caught out.

How it all came about was due to Aspie's habit of whingeing to
Zachary to divulging his sources. Eventually, Aspie's persistence
paid off and he conceded about a contact down in Hampshire
where I might be able to build a good business relationship and
source a continuous supply buying in bulk under face stamps.
These were stamps that sold at normal prices but discounted at
Post Offices.

The first time I did a deal with the Hammersford Stamp
Company was an eye-opener for me, thinking business was
conducted differently in the sticks than in London. I earned a
grand that day, surprised to find a source able to supply me with
large quantities of under face postage stamps at a similar cost to
Zachary's contact.

However, when my source said to me our first deal is the
sweetener, they had to contend with Aspie answering, 'Isn't
sweetener something you put into a cup of coffee or tea?'

'I like your humour,' was their reply.

R. I am now seeing how you take what people say to you word for
word.

H. That day, the deal was consummated over a lunch spread across the afternoon at one of the better restaurants in town. It didn't occur to me that this was a front of theirs; a misinterpretation on Aspie who assumed they were giving him the red carpet treatment. I returned three times by the end of the week and Aspie assumed our business relationship was gathering steam because of the thousands of pounds I had earned that week. Meanwhile, on the train journey back home, the smirk on his face as to how rich we were going to become was relentless.

Essentially, how the deals were consummated was I sold at fifteen per cent below face, the next time at twenty per cent and the third at twenty-five per cent. Each time I returned for more, the volume in the offering increased, until I returned the following week when I was told they were so pleased they had found a trustworthy customer they could trade with.

During the next month, we made ten trips and passed onto my customers one hundred grand of under face stamps that earned us ten grand. It was towards the end of this period of dealing with them that I made a comment, which they thought was another one of my jokes; not realising that Aspie was serious. Among Aspie's quirks are things he comes out with without thought, phrases that are said that when reheard make no sense whatsoever although, for the best of intentions, he is totally unaware.

Just after I began dealing with them, another young dealer began doing business in the same manner. It so happened I joined them for lunch one day and we spent the entire afternoon in conversation. After we left the restaurant, the other dealer went on his way and I returned with the dealers who had invited us.

Back in their shop, Aspie came out with, 'I don't understand how John Taylor arrived with you at eleven in the morning and didn't leave until five in the afternoon. It seems to me some of your clients don't understand time management like me.'

It is inevitable what a bewildered Smith and Jones said in reply. 'You do come out with some weird stuff. How is it possible for John to not understand time management when the two of you emulate each other? You come down to see us in the morning, we do the business and take you out to lunch, but for some reason you seem in a world of your own, nattering away oblivious to us and the afternoon is gone. Not surprisingly, we are rather taken back by your remark about John.'

Aspie replied, 'Sorry, guys, I don't know what you are talking about.'

Now, I must digress back to these deals, to which Aspie encouraged me to get as much supply out of. Part of my argument with Aspie is how easily he is able to coerce me to believe we were onto such a good thing, change tactics and make our trip to Hampshire a daily event. Today, warning bells would be ringing unaware a fence had found a gullible customer. About six months later, the front page of the newspapers read how some of the biggest names in philately had been found guilty of selling undertake stamps to large corporations heavily discounted.

R. I'm beginning to relate to Aspie's relationship to consequences.

A. Now that's not fair. I think you, Hartley, are trying to tell a bit of a porky. You know jolly well you were my teacher, and I can only read into consequences when you alerted me to.

H. Let's change the subject. Shamefully, Aspie enjoyed the fruits of how the other half lived. He assumed money equals happiness. Perhaps his need to show off that he could afford a similar lifestyle to his peers, whereas in fact it was a struggle for him.

A. It was worth it!

H. Can you believe what a sucker I felt? Mother was always conscious of the little money she had and saved for rainy days ahead. Sadly, Aspie was a real thorn in my backside. We were making so much money in those days, the consequential idea of rainy days were never thought about. Only when I had much less money would the day come when I could have prevented Aspie from being so easily manipulated.

A. Okay, I confess. You know how I always wanted to walk hand in hand with money!

H. Living with Aspie was like having to be permanently on my guard. Zachary, coincidentally, had been born in Bath too and Aspie enjoyed emulating his lifestyle, even though some of his antics embarrassed Aspie and he refused to participate, but on the occasions he did, he was more often than not aware of the consequences. On one occasion, Zachary decided we were going to break into a police station and pretend to lock one of us up. It all went well until Aspie panicked that he couldn't get out of the cell and he was being punished for their laughs, not the thought of getting caught or taking the blame for their actions.

Anyway, Zachary didn't drive so I became his chauffeur. For the fun of it, he encouraged me to do silly things, his ideas with Aspie actions. We found a roundabout with four exits and we found four 'No Left Turn' signs, which we placed on the exit posts and watched in hysteria as the confusion followed.

A. Absolutely. I, the spider, and you, the hopeless fly, struggling to untangle from my web. I knew you inside out and every one of your moves. Salivated as you helplessly clambered out of one predicament into another. I had hoped that my little tests could have demonstrated you have the will to teach me to change and lessen our confrontations with each other.

R. I am still confused when differentiating you from Aspie.

H. Throughout my life, but more noticeable in business, Aspie upset my colleagues and my customers. As though Aspie has one eye and ear shut so only part of a conversation was heard, and I was blind to changes in facial expression and unaware of changes in his tactics.

R. I imagine not having a mind of your own means being fed inappropriate stuff.

H. You've got it in a nutshell. Two memories stand out among the crowd. Overall my best customers bought an item based on the assumption they were the first person to see it. Aspie took over the conversation because he was worried that if he told the truth, I would lose the sale so he insisted on me saying nothing. I felt the fear of being found out to be lying and then the customer would never buy from me again. Aspie's weak link with me is a sign of his lack of confidence. I was certain his facial expressions often betrayed what I wanted to commit. Here on, he changed to anxiety mode, often stuttering and shaking with nerves. I would say calling bluff is not part of his acumen but explaining his communication complexities very trying. The outcome of any given situation was dependent on accumulated stress, lack of sleep, digestive upsets, mood swings and countless other reasons. I believed his life was either all or nothing.

R. You mean little balance can be more conducive to too much or too little?

H. Anyway, I was driving Zachary and six of our mates in a car that could only hold five at a squeeze. We visited one of the local bowling alleys, and after an hour of bowling fun, Aspie took the heaviest of the bowling balls and rolled it down two flights of stairs; not thinking about the consequences of someone wanting to exit at that precise moment.

R. Are you are going to tell me you put someone in hospital?

H. The bowling alley manager; well, I almost did. Fortunately, he jumped out of the way. All of us thought it was fun to bowl down the stairs. It was like I was back serving behind the bar and running for dear life. Just my luck I didn't hear them shout, 'Hartley's going to get himself arrested.' I was unaware of the approaching police siren and then having to run away from the two coppers who chased after us. A little later, I heard comforting words from Zachary: 'You know, guys, there was not a chance in hell we were going to get caught!'

It's a question I have often asked myself. Is autism a facet of evolution as well as why me? What I have told you is a sample of what Zachary got up to. Part of his madness was his charismatic charade to get noticed. Bad news is good news if it gets the media's attention and draws them your way; no doubt it helped his political career.

For me, spending so much time with Zachary was during a period when I was thinking about buying my first home.

Uncertain whether I wanted to live permanently in Brighton, I rented a flat close to the train station while I was still living in my parents' home. Back then, there was no M25 and it was a choice of navigating the North Circular road or the joys of driving through the centre of London. Zachary's growing business saw him moving to larger premises in the half a mile square that revolved round London's philately district.

Most days I milled around Zachary's shop or if not, I ran around the neighbourhood. The most convenient way to travel to and from London to Brighton was by train and if our timing was right, we travelled on the Brighton Belle, the equivalent of the Orient Express on a smaller scale. But our days of travelling in opulence were numbered because the Belle was to be axed. In protest, Zachary decided we were going to streak along Brighton beach. The following day, the front page of the *Echo* reads, *'Liberal Candidate for Kemp Town spends night in police cell after a streak along Brighton beach'*. Sadly, this didn't save the Belle from being put out of service and within a few months, Zachary was on his way to the US to begin a new life with his new wife.

R. Surely during your friendship with Zachary, you must have met lots of opportunities to meet girls?

H. Absolutely, but Aspie's frigidity ruined any chance. He preferred regular visits to the massage parlour in Hendon. One of Zachary's friends had a promiscuous French girlfriend who we were invited to share a bed with, under the same sheets while they humped the night away.

R. I guess you didn't lose your virginity that night!

A. Doing it again, blaming me. I have always said you needed to instruct me because I'm unable to make the first move. Shame you let the side down!

R. I've heard you talking a lot about you and your upbringing; a bit about your sexual habits; but I'm still confused as to how you digress talking about from Aspie's perspective when I consider you are one person, not two. Okay, you have some sexual deviances, but then we all do, it's part of human nature and being inquisitive and exploration of psychosexual fantasies. Anyway, you are still only a teenager and just beginning to explore your life. You're not alone having sexual inadequacies, just among a genre of young people who are late starters. Let's change the subject and talk about your relationship with your siblings.

H. It was more the case of the relationship I had with the elder of my two sisters, because the younger was older by ten years.

Although I was unaware of Aspie the bully until it was brought to my attention several years after my diagnosis, I am aware of several encounters he had with customers and staff. One of my PAs was my daughter's part-time surrogate mother. Often when I appeared to be in Aspie mode, out of the blue she would say to me, 'If you don't get out of my face, I will have my County Court ex-husband Judge have you arrested.'

Going back into my late adolescence, it was as though being bullied Aspie had to find someone else to let off steam with and he did so with my sister, who often received the brunt of his aggressive feelings. Even when we played games together, like hide and seek, Aspie somehow found a way to put my health into jeopardy, but on this occasion he did the same to her. He found my sister in a bedroom wardrobe and locked her inside. He thought it would be fun to rock the wardrobe from side to side, except there was a pane of glass on the top so I had to get it down. That was no problem, but it was when I picked the pane up, Aspie ensured I knelt into it. That little episode cost me eight stitches through my right knee and my leg was in plaster for six weeks. Meanwhile, I'm been rushed off to hospital and my sister did her best not to suffocate.

While lightning may not strike in exactly the same spot twice, it didn't mean Aspie learnt from the incident. About a year later, he was chasing my sister when she slammed a glass-paned door, which my left elbow passed through, coincidentally another eight stitches. Gratefully, these incidents didn't occur yearly, otherwise my body would have been littered with scars. Although there was always room for a next time, like falling off my bike and requiring two stitches for a ripped finger.

R. I suppose with the money you were making, what you might have paid for a sexual massage was small change in comparison, no different from going out on a date?

H. You mean short-sightedness too? Meanwhile, my stamp dealing days were coming to an end around the age of twenty-three.

R. Why did you give up stamp dealing if you were so successful?

H. Now, you've just made your faux pas. What did I say before about misleading words or phrases? You expect Aspie to make head or tails of stamps being my baby. Fortunately, this time round, I was able to connect that you were referring to philately as being my specialism?

I think the writing was on the wall back when my mother had a small antiques shop and I took an interest learning antique dealing. When asked why I gave up on philately, I turn to one incident in my life that identified with why Aspies can make very useful employees.

Picture Aspie sitting on a chair, examining the contents of a stamp lot I had bought at auction. A box of stamps he deduced based on his assumption that the box weighs fifty pounds, multiply that by sixteen into ounces makes eight hundred, multiplied by another three hundred and fifty, giving the weight of stamps to every cubic inch, and the total is around a quarter of a million stamps.

As I am sifting through with one hand, the other holding a pair of tweezers, and I come across a magnificent example of a finely used rare Mauritius one penny. Carefully, I take the tweezers and gently pick up the stamp. Here Aspie took over and there was a disturbance; he lost his focus and it somehow morphed into the camouflage of the other stamps in the box. For the next seventy hours, breakfast, lunch, dinner and sleep are taken in the box because he relentlessly searched the entire contents; except it is not found. Why, you might ask?

Since this incident, I have had some forty years to investigate what really occurred. Aspie's brain is wired differently from neuro-typical non-autistic people. He can have numerous nuances connected with his condition. I call it mind blindness; the eyes see but the brain doesn't. Similarly, the incident that almost cost my divorce from my wife-to-be, a few years later in Johannesburg when he walked through an elderly couple as though he has not seen them, just after I had proposed.

On another occasion, my brother-in-law arranged to meet me and I was on my bike cycling slowly towards him as he was walking slowly towards me. He shouted at me as we passed but Aspie carried on cycling, blind to him calling his name - let alone seeing him - yet we passed within inches.

During another occasion, I picked up valuable vases from my restorer and took them to my car with the intention of putting them into my boot. I opened my boot, might have been distracted by a bird, or a sports car driving past, but I closed the boot unaware that Aspie had left the vases on the pavement.

Once, I was really pleased with a magnificent purchase of a very rare Chinese Export European designed Hunting Bowl, which I found at an antiques fair in Atlanta. I decided to take it on the plane. As we were alighting our rental bus, Aspie didn't see a protruding metal rod, but I heard the clunking noise as the porcelain met the metal.

On a larger scale, I was pleased with an outstanding seventeenth century Japanese Imari Charger, two feet in diameter, decorated in five colours with a very imposing golden eagle at its centre.

A. Hang on a moment, I think you have forgotten about me. There's not much point to your story unless I have my say too. It all comes down to tits. You know how it is with me, I can't help it that I am addicted to them. Don't you remember that time you got chatting to Charlene on the way to the boarding gate to your domestic flight. It was my luck they didn't check your ticket until you were on the plane when it was too late. That was quite a laugh seeing you debate spending the night with her and working out how you could reconnect to get to your antiques show the following morning.

With that Imari Charger, I got you to ogle the best pair of melons we'd seen in a long time. She was sitting in the departure lounge opposite us when I pulled out my trump card, got you sitting next to her as though the two of you were an item. I was in hysterics when you are sitting comfortably in your seat and we are about to take off and you realise you are no longer in possession of your prized catch. That utter horror reaction so noticeable on your face, the arguments you had with the in-flight supervisor and your inability to have the plane turned back to the gate.

Then they got you to believe that they would do everything they could to reinstate you with the dish once it was located; it never was. On a much smaller scale, how many pairs of sunglasses, umbrellas and Bose earphones have you lost? So many, we could have opened a shop!

H. These are a sample of the sabotages happening throughout my life.

A. Got to have some fun in my life and anyway, what's the big deal? I bring you more satisfaction than trouble. The last thing I needed is a life as a stamp.

PART THREE:

MATURITY -
BUSINESSMAN AND
ANTIQUES

Chapter 17: From Stamps to Antiques

H. Let's digress for a moment to that summer so long ago, when I ate steak for breakfast every day in New York, courtesy of Carl's father, and got used to the American way of life. The money I began making the following year allowed me to travel to Bangkok, before I was even eighteen.

The sordid sexual exploits that city is so famous for were not my intention. For Aspie, visiting every brothel in the city was certainly his intention, but not for what most men may visit for; his aim was finding a masseuse who would become his girlfriend. However, coming back empty-handed, we trawled back to the massage parlour in Hendon Lane. This time, Aspie began to panic after ringing the bell several times and not getting any reaction. The sign said it was open and therefore, in his eyes, the parlour had to be open. By the time rejection had overtaken him, he was like a volcano ready to erupt and having no concern of passers-by who wondered what the fracas was about as he pounded away on the door. Feeling very disgruntled and dejected, we got back into my car and went home to look at the *Yellow Pages* to find out where his beloved might have gone to - other massage parlours! It took us a good three hours to find her and thirty miles of travelling around the suburbs.

'What are you doing here?' gullible Aspie said to her, unaware she was unlikely to be telling the truth.

'Business was bad; my expenses were not met, so my boss had no choice but to find an alternative location.'

I learnt in the years to come that they were raided by the police and got closed down as a brothel. Back then, I was very naive, not that Aspie cared.

He decided I was making a decent living, so why not use some of my money satisfying his whims? We went back to Bangkok again, and from the moment we arrived, and picked up our bags, our journey to our hotel included stopping at every brothel en route. To say I wasn't that interested would have been a bit of a lie. Being ushered into a viewing room with fifteen pretty girls wearing bathing costumes and standing behind a massive glass window would turn on most men. For Aspie, their breast cup was substantially smaller than Honey's, therefore they didn't meet his criteria! The taxi driver didn't realise he'd picked up a passenger who was unlike most other people; and who would not be satisfied sexually by any of the girls on offer and was unlikely to pick up a decent commission. Disappointed in his resolute, he took us to other brothels, but to no avail.

While, on the one hand, I would be lying if I said I didn't enjoy what was being offered at these brothels, the sight of sampling a variety of naked girls, the sensual feeling of being body washed and massaged by them, and a happy ending. Sexual intercourse was completely out as far as Aspie was concerned, and because when the paedophile groomed me, Aspie had believed his every word. He had heinous memories the paedophile had engrained in him about the purpose of a woman's vagina.

Only during the past few years while giving inspirational talks have I opened up and shared with psychologists how sexual abuse had affected my life. As well as how Aspie had believed the paedophile when he said, 'If you ever breathe a word of what I'm telling you to anyone, the goblins will come and get you.'

Aspie tried to get one better than the paedophile; he closed his eyes while the masseuse does what she does to all clients when they part with their dosh. Back in London, he was hoping Honey would become his girlfriend, unaware that to her he was simply another piece of meat.

R. I cannot begin to imagine the mental torture being violated in such a filthy way caused you when you were so young. It doesn't surprise me that memory has been buried deep in your subconscious.

A. Don't I love going back to that day and tormenting him. You see, from my perspective, it was the only way I built defences, when Hartley was willing to experiment with the idea.

H. I think, in a nutshell, Aspie has explained my predicament. Rarely a day went by when intrusive memories didn't surface in one way or other. How he manifested numerous memories of being smitten like the plague, tormented in ways I can't ever want to contemplate, is because the intrusive memories are buried too deep. If they erupted, they could get me locked up, that was the frightening part.

Between Aspie and me, I wanted financial success, and he wanted what was missing in his life; to be loved. Meanwhile, arriving back from the Far East, I had no choice but to get accustomed to living with his ideals doing what he wanted to do, and there were periods of calm.

You could say I had a close affinity with antiques before I knew what they were. I began visiting London's museums and unknowingly my interest in philately began to wither even though I was becoming one of London's successful philatelists and a member of the nouveau riche.

I think it was the different variety of antiques that fascinated me while visiting my mother at her small antique shop in the flea market in Camden Passage. When I first visited the Stamp and Coin Centre in St. Martin's Lane, all the dealers appeared alien to each other. Where my mother had her little shop, they appeared to be friendlier, although Aspie regarded her stock as menial in comparison and felt more at home with the more affluent and wealthy people in the Strand. When you have an Aspie overwhelming your life, you can never be your own boss.

Perhaps I felt that antique dealing was more lucrative than spending so much time going through heaps of little bits of paper, just trying to find the rare one that was going to secure our retirement.

Ultimately, the nail in the coffin came along when, aged twenty-three, a shop became available around the corner from my mother's shop in Temple Fortune. It could have been our first stamp shop. However, focusing on both philately and antique dealing was not something Aspie found at all easy to mentally process, and for the next few months it became a battle of the wits. It was a painful decision to drop philately altogether. Lack of confidence was one of Aspie's handicaps and once his focus was lost, it was gone forever. It was time to move on from the world of philately to our first large shop.

A couple of years went by, when a kindred spirit of Zachary's and Matt's turned up looking for a job. Danny was a retired diamond merchant and I wish I could have said to Aspie, 'This is Danny,' and to Danny, 'This is Aspie,'; both were each other's nemesis. Getting a smile out of Danny was as challenging as getting Aspie to do anything without my intervention. Although he was a valuable and loyal friend, my colleagues used to taunt him about his personality, and for me employing a man whose hands shook was a liability! However, while Danny's vice was living the life of a manic depressive, not once did he break anything, compared to my father-in-law who I was forced to employ on commencement of my marriage. He cost me substantially more with his breakages and other stuff no employer should ever have had to tolerate. He had his own affliction, which got in the way of my everyday business activities. I was commuting abroad every week to search for stock for customers, and while he was loyal and I trusted him with my money, it was his addiction to gambling that worried me. I think the differences between Danny and my father-in-law can be summed up as follows. My father-in-law cared more for the horse he was betting on than he did for my success. I am not saying he wasn't conscientious, it is just how I felt. Meanwhile, at times I felt like I was hanging off a cliff for dear life with one hand, while the other was holding on to my father-in-law, who in turn was holding on to the most expensive piece of my stock and

I was forced to watch it slowly slipping away. What was I to do? If I let go of the other hand, I might have saved the stock, but on the other hand, if my father-in-law left, my marriage would have collapsed.

R. They say that family and business relationships don't mix and what you have shared with me is a prime example. I don't think people know about the baggage they take on when they get married. Changing the subject and getting back into the real world, I imagine there were other employees you employed who tidied Aspie's disorganisation?

H. Yes. Poor Patricia, who worked for me and could have helped me get to the epitome of business success, was it not for the venomous hate Aspie threw in her direction. After a couple of years, she decided she had no choice but leave.

R. Please try to explain to me in layman's language what went wrong. For example, how did you meet and how special was she to you?

H. You have just asked the penultimate question. Aspie refused to pay her what she was worth. The real answer is more complicated. He questioned her every motive and he tried hard to form a relationship of distrust between the two of us. He didn't like how she took the initiative and ultimately he was envious of her getting results.

I remember sensing the sadness in her eyes as she waited in vain to hear that I was offering her a pay rise. Instead it was met by Aspie's detachment. He won, and I lost the best PA any employer could ever want. It was then that I felt I was slipping from the abyss' edge into hell; another prime example of Aspie's sabotages.

It wasn't as though I had found her through an employment agency or recommendation. I had known her most of my antiquing life. She was considered to be the sexy property of one of my neighbours; a restaurateur. The type of upmarket lass many a man from a building site might whistle at as she passed. How often I was goaded on a daily basis by the smile of temptation and all the fantasies of the male ego. Every time she passed me, she winked or stopped for a gentle chat but there was nothing to suggest she was looking for something anew to satisfy her. It happened unexpectedly when one day she wandered into my shop and simply said, 'Hartley, please give me a job.' To me, she was my dream come true, yet for all of her accomplishments, Aspie saw her presence as losing his hold on me and retaliated in the only way he knew how.

R. Please expand your explanation. You are talking more like you are Aspie than Hartley.

H. Patricia got on with chores. She didn't think twice about being the tea girl, the clean-up girl, the washer-up girl, the bookkeeper, or the PA, booking my travel reservations. Meanwhile, Aspie gawked at her perfectionism. He didn't attune well to what he saw in the mirror, because it showed too easily his true self and the faults that went along for the ride. Patricia was simply everything he was not.

She tried to be as diplomatic as she could with her intentions. The warning bells were clanging loud and clear when she, in the most polite manner, enquired about a salary raise. Aspie was the first to voice his objections. You could say anyone standing close by would have felt an earthquake beneath their feet as the clamber of China and other artefacts rumbled below. To say an almighty big fuck-up was on the cards was a serious understatement. She tried hard to emphasise her financial obligations, as well as that she was entitled to a raise because employer legislation said her wages should be kept in line with inflation. She knew we had a very special relationship, almost like that of a boy and girlfriend who had intended to keep their partnership intact. We were a great team for as long as it lasted. I cried the day she left, but not before I saw a hint of despair in her eyes that Aspie ensured I could not respond to.

R. Have you ever thought that she recognised the Aspie in you and felt sorry for your lament?

H. I think the bottom line was that Aspie was so envious of her efficiency, especially when she has been someone else's property for so long, that he couldn't afford on any account to have that competition in his life.

A. This is when I want to loathe you. You don't have a big business, don't need the same type of set-up, we were the only team you needed, just you and me. I often said to you, 'If you could be more objective in what you do regularly and train me as you see fit, then there wouldn't have been a requirement to have anyone else in our life and that would have saved us a lot of money.'

H. Ultimately, it was down to costs. Although, I could afford to employ her, there was also a lot of austerity around. The first year of her employment was around 1995, when I derived the largest percentage of my profit from Japanese customers, who were oblivious of the recession. It was a period when I was getting over that downturn and had taken a lot of financial hits, including a six-figure fine from the Inland Revenue!

So, as Aspie said, I didn't need Patricia, he could do her job just as well. It was a sad ending to a beneficial relationship. But if the truth be known, what really upset me was the many times she passed me by and gave me a flirtatious smile as if she was saying, 'Please, Hartley, ask me out on a date.'

R. So Patricia was the only PA you ever had?

H. Actually, no, she was the second of the two I employed. Yolanda was with me for three years. She, in some respects, I felt had her own version of Aspie. She had been working for a dentist friend of mine, that's how we met. I was told she was good at her job and the reason Aspie didn't object was that she was titless!

R. You mean flat-chested? I assume Patricia was the exact opposite, hence the jealousy and competition Aspie saw with her?

H. Yolanda wasn't the type of person who normally fitted the bill of working in an antique shop. She knew nothing about antiques, only how to answer the phone, and do the books and paper work. Asexual, as far as I was concerned, and Aspie saw her as no threat to our relationship whatsoever. More to the point, she knew she wouldn't be working for me forever!

Just mentioning a little blurb about Aspie, I think my life hung in the balance from its onset as to what the so-call professional therapists were able to convince my parents were my mental issues. Countless visits to therapists continued into my teenage years. Aspie was a genre that created absolute hell, confidence and security issues throughout my life, hence my inability of striking up any conversation with girls during my teenage years.

It might sound remarkable for you to hear that all the therapy I had over the many years, which culminating in me paying out many tens, if not hundreds, of thousands of pounds, was a complete and utter waste of time.

My mother first stopped sourcing professional help when I was eight, as you are aware. However, throughout my teens, I regularly saw an occupational therapist. My sessions didn't prevent my ongoing communication issues. I think it might have been my father who stepped in and felt I was a big boy, especially after my bar mitzvah. My therapy was concluded, except it wasn't. Within a few years, especially when money grew off trees, I privately paid for sessions.

My ultimate goal was to find out who Aspie was. I hoped in doing so, they could eject all the headaches he had me engage with and take me away from his fantasy world.

R. What you are telling me is that Aspie grew stronger and stronger, directing you to do his will?

H. You got it. I had to deal with Aspie the best way I could, and at times my life was very confrontational. Earlier on in my life at school, I was seen as a target from adult bullies who preyed on any boy who displayed any emotional weakness. During my adult years, due to Aspie's personality I was continually confronted by bullies saying to their mates, 'There's another guy waiting to be bullied!'

During the years Danny worked for me, I succumbed to bullying from a runner with a violent past. He saw through Aspie's weaknesses and used strong-arm tactics to bully whatever he liked out of me. It cost me a few grand and I was grateful when I learnt he had dropped dead from a heart attack.

R. Not in my wildest dreams could I have realised how complex your life has been and the angst Aspie caused you; yet, you appear to have been successful in business. Are you telling me success masked a different story in your personal life? If so, no wonder you encountered difficulties sustaining even basic friendships.

H. You may have gathered that many people viewed Aspie as aloof. Whenever he was asked a direct question, he rarely provided a direct answer. When we were children, we didn't see the quirks in each other's characters until well into our teenage years, and only then did we consider who we wanted as friends.

Aspie and I were brought up in a unique cul-de-sac, unlike any other in our neighbourhood. We moved there when we were three years old and my mother still lives there today. What made our road very special were the neighbours being friendly with each other and we weren't encumbered with through traffic. There were eight families who had children, mostly my age, and we got on well together. Four lived at the bottom of the road and the others lived at the top. Of these, two had parents who lived in a large detached house at the top of the street in its own grounds. We spent much time there, simply because they had more room than the other houses in the street. Stuart, who was a year younger than me, lived on my side towards the bottom of our road. He was the friend I developed a lifelong friendship with at the age of eleven, though sadly this was cut off in his prime.

I admired him, although Aspie hated to admit he was very jealous. He had the looks; the perfect example of a Jewish boy who had all the pretty girls running after him. He had a string of girlfriends who Aspie was jealous of. This was the only acumen that did me no good at all. I got it up the butt all the time from Aspie why I didn't have the same level of confidence. At the bottom of our road lived Suzanne who had an older brother, who like me had to contend with an Aspie. I really fancied her and thought she was drop-dead gorgeous.

A few doors on the opposite side of our road lived Jane. We would take it in turns as to whose home we met in. Stuart was the first of my friends who faced Aspie head-on by being present at an unacceptable incident. I was fifteen and we were in Jane's bedroom one morning, when Aspie said, 'Jane, you are not as pretty as Suzanne, otherwise I would fancy you as well.' I had no idea how emotionally damaging that was for her.

R. I imagine that didn't go down well at all. Jane must have burst into tears. If this is an example of how Aspie presented himself in your life, it is no wonder the girls stayed away from you.

H. Shortly afterwards, Stuart confronted me and said, 'Why the fuck did you say what you did?' I wished that Aspie hadn't replied, 'What the fuck are you talking about?'

A. Excuse me, but I think I've waited long enough to have my say. You talk as though everything is to my detriment. Surely not knowing about me was in your favour? You had more opportunities to get away with some of the trivial upsets I caused since I encouraged you to give anyone a blank look, as though you were the one being offended.

H. That's typical Aspie. How nice it would be if I could think like a normal neuro-typical! My life would not have been fraught with so much sabotage. It wasn't just that I had upset Jane, but Aspie's sentiment made Suzanne feel disappointed; she had seen me as a friend.

R. Thinking about what you said, did you ever get to apologise to either Jane and Suzanne?

H. You're forgetting I didn't know about Aspie and I didn't release what I needed to apologise about. Unfortunately, where social etiquette is concerned, I didn't have the innate ability to say to Aspie, 'Hey, my good friend, you can't go around telling girls they are not as pretty as their friends.'

I mentioned Suzanne's older brother. One interesting aspect of his relationship with autism was when we often played chess together, you can guess who always lost. I always maintain that everyone on the spectrum is different. Each of us has similar challenges but we handle our symptoms differently from day to day. Aspie got bored with focus quite easily in anything he was doing that he felt he didn't have control over. In chess, the lack of focus and indecision paved the way for rash moves.

A. That's nice to know now; you are telling me I am your competition.

H. As I have already mentioned, anything that meant more, and especially where money is concerned, was Aspie's ideal relationship. He would ask where anyone lived and the more affluent neighbourhood would spike his interest more. What didn't help our relationship was small talk, which Aspie was unable to relate to, which lost a friendship as quickly as it arrived. One other boy I would have loved to have as a friend lived in a luxury home around the corner. What killed the goose was some other friends saying nasty things about my new friend, which Aspie made the mistake of repeating, word for word.

Whenever anyone asked me what my biggest stumbling block was, my answer is always lack of confidence created an immense challenge that is still with me today. Allow me to digress and talk about something quite irrelevant.

At any moment, Aspie can imagine all sorts of hocus pocus that becomes reality or anxiety. For example, before it is time to turn off the light and go to sleep, I was once watching a movie where a man is imprisoned illegally for twenty years, during which time he does not get to see his captor. Aspie was already one step ahead of me. No sooner had the TV been switched off and I was in bed attempting sleep, he's become that man. I was forced to lie awake as the thought of closing my eyes and waking up to find myself in such a situation was too horrifying, and my nightmare had begun.

Why I felt the need to digress was to explain the nature of the beast. Aspie was the envy of many educated schoolboys who had got their university degrees. Meanwhile, by the age of twenty-three, I was ready to move into my first luxury two-bed apartment with Stuart willing to become my flatmate.

For the next two years, it was like living in a brothel. The coming and going of girlfriends was exhaustive. Many of them were his bed partners and the majority felt sorry for me. What was I to do? Ask one of them if they were interested in a fuck? Not on your nelly, thought Aspie!

Nevertheless, as much as I might speak badly of Aspie, he did have his talents like his uncanny ability to find me a room with a view. Every morning we woke, we went to the large window in the living room and Aspie mesmerised every brick on every building as far as my eyes could see.

Getting back to this part of my story, although Stuart had this uncanny ability of making it with every Tom, Dick and Harry in the female fraternity as though he had some magic attraction, health wise there was something very nasty growing from deep within.

My father died aged ninety-three. Although, could he have had his way, he would have preferred it ending ten years before; the worst part for him was battling with his dignity. How many times he asked me to shove a shotgun down his throat and pull the trigger. His MS demonstrated how savage an illness it could be but he had a strong heart that withstood all the ills thrown in his direction. It was dreadful for all of the family to see him suffer as he did. You might be wondering why I mention my father.

Stuart also sadly became a casualty to multiple sclerosis in his thirties, and it was his dignity that eventually killed him. He couldn't mentally handle allowing everyone who loved him to be witness to the deterioration of his physical condition. The first casualty was his full-time job. He turned to private hire chauffeuring me or my mates to the airport. As his condition progressed, he became disillusioned to the will of wanting to live; his only wish was to father a child. After that, he saw no purpose in wanting to live in his body. I guess he couldn't face the idea of wanting his child to be witness to his deterioration. He received the best care that private medication could offer and he took eighteen months to wither away.

I remember visiting him in hospital as often as I could bear. It was awfully punishing to witness his mental decline. During one of my last visits, I sat there attempting to encourage him to look on the bright side; instead he shunned me and stared at the ceiling. Towards the end, he refused visitors.

His passing reminded me of my grandmother, who in her eighties had a stroke. She developed gangrene in one leg and had to have an amputation. She too did not have the will to live on. I remember how I ordered her this most elaborate of bouquets be delivered to her bedside. Even then it cost a hundred quid, the money meant nothing if the flowers helped her live. If there is an after life, I hope I can meet up with Stuart again and he can forgive me for not successfully confronting my demons and for letting him down.

Chapter 18: Becoming of Man – For Real!

H. The last time I went through the throws of learning to become
a man was my bar mitzvah, aged thirteen. I was disappointed
because with Aspie sharing my life, the idea that I was a fully-
fledged man didn't make sense. The idea of romance was
appealing to boys and girls of my age, but Aspie kept this idea
far away from me! Why was it that only men were supposed
to make the first move, yet I was still a boy? Aspie, for selfless
reasons, refused me that transition. It took several more years -
until aged twenty-five - when I had finally lost my virginity.

R. I believe that, these days, too much emphasis is put on the
necessity of having permanent sexual relations. What I don't
know is whether you had the mental agility to thwart Aspie
manipulating you? Anyway, not wanting to change the subject,
but how did you lose your virginity?

H. One of Stuart's girlfriends suggested I put an advert in one of
the paper's lonely heart columns. A Scottish nurse answered,
looking for a place to stay the night and a man who could fuck
her during the day as alternative to paying rent. Actually, she
had a face to die for. Within minutes of her arriving, we were
on the bed and I was no longer a virgin. She told me she worked
days as a nurse and the only time she could see me was nights.
We never discussed the rent but six months later, she went back
home and our relationship ended.

R. No doubt you made up for all those lost years without sex.

H. I had one other female friend who I wished I had drummed
up the courage to keep. Sadly, Aspie put an end to that
almost before it started. I must have known her for around
eighteen months and saw her periodically. The trouble was
Aspie coerced me to believe her Cockney accent would be my
undoing. She was born under the bells of Bow. This created
huge anxiety in me because Aspie threatened me with a
meltdown and said, 'You will never be able to introduce her to
our friends, they will laugh at you, wandering around with a
bird with a weird accent.'

Before I started the changeover from philately venturing into
antiques, I decided I need a well-earned break. I took off a
couple of months to travel the world first class. The first stop
was Singapore where an easy lay was dished up for us on a plate.

R. You could afford first class? You must have been earning mega
money in those days.

H. Yes, those were good days. Aspie encouraged me to search
around, make loads of phone calls, speaking to travel agents
galore to find us a bargain. Once again, I had to take my hat
off to him. It was inevitable that travelling in the style we were
accustomed to should be repeated, indefinitely. I was grateful I
could stretch my legs but Aspie ensured this idea of travelling
would play havoc in my married life. He refused to travel
with my wife and children on package holidays so while they
travelled alone, we flew business class.

A. Can you blame me? You were making the money and I wanted
my comfort.

H. Sometimes, I think the only reason Aspie was in my life was to
fuck it up.

Singapore was very humid and thwarted with tropical storms.
There was a downpour, which caught us as we arrived and
suddenly Aspie saw a beautiful blonde. It was as though she had
chosen to wear what she was wearing hoping her well-endowed
breasts would clearly radiate through the transparency of her
very wet skimpy blouse. She must have noticed my erection

because she took me by her hand and said, 'I have the perfect place we can get dry.'

She took me into one of Singapore's high-rise buildings and we took off our clothes together down to our underwear. She simply looked at me and fell onto her bed. It was then that Aspie took over and created a dilemma. I knew she wanted me to enter the part of her body that the paedophile had told me was a no-go area so all I got to do with her was fondle her breasts. She must have thought she had a strange one here!

We travelled to Hong Kong, down under to Australia, across to Hawaii, LA, San Francisco and Phoenix, where we stayed for a couple of weeks in my apartment. Then off we went again to New York before arriving back home, but not before he had sampled every massage parlour on route, hoping to find the ideal masseuse to become his girlfriend. That was how it was with the nature of the beast. He eyed them up and down while unknowingly the wrath of God had begun to descend on me!

It was a time for me when money literally grew on trees. It was like reaching up for an apple and being showered by money. They were days when there was a customer for everything. These days, there is it an entirely different attitude towards collecting antiques. The trouble with the Internet is, it has made too many people, who have no knowledge about antiques whatsoever, believe they know as much as the specialists.

As previously mentioned, Bermondsey was the key market in London. This was because every genre of antiques dealer from every corner of the globe knew there were countless bargains available to be bought. It enabled Aspie to build a dossier of who was buying what, and from whom. There was as much fun buying decorative items than pursuing the rarities when my entire car was filled up to the brim for a matter of a few hundred pounds. The irony was since then, back in the late seventies, the majority of items sold abundantly but today they have become unfashionable and so unwanted, you are more likely to see them selling for more in charity shops.

If I thought investing in antiques was an investment for life, then it was a cruel deception. These days the majority of collectors have what they want or have died and the younger generations do not value these items for their appeal.

It wasn't too long when, watching someone buying something for a hundred and doubling their money, Aspie followed and within a year of buying at Bermondsey, I was earning a cool two grand a week.

This was not our first trip to Singapore. Once, Aspie had walked into a store and the retailer was interested in his effeminate side and promised to become a very good customer the next time he visited London. Already Aspie was coerced into believing he had made it. As it so happened, he kept his promise but even that turned to disaster. Thank you, Aspie.

During the course of that year, I travelled twice to see him, making certain Aspie got his pleasure by calling into Bangkok on route, and our trip always ended in Hong Kong for more buying. England around this time was buzzing with foreign dealers because our country was a treasure trove of antique resources. Many of the old school dealers resided outside of London. Brighton, to the south, was the second most important resource. To the North, there was Harrogate, a wealthy market town to the west of Blackburn. But actually, everywhere, there was a plethora of enough antiques to buy to satisfy every customer.

Just like the sharks in the ocean and like in philately, I was a goldfish, so I had to tread carefully; I couldn't allow Aspie to get too carried away. While in awe of the many people we came across, I was dumbstruck by the amount of constant buying and selling being maintained. It was simply incredible the volume of business that was being consummated by everyone. It didn't matter whether there were the big dealers making the big killings or the smaller ones, like me, who were picking up the trimmings.

In Brighton, many of the dealers relied on the runners who bought from Peter to sell to Paul. Or it was the knockers who raided old age pensioners' homes and enticed their savings for a pittance. They picked on something worthless and offered a fortune, and on the good stuff they bought it for nothing. Brighton became notorious for its dealers selling stuff but not asking any questions.

Out of the buying trips we particularly enjoyed were the ones further afield often requiring overnight stays. It annoyed Aspie when he found out his customers already knew his resource, thinking it was unique to him. But not before too long, we found ourselves building particular routes, like beginning our day in Leeds, continuing through the city of Harrogate then westwards to the towns of Blackburn and Preston and down to Chester. Anything between five hundred and six hundred miles was incorporated into one day.

However, it was the early morning stints at Bermondsey Market that every dealer who was anyone made a beeline for. Sadly, it is barely a shell compared to its heyday when many hundreds of dealers came from all ends of the country to sell their wares.

If by chance you bought something before 7am and it turned out to be stolen, an old English rule that is still in force today allows it to be legally sold. However, this didn't preclude Aspie for not enticing me to purchase stolen goods without my knowledge. While I never got into trouble, there were occasions we got grilled by the police. It was no pleasant experience having to prove our innocence. On one occasion, when some Irish dealers turned up with antiques to sell from the back of their lorry, it was muggins here who bought them, not because we thought the items were stolen, but because they were far too expensive. We were the last resort since everyone else had turned them down. Then the police showed up at our front door, interviewing us in a manner as if we were guilty.

Ultimately, it was a combination of the Americans and Japanese that bolstered the values. Although there were plenty of Europeans arriving to buy - particularly the Dutch and Scandinavian selling to their home market - they too were selling to America and the Far East.

Nevertheless, my entrepreneurial instinct annoyed Aspie. I might have only been a beginner in the world of antique dealing, but picking up a useful customer wasn't always up his street. His world was a contradictory one where making sense of anything could just as easily be thrown out of the window, if you know what I mean. Essentially his only interest was self-interest by benefiting him. That was the bottom line and saving for a rainy day definitely was not among his better acumens.

Anyway, back to my business dealings. I got a call from my customer in Singapore asking me to fly to him on the condition I paid for a first class ticket, which he guaranteed to reimburse me for. He wanted me to find a quarter of a million pounds from a whole range of antiques. We agreed a twenty-five per cent profit margin and the completed transaction was paid via a letter of credit. To the annoyance of many of the dealers who were my friends, I turned up at auctions bidding against them for stock they were unaware I had interest in. These included: inexpensive Edwardian and Victorian furniture; silver tea pots, tea sets and cutlery; Chinese vases and fishbowls; and a few rare pieces of Chinese Ming and Ching Imperial wares.

R. You didn't mention anything about this business opportunity?

H. Had Aspie allowed it to go as planned, it could have saved my bacon. The deal was an incredibly huge risk. I already had a hundred grand in my bank account and managed to secure a further one hundred and fifty grand overdraft. It would have secured us fifty grand profit but I was unaware the arrangement I had agreed and what payment via letter of credit actually meant. I didn't have the educational acumen to know that I had to ship the goods to him before I was paid.

R. Wow, that's some profit. Anyway, you are moving too fast, who was he and how did you meet him?

H. We met during our first travels out to the Far East. He had a shop retailing modern Bohemian crystal in the most elite shopping mall in Singapore. During this period, antique crystal was very hot; loved by the Japanese. I forgot to mention during my whirlwind trip around the world, I had included a two-week visit to Japan. Aspie had got me to do the sublime and ridiculous. With him, it was always all or nothing; somewhere in between doesn't exist in his vocabulary. I was gasped by the prices of antiques asked in Japan, although I was in my infancy of learning how much more profit I could make introducing antique glass into my range of what I bought and sold.

This new customer confessed his import export business was a front for his main business interest; his family owned a major commercial bank and he hoped he had found in me someone he could trust. I wished I could have confessed to him about Aspie. Yes, you can trust me, but you will have to watch your back, because my twin will do his best to fuck you up your arse.

R. I think what you are trying to tell me is that because you were unaware of Aspie's influences, you couldn't be aware of inappropriate bad judgement?

H. In a nutshell, you've got it. Fortunately, our business relationship didn't happen overnight, I am grateful to say, I still had much to learn. I was a baby in the world of antiques. We had got to know each other and he spent small numbers before the big one came along. It was five grand, seven grand and ten grand during the first year of doing business here and there. It was to be for me the sale of a lifetime, a quarter of a million quid with fifty big ones in profit. The deal took me two years to consummate.

While it lasted, it was as an amazing deal. However, the end outcome didn't quite go my way. Two weeks before I was due to ship him the goods, he was concerned about the cost of the forty-foot container. I had been getting quotes of four to five grand including packing, and he was not at all happy about paying that.

R. Surely it is common sense. You were doing such a big deal, you should have offered to subsidise the difference.

H. Not when you have an Aspie in your life. He would never know how to think so constructively. Eventually, I found a shipping agent who was prepared to do everything, packing and shipping. When my customer's payment reached my bank account, I was jubilant. When my customer opened his package, I don't think I would have enjoyed being a fly on the wall because I would have most probably been swatted out of existence.

R. What went wrong?

H. You mean what had Mr Ants in his Pants failed to do? And failed so miserably, he could have got a gold medal for.

R. Sorry, I don't understand, I have never heard that term before.

H. In Yiddish, it is called shpilkes, the inability to sit still, focus, concentrate, take to completion responsibilities, etc. commonly known today as ADHD. My customer asked me to find a more competitive quote. It took a lot of doing, I didn't know if it was feasible and it seemed an impossible thing to do. But Aspie had a quirky knack of finding people who would do a job on the cheap. It was once again buying stolen goods disguised in a project that was costing too little to be true. It was impossible for any shipping company to responsibly pack the hundreds of items and guarantee no breakages would occur during transportation. That was mistake number one. The other mistake was Aspie intervening during the packing. I had actually turned up early at the offices of the agents who had taken on the charade. We had the entire shipment sitting on concrete in front of the container. The important pieces of Chinese porcelain that made up one half of the entire shipment hadn't yet been packed. That was fine by me. I could see we had adequate packing material, tissue, bubble wrap, polystyrene balls. I even lent a hand, concerned for the safety of the most expensive porcelain, some costing several thousand pounds an item. I watched as the packers got to work and relentlessly packed as per my instructions. No problem here, I thought.

Then the inevitable occurred. Aspie got bored. 'You think I am going to stand here all day staring at these guys doing such boring work? What's the point? They are the experts. Leave it up to them, no point waiting round. Come back when the job is completed.'

What a mess. On my return, the container was loaded up to the hilt, yet the porcelain was still to be packed. 'No problem,' I was told, 'we have left gaps on purpose where the porcelain can be safely placed.' Famous last words. How is that possible, you might ask? Leave it to the experts, eh? If I had done some research, I might have realised I had got some incompetent boffins. Every piece had been packed well in the appropriate packing material, but had not been securely placed in the individual packages for additional protection. Apparently, when my customer finally got to open his container, there were more pieces than he had originally bought. Add together all the broken pieces of expensive porcelain. I knew if I was in his shoes, I would not have been happy to say the least.

Aspie came up with the perfect plan. Ask him if he was interested in being supplied £25,000 worth at cost, to help with the compensation. There was one problem doing this second deal. All I got in return was five grand, with a promise of the remainder being forthcoming.

Tough love, primarily what Aspie was all about. It boiled down to his confidence issues, not knowing how to stand his ground or negotiate. It reminds me of an old adage, the attitude of my father-in-law who had been a successful businessmen and believed people forgave people who wronged them. The trouble was, Aspie didn't want to learn. Anyway, I immediately got on a flight to Singapore because I wanted to inspect the damage and actually, it was not quite as bad as he made out, although what was evident was Aspie's irresponsibility.

Thankfully, he was not my only customer. I was still regularly doing the rounds of buying from Peter and selling to Paul and making thousands every week.

Whenever things didn't appear to be going my way, Aspie insisted on the perfect remedy. Since we were living in an era where money was coming in faster than Aspie could spend it, he insisted I kept hold of our image. He proved we could afford this and that. We had already treated ourselves to first class travel, and twice flown on Concorde. Since my peers lived in their mansions, drove around in their Rolls Royces and Bentleys, Aspie insisted we bought a Ferrari. Why? Because another colleague and good friend owned a Ferrari Dino. But being a two-seater, it was not my ideal car, since I required a reasonable size boot for stock and to seat four adults. So I went for a Ferrari 365 GT4 2+2. I was told I had to be crazy but would Aspie listen? It suited his need for speed and he didn't think about the cars appalling fuel consumption; typical, his relationship with the sublime and ridiculous! We owned the car for three years. It cost ten grand to buy, twelve grand interest on our loan and a further ten grand to pay for running the car. Then when I sold it, it had to pay for my honeymoon and all I got at the time was £2,500; another one of Aspie's sabotages.

Just like Aspie diving into a swimming pool to escape a paedophile, he wanted to see how well the bodywork fared with a tree, when he tested the car's acceleration up a hill on a wet road!

A. I had to; you gave me little choice. I didn't enjoy your boys' toys. It would have meant you lost touch with me.

H. It wasn't just the damage to my pride, but I wanted to keep the incident a secret. But as I keep on repeating, when you have an Aspie in your life, what you expect isn't always possible.

A. You know I can only speak the truth. I can't make up stories to please; not part of my make-up. I needed to teach you a lesson you would never forget. I hoped it would point out too that Hartley needed to take much more care of me than allowing me to go off on my own whims.

H. What Aspie said was his thoughts about our relationship. My challenge was finding the missing parts he preferred to keep hidden. It wasn't about buying a Ferrari. It was about buying the best of everything; clothes, watches, jewellery, anything he could show off.

Chapter 19: Searching For Love

H. You know, we often talked about my relationship innuendos and the women who came along. One who I hoped could be my ideal girlfriend had a shop a couple of doors away, which backed onto my rear courtyard. But if only Aspie could've realised the truth that her ideal man was far more sophisticated than me. All I could say to him was, 'Dream on!' He had to make major improvements to his social skills and day-to-day conduct. However, one day I was in for a delightful and unexpected surprise that Aspie could not put his foot into and spoil the broth. Sensing I was distraught when she walked past me, she turned round and enquired why, so I told her about my accident with the Ferrari.

That night, she became my pillow in the bed and we lay naked together, our bodies intertwined. Sex was the last thing on our minds. She was comforting me and it was most certainly massaging Aspie's mind. It was indeed a rare occasion to see him feeling so relaxed. But then he knew I was the one who needed the comforting and she was the ideal lady to give it to me. It was a one-night stand with a difference.

A. You see, it was not the accident or the money he blew on his Ferrari. It was showing how he could enhance my life to be a different person from the one I knew. He wanted to surprise me and teach me he could have any woman he wanted. In a way, I might as well add what occurred shortly before his wife took her own life shows you how I enticed him to be so insecure. It hastened him to travel five thousand miles for a date with someone he'd never met.

R. How is it one moment you are talking about deals, then we move on to cars, and suddenly we have moved on to women again?

H. One of the things you have to learn as I continue with my story are the out of context remarks Aspie makes.

Let me tell you about an episode in Miami where I had gone out with some of my colleagues and their wives for a holiday plus a buying trip. The buying part was at the world famous Miami Beach Antiques Show. The other main attraction was the Solid Gold strip club in North Miami and the neighbouring Adventura Shopping Mall.

It began with the wives having a laugh, then getting bored, but getting more excited by the Chippendales next door. Meanwhile, Aspie was in for the time of his life. I didn't know anything until one of my mates had paid for the broad with the largest tits to give him a table dance. How could I have blamed them? How could they have known the worst punishment they could give me was to feed Aspie's ego entirely!

Later on that evening, we all returned to our respective hotels. I was supposed to be heading back to mine, the Fontainebleau Hilton. However, Aspie had other plans. There was one other British dealer, who lived in America, that was notorious for trying out every brothel in every state, so the story goes. We knew which direction he was heading to the rather seedy section of Dade County west of the I-95 Fort Lauderdale.

I parked my purple Chevrolet in the parking lot, rang the front doorbell and a very scantily dressed woman appeared at the door. She led me into the reception area and, from behind her desk, said, 'Honey, it will cost you one hundred bucks for the girl. For that, you get as much sex as you desire, and I can assure you, there will be no hidden extras.'

After Sheridan had sensually undressed me, leaving not one inch of my body untouched by her lips, she prepared a bubble bath in an enormous tub where we cavorted around for the entire length of the session. Like all other nude massages, the one oddity the girls couldn't relate to was why Aspie wasn't interested in sexual intercourse. Although we know now what was the simple answer to that question. Sheridan was very different to all the other girls we met. For one thing, she was Jewish, and to Aspie that meant marriage material. I was hoping by having her phone number, we could meet up sometime in the future when I next visited New York. Sadly, the seedy strip club was the only place our eyes meet.

There was also another poignant reason Aspie ensured relationships of any sort could never work out, which was because of my first girlfriend. I was sixteen at the time and I met Svletana on a kibbutz in Israel. I spent many a night in her room sitting with her on her bunk bed. We chatted and spent much time looking into each other's eyes and cuddling and kissing, but there was nothing sexual between us. I think the idea of sex was the last thing on her mind. We eventually lost contact when she went off to university. My emotional pain was huge, the most profound loss I would ever suffer, other than that of losing Jacky.

However, Aspie insisted I kept hold of our memory. Every girl we met had to meet the merits of that lost memory of a boy and girl reaching into each other's hearts. She created a conundrum for me because Aspie looked down at every girl I met and, unless they had eyes like hers, he built up resentment towards them.

I can't begin to imagine what it is like to have cancer, but I can only say how Aspie attached his memories to mine was like one soul destroying cancer. Even today, tears can well up in my eyes thinking about those short moments we had together.

When, the following year, I asked my mother how I kissed a girl good night, it wasn't because I didn't know how; it was because she didn't match up to her beauty and she couldn't compare emotionally.

Just after Jacky died, I went on a Go-Date in New York. It was uncanny; the woman I went out with that night had a body to die for, right up my street. I don't know what Aspie said but we never kept in touch. She told me she used to know my girlfriend but had lost touch with her.

R. These things happen to us throughout our lives. Coincidences that really shock us, past memories, meeting new people who knew our first friends; but we learn to move on.

H. You tell Aspie that. I recall, among my early dates, meeting a nurse at a local dance. We arranged to go out to dinner and Aspie chose the restaurant, thinking our date would expect us to pay for her. But instead, when she looked at the menu, she was embarrassed and said. 'I'm sorry, I can't eat here. Why couldn't you have discussed a restaurant I can afford?'

R. I think it was a misconception that women expected a date to pay, although there are plenty of women who do. Equally, there are women like your date who like to know where they are being taken. They don't like hidden surprises, especially from a stranger who will probably make them feel uncertain of their safety, as you were to find out.

I am confused. You sometimes refer to yourself and other times you refer to Aspie. Now you are talking about a very special girl you meet on a kibbutz who might have been the root of your relationship crisis. How come you have never mentioned her name to me before?

H. Too emotionally painful. The funny thing is, I had set my heart on keeping in touch, visiting her, which I did, maintaining the friendship, and hoping we would eventually become an item. Svletana was the love I always carried with me, always hoping. The irony was we came so close, yet so far. It's crazy to think she sat in the back of my mind while I was married. After Jacky was gone, I hoped somehow we might meet up again through social media. Eventually, I managed to get in touch with her via the Internet. The meeting was extremely upsetting because she had grown into as opposite as I could remember her to be. I only got to see a couple of photos on her profile on LinkedIn. I asked her if she remembered me. She answered that she did but that was the first and last time we communicated.

R. Have you ever thought that she had as tough a parting as you? That when she lost contact with you, her life didn't develop in the way she expected and she, like you, built up many regrets? Maybe her memories were too emotionally painful to revisit.

H. You know what I think? You've hit it on the nail. Aspie's habitually talking about past innuendos ad-lib nuances and Svletana. I cannot begin to explain to you the sadness that continues to well up in my eyes when I remember so far back. And having to wonder how easy I was to accept that Aspie was a real person and had a completely separate identity to me. It seems that whenever I am discussing anything where Aspie felt he didn't fit in, or believed I had forgotten about him, is when I appear to digress. It is actually him who has taken over the conversation.

If I am not mistaken, the original question you asked was whether after I lost my virginity, I gave up visiting massage parlours? Sadly, sharing my life with Aspie essentially meant no chance.

R. What you are trying to say is that even when you were able to exert a little more self-discipline, Aspie's underlying controlling nature took control; that during this cycle of your life, he would do his utmost to pull you down. I suspect, though, you must have had your fair share of happier relationships?

H. Without wanting to reiterate my life story, what lay in the background to hamper any success are memories of the vile thoughts the paedophile groomed me to believing that a woman's vagina was a heinous creation by the Devil, not a beautiful creation of Gods. These thoughts continued to persist as if they were stuck down with superglue. I could never have imagined in my wildest dreams that Aspie would actually be coerced to carry out such vileness. The paedophile actually got to claim his second victim. The unimaginable occurred that following year I mentioned when by sexually exposing himself; the paedophile wished this to become an everyday occurrence and, in a way, he succeeded.

Except this couldn't be further from the truth. Yes, it is supposed to be the only time Aspie ever exposed himself, but his flies will remain open day and night of every day of my life. I cannot even begin to tell you from that moment, the prime of my adolescence was an abomination waiting for the right button to be pushed. So it's all very well saying to me most boys or girls go through a period of life just as I did when I was aged twenty-six; three years of debauchery after losing their virginity. The difference being was that I was unaware of how to identify with a monster perverting my sexual maturity.

Chapter 20: Rich Kid

R. So, you did meet with some success with women during your travels?

H. Six months before I bought my Ferrari, I was disqualified from driving for six months from the accumulation of fifteen points. I should have got more but the Judge gave me the shorter sentence because of my need to use a car for business. However, the day before, I managed to secure an International Driving License.

A. Finally, I get recognition of a good deed.

H. During my Ferrari days, I was too quick for the police. They didn't have their sophisticated speed traps and when you were in a car where the top speed is in excess of one hundred and fifty mph, there is little they can do other than radio ahead and put up roadblocks. That was my one fear that became reality.

I was driving at high speed when an unmarked police car kept up with me. I noticed ahead on a bridge a further police car, and a few miles further another one is facing towards me, and I begin to think they are closing in on me so I put my foot down and increased the speed to one hundred and twenty mph. By now, three other cars are keeping up with me so I put my foot to the floor. Although the speedometer registers in excess of one hundred and seventy mph, the supposed top speed for the car was one hundred and fifty-eight mph. At this speed, I made the M4 to Bristol in thirty-six minutes, a distance of eighty-seven miles. But I was worried that was where the police had set up their roadblock since the road converts into a single lane. So, I shoot straight across and got off at the next exit. I navigated the very narrow lanes of the country roads, almost having a head-on collision with a tractor, and twenty minutes later I rejoin the M4. However, we were very lucky to have made it as far as Bristol alive. When you are travelling at such high speeds, you pass vehicles that are adhering to the speed limit like they are standing still. God help you if one of them moves into your lane; no anti-lock brakes then.

Now I had been disqualified from driving in the UK, it was a wonderful feeling that the disqualification didn't include overseas. Being that three months of my year was actually spent in the US purchasing antiques, I spent half of the sentence there. In actual fact, when I returned home, the last three months having to get around by foot was in no way as difficult as I had thought.

Anyway, I no longer had my apartment in Phoenix. The one girl I had built up a platonic relationship with, Aspie decided she was not bed material, so we went our separate ways and I gave Phoenix a miss for a while.

R. You never mentioned her before. I guess she's another one of the other women in your life. Tell me about her.

H. We meet on a flight from LA when I was eighteen during the onset of the five consecutive summers we spent in Phoenix. But it was a shame nothing sexual developed.

R. How could something sexual develop when you didn't lose your virginity until years later?

H. That question was out of context. We did a lot of things together, and perhaps I should say she was the only girl we meet abroad and had a platonic relationship with. This part of my story reminds me of another little episode of the communication challenges prevailing with Aspie in making female friends at about this time.

I really fancied one of my sister's friends, and I was invited to see a film and sit next to her friend, who appeared very affectionate and smiling at Aspie, as though her facial expression intimated she wanted his hands cupping hers. However, his hand was rejected. There was one other of my sister's friends who Aspie was even more mesmerised by, but she wasn't Jewish. That was his criteria as to who he would allow me to wed, even though many girls he had me chat to were not Jewish. I wish I could have had some courage to go against his convictions; can you imagine how my life might have panned out differently?

R. Yes, I can, but you might not have such an amazing story to tell.

H. If only I could have had some knowledge about Aspie's anxieties. It was an unending menu of innuendos, which I took into my heart or my head without even a moment's notice for reasons beyond the scope of my imagination.

There were the odd occasions when Aspie threw something out of the box, discarding his normal criteria about the type of woman I was allowed to go out with. For example, we were on a subway train in the Chicago suburbs travelling downtown. It was the expression on her face, something in her eyes, and the next moment Aspie was responding, and we began talking and holding hands as though we had known each other for a long time. For the next two nights, we stayed at her home with her parents. It wasn't as though they lived in a mansion; on the contrary, her family lived in an impoverished area; yet, there was something about her that Aspie found inexplicably appealing. In this case, it was a lack of money that ended our short friendship; when Aspie insisted I had no relationship with a pauper.

While it could appear through lack of money or some other dislike, Aspie took to our preferred online date finder Go-Date. Frances lived in Manchester, a three-hour drive from us, so distance was never a reason a relationship ended. I wished she hadn't introduced me to one of her girlfriends who had come out of her divorce with a lot of everything; nice home, car and lots of money. It was inevitable that Aspie whinged that this was a good reason to leave. Typically too, Frances' home was only average and her job didn't pay a fortune, yet neither of these criteria were a reason our six-month relationship failed.

But when she had her appendix out, I was suddenly confronted by Aspie telling me he would not be seen with any woman who had unsightly body scars. She was an imperfect woman! This presented Aspie with a body image problem.

Anyway, getting back to having lost my driving license, no sooner had our plane landed in LAX, Aspie was feeling elated since I'm sitting in the driver's seat driving along the San Diego Expressway.

One day, Aspie and I decide to wander down to Venice Beach to do some sunbathing. Suddenly, Aspie was gazing at a particular sunbather, and it was inevitable that she had big tits. My wish was that he had the nerve to say, 'My name is Hartley,' and allow the introduction to flow and see where it led. But instead he invited her to spend an all-expenses-paid weekend with him in Las Vegas, even though the idea of going there I didn't find appealing because gambling was not our bag. While she hesitated with her answer for a moment, I was almost feeling sorry for her; saying she would love to come along but unaware she would be with a schizophrenic psychopath.

R. Isn't that a bit harsh, having those types of sentiments about your other half?

A. I am so pleased someone has the sense to come to my self-defence, even if it is only on this occasion.

R. Do you mean Aspie walked up to any stranger and expected them to say yes to him, without knowing anything about him? For all she knew, he could be an axe murderer.

H. That's another very good point. You may remember I use the term, 'Aspie doesn't take prisoners.' It's because he didn't have a conscience or interest in her safety or security, even mine, so long as he got what he wanted. What was any girl likely to say? 'Yes, I'd love to, although I would like to get to know you better before I agree to come along.'

So Aspie said to her, 'It's up to you. See that Corvette Convertible? It's mine; follow me and get in. We drive to your home, you get some clothes, and we take it from there.' You see how well Aspie made his plans. Enticed her with an expensive car and that means he must have money. Her answer was, of course, she'd love to come.

R. So, what happened?

H. We opted to stay at the Las Vegas Holiday Inn, arriving well into the evening. We had dinner and made our way back to our bedroom where things were about to get a little tricky, not like what you often see in the movies. I carried her into the bedroom; it might have broken Aspie's back, given that she was heavier than him. Furthermore, it wasn't a case of making sure she was comfortable, offering her a glass of champagne; when you have an Aspie around, there is little chance of the romantic things women lust after. They had hardly entered the room before he stripped off and got into bed, expecting her to do likewise. The sex we had was lacking in any passion or affection, and all over very quickly.

R. I'm beginning to relate to how sexual relations can be so very trying, given what the paedophile had in mind for you.

H. I think traumatising was an understatement being that foreplay was always no-play. Anyway, the following morning, when we went downstairs for brunch, we learnt why Elsie was so obese. She must have had at least five thousand calories on her plate. You know how they love their food in America? One price to pay for as much as your stomach will take. Mind you, it didn't stop Aspie eating ten thousand calories of pancakes!

We lazed by the pool for a few hours and then it was time to get ready for a show when we dressed to look our best. We were sitting among hundreds of people, each sitting at their own table waiting for the cabaret show to begin. Without warning, I was feeling as though I was about to be swallowed by hell itself. Aspie was experiencing sensory wiring overload, my worst nightmare. The motherfucker of anxiety attacks; unlike any neuro-typical non-autistic person can experience.

The sweat was gushing down my forehead and Elsie offered to call the paramedics. Actually, Aspie was comparing her figure to the many more-shapely model women sitting around us. It is as though he was on the stage, playing out an act where the audience was asking him why he was sitting there with a big fat ugly clomp!

A. Hartley, you are such a fool. So many beautiful women you could have chosen from, and you ended up with a hippo.

H. In a fraction of a moment, from a point where I was quite happy being with Elsie, my heart rate jumped as though my chest was about to explode. There was no time for explanations; Aspie didn't do apologies as he got up and dived for the nearest exit.

R. I can't imagine how your coping mechanisms worked then.

H. Only once I was outside did the heaving in my chest return to some normality. Poor Elsie could only repetitively ask if she should she call for emergency. After that, it was a case of her saying to me, 'Don't worry, I can afford the airfare home.'

A. Surely you weren't that insensitive not to give her a couple hundred dollars to see her okay? You had done so in the casino.

H. Again, it is not an Aspie done thing. It was as though his life was predestined because, barely a few hours later, we were flying to Toronto to spend a couple of weeks with cousins. From thereon, it was off to see a customer in Montreal and see if the city offered us scope for some good buying. Instead I found myself getting involved with more of Aspie's shenanigans when he began chatting to Giselle, a French Canadian in a bar in the French Quarter.

Everything seemed to be falling into place easily and naturally as we both looked into each other's eyes. Without any warning, just like what occurred on Venice beach undiplomatically, Aspie butts in and says, 'We're off to Miami this weekend. Do you fancy coming with us?' Amazingly, I think it was his eyes that women found too tantalisingly hypnotic, and by the evening Giselle was on a flight with us to Miami, telling me how she loved a man who was spontaneous, and especially being invited by a stranger more so. We checked into our hotel and because it was quite late, we decided to go straight to bed, having no qualms about stripping naked together. It wasn't long before we were snuggled up in bed canoodling together. All of a sudden, she goes on about belonging to a certain religious sect that condoned condoms and any type of protection! Just my luck! The next day, she flew home while I stayed on for an antiques show I wanted to attend, but it was another failed attempt at romance and Aspie's search for love.

Chapter 21: Wedding Day

H. I imagine if you were interviewing Aspie, he would say his nightmare day in our life was my wedding. To me, it was among the more beautiful memories; I was dressed up in a white linen suit, looking as handsome as I could, with Aspie behaving himself. Family, friends and business colleagues, many of who I still have a working relationship with, attended our wedding and we were showered with numerous wedding gifts as well as money.

R. Why aren't you mentioning your wife? Doesn't she have a place in this wedding of yours, or am I asking a rhetorical question?

H. I don't think I can ever forget how radiant she looked. I felt the same way those final moments when I had to say my goodbyes to her as well. That's why I could never forget, and another reason I could never allow, under any circumstances, Aspie ever to drive me in that direction, even if he had me enduring my worst nightmares. Our wedding day was a perfect July day, not a raindrop for miles.

I sometimes think Jacky's life could have been saved if only the parents of mine and Jacky's had opened their mouths and told some home truths when the rabbi asked if there was anyone in the congregation who believed this marriage should not be consummated. Our respective demons should have been mentioned.

My parents should have told them about me being recognised as different from the other people. Jacky's parents should have said that she required a man who can relate to empathy because their daughter had already made four attempts on her life. Only then, if we really loved each other and knew of each other's life challenges, could our marriage have had a chance to survive.

A. Hang on a moment. Would it not have been right if I had voiced my objection to them getting married? Was it blasphemy that Hartley got married when he was already married to me?

H. At the very least, it might have given our marriage a chance. But can you imagine Aspie divulging his addiction to massage parlours and what he got the masseuses to do to him? I think Jacky would have run a mile, while her parents should have mentioned she had inherited her father's suicide gene.

R. I imagine this is how it is for lots of couples that get married. Both parents are liable to be aware of something that might interfere with the marriage process that should be announced. However, whatever manifested in the past is generally kept under the carpet in the hope that it never creeps out of the woodwork!

H. I was invited to an Asperger's walk-in centre to participate in a discussion about what makes Aspies different from other neuro-typical non-autistic people. I said, 'It's like this: another person might be sad, disappointed or angry. They are sensations akin to a storm in a teacup. With an Aspie, his brain is wired differently and the sensations are amplified tenfold - akin to a hurricane in a tea cup - and you know it will inevitably spill over and be never ending!'

My answer went down a treat. I had a quantifiable explanation to give to anyone who asked me how Aspie manifested in my life. Nevertheless, all sorts of unimaginable and inexplicable situations developed, some which are inexplicably and horrifically scary.

Throughout my entire life, I wanted to find a doctor of the mind to tell me what part Aspie played in my life and how to eradicate him out of my life forever.

A. That's what I wanted to hear. My head on a chopping board!

H. I knew sooner rather than later I would be locked up. '*The menace off the streets*' would be the headlines. We could be happily walking along Oxford Street, in a park, walking past a children's playground, buying food in a supermarket, crossing the street, in a theatre, at a dinner party, and he was ready to either dangle his willy for the world to see, or uncontrollably swear out loud. I had to somehow calmly stand there and wait for my hurricane feeling to subside, not being aware of anywhere to run and hide.

I used to explain my lurid stories about Aspie to all those doctors of the mind and they told me everyone had such experiences. That's a horrific thought - the paedophile winning his bet - and Aspie joining his clan.

R. I can only begin to sympathise! What must have been going through your head, the people that would have jumped on you? I am surprised you were not wearing a straitjacket.

H. I am so pleased I heard you talking about my problems. I hope, at the very least, you are more aware of the dedicated and loving support I required one hundred per cent of the time, and why I was forced to demand it?

R. I think I am beginning to be able to better relate to your many issues. It must have been impossible for you to give in to all of Aspie's whims. Poor you! Can I give you a hug?

A. He doesn't need a hug. But I could do with a fuck, and I know I ain't going to get that from you!

H. You see how Aspie can rant out of the blue? A pure example of his immaturity. If only I could have learnt to be less confrontational with him. Be more tolerant of his hardships and make whatever necessary changes in my lifestyle were needed to focus on what he was good at instead.

A. That's all very well you saying, but I like myself as I am!

H. Anyway, the only thing I ask of you, is to remember what I have explained to you about networking and coaches being instrumental in helping me to understand my relationship with Aspie.

R. Got it!

A. I haven't.

H. I will ignore that. Let's continue. Within two days of our wedding, Jacky and I spent ten days in Bali staying at the Hyatt, before going to Singapore. However, I had an ulterior motive to help pay for our honeymoon and buy some Chinese porcelain. Of course, what Jacky was really getting was a taste at first-hand of Mr Ants in his Pants. However, the cost of our honeymoon was paid for by getting rid of my prized demon.

A. You don't have to be so sarcastic!

H. I'm talking about my Ferrari! It was our first recession, the cost of fuel rocketed, and any car that guzzled the petrol fell drastically in value while interest rates hit twenty-five per cent. For the time being, we were married, we had a baby on the way, and we enjoyed plenty of sex.

A. Thank God, I had something to live for. It was such a shame that the massage parlours offered me more satisfaction than she could ever give.

H. Another typical Aspie condescending outburst - meant to emotionally hurt me - because I am not giving him my attention. While I am certain most marriages get off to a good start, there was already serious sexual tension in ours, right from the beginning, although we are elated about the baby. If she had explained her circumstances, that the coil and pill upset her and I was expected to wear a condom, it might have helped. But Aspie decided her conditions were brought on psychologically and not physically.

R. The whole purpose of marriage is about two people agreeing terms of a life together. Best if choices and rules are set. No doubt for Jacky, having children was a priority. For you, it was about developing a career and being responsible for the keep of your family. For Aspie's, it was all about being loved and enjoyable lovemaking.

H. I don't hold any attachment to blame, but what was Aspie to do? How would you react if your husband said he had an allergic reaction that gave him hives whenever he wore a condom, and in response he is told his condition was psychological? Already the fun was taken away from our lovemaking and the only time we could safely orgasm together was when she had her period.

R. As I have said to you, marriage is a commitment. If she condoned being responsible for getting herself pregnant, either you agree with it or you don't. I imagine this is something else that was not discussed beforehand with Aspie?

H. Not my fault he takes things for granted.

R. By all account, you were already blind to the sexual tension Aspie caused. Making love is not an in-and-out affair. Among the most enjoyable parts is the foreplay that precedes the orgasm. How did you overcome the paedophile ingratiating in you not to have any relationship whatsoever with the female genitalia?

H. I admit, Aspie caused tensions, issuing me with orders so my focus was Jacky's breast area. She had sensitive nipples. I couldn't exactly say to her, 'Darling, the reason I cannot go down on you is because I was sexually molested by a paedophile and banned from your vagina.' She would likely have said, 'Best to marry a man and be homosexual.' I knew Aspie didn't enjoy the feel of massaging the vaginal area, but I did my best to overcome his sexual sentiments. My only regret was that Aspie never learnt that unconditional love meant no hanky-panky on the side.

A. Sure!

H. As time marched on, it became embarrassing enough to put up with jibes from colleagues and friends telling me Aspie needed etiquette lessons. There was the humiliation of hearing we were banned from one of Jacky's best friends because Aspie picked his nose.

R. I don't think I would have been too amused by your table manners either.

H. Aspie's, not mine, thank you!

Shortly after our wedding, Tim was conceived and, for me, the most beautiful baby born. Little did I know, one child was born, and there was another to look after that required all the attention. Being in the delivery room certainly wasn't to Aspie's taste.

R. I can remember my husband having difficulty in watching me give birth. Quite common, I believe.

H. From hereon, Jacky kept a tight leash on me. She insisted that whenever I was on my travels, be it stock buying, I checked in morning and evening to tell her how much I loved her.

R. I think it is more the case that most women know how men wander!

H. This is exactly what I had been pre-warned about. Thank God Aspie behaved.

A. That's me quietly waiting for the ideal timing for my next adventure.

H. Little did I know, Aspie was growing impetuous. Jacky's brother and sister-in-law had a baby girl the year before and they were away together monthly so either her mother or nanny looked after the baby while they are away. For an inexplicable reason, Jacky's ideology was that a mother's role was to build up her intimate role with her child, providing one hundred per cent attention. Weekends away didn't happen and I could feel the volcano inside of me showing signs of stirring.

A. Damn right. That's why I conjured up something drastic and gave you a wake-up call to listen to!

H. Aspie is referring to his jealousy. What we so often read in the papers when a person in a marriage partnership resorts to murder. Aspie didn't like the competition and decided one of us had to go. He planned for a knife to be dug deep into Jacky's heart. It was tragic. And occurred when my eldest boy, who obviously had his own version of Aspie, wanted to test if his father was his father. Not that I can believe any child of one year of age had the capacity of doing what he did. You read about it in the papers. About parents having terrible accidents with their kids, for example; driving over them, or leaving a loaded gun and the poor kid plays with it and kills himself. Should the parents go to jail, or is it enough of a testament that they have to live with the guilt for the rest of the lives?

R. I can't even begin to relate to how Jacky must have been feeling. How did this accident occur?

H. It could have been a scene out of a horror story. The poor little guy couldn't have known what hit him. He crawled out of the study door, unaware of the monster who was about to crush his life out of him. I had uncoupled a boat hinged to my car, unaware he was immediately underneath. We were both in intense shock as we made our way to our local emergency hospital. It was barely a ten-minute drive away with Jacky cradling her beloved baby, while Aspie was laughing his head off. Can you believe he had no idea of the danger our son was in, but after three days in hospital, he came out as our little miracle. We were told his age saved him from certain death because as a one-year-old, his bones were resilience and able to bounce back into shape. Little did I know, his accident was at the top of Aspie's shenanigans, with many more to follow.

A. Music to my ears. So glad it was to be the first of your married many, and I was planning my next unwelcome present.

R. Did the accident produce any long-term damage to Tim or concerns about you being a responsible father?

H. Damage to him, no; concerns about me being a responsible father, not in the beginning; more a gentle reminder of our joint parental responsibilities.

The next time, our beloved was barely three. It was our luck the au pair we receive from the agency was a druggie. I arrived home to find out she had taken Tim for a walk to our local reservoir. When I caught up with them, I was shocked to find her high on weed while he was waving, 'Over here! Can't you see I can't swim?'

You hear of stories about parents who rescue their children and risk their lives in doing so. Sadly, Aspie was not one of them. He decided it was the au pair's responsibility to save him, or for my son to learn to save himself.

R. Surely, you as a responsible father, irrespective to Aspie's demur, must have known he was in danger of drowning? Common sense should have prevailed. I guess this part of the story ends nicely?

H. Fortunately, where he had fallen in was not deep and he was not in immediate danger. Later on that evening, Jacky became aware that some money and jewellery were missing and, of course, our au pair was in denial. No doubt the weed had something to do with that! Fortunately, we called the police and she was deported.

However, Aspie continued to play a spate of childish and thoughtless pranks that terminated our family holidays altogether. I had to get used to, 'I've booked me and the children a holiday because I can't afford to be embarrassed by Aspie anymore.'

Jacky didn't have the softest of voices when she was annoyed. Not unsurprising, all our children built up an immunity to her screaming in response to bad situations. It was inevitable that poor communications developed when Aspie repetitively began saying, 'You are not communicating with me.' It wasn't that it was meant contemptuously, it was a genuine miscommunication between Jacky and I.

A. I wished you could have been more tolerant of Jacky shouting continually at the children. Then I could have built up some resilience and not allowed my sensory issues to get the better of me.

H. I believe the nail in my coffin, that sparked Jacky's interest in taking the children on holiday solo, occurred because of an incident at our local McDonald's where Aspie's lack of social manners emerged. We were being severed big fries and one falls on the floor and the boys began throwing chips at each other.

They thought it was a new game but the worst part was that Aspie joined in.

A. I have said it before, and I will say it again. It was you who I had to learn from, not me. You didn't tell me to stop; you just laughed. You thought it was funny, so I decided to continue.

H. The fun turned to the sublime and ridiculous because by now, the chips in the boy's bags had become smothered with ketchup. By the time we arrived back home, their white shirts were splattered and Aspie, Tim and Sam were in hysterics.

On another occasion, I took my eldest son on a business trip to Copenhagen. I was so excited about the purchase of a very profitable piece of Meissen and decided to celebrate that night. Our hotel was overlooking the Tivoli Gardens where Aspie encouraged me to take Tim on every ride possible, twice. I didn't see why Jacky was so angry because I kept him up past midnight.

R. As a mother and wife, I can understand Jacky's sentiments. As a father, she expected you to teach your children the differences between right and wrong, good and bad, and certainly not giving him a reason to misbehave. I easily sympathise with what she went through; being Aspie's indifferences to his behaviour and parental responsibilities in your marriage.

H. I like how insightful you are, but perhaps women are generally more so than men. Six years into our marriage, Aspie was now well endowed with his misdemeanours. I only wished I had the mental agility to walk away, realise our marriage was over, and perhaps Jacky would have been alive today. If only she could have opened up about her issues and been aware of Aspie's inability to be more empathetic to the children wearing her out mentally and physically, another reason why we had developing sexual tensions.

R. Aspie being the sexual beast of the two of you?

A. Glad I am.

H. I wish Jacky could have known about the paedophile programming Aspie. She might have been more sympathetic to his needs and overcome her issues, expecting me to protect her from becoming pregnant.

R. Do you mean to say between the pill and coil? What was her problem?

H. Psychological in that she used anxiety as her excuse too often.

A. Wasn't it amusing, when Jacky wasn't aware my antics begun?

H. When I look back at Sam's birth, I think how extraordinary it was. Why I missed it was because he was in such a hurry to announce himself to the world, by not adhering to what was expected of him. I was told Jacky would be in labour for at least eleven hours so I joined my mates for our weekly lunch.

R. Surely supporting your wife was the expected thing to do?

H. When you have Mr Ants in his Pants sharing your life, you have to expect the unexpected, regardless of the situation. Had we stayed, it would have been like Aspie giving birth because he displayed so much anxiety.

I got the surprise of my life when I returned, barely more than a couple of hours later, and couldn't understand why my mother-in law-was holding someone else's baby. I couldn't believe it when she said it was mine. Anyway, something was amiss because the doctors thought he was the wrong way up and Jacky was cut. The problem for Aspie was abstaining from sex for eighteen months. It was awkward enough, although I have to say a miracle occurred because I did abstain. However, it didn't stop Jacky from questioning my fidelity when Aspie unintentionally brought home an unwelcome present from Houston.

R. It sounds like Aspie wasn't geared up to be a family man. What occurred in Houston?

Chapter 22: Need for Adventure

H. Aspie blamed it entirely on Jacky deciding not to join us on a holiday of a lifetime. I know I keep on repeating myself, but I think it boils down to his eidetic memory. He found it very challenging separating different types of thoughts: happy thoughts; sad thoughts; fun thoughts; and annoying thoughts etc. He had already determined that Jacky could have joined us down under visiting Australia and New Zealand. But the idea of leaving our boys with the most trusted of our au pairs was out of the question. During our courtship until our marriage, we had a weekend in Paris and New York, countless weekends away at luxurious spas and the likes of the Laura Ashley Hotel near Crickhowell. However, no sooner than we return from our honeymoon, and shortly after Tim is born, our weekends away grinded to a halt. Okay, I conceded that a newborn needed their mother but for the rest of their lives it was as though she needed her children close to her breast. Aspie resented this, and his resentment festered like a disease.

It was almost like the final straw. It was almost a test to see which way her love lay; for me, or our boys. Was I a priority in her life? I brought in the bucks, paid for the au pairs, the cleaner, the gardener and the builders. Jacky's brother and sister-in-law regularly enjoyed the fruits of travelling, leaving their mother to look after their daughter, but not Jacky.

Meanwhile, my dilemma with Aspie was how to slow him down, how to get him to relax, away from business, some 'him' time. But no, of course not, it was as though he was his very own enterprise; breaking though light speed, doing the impossible. I could never have envisaged that we would visit Bangkok, Singapore, Hong Kong, Tokyo, Osaka, Kobe, Sydney, Melbourne, Brisbane, Hawaii, Los Angeles and Houston in three weeks! Little did I know, this was Dr Who navigating time travel doing the impossible; but we did it and we came back with amazing antiques.

Back in the seventies, it was pre-technology in business and reproduction antiques everything days that was to eventually kill off competition, driving the majority of smaller stores and shops out of business. In the antiques business, it was AIDS that killed off around fifty per cent of the antique dealers who regularly shopped for antiques in the UK. The other precursor of disaster was eBay and the advent of the Internet. Why buy antique if reproduction can be bought for so much less? Or alternatively, focus on individuality and the brand is what comes next in the fashion of the decorative arts scene.

As I said, I don't really want to digress to this most interesting subject, nevertheless fashion for a select number of dealers like myself was to use our knowledge to travel overseas. In particular, the US and the Far East were havens of stock to be purchased for near nothing prices because of the lack of knowledge or competition. In the Far East, where today times have changed and big prices are paid for almost anything of interest, anything that was considered decorative, be it utilitarian pieces and vases, jardinières, fish bowls and garden seats, were bought by the inch, not for what they actually were, or be it Ming, seventeenth, eighteenth or nineteenth century, with little differential in the price asked and while it lasted, stability for good profiting.

What hasn't changed over the years is the part of bartering, where anywhere outside of Europe or the West haggling was very much in force as it is today. Japan was a different kettle of fish compared to the other places we visited. If I thought money grew on trees, it rained money there. The cost of living was extortionate; beyond unbelievable. Two hundred pounds a night was nothing for a hotel. You didn't want to take a taxi ride otherwise it burnt a hole in your pocket. If you didn't speak

Japanese, there was little point in finding a restaurant, and with Aspie's lack of language skills, we ate at our hotel and could pay a hundred quid for a meal.

Although we made purchases in Japan, it was also here Aspie decided to sample a geisha. It was a memorable experience and more like a sumo wrestler than a masseur! I couldn't imagine why there was a rope attached to several rings in the ceiling immediately above our hotel bed. When the geisha arrived in our room, I learnt what it is like to be run over by a truck. My consolation prize to our little interlude in Japan was the £120 taxi ride to the airport for our flight to Melbourne.

Among my many dilemmas contending with Aspie was his rather unorthodox 'either this way or no way' attitude. He closed his eyes, put his finger on a map and that became our next destination. It was not like the days of visiting Hampshire, buying stamps and making a meal last a day. I wished time management existed among his acumens and a plan to all our travelling.

Putting Aspie's indulgences and indiscretions to one side, I admit enjoying his indigenous tools that I can only marvel at. His inbuilt compass, his ability to explore the back streets and back yards of anywhere and find the unique. As well as visiting Japan, we were regularly driving to Dordrecht in Holland for antique purchases. A friend asked to be dropped off at an address in the centre of Brussels and Aspie took him directly there, without a map and without having been there before; quite beyond my scope of thinking.

A. Thank you, it's taken me this long to get a well-deserved recognition of my achievements.

H. You see? Aspie has done it again. Now, where was I? As far as Aussie was concerned, we thought by our third trip it would bring us luck with sourcing antiques, other than spotting kangaroos and seeing if Aspie could end my life saying hi to a couple of great white sharks along the Great Barrier Reef and have my troubles eaten away.

A. Pleased to know the big white didn't have a taste for me.

H. When I look back to those days, I so badly wanted Jacky to travel with me. I believe her excuse to destinations too far away was more an indecision not to have closeness to Aspie's unruly social habits.

R. If I had been in her shoes, after that episode on the day you proposed to her, I would have imagined there was plenty more in reserve. I too might have raised the question about wanting a regular holiday with you.

H. Anyway, continuing our travels throughout Australasia, I told Jacky that with or without her, I need a holiday, so New Zealand became a ten-day marathon of enjoying adrenalin intensive sport and staying overlooking the Shotover River, Queenstown, South Island.

Our first day was hang gliding; second day, water skiing in the morning and snow skiing in the afternoon; third day, Awesome Foursome, which is flying an army helicopter down the Shotover Ravine, bungie jump high over the Shotover, high power jet ski boat, then ending the day white water rafting while chucking water into competing boats. The fifth day was a free-fall tandem jump from nine thousand feet, and day six was piste skiing. We headed to Hawaii and on to LA, where I again stayed with my cousins who asked whether Aspie had a wind-up key.

The fast-forward button was very much on, and during the next two days we crammed visiting and making purchases at antique shops in Beverley Hills, Melrose, Melrose Place, La Cienega, Pasadena, Newport, Laguna Beach and La Cholla.

However, there was a downside to our choice of first class ticket. It was affordable only because we had to follow a particular route with a final stop in Houston. Now among the many complaints I have had to suffice about Aspie's demure, was also his inability to stop talking gibberish.

I have often admired people in business with the gift of the gab and profit from the talent. But it is no talent in Aspie's life. On the contrary, he can talk someone to death if allowed. Sitting next to us in first class was a well-dressed businessman to who Aspie was all ears. It was my hard luck that the reason Aspie was so attentive was because he was being told all about what can go wrong in marriages and that the remedy was extramarital fun. 'It's a necessary evil when your wife owns every bit of your freedom.'

Aspie replied surprised: 'How do you know my wife owns my freedom?'

Our companion went on to say, 'You Brits have got some weird humour. Hmm, you tell me you are only here for one night. I commute here three times every week and encourage all of my friends to stay at the Holiday Inn on Green Street next door to a strip club. A man has needs, and every time I visit, a stripper giving me a table dance keeps me young at heart and stops me from having full-blown sex with a prostitute.'

A. I had a whale of a time, didn't I?

R. What is Aspie referring to?

H. It was supposed to be the first and last time I ever visited a strip club, to learn how professional, happily married men spend their evenings parting with dollars placed under bangles, attached to strippers' legs and bikinis. It was my luck Aspie took a fancy to a rather big busty, black stripper. Talk about leading him astray. We followed her to the rear of the club and what occurred there almost destroyed my marriage.

A. You and I sure had the fun of our lives. Got my deserved attention. Your mistake was not calling Jacky to tell her you were bringing back something rather special because you needed to extend your stay by a couple of days to make another thirty grand.

H. Aspie loved to coerce the truth. It might be fun for Aspie and other men. But simultaneously, an intrusive anxiety attack manifested as fast as a tornado erupts into fury then subsides as though never existing. My shock came when I returned to my hotel room and looked in the mirror to see a big red welt on my neck. Can you believe my luck when the first thing Jacky said was, 'Have you brought home any unwelcome presents, darling?'

I must have been even more naive to think she would not have screamed blue bloody murder at me because that is what she did. Yet, the irony was, she pounded on me that evening with some wonderful and attentive lovemaking.

R. We women have a tendency to be like a volcano erupting very quickly, and quickly simmering down. She knew you would feel fraught when she screamed at you. However, she would have discussed the incident with her mother, who from her own worldly experience concurred this among the harmless stuff wives put up with from their husbands. Above anything else, any wife is liable to have been afraid of losing their husbands so early on during their marriage, just as in your case too!

H. I'm grateful to be able to share this incident with you. It makes me want to believe there is something about self-gratification, if this makes any sense to you.

Chapter 23: Sam and Tim

H. I wish I could have related to my son, Sam, having in part his own version of Aspie, but don't all kids coming to terms with their adolescence and hormones, trying to leave the kid in them behind and attempting to be a grown-up, but being confused since the child in them is still dominant? I know from my own experiences, of wanting to spend as much time as I could in Aspie's world beyond his wall of infinite possibilities, I should have accepted Sam's behaviour in New York was nothing other than him finding his identity.

R. Why particularly Sam? What about Tim?

H. Tim could write a book about the blood he split when teenage love came along. He met a girl whose aim was to get to university and, surprise, surprise, he used his skills to bluff his way to acquiring a first-class degree in Astrophysics. Yet, why was he surprised? He certainly didn't acquire those skills from Aspie!

R. It seems rather surprising that one child can give you so little trouble and the other so much. Yet, you say your youngest has his version of you?

H. Obsessive tendencies like the rather embarrassing walking in the street while his hands were clearly down the inside of his pants holding onto his balls as though they represented his most valuable asset, and that was what we all had to get used to. Twice he accompanied us on our trip to the US. Even before the plane had landed at JFK airport, just like Big Ben he chimed on the hour throughout our trip. 'Dad, are you sure we are going to make the flight home?'

Our next stop was driving to cousins in Toronto. There was no chance of listening to the radio because our little one was waging World War Three imitating the sounds of gunfire and explosions constantly. Two years later, we made the same trip, this time with his sister, younger by four years, and we had the holiday of a lifetime!

It was during our return journey from the same cousins in Toronto that, using Aspie's inbuilt map, we found an amazing lake where we took out a speedboat for an hour or two. Driving through upstate New York, Aspie also found a swimmable river that was not on the map. It was funny how Aspie had no qualms jumping in first. Sam, on the other hand, had forgotten his trunks and had concerns his manhood might show through his underpants so he took a few minutes to build up the courage to join in. There was a fracas when his sister got caught up in the current and appeared to be drowning. It was not Aspie who came to her rescue but, surprise, surprise, Sam. Again, like the time Tim fell into the lake under the care of our au pair and Aspie decided it was her responsibility to save Tim, Aspie had taken over from me and was in anxiety mode, while Sam came to her rescue.

Slide Rock in Oak Creek Canyon, north of Sedona, where many families go with children, also has a rock sixteen metres above a pool for the more dare hardy! Aspie saw a young woman in her twenties making the jump and I had to pluck up the courage to follow. Just like years before when I did a bungy jump, Aspie did bring rewarding excitement into my life.

A. It's nice to know I am appreciated once in my life.

R. So you did, after all, have some quality family holidays? I thought you said Jacky refused to go away with you.

H. This last holiday was after Jacky and I separated. You know, women never forget, and Jacky had too many entries in her catalogue of Aspie's misdemeanours.

I digress back to a time when my eldest was eleven or nine and he was a son to make his father proud. He was gifted with many interests, except there was a nail in his coffin, so to speak, in the form of Aspie's parental skills in raising a child, which were far from the norm. He might get the little critter in their ideal direction as far as schooling was concerned but we won a Gold Medal embarrassing them all the time. How do you expect a child, who is going through puberty, then adolescence, to behave when he has a father who falls short on his social manners and eating habits? He was stuck trying to figure out where he stood and who held the truth as to the ideal path he should be on. Did he try to emulate his mother, who will be for the most part at the end of her tether, unaware her beloved husband is sharing his life with an Aspie, and simultaneously attempting to tell her children no school had yet been invented to teach Aspie good table manners, let alone be a responsible parent?

The fracas began immediately when I returned home from one of Aspie's marathon round-the-world business trips. Eager to see my son, I learnt from Jacky that he was playing tennis at our local courts. He said to me years later, 'Dad, neither you nor Mum had any inkling about the emotional damage Aspie caused. I don't believe any father would do what Aspie did that day! I had to put up with so much jeering form my mates. Pete put his hand against his throat and did a swiping movement because, just like me, he had angst with his dad. I could have murdered you but memories of that night at the Tivoli Gardens and the fun we had caused me so much confusion. And sometimes I couldn't stop laughing, the many times Mum told you off, considering you to be incompetent, and not knowing when to stop!'

R. What was the emotional damage Aspie did to your relationship with him?

H. I had been away for six weeks and Aspie didn't think twice about running up to him and swinging him over his head like he was a rag doll. I should have done it at home and not in full view of all his mates. It embarrassed him so badly, he was emotionally torn between making his mum happy and getting the respect he felt he deserved from Aspie. For the next few years, it was, sadly, a downhill struggle that resulted with unnecessary emotional damage to his mother. Nevertheless, I always knew he would turn out all right and with his head screwed on. However, as far as Aspie was concerned, anything which showed me he was doing well - be it soccer or tennis - he wanted to destroy what was left of our relationship.

A. I didn't see any wrong in what I did.

H. It was all very well, but in his mind he was a little boy growing up. The last thing he wanted was a father displaying his affections in front of his mates.

A. Not as I see it. Without me as a dad, he would never have had so much fun!

H. I hope you can begin to sense how Aspie acted like a double-edged sword. Rarely can I interpret or relate to his actions or prevent him from showing his ugly side. It took Jacky - doing her best in simple layman's language and being as compassionate as she could - asking why I didn't wait until I got home to display my affection. It was no wonder that what I did was retaliation waiting to happen.

PART FOUR:

CONSOLIDATION - TRAVEL AND SEX ADDICT

Chapter 24: Going Our Separate Ways

H. The tough part of my memory was recalling those moments when Jacky looked directly into Aspie's eyes, hoping she would sense her emotional lament. It was the terrible fear of her uncertainty, helplessness and indecision, not knowing if she was making a desirable choice. She lusted after the one thing she sensed Aspie was unable to give her; his emotional warmth that told her all she needed to know - that she would be protected from the worse kind of evil. I remember when she told me what I didn't want to hear.

'It's not my choice but I have decided we are moving house. We need a change of scenery and a fresh start may see Tim right.'

A. There she went again, trying to expect some sympathy from me.

H. A few days later, with the same look of despair in her eyes, she wrote me a note saying, *'The choice is yours, either we make a new life or we go our separate ways.'*

Looking back to those days, we married ready to start a family but I was paying for advice from every therapist I could; as much as the average plonker was earning in a salary! Little did I know it was to be the poorest of investments. It felt like somewhere deep inside my head, and well beyond my imagination, there lay a malignant disease that crossed the threshold of my mind. A time bomb set in motion, not unlike a boa constrictor, as it crushes the life out of its victims and then consumes them, and body acids dissolved what was left. Jacky's mind was slowly being disintegrated and pulled apart, little by little, and then consumed by fear, by menace, by the ultimate desire that there was something beyond death that was a better place to be. Aspie was consciously aware of this and I was powerless to prevent the inevitable!

R. Death that comes by one's own hand is something beyond terrible. Are what you are trying to tell me is that is what worried you the most?

H. During those early days, I hope I could be rid of Aspie. Set him forth into another dimension. No longer have a relationship with his selfless attitude towards our well-being. I thought moving house offered this hope. But to really understand Aspie required thinking about two identities in one person; one obsessive and controlling, and the other capable of many talents. What little chance did I have of emulating the long-distance salesman who travelled a couple of thousand miles a week around Britain and successfully sustained a family? His wife was likely to accept his habits, have children and live a hunky-dory life together. Aspie couldn't afford to provide me with that provision - another reason he showed her his true colours in Johannesburg, emulating a bull charging at a matador. He wanted to put an end to any marriage to anyone, other than him! No sooner than we returned from our honeymoon, Aspie had me commuting to the US three times a month and this lasted fifteen years! Even when our daughter came along, he could not slow down the locomotive in full steam. He couldn't show any weakness; always with a need of venting something copious as though he was the unseen monster waiting, hidden in the shadows, waiting just like you might see in a horror movie.

Aspie wanted to be what my father wasn't, a businessman contemptuous of the capitalistic society, who turned to academics to save his life. It was my unfortunate luck to have Aspie at a time when I needed his support. His shenanigans, the prostitutes and escorts he sought, searching for the constant live that would perpetually elude him. Meanwhile, the world was at war financially and I had to come to terms with a general downturn in the trade. Recession hit everyone and likewise our commuting was cut by two thirds to once a month culminating with having to downmarket.

Sadly, wherever we moved my battle with Aspie was not knowing what decision to take. Tim helplessly continued his unusual behaviour towards Aspie while sensing his mother's inner feelings, not knowing how he could quell his negative emotions, do the damage his feelings had to exert and worry about victims later. Nevertheless, our move felt a little happier, although Jacky appeared nervous; she was happier living closer to her mother who had move the previous year. However, I was scared wondering how short-lived her happiness might be.

R. Are you telling me Jacky's only friend was her mother? What about mothers she met at your children's schools?

H. You are correct. But they were her friends, not ours, and not once did they visit our home and only one became friendly, but she had an emotional punchbag, since her husband beat her up regularly. To be honest, Aspie's lack of social etiquette meant one couple she had known from ages ago decided on no account did they want to have any association with him. I believe Jacky wanted to lead a separate social life from Aspie. She might have loved me but she wanted to glue Aspie's lips together whenever we were out socialising.

I was supposed to follow on the downsize too - sell up and open a shop in the village close to where her mother lived and sell to the upmarket clientele, but this didn't happen. My life at that time was one big fuck-up.

R. Was it that bad?

H. You have to remember, I was not yet to be diagnosed and I never really knew Aspies's true identity until that happened. I didn't really know my own story. I knew the facts like I was born premature and with malformed arms and that I was prey to paedophiles and sex abusers that left me very timid, lacking in confidence, and yet I knew I had the skill set to be a successful entrepreneur.

I often mention how Aspie liked finding out what it was like living in the shoes of his best customers. Countless times he visited their shops, whether it be in New York, LA, Atlanta or Osaka. It was his lack of confidence that made me go. It was another Aspie trait, to see their smiles and shake hands, and it confirmed from his perspective that he had a strong business relationship with them.

What happened in Atlanta was not the first time I was invited to dinner at the home of a major collector who had bought a rare eighteenth century jardinière from me ten years before but had never bought anything else, and I always believed it was Aspie's doing. While I knew it was the done thing to take a gift - a bottle of wine or flowers - when invited to someone's house, Aspie could not connect to this ideology. It was beyond his scope of thinking, and so the expression of dismay I should have recognised on her face when she opened the door to me, and of course, Aspie's inappropriate table manners as his dribble and other bits of food are wiped from other guests' plates. Now you can understand why the customer did not want to associate with Aspie! However, also unbeknown to me were other events that preceded before my infancy, learning to become a dealer well versed in the art of professionalism.

I recall the sadness as though it is with me today. His eyes spoke how he felt. The only comparison I can think of is on the TV show *The Apprentice*, where there is only going to be one winner. His disappointment in me portrayed in his expression as though I had dug a knife into his heart where he had no choice but to cut off all business ties. So tragic, all because he didn't adhere well to Aspie's ways of demonstrating his loyalty.

R. What did Aspie do that was so terrible? Sounds like he was fond of you in a kind-hearted way?

H. I think you have hit the nail exactly on the mark. He used to give me these gentle bear hugs. I still feel his tenderness as though he didn't want to give me the punishment he had no choice but to give. He was a big man - must have weighted a quarter of a ton - looking very silly riding around on the smallest of mopeds.

Yet, his home was a row of terraced houses and was also his warehouse, crammed full of every denomination.

R. I hope you don't find me a bit disparaging. How you appear to jump from one story to another. I appreciate your attempting to tell me your life problems, yet you appear not to give a direct answer to many of my questions!

H. I think it is because I am trying to show the relationship between the big man and the incident in Atlanta. Sometimes I feel a need to kick up the butt, metaphorically speaking, like the repetitiveness in my story.

The big man asked me to find a selection of broken Oriental vases for him to display on his furniture. Aspie assumed broken meant the more broken, the more profit. When I delivered the order he expected within his purchase, some common sense at least with a selection of less damaged rather than all very damaged.

R. So, Aspie did exactly what he was told because he was unable to relate to what the big man may have meant?

H. Exactly, but sadly the damage was done. I saw tears in the big man's eyes. I felt something was wrong but I had to learn the hard way!

R. Surely, the big man could have said no!

H. Not so easy when he had already parted with his money. But what Aspie was doing after disappointment was burying them so they accumulated to build his eidetic memory bank. How many times he got me to count on my fingers and toes the blow jobs, the unprotected sex, the paedophiles, the teachers he felt had wronged him, the bullying he couldn't understand. These all went really deep into the back of his mind, waiting for the right moment to erupt.

R. He was unable to filter out what he didn't want to remember?

H. Yes, but that's an understatement. I needed more fingers and toes to count them all! But this is what he did only while he had me to myself, and he was conniving too; he made me feel guilty. That was the real reason behind me staying in my relationship with Jacky; the thought that one of his whores might have given him AIDS.

A. AIDS, I like that! I'd always wanted to experience death.

H. Basically, it boiled down to him wanting to try out everything the world had to offer, experience it, and hopefully survive. It was like reading the news in the US; '*No remains found in acid lake in Yellowstone after man falls in.*'

It reminds me of among my early travels around the world. We were visiting Hawaii, when Aspie decided to see how hot the advancing lava was. I had to stop him running up to the lava flow as though he was under a hypnotic spell, let alone inspect a steaming foul and noxious vent, leaving me with the vilest taste in my mouth and a heaving cough. How often do we see on the news of an erupting volcano and hear about tourists who get too close? Again, Aspie nearly had me killed.

It is these types of stupidity I am referring to when he felt the need to experience that I sometimes felt powerless to prevent. There was the direct relationship I had with him and his answer was always, 'I can only learn from you.' That was a tough one to deal with, and I always answered him, 'I wished you could learn to stand on your own two feet and our life together would have most probably panned out for the better.'

Ten years passed, and my customer from Atlanta visited my shop unexpectedly. She had aged and was not the same woman I knew. She told me about losing her husband and gave me the opportunity of telling her about Aspie. No doubt, spending ten grand was her way of being empathetic and realising my communication changes.

A. What do you mean when you say, 'I don't say thank you.' I thanked those queers for giving you a repeat performance of what Joshua and his mates did back in LA.

R. Is this typical of Aspie's butting in with his innuendo of sarcastic remarks?

H. I think if he could have had his way with me, he would have preferred me to be ACDC. He was referring to a couple of nights later wondering why my Atlanta customer hadn't invited us back to dinner so he got us invited out by this gay couple, convincing me I should spend as much time as I could with customers who owned mansions and Rolls Royces as they were the customers worth doing anything for. I had an idea that I might be dessert. As far as I was concerned, I was being invited back to their house to inspect their wealth, so I was blind to what happened next. A repeat performance of what occurred so long ago in the gay home in LA, when I because their pet for the night. This time, there was no running away. We were somewhere I didn't recognise and in the middle of nowhere. There were large electronic gates, which we drove through, and what appeared to be a deep ravine winding its way through a valley and then we came to a stop, and I heard the words, 'Which of the two of us would you like to do first?'

R. Perhaps you have bisexual tendencies?

H. You know I jolly well don't!

A. Don't be daft! Those queers told me what that was like years ago.

H. My qualms with Aspie is how his opinion can change as quickly as unannounced as the wind. Back in the seventies and eighties, before the AIDS epidemic, half of all my customers were gay and most of these we got on really well with. But there were a minority he didn't like. They walked past my shop and every time they did, my heart missed a beat, not understanding why they were giving me a miss. It boiled down to the fact that Aspie's sensory system played havoc with some of the looks they exchanged with them.

The other challenge was the fear of rejection, thinking my business colleagues or friends might be appalled by my choice of sexual orientation. Most certainly, my father would have disowned any relationship with me whatsoever.

Sometimes, I used to think Aspie saw his relationship with me like he was playing a game of charades, getting me to try it on with every fucker of a personality and character just to see if I played out the part he had intended, then he would turn round and appear to be sympathetic to the cause and say to me, in his so-called derisory condescending loving way, 'You know why I do this? It's because emotionally I know you are weak, and I hope, by doing so, it will strengthen you so one day you will turn round and stop me dead in my tracks. Then I can be proud that you have thwarted my attack.'

What I was unaware of was that Aspie had no recognition of consequences whatsoever. He didn't see other people as neuro-typical (non-autistics) did. He had no chance of recognising facial expressions and even worse was that emotions and feelings were all amplified. What this meant was that he saw everyone as a loving invitation as though they would fall in love with him, male or female, it made no difference to him. Meanwhile, I had an impossible task to keep Aspie in Aspie mode from my parents, siblings, children and my friends; bite the bullet with his antics, and keep my marriage intact.

Chapter 25: Marriage Vows

H. I've already discussed the qualms of getting married, the responsibilities a husband has to make to his wife and vice versa. If I had known about Aspie's philandering personality, I would have decided the terms of our marriage had been broken and that we could have agreed to go our separate ways within a few years. However, hey ho, such is life. Our marriage continued, while Aspie coerced me to believe Jacky would have a change of heart and our love life would return soon. Sadly, as our marriage progressed and we worked our way through Aspie's transgressions, it was almost as though Jacky was prepared to overlook them while I was having a challenging time getting her to admit she had her own demon, although for most of my marriage I was unaware of Aspie's presence. In nearly all cases, her demon showered her with all its colours after we had put the children to bed and were having our own time, watching TV; that's when the mayhem was set lose. It was often after I had been travelling abroad. I put my arm around her shoulders and the fireworks began. She made it obvious that she begrudged me sitting so close and moved away, simultaneously hinting it was entirely her problem, which she needed the space to deal with.

It was inevitable that Aspie felt shunned. You can imagine, he had just returned home after the exchange of many bodily fluids. If her stupor lasted for more than a day, Aspie went love searching. His antics weren't just the cost of the woman of the night but also shrinks, who didn't come cheap and who I often visited twice a week. I know it all sounds very dramatic, but I had albeit only two options: to go along with Aspie's journey, or to take extreme actions and slit my throat!

R. You obviously didn't because you are still here.

H. Here in a physical form, but I debate whether I am mentally.

A. Shame, I always wanted to know what it was like to die!

H. I often mention my marriage as being a dangerous one, and I didn't know my comeuppance almost came to be.

R. I don't understand how that is possible?

H. Not trying to digress by blaming Aspie.

A. Thank you. I love it whenever my name is mentioned. Hmm, responsible for your death, love it! Music to my ears!

R. How did Aspie aspire to almost commit murder on you?

H. It was a mistaken belief that our move was to a quieter place because we came up against an unseen problem about where our children were going to let off steam. Tim relied on the gaming machines and betting shops in the High Street, while Sam appeared to be content. Ever since that embarrassing day with Tim and his friends, he did his best to cause me as much angst as he could. If he felt I found it rewarding when he pursued any hobby with interest and became proficient, he did his best to do the exact opposite. The worse example being when he was going through adolescence and he learnt Taekwondo. He asserted his position as king pin at school and it wasn't too long before he had a rather unsavoury following. We went through a series of moving schools to no avail since he refused to change his attitude. Jacky and I hoped our move out of the city suburbs to a country village would see him off on a safer course, but how wrong we were!

Once, I had returned form New York, worse for wear from the overnight flight and the two hundred mile drive. As I walked into the breakfast room, Aspie barged through both our boys as though they were nothing more than skittles being subjected to a bowling ball hitting their mark. It was inevitable that Jacky blamed me, never the children, and it became another cog in her wheel to divorce me! The trouble was that Aspie tried to hug both the boys without realising that their mates were there too. The mates could not stop laughing and our boys just resented me for showing affection again! That night, Aspie gave me the most absurd nightmare. He had me believe that I wouldn't be waking up in the morning because the likely chance was that I would be getting a visit from the boys' bogeyman. It was little wonder that our married relationship was so strained, as well as my inability to have a sensible conversation.

A. Hang on a moment. I think I am entitled to say a few words here. If you want my honest opinion, I reckon the boys' angst with you was assimilating why I embarrassed them in front of their friends. It, no doubt, didn't help you as the father figure being more abroad than at home. For me, that was more down to simple arithmetic. I saw the money rolling in, but meanwhile a tenuous relationship was developing between them and you were blind to it. The pressure, from you being away so often, meant you were not there offering Jacky your presence. With her distancing herself from you, something had occurred in her past that she was reluctant to share with you. Perhaps she didn't trust me and was not prepared to discuss it with us. This added angst and caused a salient approach in her relationship with you. I found her attitude too disconcerting, especially when I sensed her resorting to unwifely tactics. While I accepted to a point that any mother's main priority was her children, it was as though she was using this as an excuse for not giving you attention. You often accused me of being a double-edged sword, and I saw this in her too. I was protecting you and hoping that the emotional love she was denying you would return. I wished you could have been a little more understanding about those business trips you returned from and had attempted to give her a loving cuddle first, but you were always rebuffed! Now tell me how that made me feel! Is it no wonder I derived happiness from any skirt I found walking the streets, so to speak.

A boy experiencing puberty is suddenly no longer a child, but throughout his adolescent years has difficulties learning how to handle emotions he is unfamiliar with. As you rejected me, this resulted in Tim seeing revulsion in the part I played in your life. During his adolescence is when sexual maturity is acknowledged. Surely you remember the first time you wouldn't let your mother see you naked? Alas, when you returned from your trips away, it was the icing on the cake for him to blow his fuse. With that alteration, he needed to get rid of his frustrations so wreaking havoc on the streets was the only way he could safely keep away from you. What I had demonstrated on the one hand was genuine concern for your personal safety and a need to realise that as long as he had you as his father, he had to respect you regardless. That he chose to make his aggressive display in front of his mates was even more of a reason for him to be aware that you would always be the master of your household while he lived there and that was why I worried that he might try to take your life!

R. It seems to me that Aspie didn't consider his relationship from being that of a supportive father, from listening to his version of the facts, and that you feared attempting any peaceful compromise.

H. Why do our lives have to be so complex? When I look back to my relationship with my boys - the youngest one who appeared far more resilient and quieter in temperament to his older brother - it's little wonder that Jacky was never aware of my plight!

R. Didn't you tell me you had three children?

H. You mean our beautiful accident, a little miracle who came close to my rescue? I believe Aspie resented the thought of even more competition but I hoped Julie's birth was the answer to our already fragile marriage.

R. From a mother's perspective, raising three kids can be an exhausting experience and that can result in a temporary loss in the attraction of sexual stimulus.

H. From the onset, there was no denying my attraction to Jacky's curvaceous body. But she put up protocols on how our sexual liaison developed, and it was the ongoing sexual tension that Aspie objected to that had a significant negative impact throughout our marriage. From the first time we spent the night together, it was perfect timing. The lovemaking we enjoyed couldn't have been more pleasurable and I thought about it every day. But I sensed a problem for Aspie when Jacky first told me she had an allergy problem with all types of birth control and wanted me to use a condom. Unbeknown to me, Aspie condoned the use of any male contraception and we enjoyed lovemaking without any protection and took the risks, and simply hoped for the best!

R. Sounds a bit too convoluted for my way of thinking. Sexual intercourse is an agreeable lovemaking activity between two people, which should be sexually stimulating to both participating parties, respecting each other's sexual idiosyncrasies.

H. Well, it was, even though I had to deal with Aspie's objections so they didn't get noticed by Jacky. Please allow me to elaborate. One of the main traits Aspie suffered with, that I was unaware of until after my diagnosis, was his ability to fall in love with any woman. Jacky was no exception. However, she presented this different set of rules on only our second lovemaking night, saying that the first wonderful night was fine because she had her period and it was therefore safe. But for Aspie, he was suddenly no longer in control of these situations and his behaviour was unlike the average male, since he made the rules to appease himself and his brain was wired totally differently to a neuro-typical (non-autistic) person.

Not wanting to hurt Jacky's feelings, I wanted her to see me as a man she could receive much pleasure from so I forced myself to look past Aspie's angst.

R. It was obviously good that you were able to do that. Sometimes it is the case that we do things we don't want to do. It is the ups and downs of life. And after all, you two conceived three beautiful children.

H. Yes, you are right, but it didn't change the angst that Aspie pushed down my throat, so to speak. Jacky was the root cause of much unnecessary sexual stress because of her unwillingness to use any form of birth control. This invariably meant that our lovemaking was under sexual pressure.

R. As I have said, in my opinion, when a successful marriage works it is because both consenting partners are able to discuss the most intimate of sexual woes or desires and these are accepted and worked on, where necessary.

H. We did talk about it, but there was other stuff at play that created a hostile environment during our lovemaking that I always thought was a natural part of sexual intimacy.

R. I assume you are referring to masturbation and, by account if what you have said I am basing my supposition, that Jacky frowned on this pastime? Yet, we all do it, or have done so at some point in our lives.

H. Yes, Jacky condoned the idea of me having to masturbate while she was in bed with me. Her view was that she satisfied me with the sex she offered and felt it was an insult when I did, so I had to stop!

R. Did you?

H. I didn't want to disrespect her decision so yes, I did.

R. But Aspie didn't, I am guessing?

H. I have already said that Aspie lived in a world of his own where he was the only person he listened to, and that excluded me.

R. Would I be correct that throughout your entire marriage, Aspie's attitude towards sex created your sexual tension?

H. I think it was more a case of my lack of knowledge of his existence. I didn't know how he processed information until later in my life, let alone the rules of marriage, protocols and agreements between two consenting people. Also, his sensory wiring caused sensations to be amplified. The idea that he needed to talk about such things as sexual relations, lack of trust, the possibility of rejection or what was acceptable and what was not, were way beyond his comprehension. Because Aspie though Jacky and I were an item meant there were no boundaries to what was acceptable, while Jacky accused me of being disrespectful.

R. Seems so sad that you were not able to discuss what is so natural between two consenting people. We all have our individual hang-ups, just as you have explained yours and your relationship with the female genitalia. Did you never consider that she had a similar hang-up?

H. I think you have got me on this one. I blame it entirely on Aspie because not once did he consider that he was the one who had the hang-ups. He thought they were all hers.

R. What I think you are trying to tell me, is that because he wasn't getting what he wanted from Jacky and not being able to talk about it, he returned to his love searching ways while still married to her. I don't want to sound demeaning but if you ask me, you could have prevented Aspie from looking elsewhere. There are other ways, you know, and one that comes to mind was masturbating in the shower or bathroom instead?

H. While I fully agree, you know the adage: *Old habits die hard.*

A. I know Hartley blamed me but I think it was damn unfair that I had to take the blame for everything in his life that went ape shit. I only had him to learn from.

R. While I value what Aspie says, you have demonstrated that your marriage was not a healthy one.

H. I have to reluctantly agree with you, but I was in no position to object, had I the capabilities to do otherwise. The simple fact of the matter - although it may sound rather cynical - was that when I began courting Jacky, Aspie was mesmerised by the size of her mammary glands.

R. You will have to excuse me, but I have to interrupt you here. I think Aspie joined the conversation without you even being aware. I can only imagine this must have been typical of his style that created havoc in your life, and since we are talking about your marriage sent you on the road to ruin.

A. Can you blame me?

H. This was only the start of your problems, and I never expected Jacky to set such strict protocols so early in our marriage.

Chapter 26: The New York Affair

H. Two years after my youngest boy was born, common sense should have severed the marriage. We were not a well-matched couple, and given the rise in sexual tension, our marriage was heading towards meltdown mode. When I look back, I compare my life to a worker ant; where thousands of ants are aware of their role as the gatherers in their tribe. Although America was where my heart lay, I was constantly plagued by Aspie's contentious attitude as though he needed no one else in his life other than me. That my spouse and my children were of no importance and he resented anything that threatened his world and he would fight to the death if needs be.

In all the years Aspie had me commuting across the Atlantic, I calculated somewhere in the region of around a thousand round trips, of which three quarters went via New York. It was a period of my life when he was desperate for me to find a new wife, while I had hoped we could start a new family life moving to Paradise Valley, Arizona.

Her cousin had done exactly that and after I stayed with them, I was supposed to report back home what my experience was like. But, sadly, Aspie had decided to resort to tactics and they took an immediate dislike to me, which meant I never stayed there again. Their home was not unlike many of their neighbours, fitted out to the epitome of luxury. When I returned home, Jacky put me through the Spanish Inquisition and read the riot act. She told me that I was an unwelcome pig who should find a sty to visit next time!

It's only with hindsight that I was able to work out what went wrong. In front of Jacky, Aspie was defiant, trying to piece together snippets of transcripts of what was said behind his back. Having a relationship with feelings meant solely to describe his loutish behaviour while staying with her cousins. I sat in the middle of the fracas, unaware that a case was building up. One that would have longer lasting ramifications than the financial loss from losing my Atlanta customer; we were talking about the survival of my marriage.

Without wanting to appear sexist, you know how you women have a tendency to invite something completely out of context into the conversation as though you have a right to satisfy your whims, and we men don't?

Here I was being transported to the heart of Wales. It was an enjoyable family holiday, as far as I was concerned, until Aspie decided to vent his fury on Jacky. She once again was exasperated by his bad table manners and, without warning, I was overwhelmed with an emotional tidal wave that moments before looked like it would swat the life out of me. I saw a ruin in a field that I decided must be investigated, although part of the reason I was stopping the car was to defuse an untenable situation. Since we had left, Jacky had been going on about never going on another family holiday again, if it involved taking Aspie along.

Aspie was totally ignoring her rantings and ravings that I should get back into the car and continue our journey, otherwise she would continue without me and not return. Meanwhile, I was standing in the heart of the ruin, feeling very pleased I had moved away from the tension. For a while, I was left wondering whether she will return or am I really stranded. Thirty-five minutes later, to be precise, she returned; the volcano had simmered down. She and the children got out of the car and we took some family photos. It seems that all is forgotten; except it isn't really. The incident of that day was added to her erroneous catalogue that I would only get to see, sadly, when she had left the planet.

A. Only doing what I know I do so well, a job to be pleased with! Not wanting to digress, I think it would be apt timing to talk about you and the female passenger sitting in the adjacent seat on that flight to New York. She was the sexiest bit I had seen around you for a long time and she asked you to get up so she could sit in her seat. We are really going to have some fun on this flight to New York, is what I thought.

H. I had to remind to Aspie that I was a married man but before I could, he got me back on the guilt factor. He reminded me of the years I spent roaming the streets of London, telling Jacky that I was doing evening house clearances because during the day people worked, while in reality I was going from one massage parlour to another, looking for the bitches with the biggest tits for Aspie to get off with. What most men want to do with prostitutes, but Aspie convinced me that was dirty, and until now I was yet to have sex with any of them.

R. I can see how Aspie convoluted your thinking. You no longer had to concern yourself about family commitment or responsibilities. You could have allowed his kindred spirit to guide you in a direction that suited him the best, chatting up the lady sitting next to you.

H. I felt seriously embarrassed when Aspie came out with, 'Hello, darling, my name is Aspie. Do you want to join me in the mile high club?'

R. Did anything actually happen between you and the attractive passenger sitting next to you?

H. You mean once she'd seen Aspie staring down her cleavage? It was never quite that simple. I would like to say Aspie was getting quite fraught with me because my interest was not on him gesticulating in the direction of her tits, but on aspects outside of the plane window.

It all goes back to when I was very young. You may recall how I bamboozled the nursery school teacher who often found me sitting on my own, staring at the wall. I was looking at something my eyes couldn't see, although what I was looking at were myriad outlines, while repetitively counting every tile on the floor or wall. It reminds me of *Star Trek* and the character, Shapeshifter. I could not have known about him because he was yet to be invented, but in my world I was acting out his part. Most certainly when the mobile became invented, it became my spaceship.

What Aspie got me to do was count every floor on a skyscraper and if he thought I got the counting wrong, he'd get me to repeat the process until he decided I was correct. It didn't end with floors, it could be railway lines, and while sitting in my plane taxiing, I was counting all the windows along the fuselage of all the planes taxiing around us. If we were watching a Concorde land or take-off, it reminded me of the times I had flown that bird with its mighty roar and thrust of its giant Rolls Royce engines.

A. Boring! I'm more interesting about the thrusting we were going to be doing later.

H. I remember thinking how lucky I was to be able to afford Concorde. The first time I flew was the bargain of a lifetime, an extra two hundred and fifty smackers on top of the round-the-world flight, and it was during the last leg home. The second time was because of a funeral; I wanted to show my respects, even though that cost £1,600.

A. Herby, my boy, I think you have had your say. Whether you liked it or not, we were about to have some fun.

H. Conscious of Aspie's thoughts on what he wanted me to do, the first thing I checked was to see whether she was wearing a ring on her fourth finger. Luck was on my side; she wasn't. He said to her, 'Would you mind if I said you are the sexiest woman I have seen for a long time?'

She replied, 'Wow, I can't remember the last time a man said that to me, and especially on a flight to New York. Do you fly this route often? Are you married?'

'Why do you ask?'

'It seems to me a man who commutes to New York could never be married, let alone lead a family life. If so, how do you find the time to spend quality time with your family?'

'That's a very good question and, to be honest, sometimes I don't know. Perhaps I have youth on my side.'

'How many children do you have?'

'I have two boys, aged eight and six, and a daughter of one.'

'I still don't see how you have the time to travel and be very happy.'

At which point, Aspie whispers to me, 'Go on, now is your opportunity. Tell her you are not happy and you wish you could find a woman who really understands you.'

'Am I interrupting your train of thought because you seem to be a little distant?'

'No, I thinking how tough life can be trying to raise a family, spend quality time with my kids and get quality attention from my wife.'

'I don't suppose she has much time to do that. I hear being a mother is a full-time job.'

'You don't have children?'

'No, I chose to be a career woman and it became my way of life. I also do my fair share of travelling.'

'What do you do?'

'I'm a travel consultant.'

'What is that?'

'I arrange corporate travel for companies who use us to make all their employees' travel arrangements. I have been attending a travel conference in London. It's a wonderful city - it has so much more character than New York and is more peaceful too.'

She shed a silent tear and then continued, 'I'm sorry. Excuse me, I don't really get like this but it is rare when a handsome man asks me such personal questions. Especially a happily married one and it's the first time I have spent any time in your city and I feel a little embarrassed.'

Aspie spoke to me again. 'I think she likes you. You have it made, mate.'

'You are making me feel I have said something wrong. Now I am the one who is rather embarrassed.'

'Please don't. You haven't. On the contrary, it is I who touched on a raw nerve in my life and I was thinking how lucky you are to have your children and a wife.'

So I continued the conversation.

'Can we start again? My name is Hartley, what's yours?'

'Francesca.'

'Pleased to meet you. I hope you don't mind me kissing the back of your right hand.'

R. Given what I know about Aspie, I am surprised you felt comfortable kissing the back of her hand, let alone introducing yourself?

H. Then you don't really know him. He wanted to make me even more uncomfortable, perplexing me to feel guiltier than I was already feeling.

R. What I think you are trying to hint is, 'The axeman bringeth his axe down.'

H. Yes, that is exactly his play. He wanted to test how I would react.

She continued, 'Are English men all this romantic?'

'I only do this to women I find very attractive.'

'You have very big hands, do you mind if I feel them? I like caressing the hands of men with big hands! If only you weren't married.'

'I am sorry.'

'No, it's me who should be sorry. I've said something out of place. Have I put you in an embarrassing spot?'

'To be honest, I never thought I would be having the type of conversation we are having when I sat down on this flight. Talking about my marriage is not normally something I discuss with a stranger, even one who has such attractive eyes.'

'Is what you are saying is that if you weren't married, you might consider what is happening between us is love at first sight?'

'That's a very hypothetical question. Perhaps two people who have found common interest in each other?'

'My fantasy is that our conversation will develop into something more.'

It was here I became a bit coy. Aspie wanted me to commit to her, but I needed the inner strength to hold back.

R. But you couldn't, since Aspie at times had a very strong influence over you.

H. You are becoming far more insightful into my life affairs. I wanted to say to Francesca, 'Look, I am aware I am attracted to you, but because I am happily married, there is no chance of that happening.' But I knew I couldn't because I would be lying to myself. Her questions and Aspie's interruptions made me feel so very alone. I was so upset with Jacky. Many times I had said to her how nice it would be if we could go away that weekend, like her brother and his wife do. He and his wife found time for each other, but Jacky always had some convoluted excuse as to why she couldn't leave the kids. Even on a business trip, she came up with the same story.

R. You mean Aspie's mannerisms were driving a wedge between the two of you?

H. Yes, you got it, here I am repeating myself. Jacky wanted to come away with me on the condition that I left Aspie at home. It was difficult enough when either of our boys went into a temper tantrum when they weren't getting their way, but not in her wildest dreams did she ever expect such embarrassing behaviour from her husband.

She thought she'd married a husband fit enough to be a father but instead she found out that she'd married two people; one kind, considerate and well-mannered, and the other where embarrassing appears to be his second nature.

Anyway, back to Francesca. While Aspie didn't get his oats during that flight, he ensured I was being seduced. It was only after the plane had landed that Francesca suggested we share a taxi since her apartment was on the way into the city. When it stopped, she said what Aspie was waiting to hear.

'Would you like to join me in the shower?'

Meanwhile, I knew I should be checking in at my hotel because Jacky would be expecting a call from me.

R. But temptation was too strong for you?

A. Are you a fucking idiot? She'd invited you in for a fuck, and you were thinking of turning her away?

We went inside, and she said to me, 'I'm going to put on some fresh clothes.'

I could see through the gap of her bedroom door that she was only wearing a towel and bra. Look those amazing pair of tits! They are just up my street!

H. Just my luck I am lumbered with a big tit pervert.

A. What do you mean? It is me who brought you so much sexual satisfaction. You would have got very frustrated if you didn't have me in your life.

H. Why is it you always have to have an answer for every one of my questions?

Okay, I concede on this one. Yes, I had a dull marriage so getting me romping around extramarital sexual encounters, was it to appease you, or me?

Francesca returned and said, 'There's a nice shower waiting for you and fresh towels on my bed.'

I came up with this line! 'Francesca, since it was you who invited me into your home, and it was you who offered me a shower, I have to confess something. I have a disability and I can't wash my back.'

'I know this sounds a bit ridiculous, but wow! I can't believe the size of it! It's been a long time since I have had such a large cock rubbing up against me. Am I going to see how well it's going to perform?'

A. I have to tell you one thing. I have had sex in all sorts of places but never up against the gas stove.

'Am I presuming correctly that you would like to have a relationship with me and we are going to go through all of the positions in the Kama Sutra?'

'I'm game if you are?'

H. I had no conception my dull life was no longer dead. I hadn't the slightest inkling that Aspie had begun his biggest retaliation my life had seen up till now.

'Why don't you spend the rest of your stay in my apartment?'

'I would like to, but I have a problem.'

'I hope you won't mind but there is one thing I have to say to you. I never in my wildest dreams imagined I would be having a relationship with a toy boy.'

A. Yes, and I didn't imagine I was beginning an affair with a woman who was old enough to be my mother.

H. Just typical of the remarks I expected Aspie to make. I gasped in amazement and thought, 'That's it.' She'd be showing me the front door - from the expression on her face - it belied her astonishment. Whenever he did that to me, I invariably stepped in and said, 'Only joking!'

'I hope you are joking. I'm only eight years older than you and I don't know a place on the planet where mothers have babies that young.'

H. Two nights later, Aspie was over the moon. He had already convinced Jacky that he'd had a great buying experience, would be making at least £20,000, and could make an extra ten by staying an extra few more days. Although I wasn't lying about the profit, Aspie coerced me into spending as many sinful days as he could get away with every time we commuted to New York. He might have had an insatiable appetite, but I was wearing thin the cumulative effects of too much sex and jet lag.

Chapter 27: Family Man

H. In no time at all, my relationship with Francesca was causing much havoc, while for Aspie it was deriving the most sordid pleasure.

R. I hope you don't mind me saying, but how is it possible for you to say to me that it was only Aspie who was deriving pleasure, when you are the physical person? You are the family man who has responsibilities. Your wife, on the other hand, has mothered your children. Giving birth is no simple process. As much as it is nature's most wonderful gift - as a mother who knows - it can be equally mentally traumatising, let alone exhausting. As a father to your children, and a husband to your wife, you should be able to respect her decision. If she cannot offer you sexual intercourse, there was probably a valid reason. But what happened to you, the Aspie part of your brain decided it must have sexual relief and, hey presto, you are seduced on a flight to New York. You men are full of some of the feeblest excuses on the planet. Except I am aware, from what you are telling me, that Jacky had her own version of you that she was in denial of. So, I will let you off from the critique of your lifestyle.

H. Perhaps I should say it was Sod's Law my meeting her.

R. Or you could put it down to fate, yes?

H. I wonder what percentage of men can stand by their wives and fulfil their marital obligations? I would say only a remarkably low percentage. Especially as I had given it nearly two years without intercourse, an achievement, wouldn't you say? Even Jacky asked me how I lasted that long.

R. Now you are showing a little bit of your nativity. Anyway, at least your story is getting a little more interesting; perhaps it was meant to be. You meet Francesca and you realised you're not suited to being a family man after all, and a little bit of nookie on the side can't do you any harm. But as time marches on, Aspie coerced you to believe you would be better off jacking it in with Jacky and focusing your attention solely on Francesca. This created a dilemma for you, as to how Aspie will be about you being put up in front of a firing squad, whatever your decision was. So, you give your marriage another chance and he will carry on with his ill ways. You tell Jacky you have fallen in love with another woman and you give yourself a predicament about what to do about your responsibilities to your children.

H. You are correct about Aspie. He found a new fuck partner and couldn't remember when sex was so good. Meanwhile, to convince Jacky I paid for my hotel duration, just in case she tried some sneaky going through my receipts, I got the hotel reception to divert my calls to a carefully prepared answering machine.

I suppose it appears to you that I'm being disrespectful by commuting to New York, but my addictions to flying bore no relation to Aspie's interest in Francesca.

You just made a number of comments about my marriage vows. What made me feel so sad was that we couldn't make things work out. How was I to know that Aspie was a sex maniac?

A. That's me, my name being mentioned?

H. It's almost as though he sequenced me to wait for so long to lose my virginity, and then attracted a wife who was not on his wavelength, sexually speaking.

R. You have mentioned various aspects of your sexual incompatibility but it appears to me that it was more a case of being delicately flawed to satisfy her demands. Aspie made certain there would be no solution for you. From my perspective,

I see marriage as a partnership of commitment. This means a mutual learning about each other intimately is part of the arrangement that is satisfied by trust alone. How did you feel when she wasn't giving you everything you wanted sexually, but expected you to satisfy her demands and remain together, just to have kids?

H. I respected her wishes, but I believe part of our sexual tension originated from not wanting to give Aspie oral sex. I think among my blindness was my unawareness to his manipulation of my mind. He was a total control freak who mastered the art of intimidation, by masterly conceiving his mischievous acts without my knowledge with sole role to fuck-up the life of his master.

Francesca said to me, 'I am very curious about something else you said. That you are happily married. Why are you spending so much time with me?'

'I can't remember saying that. Anyway, you were the one who invited me to have sex with you.'

'That is true, but it doesn't answer my question. Don't you see the point I am making? Wouldn't it be better to tell me the truth, that the reason you are seeing me is that I can offer you something your wife can't?'

A. Cat cut your tongue. Talk about me manipulating you, and now I see she has really got you where she wants you to be!

'Francesca, something I don't understand is how you come into my life and continually fuck it up, just like you are doing right now. Francesca, you promise you are not going to laugh at me?'

'I promise.'

It's the idea of cunnilingus. It's not just about every time I go down on a woman's fanny, their vaginal hairs get stuck in the back of my throat and I start gagging. I see the ghoulish face of the Scoutmaster who abruptly appears as if out of nowhere, staring at me abhorrently and shouting out so insanely loudly. I try to cover my ears, only to realise the voices are coming from the inside of my head. Have you any conceivable idea? Hearing the words, 'You fucking lunatic, are you fucking out of your fucking mind? You want me to fuck the shit out of you because you have broken your promise to me?'

That's the real reason why I paid so many visits to therapists. You have no idea how much his tortuous taunting cut me up, and I had to put up with his thoughts whenever I went down on any woman. I know what I am saying to you spells that this guy needed locking up in a lunatic asylum. But no quack of the mind, no matter what fucking therapy they have tried, including hypnosis, has quashed the back queue of the most evil thoughts. It's as though the paedophile succeeded in brainwashing me into believing that God conjured up the idea for a woman's fanny from the vilest of unearthly creatures.

What can I say? I do what I do because I love taunting Hartley. It's just that I was addicted to saying, 'I love you, I love you, I love you, Hartley.' Can't help it. You must admit, I had an unquenchable talent, to ensure his affair was to be fucked up. I fucked him when he was in New York, and I fucked him when he was at home, and I fucked him when he was in public places, trying to hide his relationship with Francesca.

Francesca said to me, 'You must have noticed I have been getting a bit pissed off with you mentioning your wife's name while in my company. You carry on in this manner if you want me to leave you.'

'You are aware you are making it very uncomfortable for me. I am not married to you, I have a wife and children, and I have responsibilities to them.'

'I am going to ask you again. Why are you with me?'

'Because you are a good fuck!'

'I don't know how to put it, but I'm not going to be able to change you, am I? So, sorry, but I think our relationship is not going to work out. We will have a clean break, you go back to Jacky, and I will get over you in time. Look, I am sorry, it's hard work for me to sustain our relationship when I hear you talk about feeling guilty, missing your kids, or accidentally mention your children's or Jacky's names.'

You couldn't let her treat you like this. If I were you, I would have turned around, picked up your bags and slammed the door shut.

H. It frustrated me when Aspie played me, got into my mind and before I knew it, I had slammed the door. He knew there was a safe haven for him to descend into, our hotel room that I had paid for just in case of difficult days.

R. Don't tell me what I was thinking.

H. Yes, it was back to Hendon Lane, except we were in New York and I've being coerced again to being up late watching the adult channels. Aspie learnt about a great swingers' club called Caligula. We found ourselves at a news stand that was home to an underground world, where every imaginable bit of porn and sex is available at a price. Aspie got it in his head that Francesca needed to be taught a lesson never to forget and told me to tell her that next time we visit New York, we wouldn't be paying her a visit, instead saying we have business priorities to attend to.

Actually part of the lure of New York was the fast-paced restless atmosphere. It's a city to walk around if the weather allows. For Aspie, it was another chance of losing himself in his world while walking hundreds of blocks, to which our destination antique shops were on route. When I think about it, for Aspie it was all about cramming the most out of any one trip. No thought about quality, it was all about quantity. He didn't like competition. I'm not talking about from my competitors, it could be anyone, strangers. As you know, we flew excessively. Often, we sat next to salespeople who flew to work and they could take multiple flights during the course of their working week. Aspie decided he had a need to outdo them. I counted during one crazy week, of hopping from one city to another, an unbelievable thirty-two internal flights.

R. Something I don't understand that you might be able to educate me about. Surely America has fewer antiques, compared to Europe? They are a young country. Are you trying to tell me there was interest in American antiques and this is what you profited from? I thought too that all you antique dealers made your money out of the many gullible American tourists who visited you?

H. The second of your questions is the easier to answer. In a nutshell, there's a name we dealers have for the majority of tourists, be them American or anyone else. TWs, short for time-wasters.

To answer your first question requires more of an explanation. We found ourselves in the era when the railroad phenomena was overtaking America. Until the beginning of the twentieth century, Britain was seen by America as the world powerhouse and America decided to take its place. Americans, with their unlimited wealth, began taking back what they decided they deserved, interrupted by two world wars. This greed of theirs resumed towards buying everything antique in sight, relentlessly every genre within the field of antiques and art. I was one of a handful of British, European and Japanese dealers who saw an opportunity using our specialist knowledge to buy bargains, sometimes at a fraction of the real value. While Americans cultivated mammoth stocks of every genre in the field of antiques, few of them had our experience, let alone specialisms. Often prices asked were based on their decorative value. We picked out the rarities and the more fashionable using our more extensive knowledge.

By the beginning of the eighties, weekly antique shows raged in every major city in every state. This didn't mean I was successful at every one of them. Among the more boring aspect of my business was visiting the countless antique malls that began popping up everywhere. Here, anything - including the kitchen sink - was on offer. I remember visiting an antiques show in Philadelphia, paying $6 to get in. On our way out, we were asked if we bought anything. It was Aspie who answered. 'Yes, sir, really successful. The ticket to get us in.'

Anyway, getting back to my relationship with Francesca and Aspie's addiction to visiting whores reminded me of the movie *Crank* starring Jason Statham. He played a person who had been injected with a drug that would kill him if he is forced to slow down. Public sex acts became the norm for him. This is typically what Aspie did to me; reached down into the deepest depths of my mind with an imaginary force, just like comparing the Persian Army invading the Greeks in the movie *300*.

That is why I found it so challenging to do anything that required focus unless he was not Mr Ants in the Pants. During this part of my life, Aspie was eager to find out what part he played in my life. During those periods of our life together, he had me cooing with every conceivable therapist, psychotherapists, psychologists and counsellors. What did all of these visits do for me? Nothing, just made my life more miserable. Aspie was told he was a figment of my imagination. Of course, this was before more of the population was to be diagnosed Aspie's autism - the plague of the mind - that medical science had little knowledge of. I had to somehow earn enough money for Aspie's philandering and then pay all the doctors of the mind to tell me that he didn't exist. Hallucinations causing anxieties caused by the excessiveness endured from too fast a life. While in my relationship with Francesca, I often wondered - with Aspie and all his antics - whether a day would come when he really got out of control and I would be put away into a lunatic asylum and the key thrown away. The bottom line was Aspie could produce any number of angsts as quickly as a magician takes a rabbit out of a hat.

However, fate came to my rescue. Recession dominated the western world; the value of the pound plummeted almost to a par with the dollar; and I catapulted from being an obsessive commuter to almost becoming a hermit in comparison.

R. So this meant that Francesca began thinking there was no point in her affair with you continuing?

H. Not exactly, it was more a change of tactics. You see, she didn't want to lose me. To her, I was her gift horse. She never married;

told me she was too old to have children and found few men interested her. During the next six months, I only got to see her a couple of times. This was a very stressful period for me because Aspie wanted both the cake and to eat it. He wanted to continue visiting his whores, put up with me visiting Francesca, and supporting Jacky and our children. You see, he didn't really care about me. He only had his interests at heart.

I wish I could have had the strength to say to Jacky, 'Things aren't working out for us. You have your issues and have chosen to show no interest whatsoever in your marital duties to your husband.' It was as though we were strangers. 'You might be a wonderful mother but a poor excuse as a wife. I have met a lady in New York who I have fallen in love with.'

Chapter 28: Aspie's Antics

H. I arrived home from one trip, after my affair with Francesca was finished and Tim was about five and Sam was two, when Jacky was recovered from the birthing operation. She said to me, 'Come on, darling, we've been together this long. What do you think I am going to do, bite your head off? All I want you to do is tell me you have been seeing a woman behind my back, since I doubt many husbands can go without sex for two years.'

One of Aspie's acumens was the inability to lie. It was a feature of his I often found highly embarrassing because I was unable to counteract against it. He caused me to grimace, often feeling the fear of what was coming, as though my head was on a chopping board and I was praying the axe would miss its mark. Meanwhile, my expression became even more contorted, as though my involuntary spasm was exaggerating a lie.

R. Did she find out about your affair? By all accounts, I would guess she realised she'd neglected you, felt very guilty, blamed her actions on you getting sex elsewhere, and then wanted to make it up to you. The truth of the matter is, she had her own demon to contend with and desperately needed you to become her loving husband again!

H. Perhaps you are right. The toughest memory I remember takes me back to a few months before she took her life. I looked into her eyes and what I saw scared me. I didn't have anything that I could offer her as respite. Then Aspie interrupted my focus and reminded me she was not the amazingly beautiful woman I once knew. Now her beauty had been replaced with pity; she was an ashen empty shell compared to how she looked on our wedding day. It was an emotion he was unable to handle and almost before you could say, 'Jack Robinson,' we were driving to the airport and taking the next flight out to Los Angeles.

R. It appears to me you were very wrapped up in your personal life, that your travels were more about soul searching than anything else.

H. As I have mentioned to you, my love for Phoenix, Arizona. I even rented a home there in my late teens. I think the problem Aspie feared was settling down.

R. Settling down?

H. Sometimes, I believe he was misguided. There was more going wrong for him than met the eye. If he could have broken away from Jacky, Francesca might have made a better match. She gave him what he lusted after, constant attention. It is something I couldn't have offered him. My time was split between business and a family life, and he was somewhere in-between. Ideally, he was looking for a woman who could give him one hundred per cent attention. But even this would not have been enough because he would have realised once he had his lover's devoted attention that I would be happy and content. These are qualities he cannot afford to have a relationship with.

I think the truth was Aspie's lack of moral strength. He knew I would be happy with Francesca and live happily ever after; but he could never contemplate losing his control over me. It was like living in a never-ending cycle, one fucked-up relationship after another, and my marriage being the granddaddy of them all!

R. You just mentioned LA?

H. Trans World Airlines was my preferred airline because they offered upgrade to business class when the full economy was paid. It was expensive, but cheap for the business class seat, although on board service were the same as cattle class.

Southwest offered a remarkable one-way $29 to Phoenix, which was good value for me and for Aspie, who enjoyed staring at the staff's legs in the micro shorts that was part of their uniform. Going to Los Angeles also meant being seen with a celebrity because we once did business with Sidney Poitier's wife and Aspie lusted after her money.

A. You know I always want to walk with the best!

H. When you are sharing your life with an Aspie, it is prudent to be aware of any misfortune you can pre-empt. All Aspie's are akin to wizards performing magic tricks that even magicians daren't perform.

On another occasion, I sold to Sidney Poitier's wife six Chinese export plates each illustrating a Negro. Delivery was to a store in Melrose Place, LA, where around the corner there were other competitors who sold to the rich and famous regularly. They marked up their purchases by a thousand per cent, but there was a downside. The reason stock was marked up so high was because customers were liable to change their mind. But this high mark-up could work in our favour too. When it sat too long in their stock, they down priced by extraordinary percentages. One item I bought retailed for $25,000, was sold to us for $5,000, and we resold it for $20,000.

During this period of my life, while I was continuing purchasing antiques, Aspie had another idea. You could say he had an ulterior motive. It was a photo in the window of the Ultimate Dating Club, which he made me pay two hundred bucks to become a member.

R. I think I am getting more of an understanding that Aspie was really a big thorn in your backside whose only interest was finding a whore who he could marry. Although I have heard other stories of men who have found their loving life partner this way, it seems to me this was the last thing on Aspie's mind.

H. Anyway, the following day after arriving in Phoenix, we learn of a great antique collection in Albuquerque. The last time I got a call from my contact in Phoenix earned me fifty grand. However, we also had to attend an important auction the day after the following day in Chester, North Wales. In theory, Aspie decided it was doable. We went to our meeting in Spokane at 2am, made our purchases, connected to a flight to San Francisco and took the red-eye to London that afternoon.

My complaint with Aspie was not allowing room for delays or any consideration of my physical health; driving one hundred and eighty miles without a nap. Fortunately, common sense got the better of him, or so I thought, but I knew too there was always an ulterior motive to his decision-making.

This time round, we were on a night flight to Albuquerque, barely an hour away, but we didn't arrive until midnight. It was nothing new and Aspie made a beeline for the *Yellow Pages*, looking for the whorehouses. He found twenty-four of them along Two Mile Road, each with a neon-lit sign overlooking a red door within a wooden framed building. Ringing the doorbell of the first one, we were greeted by the madam who showed us into her lounge and invited the wannabes for Aspie to take an interest in.

'Is there any girl who takes your fancy?' she said.

But Aspie was not happy. 'I'm looking for a girl with bigger breasts.'

'You had better come back at 4am. I have what you desire.'

Now I had a problem with 4am because it required Mr Ants in his Pants to wait around twiddling his thumbs. Of course, he decided he was better off checking the other whorehouses. We found one with a swimming pool and decided that was fun. You have to remember, I'm past exhaustion but Aspie took no prisoners, just victims.

I got a massage from an angel blessed by God. She had a perfect body with the melons made to Aspie's specifications. It was love at first sight and he desperately wanted to make her my wife. What remained of the night was spent at a local luxury resort, a quick wake-up dip in the morning, followed by an hour's drive to Santa Fe where we bought some very profitable antiques, certainly enough to buy a ring for Aspie's new love interest, except when we returned the following evening, she wasn't there. Aspie was livid. He felt let down. We were supposed to be on a flight to London from Los Angeles.

At about this point in our lives together, we had undergone immense trauma; gallivanting to make my business work, while Aspie searched every brothel he could for wife material. It was a year after Jacky had taken her life and I had endured two six-month long relationships that went nowhere and found myself living temporarily at my parents; home and attending a Jewish Support Group. We met other men and women who had undergone damaging divorces, marriages and relationships, some I felt were worse than ours. Once a month, the group psychiatrist sat in the centre of a circle and each of us had to have the courage to say our name and something unusual about ourselves. I talked about an unusual vegetarian indulgence I had enjoyed, my grandmother's chopped liver; irrespective of the diet I was on, I wouldn't stop eating in the memory of the love she brought me; and the flight to New York on Yom Kippur when I thought the plane was going to crash and God was paying me back for my crimes.

After several months of going every week, Aspie fell in love with a new woman and we agreed to meet up the following week to walks her dogs in the local woods. She was very inquisitive and Aspie believed she was happy to listen to his worst nightmares. He shared the most intimate but also the most morbid of his emotional traumas, being the paedophile grooming episode. As we walked further into the wood, it was though I had finally found a woman who was really interested in listening to my nightmares. Aspie continued to go deeper into my no-go zone. You have to realise, I had told no one, not my parents or siblings, or the hundreds of psychotherapists, and I'm feeling terribly ashamed. I didn't want to go that deep; it was too much for me to bear, emotionally. But Aspie is in love, he is beyond trust, and his OCD took over. I told her how Aspie manifested the paedophile into my head and how he was no longer in control of my thoughts and that there would be ample opportunity to emulate what he enjoyed doing most.

Without warning, I was myself drowning in the deepest of sexually intrusive thoughts. I thought I was standing there completely naked and getting horrified stares. Somehow, in my mind I had become not only the paedophile, but also a sex abuser. I had horrifying thoughts at night about young girls and finding myself in their bedrooms, unaware of how I had got there. As my anxieties died down, I believed I had been given a reprieve. However, I knew these awful thoughts could return at any time. There were the nights when I believed I was being wholly consumed by spontaneous combustion and I'd wake soaked by sweat with sweaty bed sheets. It was no wonder I felt like I was a mental retard!

Anyway, back to our walk in the woods, because she listened to me with compassionate ears. But again, this was Aspie playing with my sensory wiring. If only I could have held back and not divulged so much about my terrifying anxiety attacks. It was her text the following day that I didn't want to read.

'You are a brave man for sharing Aspie with me. Sadly though I have four children and I can't take the risk!'

Now Aspie was deeply hurt and convinced me I was so much better off paying for sex than the anguish of a relationship, and we went back to Chicago for an antiques show.

R. For more sex?

H. Well, listen to this. I was walking to my intended gate when Aspie started chatting to this woman and the next moment I find myself flying to Phoenix.

R. Without a ticket?

H. It was at a time when I could buy the ticket on the flight.

R. Wow, that was a bit of luck.

H. Not really. By the time we landed, I had learnt she was gay. You see, Aspie was not always good at recognising facial expressions. She smiled, he smiled, and he decided they are an item. My only consolation was earning £20,000 from an antique shop.

R. Surely that is a worthy consolation? Nevertheless, you were blind to the genre of women you were addictively attracted to because you each had similar needs.

H. Yes, you are correct again. I was a needy man then, who was successfully coerced into believing this by Aspie, who took me away from what I was focusing on.

R. Your family!

H. I think I would be correct in saying that Aspie wasn't good at dealing with life's complications. He made poor progress where recognition of normal cognitive behaviour or communication was concerned.

Our flight back to London was like one of many. I was in tears repeating to myself, 'Why do I have to endure Aspie in my life?'

For me, it was an unanswerable question. No words were forthcoming no matter how often I repeated the question. My angst with Aspie resided on his inability to filter out memories that reminded me of having a noose around my neck with a trapdoor beneath me.

The year 2000 might, for many people, have marked the most auspicious year of their lives. For Jacky, it became one of her worst nightmares and may have marked her decision that, unless someone came to her rescue, she was beyond hope. She was watching a documentary about a new psychological condition that caused men to lack characteristics of being ideal husbands because they lacked empathy, and had limited social manners. I was playing with the kids at the time and she came rushing to me and said, 'You should be watching this documentary because it is all about you!' I think she must have thought, 'Oh my God, who am I married to? How am I going to get out? What hope is there left for me?'

The following year, she met James, a psychopath. He'd had a string of women who had all died on him. She ended the relationship two years later, and during the following year made three attempts on her life. About a year later, I dropped in to see my parents and my mother told me about their new neighbours, who had two boys with Asperger's Syndrome. I turned to her and asked, 'Do I have Asperger's Syndrome?'

She told me more about my childhood and the five years I spent seeing a child psychiatrist. Suddenly, Aspie decided he had to ask the new neighbour about her sons' diagnoses. He announced himself as though he was a most important person who could benefit and he hoped she could tell him everything about child Aspies, which he had been too afraid to ask previously.

R. My dear Hartley, I still have difficulty recognising you being as two completely diverse personalities.

H. It is deeply and psychologically complex. And the ultimate for me was my near-death experience when I attempted to cut my brain in half to understand what part Aspie was playing in my life.

Let's, for argument sake, say his capabilities compare to Leonardo da Vinci, Jim Thorpe, Yuri Gagarin and Stephen Hawking. Why these four minds? Leonardo da Vinci was considered one of the greatest minds of all time. Jim Thorpe was the greatest athlete of the twentieth century. Yuri Gagarin, you've got to be very crazy to risk your life to be the first man in space, and Stephen Hawking takes us to the farthest reaches of the universe. Try to appreciate that Aspie lived in a labyrinthine world and needed to explore Pandora's Box. He wanted to push the boundaries of everything that can physically exist. I was the one who had to make head or tails of the seemingly doable Herculaneum challenges Aspie presented me with.

I personally believe related symptoms of ADHD and OCD were nothing more than his mind running out of ideas and becoming perplexedly confused. It was like a fuse that had too much electricity moving through its circuits at any one time before it explodes. This is what I believe ADHD, OCD or any other related label is. The product is sound but when one or more symptoms are added to it, it cannot hold itself in place. It is as though people who are labelled as such swing their fishing rod and the line hits its desired mark. Aspie took the bait and I was the one hung out to dry. Looking back at my childhood, I was young and innocent, but blind to a certain type of individual who got off delivering pain to their victims. I had one friend who I had grown up with, unaware he was going to turn out to be a real Schadenfreude and nearly kill me.

He put me too close to comfort at the entrance of the tunnel of death in a submerged car accident. He was driving my car back from the airport one night when there was black ice on the roads. He lost control as the car hit a low wall and rolled over a number of times and down an embankment. We hit the water upside down and were quickly submerged into a icy river. The force of impact made the boot open and I felt the rush of ice-cold water. We were upside down and strapped in by our seat belts. Neither the window nor the door would open. My face was squirmed against the window, sensing the last breaths of air leaving my lungs and finality, and thinking Aspie had finally got what he wanted; to experience death.

Suddenly, I heard in my head the words of my scuba diving instructor: 'Never panic in an emergency.' People have asked me how I got out, but I somehow managed to open the door slightly and squeeze out, and my friend followed me.

Miraculously, our injuries were barely scratches, albeit we were extremely cold and soaked. Luckily for us, it had not been a raging river and the car was only partially submerged. Amazingly, when we returned the following morning, the engine was still running and our stock of china was found floating down the river, more or less still intact! However, the following day, I learnt that my friend was not insured to drive my car and I had to endure humiliation from the police by pretending to be the driver.

R. What do you think went wrong in your friend's life?

H. I knew his wife and family, although we were not close friends. To be honest with you, with all of the shenanigans in his life, who knows what went on under the sheets. At the beginning of my friend's relationship, he had pots of money and a loving family. How he developed into a Schadenfreude, I don't know.

R. You can't hold yourself responsible for your friend's inadequacies.

H. I think, like Aspie, he was born from a different planet. Aspie always took control of my focus and thoughts. I only learnt about the consequences after they had occurred, and only on the odd occasion was I lucky enough to be aware of his coercing and stabilise the symptoms.

R. Can you be more specific and give me some examples of his obsessive nature?

H. I'm aware that many people play pointless computer games that perhaps replace boredom, which I believe to this day were part of Aspie's problem. He was not capable of knowing what to do with the feeling, and whatever he focused on replaced the boredom. It could have been a partial reason he was addicted to prostitutes. Some computer games attached themselves to the sensory wiring in his brain and he was unable to switch it off or move away out of the danger. Pinball was the first game he fell for, imagining a force he had to conquer at all costs. I was the ball catapulted around a field of obstacles he had to navigate. Getting him to leave it is was as challenging as taking a doll or teddy bear away from a child who is likely to demonstrate vocally to stay in the game. He had the perfect solution to ensure he played relentlessly, by telling me playing these games was in my interest because they would enhance his cognitive skills. But these games left me feeling he was the Devil in disguise in my life.

A. I like the idea of being the Devil.

H. Two criteria occupied Aspie's mind; money and sex. Money was necessary to travel, and sex was for his happiness, which my antique dealing paid for.

After Jacky died, I discovered her catalogue of events and incidents, which she had seen in Aspie and didn't like.

One, which stands out like a sore thumb, was when we were eight years into our marriage and the city of my dreams was looming close to becoming a reality. A few months after my relationship with Francesca had ended, I was planned the holiday of our married life that I hoped would guarantee our future. A new lease to a doomed marriage, although unknowingly it was the doomed part.

Our destination was Phoenix and we were flying Trans World Atlantic on accumulated air miles in first class. I was with Jacky, my two boys, their little sister and my mother-in-law.

We arrived in Miami and took the kids to play in the pool, where they were having a water fight. A waiter asked me to go to reception. Unbeknown to me, Aspie was jealous that he had not thought of this diversion from family harmony and he decided to act in my worse interests. Several hours later, her mother made an apt comment: 'Your husband must have been kidnapped by some big bosomed blonde.'

It was lunchtime and Jacky decided to go back to the room but there was no husband there, and the reality of kidnap seemed real. However, when I returned, I hoped the grin on my face would convince Jacky and her mother that I had exciting news. But instead, I got., 'Where the fuck did you get to? You had us so worried, we called the police. You could have had the decency to come back and explain what you wanted to do, at least given us an opportunity for discussion.'

R. From what I am learning about Aspie, I imagine he returned as though he had done nothing out of the ordinary.

H. Jacky instigated immediate divorce proceedings. Aspie had not even left a note in our room or had the slightest awareness of the scare he caused because we had flown to New York to buy a collection of Meissen.

R. I think I would have wanted to divorce you too. I can't think of any wife who would want to remain with a lunatic of a husband who had lost sight of his family responsibilities.

H. You already have heard me discuss a volcano. After the first eruption, and the eventual simmering down, she asked me how much profit I had made and when I said £25,000, she claimed it as hers!

I was making so much money in those days that £25,000 was

under a month's work and the following month I did a deal that made that look inconsequential in comparison. Nevertheless, what occurred in Miami had consequences I would pay dearly for later.

R. It sounds like you brought Jacky's mother along to help look after the kids and bring some peace of mind?

H. Isn't that why mother-in-laws are for? Good at diffusing situations? Actually, so early on in my marriage, I learnt about Jacky's volcanic mouth when things didn't go her way. She rarely thought things through. The kids saw it as a way they could extract whatever they wanted from her. It drove Aspie to despair; we preferred peace and quiet, rather than listening to her constant gibberish.

R. I am getting more of a sense of the part Aspie played in your life. Incalculable manipulation exerting such a very strong hold over your will, leaving you completely incapacitated to do otherwise.

H. I only wish I could have found a miraculous method to quell his irresponsible lust for attention seeking; be tolerant towards consequences; and hopefully value the art of making money to save, instead of spending it all on his desires.

Often, my mother-in-law was on my side. But so often I was tortured by the memory of her amazing eyes, while Aspie tormented me saying it was a matter of only time before my marriage was over. Although, a real callous truth and emotionally painful, I hoped if God existed he would have shown me a way to ditch Aspie and keep Jacky with mutual and eternal love. But that was not to be.

In 1989, eight years after our marriage started, Aspie delivered the Krakatoa of financial blows, losing me a cool two hundred grand. The bargain of a lifetime blown away faster than a dying flower shreds a petal. We were in Dublin, a city I enjoyed, particularly the annual antiques fair and the upmarket dinner that followed. Aspie lusted to be seen amongst the Irish aristocracy. The majority of Irish dealers only tolerated us English, but Aspie was blind to all that.

Chapter 29: The Nabeshima Dish

R. Before you tell me about the calamity in this stage of your life, would you mind painting a picture of what life was like in the world of antiques?

H. After I outgrew my first premises at Pierrepont Row, I moved to Camden Passage, where I was selling Chinese and Japanese works of art and European and English ceramics. My neighbours consisted of a selection of dealers selling English furniture, decorative and general antiques, Oriental works of art, decorative arts, silver, jewellery, military, music boxes, and vintage clothing. The majority of my peers I got on well with, but there were a handful who could not take Aspie's wayward ways. They avoided my shop like the plague, which left me feeling frustrated. The remaining specialists who bought from me accepted me and rewarded me handsomely. Later my diagnosis helped them have a better understanding of Aspie's strange mannerisms, as well as providing a window to look into his world.

In Aspie's world, he required answers to everything. This meant he expected my customers to repeat to him why they bought from him and why they refused to pay a higher price. When he found this style of learning didn't have any effect, he changed his pattern by generally creating such a nuisance my customers let him into their pants, metaphorically speaking.

Eventually, greed got the better of Aspie and, fed up with me being the middle man for customers who were buying my goods from my neighbours, he chose to be seen as the new kid on the block who everyone else had to take notice of. So I was no longer selling to my neighbours, but playing the waiting game for bigger profits from their customers. What I was unaware of was how business relationships were built. The most probable reason why many of my foreign and predominately gay customers refused to acknowledge buying from Aspie was because they had experienced what they considered to be non-business-like behaviour.

Until the Internet and eBay took over the retail market for selling everything, solid relationships were built on having a good business acumen and budding one's wits, knowledge and a bit of luck, interacting with real people, with real faces. They too shared some of Aspie's sensory challenges.

R. Although the Internet and EBay changed the business, how did the customers find you?

H. Word of mouth and foreign dealers were escorted by couriers, whose job it was to ferry customers to their desired locations. How life has changed in a matter of twenty-five years. Once upon a time, there were many thousands of antique shops in London, now only a matter of hundreds. It was a bygone era where there was room for every genre of specialist to make a living; compared to these days when higher rents forces most dealers to look to new means. Some of them do fairs while others use the Internet.

For much of my career, as a successful antiques dealer and budding Meissen porcelain specialist, I primarily made money selling to some of the upper echelons in the society of antique dealers. Among the more popular items were decorative Chinese porcelain from the seventeenth, eighteenth and nineteenth century; eighteenth century English porcelain and nineteenth century English ceramics; particularly ironstone and blue and white English dinner services, which were very popular with the American trade. The reason this china was of so much interest was because it sat in the homes of the rich and famous, particularly the aristocracy, royalty and well-known celebrities. Therefore if it was fitting for the British, the wealthy Americans wanted a piece of what Britain had.

If you visited stately homes, you saw an abundance of the finest antiques money could buy or items of utilitarian use, and it was this that made up much of the collections the public were invited to see. Given that Americans were jealous of our heritage, since the majority of their cultural is very young in comparison, it was not surprising when they saw what their money could buy. They came over to England in droves and shipped back all that they could muster before returning for more. However, the majority of Americans in their quest to acquire the plenty had little knowledge, and for this sole reason a small genre of European dealers like myself found buying among the plenty very profitable. This desire of theirs for plenty overruled the desire of value; hence the desire of decoration was so plentiful that much porcelain was actually used as opposed to simply being admired. Rare Chinese vases were drilled into and converted to make lamps; another reason decoration was seen as a more useful quality than provenance or rarity. This meant we could purchase them for a fraction of the real value and ship back to London to sell to dealers from the orient.

However, getting back to Aspie, I have already mentioned how easy it was for him to corrode my mind without consideration to consequences. He loathed seeing in Irish shops what he couldn't afford to profit from.

A. How wonderfully patronising.

H. Knowing who to trust was a problem in those days. I preferred dealing with an art dealer who also on the side had an interest in antiques. He dealt from a beautiful Georgian home and dressed impeccably to impress and had a fine relationship with some of the higher echelons in society. Aspie, on the other hand, preferred a dealer who was at the opposite end of the scale; rarely dressed to impress and preferred the informal look. The icing on the cake for me was feeling like piggy in the middle, which resulted in the biggest disaster in my career as an antiques dealer. I was at the famous Adam's sales rooms in Dublin and, searching along a table in one of their basement rooms, I found an interesting Japanese dish. Although I have expertise in a host of different types of ceramics, I was unaware that what I was looking at was one of the rarest finds of the century. I liked the dish, which was around ten inches in diameter with a gold leaf repair to a crack, which probably was why it had escaped other people's attention.

Aspie's attitude was quite contemptuous; in his eyes, it was a bit of crap that might be worth a gamble. We left a bid of £200 with the clerk at the sales room and returned home to wait and hear if we were the successful purchasers. But because I heard nothing, I assumed the lot had been sold to a buyer who was prepared to pay more.

Back in the eighties, there were many disreputable auctioneers running sales rooms where the bid you left was the price you paid. Normally, I tried to either buy in person by attending the sale or bid over the phone. Buying at auction offered the opportunity of buying lots at bargain prices because other than the specialist collectors and trade, few of the public knew the real value. This also meant making a purchase for the cheapest price possible if there is no reserve and no interest. Alternatively, it was a case of local interest in the room, other telephone bidders or entrusting bids with members of the staff. Nevertheless, there were still a good number of auction sales rooms that abided by a good conduct.

I was not notified of my purchase and Aspie didn't have the time to find out if my purchase was a unique Nabeshima dish; which I had actually just purchased for only £77 plus a buyer's premium. The only problem was, I was unaware of this until it was leaked out a few days before the lot came up for sale again, when I heard the story that the dish was re-offered and resold for £44 plus the buyer's premium. To make it worse for me, it went up for international auction at Sotheby's and sold for £200,000 which was a world record price at that time! I learnt that my peers could have told me about the resale well in time and perhaps prevented the dish from coming up for sale again. I was warned not to prevent its resale because if I did, I would never be allowed to walk into the sales room again. By now I was depleted of all confidence. I should have stood up to this warning and called the lawyers in to fight it out, but British law had no jurisdiction on Irish soil and I had to let the whole incident go, with no purchase and no profit, although it had legally been mine.

During a subsequent visit to Japan, I was offered consolation the Japanese way. I was due to be met by the manager of a customer who apologised for not meeting me at the airport in person. He had too much to drink and had unwittingly insulted a friend of a friend who refused to lose face. They chose to settle their indifferences the way of the Yakuza, each armed with a katana but they were caught by the police.

When Aspie was offered seppuku, he didn't see it as a joke. Later, I got a hard pat on my back with a big grunting laugh and an invitation to a very special Japanese restaurant where the Yakuza were purported to have been customers in the past.

On most occasions, Aspie and I aren't drinking men, but I was glad I made an exception on this occasion as the three large bottles of warm sake arrived. I was glad I was somewhat goggly-eyed by the time the main event arrived with video camera to hand.

A. I have to interrupt here that it is with joy that I was given some deserved attention, finding the next course more satiating than the Nabeshima dish. Here was my Hartley, with a plastic bib hung around his neck and it extended downwards and draped over the table in front of him. This had to be some initiating ritual, was the first thought that went through my head. A waiter came along and tilted Hartley's head backwards - not for the guillotine, I joked - but with this large goldfish bowl filled up with goldfish. It couldn't have been much longer than a blink of an eyelid but Hartley's head was sitting there transfixed in disbelief.

R. Sounds typical of one of those Japanese endurance shows. Perhaps you were being sounded out to becoming one of its latest contestants?

H. I needed the liquor. I was out for the count. Must be what it is like for a whale swallowing its prey. Even the thought of their callous joke made me want to puke. It was all because of my aversion to eating meat and they had taken me to one of the top restaurants in Japan where Kobe steaks cost five hundred quid a throw.

R. He obviously made a lot of money out of you.

H. Or he felt sorry for me, in a sarcastic way. You know the Japanese with their heinous teases. The only upside that year, financially speaking, was that my profit exceeded three hundred grand after tax. Aspie argued that he was given no choice but to visit every call girl the world had to offer. Back then, earning £70,000 from an extremely rare Ming period rhinoceros horn carving of a Guanyin might be a pittance compared to what it might have made ten years later. How misconceptions have changed the world, where ivory and rhino horn are virtually banned from selling, regardless of their antiquity. Yet, back then, it was a small consolation.

A. Sorry to butt in here, lad, but if you didn't have me in your life, you might be dead!

H. Another typical Aspie remark. I can say I was very lucky to have purchased the rhino horn for the $1,700. We did this while zooming round an antique show in Cleveland. Two hours later, we hopped onto a plane for the seven hundred mile-flight to Atlanta, where I would hop into another rental car to get me to another show an hour before closing time; all thanks to Aspie's OCD acumen.

Looking back at my years of travelling throughout forty-two states in continental America, I wish Aspie had a slow down button and we'd taken a closer look at the local culture and scenery. During our fifteen years of travelling to the US, we clocked up an astonishing 9,995,233 miles. No matter what part of the country we were in, Phoenix - the city of my dreams - was always included.

Chapter 30: Double Diagnosis

H. I wasn't interested in getting myself diagnosed but felt I had to because I mistakenly thought Sam was on the spectrum. This was the sole reason I decided to get diagnosed. There were so many similarities between Aspie and Sam, although Aspie considered my boys as competition. Aspie was jealous of Sam's adorable face and how he received constant affection from me. Aspie had to join in on the party and he did an Aspie thing that few children were likely to have tolerated for long. He found sordid pleasure in nibbling Sam's ears. Even when Sam retaliated by giving him a dead arm, it was to no avail, and a solid punch followed.

R. Surely you must have found Sam's response annoyingly painful.

H. Aspie was beyond pain and left the physical stuff to me.

R. It seems ludicrous to me you allowed this?

H. That's your mistake. Not me, Aspie. It was as though Sam had his own version of Aspie and wanted to emulate certain Aspie traits.

R. What I don't understand is how you appear to contradict yourself. Why would you want to hope that one of your children was labelled?

H. It was Aspie's insistence. He got very obsessive about Sam holding on to his manhood all the time and wouldn't stop goading me until I was forced to have Sam tested.

A. There he does it again, passing the buck my way.

H. Sam has wonderful memories of the fun times we had together. He was on my planet, so to speak, and guided by me. Until his mother's untimely death, he had been her emotional crutch.

R. I think we, as parents, find some of the things our children do embarrassing, although the reality is they are quite comfortable in their own skins. However, if I had a son, I would explain to him that what Sam was doing was not a manly thing to do.

H. During those strenuous periods of loneliness that Jacky endured when she withdrew into her world of depression, although we shared a bed, it was like sleeping with a volcano during the final moments before it erupts. Aspie was so bottled up because I was unable to reach out to Jacky and give her some quality hands on warmth. Instead she rebuffed me, which in turn drove him towards finding the appropriate prostitute for his immoral pleasure. It was about a year later, after she returned from visiting her sister in Cyprus, that I got the real hard kick in the nuts.

R. You mean, she told you she had fallen in love and wanted a change in scenery with her new man?

H. I discovered a letter my daughter had written to her mother.

R. How old was she?

H. A thirteen-year-old living in an eleven-year-old's body. Her writings were an understatement of how she felt emotionally. They were so poetic. You can appreciate it's a difficult age for any girl going through their hormonal changes, let alone deal with the needless stress imposed on her by being so close to her mother's deteriorating mental health. Her writings indicated how she would give everything up to focus on her mother's well-being. But it was during the night when she twisted and turned that her own demons came out to play. I can only sympathise with waking up and trying to work out how to get out of her head thoughts of anguish she didn't want there. It reminds me of an Aspie thing when he used to go into meltdown more often when we were travelling with the family. Aspie had no concern for the emotional damage his actions did to our children and all it needed was the change in the tone of Jacky's voice and he'd be jumping out of the car at speed, regardless of the risk to my health or any consequences to my safety. I imagine this was the same for Julie. When we later investigated with her doctor, it was a form of sleepwalking to which at the time she had no memory of. The police found her on the beach gazing far out into the surf and the heavens, dressed only in her nightie, at two in the morning. Apparently, she heard voices in our bedroom, which were alien to her, and the following morning she was confronted by a stranger who her mother told her she was in a relationship with. Julie continued this behaviour repetitively, while trying to coming to terms with her mother's new partner, someone she never wanted to become attached to, and she despised.

R. I imagine she felt safe on the beach; found solace with the stillness of the sky and sound of the surf.

H. Remember, I had no knowledge about the trauma that had set her off. This was only reiterated to me when she was older and emotionally prepared to talk about her relationship with her mother. She was eleven when she developed this disturbing habit. We normally checked to make sure our children were tucked in and sleeping soundly and, to our shock, her bed was empty and she couldn't be found anywhere in the house.

R. Perhaps she was psychic and sensed an invisible separation in your relationship that traumatised her at an unconscious level.

H. What you have said makes such sense. I wonder whether Aspie passed on to her the traumatising gene that caused unimaginable nightmares, anxieties that had caused him to run out of the room, or even the house. Perhaps when she experienced such episodes, her way of dealing with it was to run away until she was out of breath, and it happens to be that she got to the beach. Much of this time, I was away travelling. For Jacky, it was very traumatic wondering what she had done wrong. Yet, when our daughter was seen by the doctors, no psychological conditions were found.

R. Our children too can be very perceptive. They can pick up on our emotions, traits and all sorts of other stuff that can be an innate danger to us as parents. We want the best for our children. However, when our marriage fails, we are often blind to their torment. I imagine it must have been the same for the two of you. Perhaps her running away at night was a culmination of that; hoping when she returned home, her nightmare would be gone.

H. Except her nightmare was repeating itself. Anyway, the following year, I had myself diagnosed at the Priory Hospital in Southgate, with the symptoms of Asperger's Syndrome, partial ADHD, ADD and other afflictions.

R. It must have been a lot for Jacky to emotionally relate to. If I had been privy to read your diagnoses and I was in her state of mind, I am not sure I would have been able to see a future being married to you. I realise this might sound a bit cruel, but put yourself in Jacky's shoes, if you can. Anyway, how did your diagnoses affect you?

H. Primarily, my diagnoses gave me an opportunity to cleanse my past, an explanation for every one of Aspie's misdemeanours.

A. Hallelujah! God has spoken and I have at last been recognised as the demon sitting on Hartley's shoulder, and he is not at all happy. At least I knew I had a life. At last I can now announce myself in person.

H. I had known for a long time that I hadn't considered myself normal. The looks people gave made me feel conspicuous in public, even among friends. My diagnosis of Asperger's Syndrome, I thought, would offer me some respite, the penultimate answers to all of my unsolved riddles and unanswerable questions I had been asking myself on a daily basis.

The irony of a diagnosis of a mental disorder is that you may perceive you know everything there is to know about the condition you have been diagnosed with, and you believe it translates into knowing everything there is to know about yourself. Anyone, reading those five pages of my diagnoses might have thought that my saviour had arrived. Little did they know, it simply made the devil in me even more apparent than he was before.

A. So lovely being referred to as the Devil again!

H. I hoped a new chapter had begun in my life, where I could shed my vulnerable past and replace it with a solid foundation.

R. Except our past rarely vanishes completely. How do you separate those memories you want to remember, and those you don't? I would have thought that was impossible.

H. So true. While my diagnoses may have answered a lot of questions, it became the perfect excuse for Jacky. What hope was there left being in a relationship with me?

A. None, mate, from the way I saw it. I was laughing at you, thinking how funny it was for you to come back home to such an unwelcoming coming home present. You had to cope with jet lag, separation and your kids getting used to seeing their mother with a stranger.

R. I imagine it was a case of packing your bags and finding somewhere else to live.

H. I was penniless. Mr Anxiety took over, suggesting the best thing was to slit my throat and end my suffering. He got me down on my hands and knees, snivelling, begging for forgiveness, and hoping she'd changed her mind.

However, as generally happens when couples part, one has to find alternative accommodation. I tried to convince Aspie that The Bishops Avenue was not the ideal place to go looking.

R. How long was it before you found a place?

H. What you should be asking is, how long was it before Aspie found himself in a woman's bed? I hate to admit that during those first months of lonesome, Aspie became more dominant in my life. I all but gave up on myself and felt quite useless. An angel in the form of my mother came to my rescue and found a home she thought was suitable for me, a stone's throw away from my old junior school in a street that Cliff Richard lived when I was young. However, Aspie sought whatever wrench's bed he could find, getting me a date that turned into a six month relationship.

R. I find it sad you had to rely on your mother finding you a home.

H. Finding, yes; acceptable to Aspie, no.

A. You expected me to be happy in that hovel?

H. I think his angst goes way back into his childhood years when he refused to use the toilets at school. I don't think our mother realised what she was getting herself into, giving birth to me. Schizophrenic twins sharing one body. Talk about conflict of interest.

A. Always whingeing, aren't you? Come on, you had everything you could ever want in life, and just because now you have less doesn't mean you have to live in a dungeon of a place. You were also very aware that I needed space and a healthy outlook, otherwise I became Mr Anxiety.

H. It was tough, and with Aspie's angst it made my life hellish, and I did think the place my mother found was a bit of a dump. It's just her selfless nature; any luxury is wasteful with more emphasis on being provided with a loving family being around you, although I was being deprived of the family I loved.

At least my diagnosis brought a restitute silence from Aspie. He was no longer perpetually in my face, due to the sympathetic attention I received from every Tom, Dick and Harry; realising it was the thingy inside of my head that had upset them so many times.

Did I feel out in the cold? Bloody Antarctica, as far as my personal life was concerned. Wasn't like from the fireplace into the fire, it was from the security of having a family home and living within the confines of the family, into the most isolated place on the planet, and all I had for company was Aspie!

A. That's a bit of a fib. I bestowed on to you the art of online dating at Go-Date. You've got to hand it to me for saving your bacon!

H. This is where my argument agreeing with Aspie got rather complicated. There was a difference between my ideal relationship and his. In mine, I was looking for a woman who is loyal, interesting, supportive and has common interests and, if everything clicks with me, we can nurture our relationship into a full-blown partnership. That, of course, is something Aspie didn't want with any relationship, which did not involve him in any one way or other.

Losing control of his authority in my life was something Aspie couldn't bear so he set me up with any needy women he could find; the more baggage, the happier he was. Therefore if they had big tits, blonde hair and a shapely figure or their profile intimated a sexual desire, it was a worthy relationship to pursue, and anything else fell well short of his values.

I, on the other hand, although distracted by his sentiments, sought women that appeared to have a bit of intellect and in an arena that had a relationship with my lifestyle. Finding these women in my state of mind was entirely a different matter, hence I found myself lumbered with women who unbeknown to me had a somewhat ambiguous lifestyle, be it their fault or for other reason. As a result of Aspie's ideas while looking for that relationship that would work for him, I had to kiss many ugly frogs before he found one he believed was the ideal relationship blessed with loyalty until she too joined the club of the disloyal.

A. How ironic that your very first date was with a pair of pancakes? Love at first sight, but for the wrong reasons.

H. It was during the Christmas and New Year period, and I had become excited by a woman I was chatting to on Go-Date who I met up with in New York. Anyway, one of the conundrums I had with Aspie was his convincing me of the importance of only being seen with Jewish women. By the time we had eaten dinner on our first date, she invited me back to her home, the top floor of a warehouse. Aspie had become completely besotted by her seduction and she invited me to give up the rental of my apartment. The catch was, I had to fuck her every night during the six weeks I stayed there.

R. Seems to me, other than being sexually worn out, a rather inexpensive compromise to paying rent. Knowing so much about Aspie, he must have leapt at the chance?

H. You are completely correct, except you may have forgotten about Aspie's ideas of jumping in at the deep end and not worrying about the consequences. The trouble was, she didn't want to stop, and I was expected to give her multiple orgasms all night!

R. Must have had a tough condom!

H. Are you joking? Aspie wear a condom? In all of his years of shenanigans, he had never worn one.

R. I am surprised you are still here and that Aids didn't catch up with you!

H. I became exhausted, hoping for a get-out clause, except was too late. Aspie had accepted her invitation and I was doomed to carry out her whims to her heart's content. The following night, I preferred respite in my apartment but after midnight, her pounding the outside window of my ground floor apartment in sub-zero temperatures woke me up. Ten seconds later, she was on top of me and I realised I was dealing with a sex maniac who had injected herself with Viagra. I tried to convince her that enough was enough and I wanted out. Anyway, I called her later that day and told her I needed my beauty sleep in preparation for the antique show the following day. By the end of the week, I had her locked up by the police for stalking me. The story made it into one of the local seedy village newspapers; *'Jew-boy ravaged by excessive nymphomaniac.'*

R. You know, in my trade, I get to hear all sorts of things, so the stories you are telling me don't surprise me. You have to remember, some of us are different in our sexual morals. People have their own little vices, just like you have with Aspie. It is only when addictiveness and obsessions lead onto more lewd situations where behaviour becomes unwelcome.

H. But it was back to Hendon; love at first sight with any female, form, shape and size unimportant, but big tits essential. The next one spoke six languages and worked for an insurance company. This meant money and more transgressions for Aspie. But I was missing tucking my children into their beds and doing all the things happily married couples do while doting over their children.

It was the same with all of my relationships. Aspie was conniving and highly manipulative. I wish I could say he was predictable. It was like standing on a street where every corner looked different, although each corner is actually identical. Why was it impossible to predict his next move?

You also asked me whether I could thwart some of Aspie's manipulation. I thought this could be achieved after I was diagnosed, when I attended a special school twice a week for the next six months to learn how to live with him. I began seeing Aspie as the ultimate predator hunting his ideal victim; me. Love is what he craved and it was my downfall. I had hoped distance wouldn't prevent any long-term relationship working out.

R. Aspie had other plans?

H. Control! I couldn't be in two places at once and he chose to be in the wrong place, New York. She wanted to go to the Big Apple for her fiftieth; seemed ideal for her, but not for me.

A. But for me.

H. It was quite a learning experience when a woman puts her vanity before sensibility. It was ironic that by the end of the first day, I pitied her blistered feet, yet she insisted heels were her ideal choice for Central Park. However, by the end of the day, her last words were, 'Your bags with your clothes inside will be waiting the next time you pass.' When I rang her doorbell, an arm extended out without one word being spoken. Meanwhile, Aspie convinced me time would heal and all would be forgiven.

R. You flew back to Phoenix?

H. Yes and no. I knew Aspie would be gloating and I had to do something about that. I allowed Aspie to do what he had to do and that was get me on a plane and spend a week with my cousins in Toronto.

I knew Phoenix could wait. Allowing Aspie to believe he had me exactly where he wanted me meant I could focus my energies on my business needs. Fortunately, Miami was barely a few weeks away so immediately after that, I planned to travel back to Phoenix.

R. Miami?

H. The Miami Beach Antiques Show was like going to shul for all of the Jewish antiques dealers. Regular as clockwork, the one antiques show of the year,not to be missed.

R. You went to Miami via Toronto?

H. Having Aspie around my neck always accompanied an ulterior motive. But the answer to your question is we did fly to Toronto. Four days of pure relaxation. We went with my cousin in his plane over Niagara Falls and another day out on his yacht on Lake Ontario. Business-wise, from past experience, Montréal was not a profitable destination, but it was another place on Aspie's map enticing me to believe I was missing some fantastic pair of tits, wandering the French Quarter looking especially for the likes of me.

R. Who was this lady?

H. She owned a vegan restaurant and we appeared to get on so well together, talking about our personal lives and how much we wished to find our ideal life partners. Aspie, of course, couldn't stop staring at her body curves, to say the least. I quite enjoyed being aware of a lot of body language and eye contact, but my one regret was not asking her out.

I thought getting her phone number would be enough to make her realise I was interested in her. Luck would have it that she didn't have time to go out for a drink until the following Wednesday. That was four days away. Aspie was letting me off that easily and instead thought we could travel up to the

Ashuapmushuan Wildlife Reserve and get a real taste of the Canadian outback.

R. That sounds really exciting. I would have loved to go there with you.

H. Except, I knew he was diverting my intentions from making the ideal choice. The bottom line was spending the night at my hotel alone. In a lewd way, he got his way. The Canadian outback became a dream. Instead, he decided the easiest way of keeping an eye on me was getting us on to a flight to Miami the following afternoon.

R. Sounds life together it was a real holiday.

H. You make everything sound so easy. Where else in the world could I go, and have great weather and do business, and along the way where Aspie's whims are catered for?

R. I see what you mean; strip clubs, whorehouses etc.

H. Regrettably, the police clamped down and the majority of unlicensed clubs vanished. It was no longer the same as those early years visiting Miami. Meanwhile, I yearned for some normality in my life. I was sure my colleagues must have had an inkling of his shenanigans, not that they ever let on.

I have so many memories I could do without. Whenever I was asked why Miami, New York, LA or Phoenix, it was more feeling spaciousness around us: whether it be the mountains; the desert; the cities, and that everywhere was so spread out.

That's another thing, being aware of what society accepts in everyday life. Here I was referring to the sublime and ridiculous, normally over something very trivial. It reminded me of a rare time when it was acceptable to Aspie to stand in a queue and wait for his turn; normally he pushed in to the front. Brushed past everyone as though he was the only person who had walked into the cafe to be served, ignoring everyone in front, a typical Asperger's gesture.

Aspie did it to me all the time with parking tickets every time he got them. First procrastination set in and, by the time any acceptable appeal could be made, the twenty-eight days had been long gone. Can you imagine Aspie telling the Judge to look at my diagnoses so he can be more understanding to his issues? Yes, there were the days that we got off, but how many times Judges had suggested that given my handicaps I was a dangerous driver, that if Aspie didn't see the signs he might not be too aware of all the other road users, pedestrians or other vehicles. A better solution was to remove his license as well as have him retake his test to see if he knew how to comply with driving rules. My defence began with me kissing the Judge's feet, so to speak, and explaining that Aspie's inability to be unaware of the road bore no relationship whatsoever to my not being a safe driver.

ADHD somehow crossed over the sensory wiring in the brain. While Aspie was unable to read correctly the connotations of parking restriction signs or be aware he is speeding or being chased by police, it didn't mean he wasn't aware of the danger of injury to pedestrians or other drivers. On the contrary, he had highly tuned in senses that gave him incredible abilities of spacial awareness,where he could risk taking life-threatening chances safely!

PART FIVE:

SCHADENFREUDES AND MURDERERS

Chapter 31: Psychopathic Challenges

H. Back in my days of learning to become a philatelist, it was Zachary who was the first person to explain the rules to the art of honesty. He told me, 'If you want to lose a customer fast, tell him a porky. Your integrity will disappear fast as will the chance of building up a reputable business with a foundation built on trust and transparency.' While I had no trouble adhering to his words, there were no guarantees when you had an Aspie sharing your life.

On a number of occasions, I questioned him when I overheard him telling someone a story that he could profit from. He replied that there was an art of fibbing in stories without promoting the lie. That ultimately repeating false stories was for losers whose only interest was to display a weakness in their character that promoted coercing the truth too much for comfort.

He was also my teacher in showing me how to convince a customer the items I was selling were a worthwhile purchase even though I might be making a huge profit. Nevertheless, he taught me to always leave some room for a trader. Sadly, though, I had to contend with Aspie making up his own rules as each day passed. It was just unfortunate timing when a customer called Astrid had come to pick up her pieces. It was Aspie who greeted her and caused her to get emotionally tearful on the spot, insisting she hadn't paid for them. I had to run after her and apologise for Aspie's inadequacies.

R. Did you learn from that incident?

H. It disappointed me to say that Aspie was repetitively doing this and she was one of many of my customers getting away with unpaid purchases.

R. Could that be so?

H. I don't think so, although it was pre-written on each invoice 'to pay' or 'paid'. Sadly, it was the first and last time I saw that lovely customer, and perhaps this same problem existed in personal relationships

R. Please explain.

H. With hindsight, I had always felt a lack of confidence followed my business career. Somehow, Aspie's facial cues betrayed me as my customers saw through his weaknesses, and rarely did I get the same ultimate prices my compatriots could get. This developed into an unchangeable pattern and rubbed onto my personal life. I was certain women saw me as a needy man so the universe sends women in Aspie's direction with similar needs.

R. Yes, no woman wanted to nurture a relationship with a needy man.

H. Anyway, the following day, I was flying to Pensacola to inspect a fine collection of eighteenth century Chinese export porcelain. With most of my luggage left in Miami, I arrive into the arrivals terminal to see Frank, who I believed to be Ingrid's husband, dressed as though he is going into battle. Camouflaged outfit, boots, cap to match, and a holster attached to his belt. On the way to his customer's home, who he had me believe is allowing us to stay the night, he told me he dressed that way because he used to be a fighter pilot in Vietnam.

The first strange thing was, I found him asking me whether I liked my eggs sunny side up. It was as though my kindred spirit had stepped in and said, 'Be on your guard; you might be dealing with a psychopath.' We arrived at his home and I presumed I was being introduced to the elderly collector to whom the collection belongs. She must have thought I was some dumb-arse, that her young man had cleverly taken for a ride, unaware of their deceptive intentions!

What really saved my bacon was their greed. He had convinced her to price her collection at my retail price. I had to hand it to Aspie, I might have initially thought he got me into the mess, but it left an unsavoury taste that resulted in me asking for a couple of days to think about how best I could take on the entire collection. It was almost as though this was Aspie's ploy, knowing we had been manipulated to travelling on what was looking like a wild goose chase.

This was where lack of commitment paid off in my favour. Whenever Aspie felt out of his depth, alarm bells began ringing with anxiety attacks in the making. That night, Aspie had me pacing up and down the room, thinking there was no viable way for me to profit from this customer's collection.

It was only with hindsight that I compared Aspie to a cat using up one of its nine lives. I was once again feeling the effects of being in an untenable situation where I didn't want to give in to the enemy's whims and purchase a collection priced insanely high. Quite different from being an expert in buying and selling Chinese export porcelain.

Only after we were safely on the flight back to Miami did I feel terror had finished stalking me. The most annoying part of the deal was thinking I would make a good profit on the one item he allowed me to take on sale or return, a rare pair of Meissen Kakiemon-style Monteiths.

In an unkind way, it was as though Aspie was unable to heed the advice Zachary tried hard to implore; never to be taken in by illicit trust. I wished Aspie could have learnt that acumen, then I more than likely would never have endured the unnecessary ways Schadenfreude had their way with me, with their evil or manipulative intentions. But I feel sad that, with the lifetime of psychotherapy, not one person has able to demonstrate to me that there was a way to change the outcome of this unfortunate acumen Aspie owned.

R. You have already mentioned Aspie had an addiction to experience everything, including death. All I can say is perhaps he wanted you to die and be reborn without his kindred spirit playing you with so many thoughtless innuendos. I read about climbers dying, doing what they enjoy. Maybe they have their own version of Aspie and choose their demise to be camouflaged by attempting an impossible feat.

H. Sometimes I think of my life compared to a Beethoven piano sonata. It can go on and on with no resolute of actually ending.

Anyway, getting back to my story, about a year later I bumped into Ingrid and mention her husband's name and how I was in possession of a pair of Monteiths. The shock was obvious on her face, and firstly I discovered that Frank was never her husband, just another man servicing her nymphomania. Secondly, I learn his latest wife was old enough to be his grandmother and he had contrived to steal stock from her. For the next two years, the Monteiths became the property of the FBI.

R. That's awful. I hope you got them back.

H. I wish I hadn't got involved in the first place.

R. Surely not?

H. After the fiasco in Florida, it was back to jolly old England and focusing on the art of buying and selling items, where a profit was guaranteed and not being coerced by Aspie into spending time overseas on fruitless exercises. Meanwhile, after a couple of months, Aspie was getting itchy fingers, so off we went once again to Phoenix where I met Alexa.

The trouble with Aspie was sitting still. No doubt many a man would think Aspie had a colourful life, jumping into bed with a woman and jumping out with another. The fact was, he saw no difference between a one-night stand or a full-blown relationship. My troubles related to his unfortunate talent of love at first sight with every woman we went on a date with. It became tough luck for me that, whereas many women might look at a man to offer them financial security, he hoped the ideal woman might be able to offer the same.

Throughout my story, I have spoken about his many sexual exploits. 'I love you,' became part of his vocabulary. Often women might feel sorry for me while I wished I could see how things actually were, as opposed to how Aspie interpreted them.

A. I only demonstrated this weakness in the hope you would stop causing yourself so much emotional grief.

H. I have already mentioned how Aspie's relationship with love at first sight was very unnerving for me. Such exaggerated feelings followed me throughout my life, making me feel very conspicuous and embarrassed when I was left unable to pursue any more intimate contact, be it casual contact with a girl or woman, friendship or relationship. It was all or nothing with Aspie.

Throughout my single life, I wondered whether Aspie set me up on purpose with problematic women or with ones looking for their next victim. During this cycle of getting introduced to so many different women to whom I had no control over, and Aspie falling in love with them, meant relationships could last anything from a day or two, to a maximum of six months. Eventually Aspie's tactics changed when business slowed and our lifestyle had to change to accommodate it

With Jacky's continued bouts of distancing herself from me, trying to convince me it had nothing whatsoever to do with me, I was looking into eyes full of despair, unable to prevent a life that had begun ebbing out of her. All Aspie could sense was what he thought was the most important criteria, which was to ensure our marriage continued, dishing out unlimited unconditional love. On those days our children were in need of her attention, she couldn't have been more content, and we couldn't have been more of a family if we tried. But when we were on our own was when the ghost in her reappeared. She became very distant, perhaps withdrawing somewhere into her past where she seemed safe, and a week might go by before she became my loving wife again.

I long ago had to get used to hearing the same words repeated over and over again. 'It's got nothing whatsoever to do with you. It is my problem to take care of.' No wonder Aspie got so restless. I wonder how much angst a neuro-typical non-autistic husband could have taken without having an Aspie sharing their lives.

I think with her demon and Aspie, unconditional love was depended where on the roller coaster we were. Still, that worst memory of her will continue to haunt me until the day I die. The day I was looking at a chilling emptiness in the eyes of the most beautiful mother of my children. I remember taking her in my arms and holding her so tight, I didn't want to let go. We both cried our eyes out, exchanged our sorrows. Then she admitted there was stuff in her past she regretted never speaking about. It had prevented her from going to therapy. I couldn't look at the torment in her eyes, and it lay there getting buried deeper and deeper. She had long ago seen our marriage fall apart but was powerless to do anything other than wait and hope a miracle might come along. But as much as she had felt damaged too, I felt the same, like a jigsaw puzzle with the pieces fitted into the incorrect places, more so made to stay in place than anything else.

The irony in having to wait until her inquest was that we learnt what Aspie had suspected all along; we had been living with a psychopathic schizophrenic liar. We were appalled too at her father's notion that her suicide was completely her own doing. I knew her parents were the real culprits who had seen her marriage as a release from their own misery. Now their little secret was out and they had me to blame.

R. I can't even begin to imagine the suffering of your children, let alone yours.

H. It's not something I like to think about, but you know children have a tendency of developing their own coping mechanisms. What Aspie was blind to was they could never get over what their mother had done and the start of their own emotional nightmares. How is a child supposed to react to a suicidal history in their genes? That their mother took her life on her eighth attempt? Worse happened three years before she met

James, who she thought was going to rekindle the love that had lost its way and he would take her with him into eternity. The following year was to be Jacky's fiftieth. Yet, weeks before, she fell out of love with him and was forced to endure serious therapy and medication for her own protection. James, who had supported her emotional needs, was not willing to let her go so easily. I too have on occasions experienced such hollowness. Not that I suffer from depression, but more of a feeling as though my brain has been removed from my head and there is consciousness; a blank void in its place. There have been times I might have succumbed to suicide. It is a very unnerving experience.

R. Sounds rather drastic!

H. Learning at her inquest about her making four attempts on her life before she was seventeen told me how serious this had been. When she ended her relationship with James, Sam became her emotional crutch, yet she had few qualms putting an end to her lament directly in front of him.

Then I have to suffer my own comeuppance on the account of the dreadful James, who inherited my wife's life insurance policy and demanded a further hundred grand to buy himself out of my children's life. This was a period when I was living the nightmare of nightmares. I had hoped some retribution from suing the psychiatrist who let her out of the hospital into harm's way. I might have got a cheque for fifty grand because of his irresponsibility, but it was too much emotional pain for the kids to bear.

After I inherited a new home, I was shocked to see what terrible condition he had left my children's home in, as though he purposely left them a reminder of her suicide attempts.

A. Typical, you didn't drown in your car accident so she wanted to show you how it was done.

H. While our eldest son was at university, his mother was in her depressive state and he was deprived of her madness. Instead, Sam took his place; can you imagine what it did to his mind with bottles of pills everywhere and his mother lying on the floor spaced out?

However, it was the graphic writing of his sister that really surprised me, sadly written by the hand of someone so young and so tormented. In the first of those papers, it discussed the difficulties she encountered having to come to terms with her mother sharing her bedroom with a man other than me. During the couple of years her mother went out with James, they made their home together as they bought a flat and went on holidays together, and no doubt expected to live happily ever after together. However, in her diary of poems, she told a very different story of her mother's unhappiness. I think getting lost in some of her most beautiful poems was her way of surviving what her mother had done.

R. It appears to me you have a story within a life of mega issues. I am grateful you are able to share with me this saga of yours. Now that Jacky is no longer with you, how did you cope, given that you also had Aspie to contend with?

H. After what Jacky had done, I was at the point of despair as to how best I could support my children, emotionally. I was deeply grateful for the moral support at her wonderful send-off, with so many of my friends turning up for her funeral. The children dressed to impress, even though their hearts were reeling with the horrors of what their mother had done. Even James showed what sympathy he could to the children, but I did wonder if he had an ulterior motive and within a few weeks his true colours were revealed, when he received a cash settlement from Jacky's life insurance policy.

Back in 2004, so little was known about Asperger's Syndrome so he convinced the social services that I was an incompetent retard. He convinced a Judge that the children were safer living with him than with me, and for the next twelve months a court order put in place an injunction against me visiting my children in their own home, with worse to come.

R. That sounds preposterous, almost barbarian. You are telling me they considered your diagnosis as though it was a virus your children needed protection from, in case it was passed onto them? I first knew you long before Jacky, and I never imagined you as a bad parent.

H. You can imagine the terror my daughter had to endure, being put into the custody of James by the social services because I'm deemed mentally unbalanced to look after her. Meanwhile, Tim is deemed safe, being a couple of years older, and Sam's at university spared of the grievances.

If it was tenuous in their relationship that he didn't make the smallest effort to offer her his sympathy, he decided it was all about his own home comforts, not hers. That she was an irritant in his life and, to quash his anxieties, he returned home every evening drunk. It was even worse because he spread more lies to the social services and managed to convince them that her being home alone most nights was my doing so they decided to have her fostered.

R. I can't bear to think of you losing your daughter to foster parents.

H. How often do you hear about the inadequacies of the social services failing to do their homework properly and, only after a situation goes out of control, is it picked up in the media? Primarily, it was all about James' convincing story. I, the lousy father, never around for my children, was the reason Jacky found him more promising as a father figure.

R. How long was she in foster care?

H. A saving grace came along. Also, luck came my way in that Jacky and I had given her the best education money could buy and she had a good circle of supportive friends. One of them offered to take up the role of parental responsibilities and, a few months later, another was my PA. But she did a lot more than that because she had a daughter of the similar age and took off a lot of the pressure when I was travelling. However, in her spare time she ran singles parties and I picked up one or two relationships from her events.

R. That's a funny one.

H. I don't know how Aspie always got attracted to the weirdos. First I strike up this relationship with….

R. Can you explain to me how we are supposed to be talking about your daughter's welfare and now you have deviated back to talking about your own relationships? Do you have a problem with this? Is this Aspie's doing?

H. The bottom line was I took over the mortgage from James after handing over one hundred grand. What I inherited was a four-bedroom dump. I'm broke and ordered back to school to learn how to appease my daughter. Can you imagine having to sign in with the local social services twice a week for three months? But, at the very least I am grateful for them too; given my baby's circumstances, a surrogate mother is better in the long-term than fostering offered.

But this period bought me close to my daughter again, although she was a very troubled girl; she followed in her mother's footsteps. Jacky had been an accomplished dancer in her youth, appearing regularly in *The Morecombe and Wise Show* and Julie had inherited her mother's creative genes. She was outstanding at acting, art and English, and she had supportive teachers at her school. Slowly, the love between us returned and she regained her trust in me. Aspie had never failed to excel at finding the most exciting places to travel to, one of his better acumens. I can reverently say Aspie proved his worth in proving to her I was the responsible father she never knew.

It was also a lesson for me learning new tricks the that teen girls generally don't see eye to eye with boys' stuff. This I learnt when Aspie decided to show off the Empire State Building. 'Dad, why are we standing in front of another skyscraper? It's as boring as a cup of tea?' I wished Aspie could have realised that she had reiterated many times how she hoped before we returned she would able to go clothes shopping. Our next stop was therefore Macy's, which guaranteed a smiling daughter for the remainder of our trip.

A few years before, when Aspie discovered the Sheraton Phoenician Resort was geared up to entertain all the family and was a stone's throw away from Camelback Mountain, we regularly hiked. All I had to do was tell my little baby not to go mad on our unlimited tab and make friends, which she did, and that allowed me to do some antiquing, knowing she was safe.

A few weeks after we had returned from our holiday, it was good to see a happier expression on my daughter's face. But it was a smile that always annoyed Aspie because it felt for him it was taking my attention away from him. I hoped it was long-lasting.

Chapter 32: Chantal

H. Meanwhile, I had my own women problems; three women in
my life, and my girlfriend Chantal was at war with Jennifer,
my PA! Jennifer will always be a very dear friend to me, and
Chantal was the longest on/off relationship I ever endured.
Jennifer also cared about me and wanted me to be in a more
stable relationship. Many times I had reservations about my
relationship with Chantal lasting, but what I resented was how
whenever I visited her, she demanded one hundred per cent of
me. Take her out for dinner; see a movie; if I wanted a fuck;
everything was on her terms, or kiss the relationship goodbye.

R. Sounded like Chantal was emotionally blackmailing you.

H. Not me, Aspie. Three years into learning where Aspie fitted
into my life, along comes Chantal. Apart from my marriage, no
other relationship lasted longer than six months, so while he was
manipulating me to remain, my closest friends told me to leave
for my own well-being.

R. How come your relationship with Chantal lasted so long?

H. During the first couple of months, it was uncanny, how quiet
as a mouse she was. Never bad-mouthed; accepted everything
as though we were the happiest couple on earth. However,
during the first month, she never offered to pay for anything, not
even a cup of coffee. Aspie was livid and insisted on choosing
the restaurant when she has to pay. This episode gave me an
insight into the life she led with her husband, who treated her

like a bit of muck off the back of one of his shoes. She didn't say anything, as though she was content in paying the eighty-five pound bill but her abhorrent look told me our honeymoon period was finished. I had to learn fast when to hike the dormant volcano and avoid it when it erupted.

Just as Aspie had me in a relationship with a problem woman, Chantal was no different. She had endured a sexless marriage with another control freak, who regularly beat up his children. By the time I came along, they chose to disown him and her daughter found a new friend in Aspie, although not me. Meanwhile, her plight was being a motherless teen contending with raging hormones and her inheriting her mother's genes and being a friend to me emotionally in my contest with Aspie.

A. But that is why I am in your life, I didn't say it was going to be easy and you did admit to me you enjoyed seeing your life as one big challenge!

H. Once our honeymoon period was over, it became a battle of wits. When Chantal was not in the mood to talk, it got on Aspie's nerves and when her talking switch was on, it could go on and on, which got to him too.

While I don't want to appear sexist, Chantal had this ridiculous relationship with her job, telling me she wasn't allowed to call in sick on any two subsequent days. Later on I found out that this was her ploy of getting around me so many times when we aren't together. She called in sick when she wanted an excuse to do something else without me.

On two trips coming back from Edinburgh to London, words came out of her mouth as violently as a pyroclastic flowing out of an erupting volcano, demanding I drive through the night to get her to work. We stopped at every service station on our route home and I arrived feeling an absolute wreck and decided there was not going to be a next time, only for Aspie to overrule my decision.

R. You and your relationships!

H. Here we are driving back from having a glorious long weekend in Scotland. We run into a blizzard and we are forced to find a motel and settle for the night. Gratefully, in the morning, it seemed the snow had thawed and we drove further on, but I was concerned there was a lot of ice on the road and the radio was warning of more snow on the way so I slowed down and Chantal got agitated. 'What the fuck do you think you are doing? I've got to get to work.'

This time I decided to put an end to her conceited moaning by telling her that I was not prepared to put our lives at risk. She replied, 'My managers don't care about the weather. Fuck you! If you won't get me to work, I'll take a train.'

At this point, we are 260 miles from London, driving through Northumberland, and we passed through a small village with a railway station. Chantal was told it would cost her £81 to take the train, with a journey of seven hours. Her wage for the day was £65!

R. Perhaps she wanted to show to her managers that she made the effort.

H. I was amazed that my relationship with Chantal lasted as long as it did because she didn't get on well with Aspie, who objected to her never putting her hand in her pocket. And when I objected, her mannerisms changed and she was pretty highly-strung and always on the offensive. But when I let her have her own way, she would be as quiet as a mouse, which Aspie developed an objection to.

A. Absolutely. It was like you having a conversation with a brick wall. You deserved more respect than that, yet you didn't seem to care.

Another day, we were cycling on Horsenden Common, close to the canal. The park's summit offered sweeping views across London. At the top was a little stone compass that gives distances in every direction. She decided to take a short rest, which might have been a good thing, had not a bull terrier decided to take a liking to her and began seriously attacking one of her cheeks. Had she remained calm, the dog would have probably got bored, but very soon there was pandemonium and blood everywhere, and the concerned dog walker made his excuses, not being the owner, but I made him walk with me until I was able to get a mobile phone signal. Once the ambulance was on its way, the dog walker made his escape. The situation was made worse by an appeal in the local paper for any witnesses to come forward, which came to no avail. Chantal had four operations cutting skin grafts from various part of her body during an eighteen month period before surgeons put her cheek back together again!

During my relationship with Chantal, I was building a pretty good friendship with her daughter, Zara, who was using me as her confidant, finding it impossible to speak to her mother about what mothers and daughters normally speak about. I was also replacing her selfish father, who had decided that now his wife was in a new relationship, she could take on the burden of looking after their daughter alone.

In many ways, although they were completely different circumstances, there was a similarity between Zara's behaviour and my son Tim's. Both wanting total control of their lives but causing as much disruption to their parents as they possibly could. In a nutshell, I had suddenly inherited a sort of stepdaughter because we had developed a trusting bond.

A. Okay, I concede. I didn't mind it at first when you are being supportive towards Zara, seemed nice. But I was torn between you offering her the emotional support she wasn't getting from her mother and her being very OCD with the whole business. Also, it wasn't helping me feel emotionally strong, zapping me of a lot of mental energy.

Chapter 33: Schadenfreudes

H. If a path leads to hell, Aspie had taken us the most direct route. Out of all of my regrets, one stands out more than all the others; leaving my shop in Camden Passage. While I have been immortalised in a photo on a wall there, I wish I'd had the courage to remain.

It couldn't have been more of a beautiful spring day, and just my luck Aspie spots a very sexy lady wearing little more than a miniskirt standing directly outside of a shop that was once ours. Aspie was tantalised by her alluring look. If with hindsight I could have learnt a lesson, she clutched a handkerchief to her cheek whenever she felt she needed the attention of a man coming to her rescue. Just my luck it had to be Aspie.

'I've been dumped by my boyfriend. Would you like to go out for a drink with me?' she said.

Little did I know I was being seduced, or that Aspie would end up in her bed. But more importantly, neither of us were aware of the half a dozen drinks she had drunk that she hadn't paid for. During the evening at the bar, I couldn't believe what she was telling me about her previous boyfriends who all seemed to be in the same bar as us!

'You see that man over there? He was my boyfriend for five years. And that one over there? For three years.' I was quite astounded because they were both at least ten years younger than her. Also, she told me her life story and how she had raised her son alone before meeting a kind man who she purported to be Princess Diana's accountant. They had lived off Sloane Square and travelled the world in luxury. It reminded me of Chantal's first husband, who was supposed to have been one of the Prime Minister's PAs. She was nineteen at the time; does it surprise you their marriage only lasted a year?

Little did I know that telling me her life story was her deception to get Aspie to become her permanent bed partner. Do you remember I said that, apart from Jacky and Chantal, no relationship lasted more than six months? This one would be no different, and in fact, in retrospect, I was lucky to escape with my life. If getting scorched by the fire isn't enough of a warning, Aspie had chosen a path that sat in the heart of a volcano.

When I was first close to her, I was frustrated because I couldn't see whether her breasts were small or large due to the cape she was wearing. The last thing I needed from Aspie was his whingeing that I had chosen a small-breasted woman again. However, this relationship was to give me trouble for other reasons. I had fallen in love with Coco, her poodle, with whom I formed an unbreakable friendship.

R. Such a pity; you know I'm a pet person. By all accounts, it was Aspie who decided on getting into bed with her while you wanted to show Coco how she should be treated.

H. That first time Mania walked me into her flat, I thought, 'Oh my God, what am I letting myself in for?' The she-devil convinced Aspie that all is not as bad as it appears and she didn't normally leave her home in such a mess. Yet, surprisingly, she had a lodger who she had given her best room to. Ours appeared not to have been cleaned for years. Her excuse was that she was still in mourning for the one that got away.

Anyway, now I had befriended Coco, the fly had unknowingly been caught in the spider's web. It wasn't long before her friends all hated Aspie, as though they knew our relationship wouldn't last.

The irony of what I am telling you is learning who your real friends are. Mania was known to attract every down and out, and get drunk in the process. I had to learn the hard way, as rarely do friends try to pull two people apart, hoping love will pull together two hopeless people. Meanwhile, Aspie had found for himself his ideal nymphomaniac who enjoyed fucking every position in the Kama Sutra!

A. Absolutely, my dear. For once in my life, I had found a woman who could compete on my level, except she wasn't competing on my terms and I needed to demonstrate who was the boss! It's a pity you got in the way.

H. If I can be candid, I was enticed by the three homes she owned but equally shocked at her being as selfless as a woman can be. Frugal was an understatement. How any lodger could put up with a dog and a cat shitting in the kitchen showed me she didn't give a damn, and she was overjoyed when Aspie gave her a good seeing to up the arse. If you believe the sex was enjoyable, you are mistaken. Something else new I learnt about Aspie. My dick felt like I'd been doped by a dozen Viagras and who knows, perhaps part of her plan was to get rid of me when it fell apart, while Aspie was having the time of his life.

Three months into our relationship, a serious predicament was blooming. Mania decided to give Coco away to one of her gay friends. She was aware she couldn't give her the love the dog deserved while I began wondering how I could get out of the chaos of Mania's life. Two reasons kept me there: running my business from her shop, but also Coco and I were inseparable and I enjoyed my daily cycling along the adjacent Grand Union Canal with Coco running closely behind.

The following month was my birthday and Mania had already shown me her stingy side on more than one occasion. My kids were taking me out for dinner and I agreed she could come along on the condition that she paid her way. Just before the bill arrived, she said, 'I need to go to the loo.' On her return, learning that Tom had paid, she said, 'Next time, my turn!'

It was a gorgeous night and I wanted to walk the couple of miles home; it could have been most romantic. But there was to be no walking for Mania. I knew this was her ruse to get more sploshed on the way home and so I walked anyway. Three hours later, at 2.30am, I was concerned for her well-being. Aspie insisted on calling the police but, of course, Sod's Law, – he gets arrested. He's upset with her antics because what should have been my night was ruined by her drunken arrival home and he throws her into the shower. She tripped and cut her knees and had blood pouring down her legs when the police turned up, who think I have battered her! With her in the state she was in, they had no choice but to lock me up. Staying in that cell was a nightmare for Aspie.

From there onwards, my relationship with Mania was on the way out. Returning home every evening was akin to jumping into a cauldron of lava in comparison. When she had my full attention, she was very much a loving partner, but as soon as my back was turned, her face turned into the contorted look that Medusa gave to her victims before turning them into stone.

But my situation was about to turn dire. We stopped in a traffic jam in central London and she was ranting like there was no tomorrow. No doubt if I had died then, she would have continued carrying on with her antics, talking to my corpse. Meanwhile, I fear Aspie was bringing on another anxiety attack and I was trapped, looking for a way out. There wasn't one. I knew I had to make a radical decision, otherwise Aspie would take control of the driving seat. I could not risk certain death via him doing something radically stupid, like mowing into a crowd of people and not caring about their injuries, or slamming the car into a brick wall. In his state of mind, I knew how easy it would be for him to become a hand grenade with the pin already taken out.

It became a split second life-saving must-do moment. I undid Mania's safety belt and threw open her door. I did this by reclining my driver's seat and pushing myself against the nearside back seat, which gave my legs enough kicking room to push her out of the car.

It wasn't as though I was listening to her objections, since there were none. No defiance on her part; not anger nor frustration or anything, other than repetitively telling me how much she loved me, although she was trying to clamber back into the car as I put my foot back on the pedal. I was grateful when the traffic began moving again.

By now, it had become obvious that she had serious alcohol problems with no desire to make an effort to change. She simply returned home later the following evening; again, very intoxicated. I needed to be up early the following morning but she wanted my full attention. It didn't take much whingeing for Aspie to snap. He grabbed hold of her and shook her around by the neck as though she was a rag doll. I had never seen Aspie before in this state of mind. It was about to get worse as his hands begun to clasp her neck tightly with the full extent of what he was doing becoming obvious because her feet had lifted off the floor and her life was ebbing out of her.

I knew if I didn't intervene, I might hear the sound of her neck snapping. That would be it. I began imagining the headlines; *Asperger's Antiques Dealer Convicted of Murdering Girlfriend.* So I took control and threw her onto our bed. She simply begged for more!

R. Sounds like a nightmare gone mad. How were you able to hold on to your sanity?

H. A good question, to which I have no answer.

Chapter 34: T-Rex and Trees In The Sky

R. What connection could T-Rex have in your life?

H. A very good question, with a rather complex answer. You know how terrifying watching *Jurassic Park* can be? Somehow, Aspie has the ability to transport T-Rex into the present, and the anxiety that produced became as real as playing the victim for its next meal.

Why T-Rex appears is complicated, and while I have some theories, they are more conjectures than anything else. Possibly an extension of how Aspie imagined some terrible beast is out to get him while driving in the countryside. You know, how the media pick up on some lion-type animal that is supposed to have been spotted, but not actually caught.

On the day in question, the morning couldn't have been more peaceful cycling along a route we took when the weather was fine, and there wasn't a cloud in the sky. It was my preferred route leaving Chantal's home in Harrow and cycling along the roads that led into parks as we approached the Grand Union Canal at Greenford on our way to Portobello Road. The canal took us most of the way and was a lot safer than using the main roads. Although most of the cycle is not picturesque, there certainly are a lot less fumes to take in. When the canal crosses over the North Circular Road, there is at least a mile of winding through an industrial estate. There was a lot of smoke and steam billowing out from extensive pipes that camouflaged the sky as I cycled into this eerie atmosphere. Somehow, Aspie turned this part of our cycle into something more sinister. Without warning,

I was engrossed with the most devastating sensation; not an illusion, but the aberration, very real. I closed my eyes, knowing by the time my bike ground to a halt, I would be held in its mighty jaws. Suddenly, I was catapulted into the air as the back wheels of my bike skid over the canal edge and only coming to a halt when I hear a gentle thud as my shoulder met concrete. I lay contorted in a heap, my feet dangling above my head and my heart pounding as though it was about to explode. I was astounded I was alive, but only just. I still felt the monster's breath reaching down from the bridge above.

I have previously discussed my grandparents and other elder relatives being members of the Communist Party whose ideals were handed down to my parents, and the reason they one day would take the position of being the bookkeeper and secretary for their local branch. Why this is relevant is because they supported anyone with a plight and likewise some of those dearest friends of theirs lodged with us. I could have only been about eight years old at the time and I remember how I said to my mother that one of my parent's friends had come into my bedroom and drew me close in a cuddle with one of his hands resting high on my thigh. 'Don't be so ridiculous,' she said. 'Don't ever mention anything so absurd to me again.'

Now you tell me how an Aspie boy was supposed to react, accepting that he was being touched and knowing how the slightest ruffling of noise will send him into an immediate anxiety attack. In this instance, Aspie had ran out of the room, scared as hell, straight into my mother's arms looking for her protection. But her reaction was not what he expected. 'Don't be so absurd. David is probably the kindest man I know, and I know jolly well he wouldn't do anything to harm you.'

However, the unseen damage had hit its target and it festered whenever I came into contact with the sexual predators I met growing up. So many psychological anomalies attacked Aspie. It was no wonder I couldn't make head or tail of what part he played in my life.

R. Without wanting to appear demonstrative, by all accounts you have had too much to bear mentally. I am surprised you are still around to tell your tale.

H. By the time I had been going out with Chantal for a couple of years, Aspie was convinced I had to find a way to marry her. We went to Death Valley in the States, arriving during the hottest month of the year, where scorching temperatures of 48 °C are not unusual. We stayed at the Death Valley Resort for a couple of nights before touring Bryce Canyon and Monument Valley on our way to Seattle. It was while we were driving through the spectacular Columbia River Gorge and Aspie was jealous that my attention was on Chantal, so he orders me to explore the six hundred and twenty-foot Multnomah Falls, or else! Chantal had never been one for hiking and so I went on ahead and waited at the summit for her to appear. Aspie gestured me across a small bridge and got me to climb onto a fallen branch that traversed a stream before it became a torrent falling far below. By the time Chantal arrived, Aspie had walked to the end of the branch and suggested she takes photos of her daredevil boyfriend.

Suddenly, it was no longer Aspie standing on the branch. Instead, I realised I'm in a rather precarious predicament. If I slipped and was caught by the current, I would learn what it feels like akin to absolving down Niagara Falls, but without the protection of a barrel. Suddenly, I was Aspie again in panic mode; there was no room for my feet to turn but instead I had to move backwards, inch by inch. All went well until I felt an almighty burning sensation as the thick rubber sole of my left sandal and the sole of my foot is pierced by an unseen protruding mistletoe. It is fascinating that Aspie joked about the consequences of not considering danger to life other people find themselves in, but not his own.

Quartzite is not your typical tourist attraction, situated halfway between Phoenix and Palm Springs, along the 90 Freeway. It was my luck that Aspie spotted a radio mast in the mountains and wanted to investigate. This meant driving along a dirt track for several miles. Thank God, before he lost his senses, we came across a sign that read Kofa National Wildlife Refuge.

R. Is one of Aspie's major problems being addicted to distractions?

H. It was part of his need to do everything, or see everywhere, before I die, and Palm Canyon is the epitome of what Aspie was addicted to in the Arizonian desert. Anyway, we eventually arrived at our destination after getting back to the main road and driving eight miles south and back onto another dirt road. We found a sign which read: *Palm Canyon is the most visited location within the Kofa National Wildlife Refuge, as well as being the last place in the state of Arizona where native California palm trees grow in their natural habitat.*

Aspie was fascinated that palm trees could exist in a canyon where there was more chance of a single cactus than a palm tree. I wish he could have stopped analysing not being able to get everywhere and simply be grateful for the uniqueness of wherever we were.

We arrived at 10am and already the temperature was 100 °F. We ascended along a trail of a couple of hundred yards when without warning the trail vanished into thin air and we were surrounded by enormous boulders; some we were able to clamber up and enjoy a spectacular view from the top. Spotting the indigenous palm trees, Aspie was more focused on venturing further into the canyon than clambering over the huge boulders, as though he wanted to show off his climbing ability. Suddenly the inevitable occurred and we heard a rustle in the bushes. My heart missed a beat because I wondered if it was a rattlesnake or a scorpion and momentarily I lost my balance. It would have required another transatlantic flight and more focused awareness to discover these palm trees we had missed before, because it required looking a hundred feet up the cliff face where they sprung forth. Thanks again, Aspie!

Already Aspie had driven us an astonishing six thousand miles, taking in every different type of scenery imaginable. One day, we drove to Bakersfield, and another day through Kings Canyon and Sequoia National Park, where I had hoped Aspie learnt about the consequences of people's actions, after hearing on the radio about two young women who thought it would be a fun July 4th to raft the violent river tormented by rapids.

We were driving adjacent to the river and into the heart of the canyon when he got a telling off by the park ranger for exceeding the thirty mph limit.

'Our park's low speed limit is to ensure idiots like you don't collide with the bears and elks that are more frequently seen than people like you.'

About three thousand miles later, at 3am, we check in to Motel 6, one of the well-known motel chains with rooms from $29, not realising it was next to one of the busiest railways in the state. Barely fifty feet away, two hundred trucks, or two miles of train, thundered past us every thirty minutes. That night, we were lucky to get a full three hours of sleep.

R. Sounds like that, between you and Aspie, you had the time of your life.

H. Absolutely. Anyway, you may recall Aspie's addiction to counting floors of every skyscraper we pass. Drawing the curtains in the morning brought another dilemma for him. From our motel to the horizon, in every direction were windmills, and so we had to drive twelve miles up the first road to count the thousands of windmills we passed, which was quite impossible because it was the largest project of its kind in North America. The windmill farm was located on land belonging to the GE Corporation in the vicinity of Tehachapi and Mojave. We drove up Horn Toad Hill to a T-junction and then it was like tossing a coin and choosing to drive to the right to see where the road went, similar to Aspie's talent of pinpointing a place on a map and that's where we head off, to as though he has a sixth sense that there is something that will be worthwhile to see.

In this instance, we found the graveyard for aeroplanes that have come to the end of their life. Our personal guide told us, 'All the planes you see here are either ones that have outlived their usefulness or have been parked by their owners because it is so much cheaper here. Some of the carcasses were broken up and used as spare parts and others were left as tangled pieces of metal. A few are in better shape and are used as movie settings for those who can afford it.'

Having forgotten breakfast - because, out in the sticks, healthy eating is barely known - our saving grace was to enjoy a relatively healthy lunch in The Graveyard Restaurant. Shortly afterwards, we were back on the road heading eastwards along the 58 Freeway. Two miles past the sign that read Boron, for some Aspie-inspired reason, we do a U-turn. There were odd, thin cigar-looking objects peering out of the peaks of small mountains that peaked his interest, although I was concerned by the ominous sign that read; *Authorised traffic only, offenders arrested on the spot.* A few moments later, we find ourselves standing in the foyer of the Twenty Mule Team Museum, in the only street running through Boron.

It is as though every glass cabinet in the museum was about to shatter. The thundering eardrum bursting noise we heard was their key exhibit. Many times throughout the day, phantom jets break the sound barrier overhead. The historical photos on the wall were a reflection of a once thriving community who were responsible for the entire world's production of Borax.

We were told about an amazing shortcut on our way to Phoenix that would shed thirty miles off our journey past the Edwards Air Force Base, with no unauthorised traffic allowed. However, as long as drivers adhered to the twenty mph speed limit, it was meant to be unlikely they would be stopped.

R. It's interesting how your desire to settle permanently in Phoenix never materialised. You told me you rented an apartment there. Tell me about Alexa; is she the missing link?

Chapter 35: Alexa

H. Hardly. It wasn't about her. For Aspie and I, it was the one magical place we set our hearts on, since the very first five summers we spend there. The only way I can explain the sensation was the moment you step off the plane and you feel the unimaginable heat, with the horizon being mountains in the distance. The desert will always be our most spiritual place. I can only describe it as a place where we most felt at peace with nature, amazing mountain scenery, spectacular sunsets and sunrises, while listening to the likes of Pink Floyd, Led Zeppelin and John Mayall at full volume.

To be honest, I think Phoenix was at one end of a war of my emotions. Throughout my life, I had been asked that penultimate question so many times, and I had always come up with the same answer. When I was in any city that houses culture, I wanted to investigate; when I was in countryside, I wanted to enjoy the scenery; and when by the sea, I wanted to enjoy its madness.

Phoenix for me was unlike any other city I knew anywhere. The city sat in a gigantic ancient volcanic basin that was all desert. Fifteen miles from downtown was the spectacular South Mountain Park, the largest of its kind in the world that sat on the inner ridges. At night, I always saw the red lights of the radio masts on its summit that could be seen thirty miles away. Twenty miles to the north, past Pinnacle Peak, was among my favourite resorts, the Boulders, so called because once a historical volcanic eruption threw giant boulders that sat there as a reminder. To the east was Superstition Mountain, an area that fascinated me in my youth during my hill-billy days, and to the west was an awe-inspiring desert, stretching as far as the eye could see, towards Los Angeles.

Aspie was still addicted to visiting Phoenix every time we travelled to the US. His tactics hadn't changed. During those years, my business was doing well and we flew into Sky Harbor, rented a car, and visited every antique destination within a couple of hours. When time permitted, we enjoyed relaxing at the Scottsdale Phoenician or the Frank Lloyd Wright, Biltmore. We woke up at dawn, the temperature already hotter than the recorded hottest day in London, got into the car, and drove the few miles to hike Camelback via Echo Canyon before breakfast. We were at Squaw Peak by lunch and, at dusk we were at the Praying Monk, just to prove how extreme Aspie believed he was!

A. But would we get enough?

R. What is Aspie referring to?

H. I would have thought that was a question you needn't ask?

R. Pussy?

H. What else!

A. You don't have to be so sarcastic. Think about all the pleasure I brought into your life and, if I hadn't strayed in her direction, you would not have met Alexa?

H. The morning our eyes meet, we are supposed to be thirty thousand feet in the sky a couple of hours later. Little do I know, Aspie was being seduced by the look in her eyes. We had just eaten breakfast, had already had our last swim earlier and dressed as though we are leaving. But I was enticed to dip a finger into the water and find myself escaping; reminiscing about what attracted us here. Thinking about the amazing cacti garden that spanned the entire width of the reception, or was it a combination of the resort's pools, lawns and large ponds, streams and waterfalls, filled up with hundreds of carp, set against the red rock of Camelback. My eyes began their last searching for the illusive 'whatever is missing in my life' and there she was, cavorting with a group of young people - aged between fifteen and twenty-five - playing water basketball. I watched the game and, after a short while, she sat on the steps by the edge of the pool. She asked when was I leaving and before I could answer, there were three words: 'You should stay.' It was later that I discovered her name was Alexa and she volunteered her free time to support teens with autism. At first, I didn't understand the connotations of what she was saying. Again, it was Aspie in 'love at first sight' mode, not believing what she had said and what it might mean. But while it was her eyes that peaked my interest, Aspie's focus was on her tits.

R. More tit talk, eh?

H. Admittedly, Aspie's interest in the largeness of her tits was the reason we never made our flight, but it was as though because of meeting Alexa my life was going to pan out differently; that our chance meeting would be different from the rest.

While we enjoyed the summer heat, it was also the only time the resort became affordable where room prices were down to around the hundred mark. But when staying in a city when the daytime temperature is unlikely to fall below a hundred, only people like us, who rarely saw hot weather, are mad enough to want to stay here.

As soon as Alexa realised I was no longer going to make my flight, we went back to reception to reserve a room for another three nights, then back into the swimming pool where we cavorted for the next couple of hours. By the time she left the pool, dinner together had been arranged at her home later that evening.

Like much of America, it is all too easy to believe the majority of the population live in luxury, compared to the UK. The first notification Aspie and I had that we had arrived was when we were announced at the security gatehouse, at the entrance to the condominium, where she lived.

No sooner had I stepped inside Alexa's hall than I got a measure of the luxury of her home. It was bathed in solid marble floors, a characteristic no doubt seen in her neighbours' homes too. However, there was one impossible task that remained of how to leave Aspie behind. I had to ensure his visibility would not cause me any embarrassment and I was grateful that no sooner had she opened the door and our eyes met that the rest of the night was spent caressing each other's mind. For the first time for a long time, I genuinely felt our body language and saw to it that nothing interfered. For the most part, we did this outside, indulging in a swim in her pool, sitting in the jacuzzi and chatting until our hunger pangs set in.

It was on rare occasions that I felt it was truly me acting in the most natural and responsible way uninhibited by Aspie's presence. Needless to say, during our conversation we got down to the nitty-gritty of my life and all of my emotional beans spilt out. Feelings that had been kept deep, no doubt, she sensed my vulnerable weaknesses as she held me tight and caressed my mind. For me, it was the deepest sense of sensual serenity and, above everything else, felt very safe. Sadly, though, whatever time we were spending would be nothing more than a fleeting visit, akin to the time it takes for someone swatting a mosquito out of existence before it could do any harm. That evening, I learnt that Alexa was into way-out complimentary therapy when she said to me, 'Do I know what rebirthing is?'

Now was the chance of spilling the last of my emotional beans. Alexa said, 'Suicide is the most selfish and damaging way out to those people who are closest to the victims. Your children needed their mother and, in their eyes you couldn't be her replacement. Every negative emotion was attacking you from every angle, and it was aimed at your inability to understand why your children's mother chose such a tumultuous exit from her life. No one in her life mattered anymore, be it her children, her mother and anyone else who may have been close to her heart. You could not have been aware of her emotional pain that living outweighed the pain of dying, and that is why those moments before she died, her children's lives and your life were of no consequence. Instead, her mind was set on where she was going as being a better place.

'However, if we are to continue with the healing process, you need to completely exonerate her for what she had to do. Your forgiveness has to come from my heart. I'm now going to make us some dinner and when I return, I want you to be able to say out aloud that you have completely forgiven her and that you promise never to utter a distasteful expression about her again; either to yourself or anyone else, family, friend or stranger.'

I don't know why, but somehow I thought it was one of Aspie's weaknesses that I was able to do this; that during my life I had some experience. I think it goes back to my childhood, to those days I was bulled and humiliated, and I wanted my attackers to realise I was not worth kicking the living shit out of; that the wrath of the emotive words they spoke and their vengeance completed the damage I felt. I think this action of Aspie's enabled me later on to be able to humble myself when I felt it was necessary as I was demonstrating once again this ability to Alexa.

A. This is what I mean about you. You can't stand up to your own beliefs and this is what I wanted you to do. Not the poppycock you have just mentioned.

H. In a way, Aspie has raised an interesting hypothesis. I was afraid to give any answer other than the one I gave, in case it spoilt a good thing. It suggested that these sentiments of mine were of little consequence to what Aspie had in mind for me; as though whatever the conclusion of the evening, he always had a back-up plan to wreak havoc my way.

Two years had passed since Jacky's death, and I thought I had grieved enough, unaware grief wasn't going to go away just because I was prepared to forgive. I still had a huge challenge with Aspie who could never condone what Jacky had done, and it would be another couple of years before he learnt to stop repeating the words, 'You fucking stupid cow!'

However, on Alexa's return, I found the courage to say, 'Jacky, my love, I forgive you for taking your life and hope that wherever you are, you are at peace with yourself.'

A little after midnight, we ate. Alexa made herself some chicken, and, for me, all she could offer was some rather bland tuna. Yet, our snack was a brief necessity to aiding us to waffle the night away, relaxing intertwined in her hammock looking up at a perfect view of the enchanting heavens. Meanwhile, I had to fend off Aspie, wanting me to hold her breasts tight and hope, as we gently rocked to and fro, to get into her knickers. Instead, the night sky took our thoughts on an enchanting journey. It was here that she spoke softly about her own concerns

She was hoping ours would be different from other men she met and would unfold like a flower in bloom and not end up like a weed. She did have concerns that Geminis meant trouble, although she was looking into the eyes of a man who interested her. Little did I know, Aspie had other plans for me. I only wish Aspie had more self-control and could have acted like cool-handed Luke! Because all of a sudden, it was time to go to bed.

'Make yourself comfortable in bed while I take a shower,' she said to me. Meanwhile, it was clear Aspie had no intent of going away.

A. Damn true! It is what I don't like in our relationship. She was inviting you to take a shower with her, a missed opportunity. Sex was being given to you on a plate, and you fucked that one up, didn't you, just like you did in Singapore?

R. But you saw past Aspie's sentiments and wanted this night of yours to be remembered as special?

H. Her super king-sized four-poster bed reminded us of the bed I had specially custom built for me and Jacky with the finest Egyptian cotton sprawling on a sumptuously comfortable mattress, with similar white pillows. When Alexa emerged from her bathroom, she was wearing a towel that barely covered her substantial bosoms. It was as she got herself into bed I told her of my embarrassment that I wasn't wearing underwear under my jeans. She replied, 'Don't worry, I won't fondle you.'

A. Another bloody missed opportunity!

H. Remarkably, she was true to her word and, needless to say, it wasn't long before our bodies were truly snuggled up together. We knew sleep wouldn't come easy, more the case of gentle caressing and getting used to each other's touch. It wasn't long before Aspie moved his hands in the attempt of cupping her breasts, only for them to be gently removed and placed below.

The following morning, I was asked to be out before breakfast because she had an early appointment. However, I didn't have long to wait. By the afternoon, I was invited round to her home again. To my surprise, her front door was open but what I was not prepared for was seeing a little Oriental girl sitting on her bed behaving in a manner which required Alexa's complete attention.

'Allow me to introduce my daughter.' It took about an hour of sudoku, caressing her mother's feet, before I became acceptable to her.

R. What happened between you and Alexa?

A. Go on. Blame it on me again, as you always do!

H. It didn't take her too long to realise Aspie was a needy man. Of course, she was unaware I was sharing my life with Aspie and that he had OCD to contend with. Basically, she created a dilemma for Aspie. No sooner had I returned home, she told me how much she was missing me and invited me to stay with her. I had no problem with that. Aspie, on the other hand, was already in panic mode, reminding me it was August and that the chance of getting a seat, at any price, at such short notice, was highly unlikely.

Understand I was very aware of the ins and outs of flying; no flight reservations work, not when I can break through airlines protocols. I knew if I turned up as a standby passenger, the chances were there would be a seat for me since they oversell tickets. The problem Aspie had was in not being able to see a logical way he could explain to Alexa that it is unlikely they would be able to meet up, unless she could confirm the dates.

That was the first part of the problem. The next, and in a way more prevalent, was being Mr Cool. During the following week, there was no communication whatsoever from her. He started going on at me that I must have said something inappropriate to her without being aware of it. Without warning, his OCD locked to find out what was going on and he acted like a viper that won't let go of its victim, until its prey was dead within its jaws!

R. What are you trying to say? Did Aspie continually phone and email her?

H. Yes, but this had always been Aspie's way. Be it with Alexa or any relationship, personal or business. There was no such thing as etiquette in an Aspie's life. No thinking about the cultures of my Japanese or gay customers. The Japanese, in particular, because they play by their cultural rules and dislike weaknesses or anyone running after them. You remember I told you about Aspie knocking at the hotel room of one of my customers when he failed to turn up at our shop? That is one example of his behaviour. My gay customers also found this attitude of his too claustrophobic and saw it as an invasion of their privacy.

It amused me, though, the embarrassments Aspie caused. We were visiting Japan once and it was common knowledge among antique dealers that the best lots in any shop are likely to be hidden away. We were in Kyoto and, uninvited, Aspie made a beeline to the office at the rear of the shop and gets the beating of his life.

R. A beating?

H. It was customary in all shops with a raised step-up, which marks a boundary between retail space and the private space of the seller. Part of the custom required anyone who wished to enter to announce their presence. There was a courtesy and a bowing procedure to follow, or for a foreigner to respect these customs. The trouble was Aspie had no knowledge of this and, intrigued by what was in the back room, he overstepped his welcome. No sooner than his right shoe touched the step, he was met by this little old lady, half his size, shouting, trying hard to shoo him back into her shop. He ignored her, until he felt the sensation of a broom being repetitively hit over the back of his head!

R. Yes, I imagine that must have been quite a sight. I suppose there is no difference really from seeing the back office in any shop. You don't go in unless invited. It was common courtesy. In a nutshell, what you mean is he cannot differentiate body language between right or wrong? I imagine that is quite a conundrum for you at times?

H. It has caused me quite a dilemma in many walks of my life. If this Japanese woman thought Aspie's mannerisms were typical of an Englishman, it is no wonder my Japanese customers found difficulties and always questioned my judgement!

The bottom line between me and Alexa was that Aspie was so worried with her unresponsive communication and that there would be no room on the plane at a time she wanted to meet again. You can imagine after the barrage of calls and emails she received, I received an email that a business deal went amiss because of Aspie's obsessiveness.

R. No doubt her communication also intimated she never wanted to hear from you again.

H. Actually, yes, and no. At first, that was the case, and it caused me much frustrating and upset. I thought Aspie had killed off another relationship; will his madness ever end? However, I had to be in Phoenix again, so I suggested we meet up, no-strings attached, and I explained about my relationship with Aspie.

Sadly, she reiterated what she had mentioned earlier when we met that she was worried by Geminis and knew who ever she met it never worked. The final nail in my coffin from her was, 'Without wanting to seem offensive, I cannot have a relationship with a man who has emotional issues like yours.'

I had hoped that, as a volunteer working with mentally handicapped people, she would be more sympathetic and work with me at our relationship. Nevertheless, we did keep in touch and I got to see her on all of my subsequent visits to Phoenix.

R. Surely, long-distance relationships are among the most challenging to work?

H. I think this is a question that is not so easily answered. Jacky had a cousin who lived in London while her long-term partner lived and worked in Hong Kong. They only saw each other twice a year for a couple of weeks at a time. That's commitment for you.

R. No doubt her partner wasn't a sex mad Aspie.

H. Somehow they were able to persevere with their separate lives. She was a very creative sculptor who built up a respectable following from her studio in London, and her partner respected her wishes until she was able to join him. They now live permanently in Hong Kong.

I craved the Phoenix lifestyle, the desert and the mountains and the Pacific Ocean, just an hour's flight away. But the one thing missing in my life was ultimately my downfall; Aspie's inability to relate to stillness, knowing how to relax, always acting out Mr Ants in his Pants. After I was dumped by Alexa, I came to the conclusion that as a Gemini, it made sense that Aspie was the schizophrenic part of my life.

R. I think you are being too hard on yourself. Astrologically speaking, you may be of two minds. In my opinion, you are one person who thinks differently. Try to identify with what your life coach said to you: 'Stop being who you think you are; be who you are. You are aware that Aspie has strengths as well as weaknesses. Acknowledge rather than fight them.' Isn't that what she said to you?

H. The idea of being one person would be so in an ideal world. I think my difficulty is differentiating between my attitude towards him and his responsibilities towards me.

R. If we are to continue with you being two persons with rather a selfish attitude, wouldn't you agree?

H. Perhaps, but I'm dealing with all of Aspie's emotional ups and down, which leaves little room to think about the emotional well-being of my children.

R. But they had no mother, only you to rely on. While I don't want to appear demonstrative, it seems to me your ethics are no different from the husbands of the women you ended up having relationships with, who don't put their children first.

H. The last thing I need now is you putting me on a guilt trip. I was learning to come to terms with who I really was. Accepting that I had to live with a madman at times, an entity that took no prisoners, his actions saw to it that I was drowning in a sea of anxieties. A no-way out situation for me, that's how it was! I am sure you know how it is with divorces. First comes the alienation. Here I am at my lowest ebb. Aspie's my friend and the dating website Go-Date gets me hooked up with fucked-up relationships because he craves bodily contact that I missed during my marriage to Jacky.

Now I have virtually told you my entire life story, it leaves me simply to talk about my last recourse; ending my emotional suffering. My kids would in time get over what I had to do. It was no easy task; the most difficult choice in my life. I was so emotionally devastated by how Aspie succeeded in permanently depriving me of the one woman who meant more to me than any one I met. Yes, I was prepared to take my own life. Where Aspie fits into the picture is the method he chose for me to take this route. By no means conventional, built by his rules, he didn't want to make it an easy choice. I would even go on to say a test of his to see if I could achieve him giving me obstacles to overcome.

Never in my wildest dreams did I think Aspie was capable of conceiving the plan for the perfect murder, yet that is what the conniving cunt planned.

Sorry, I was laughing, it was a nervous reaction. It was in the moment, the milliseconds before the axe fell and did its deed. In the time it takes a doomed man who has gulped their last breath of air as their lungs are completely depleted of air, they see their life go past them, as did mine. Before that final moment, I realised he found all the information he required freely available. Can you believe that if you want to murder someone, you simply search for it on Google?

It was his covering up of every type of anxiety and panic attack caused by extremely intrusive feelings he was subjected to. It meant he didn't need to apologise for the countless menacing culmination of charades he performed on me on a daily basis. The culmination of which would dictate whether I end up psychotic or psychopathic. It's all very well saying I was a delusionary, but the fact of the matter was, if Aspie was me, and I am just one person and the symptoms are very real, then my inner commands I have no choice but to obey.

Epilogue: The Perfect Murder

H. The morning began like the trip to Bristol, instead we were going for a cycle and had chosen to do so along a path in the heart of Princes Park, about three quarters of a mile from where we lived. It ran adjacent to the golf course, but hidden by thickly grown fir trees so it made sense to be the perfect place where he was going to prepare his lair. It was as though the route had been pre-planned. The route, yes, we had cycled it a number of times. It happened to be Aspie's good fortune that his proposed victim was the only woman in our vicinity and her dog, a small one at that.

Aspie lay this plastic sheet beside a tree trunk that is hidden from the path. I had actually thought those previous cycles were his test runs to see if he got the same adrenalin rush; that the idea of actually the real doing was not preposterous, but quite feasible.

It was only after what he did that I saw his jigsaw fit into place; that final piece was the missing clue of my life. He ventured to tell me about the story he read about a psychopath who had got caught and had shown no remorse for murdering several prostitutes, and this was how he had come up with today's stunt. He required the knowledge of learning how it felt to consummate the perfect murder. It was Alexa he said who put him up to this idea. He needed her gone permanently, but someone in her place would do because he was horrified by her attitude towards him. He had thought she was a hypocrite. On the one hand, she had shown the commitment to freely give as much of her own personal time helping people with mental difficulties, but on the other hand, she had vilified him when she learnt he was of the same breed. While it was not ideal trying to take her life out, it was acceptable that another life was taken in recompense. He said it was important too, for me to feel his own self-gratification, but not the slightest bit of concern or guilt, or sign of emotional torment.

So, there she was, and as she drew closer, he could see she was wearing a red skirt beneath a white blouse. It was the third time she had worn it. He wondered if he revered throughout his life with the number three? Would this be the first of three murders he felt compelled to commit?

Looking around him as far and wide as his eyesight could see, he was assured there was absolutely no one at all in his vicinity. Therefore there would be no witnesses. He already knew there would be no screaming since he had already followed and seen her converse with people through sign language.

He knew he didn't have to be concerned about her small dog. It would not offer her the slightest protection or be able to deliver him any physical harm. The noise of the forest would muffle out any barking it made. He had planned the trap very well and it would be over before she realised what was happening. The course of martial arts he had begun the year before, learning self-defence tactics, had taught him how to get out of a headlock, but also how to use it against any foe. It would be that simple; coming up from behind, placing his arm around her neck, and feeling it snap with very little exertion. A quick pulse test with his finger placed on her neck to complete the remaining part of his task. My concerns were not about taking away a life of a woman who was in the prime of her life, but finally learning what it felt like being Aspie.

R. Now you are telling me after all that you have told me Aspie is a psychopath, or are you saying something blasphemous anyway he did was an act of God?

H. Makes interesting hypothesis, doesn't it?

R. All I can say it that I am grateful you didn't choose me to become your first victim, and hopefully I won't be your next. I will never forgive you for taking an innocent life, but I will always be your most trusted friend. Anyway, let's not heckle; I do not want to appear like the local nag, but what happened next?

Resources and Additional Information

The author has established several website to help other people in similar situations to his own.

www.aspieandme.com

Here, you will find references pertinent to pages and chapters throughout his story, *Aspie and Me*. These include: translations of certain vocabulary; analysis of incidents and situations; and precautions to develop the best strategies for promoting a more rewarding relationship with your Aspie self. This includes neuro-typical people who may have their own Aspie living with them too.

www.lifewithoutlabels.co.uk

This website takes readers on a surreal journey into the heart of a creative mind rife with dyslexia and ADHD.

Research Autism: www.researchautism.net

The National Autistic Society: www.autism.org.uk

The Autism Show: www.autismshow.co.uk

The Welsh Autism Show: www.thewelshautismshows.co.uk

International Society of Autism Research (IMFAR): www.autism-insar.org

Autism One: www.autismone.org

The Autism Society of America: www.autism-society.org

You can also view the following videos online.

Research Autism Conference, 2001: <u>www.researchautism.net/</u>
<u>about-us-research-autism/research-autism-videos/videos-disorder-</u>
<u>or-difference-conference</u>

Life before and after diagnosis with Asperger's Syndrome, from
Laurence Mitchell, Freelance Trainer

<u>www.youtube.com/watch?v=a-P79jRBJIA</u>

Collaboration with Dr Rory Allen

<u>www.youtube.com/watch?v=H3RwEF8UtYU</u>

The author's experience of being diagnosed with Aspergers
Syndrome, courtesy of Valentine Palmer

<u>www.youtube.com/watch?v=uBFt3JzNV0A</u>